**Praise for the novels of Joyce Lamb**

## FOUND WANTING

"Top-notch suspense . . . Believable characters in an action-packed plot will enthrall readers. Like Tami Hoag and Iris Johansen, Lamb weaves the textures of romance and suspense together in a satisfying read."　　　—*Booklist*

"This wonderfully written story is a must read for any fan of romantic suspense! Joyce Lamb is a master storyteller . . . Don't miss out on one of the best novels ever written!"　　　—*Romance Junkies*

"Fast-paced suspense, full of twists and turns and nonstop action . . . To find out the many other fabulous nuances of this story, you'll just have to go and grab yourself a copy!"　　　—LoveRomances.com

## CAUGHT IN THE ACT

"Page-turning suspense and a rewarding romance make for a riveting read."　　　—*Booklist*

"Captures readers' interest from the opening pages."
　　　—*Romance Reviews Today*

*continued . . .*

# COLD
# MIDNIGHT

## JOYCE LAMB

BERKLEY SENSATION, NEW YORK

**THE BERKLEY PUBLISHING GROUP**
**Published by the Penguin Group**
**Penguin Group (USA) Inc.**
**375 Hudson Street, New York, New York 10014, USA**
Penguin Group (Canada), 90 Eglinton Avenue East, Suite 700, Toronto, Ontario M4P 2Y3, Canada
(a division of Pearson Penguin Canada Inc.)
Penguin Books Ltd., 80 Strand, London WC2R 0RL, England
Penguin Group Ireland, 25 St. Stephen's Green, Dublin 2, Ireland (a division of Penguin Books Ltd.)
Penguin Group (Australia), 250 Camberwell Road, Camberwell, Victoria 3124, Australia
(a division of Pearson Australia Group Pty. Ltd.)
Penguin Books India Pvt. Ltd., 11 Community Centre, Panchsheel Park, New Delhi—110 017, India
Penguin Group (NZ), 67 Apollo Drive, Rosedale, North Shore 0632, New Zealand
(a division of Pearson New Zealand Ltd.)
Penguin Books (South Africa) (Pty.) Ltd., 24 Sturdee Avenue, Rosebank, Johannesburg 2196,
South Africa

Penguin Books Ltd., Registered Offices: 80 Strand, London WC2R 0RL, England

This is a work of fiction. Names, characters, places, and incidents either are the product of the author's imagination or are used fictitiously, and any resemblance to actual persons, living or dead, business establishments, events, or locales is entirely coincidental. The publisher does not have any control over and does not assume any responsibility for author or third-party websites or their content.

COLD MIDNIGHT

A Berkley Sensation Book / published by arrangement with the author

PRINTING HISTORY
Berkley Sensation mass-market edition / August 2009

Copyright © 2009 by Joyce Lamb.
Cover photo by Image Source Black/Jupiter Images.
Cover design by Annette Fiore Defex.
Interior text design by Kristin del Rosario.

ISBN: 978-0-425-23024-4

BERKLEY® SENSATION
Berkley Sensation Books are published by The Berkley Publishing Group,
a division of Penguin Group (USA) Inc.,
375 Hudson Street, New York, New York 10014.
BERKLEY® SENSATION and the "B" design are trademarks of Penguin Group (USA) Inc.

PRINTED IN THE UNITED STATES OF AMERICA

10  9  8  7  6  5  4  3  2  1

*For Mom.*
*You're the absolute best.*

# Acknowledgments

Thank you to:

- Mike Becknell and Jim Royals for their cop expertise.

- Julie Snider, Shari Grace and Jennie Pollock for their help getting the word out.

- Tim Loehrke for being an awesome photographer.

- Diane Amos, Joan Goodman, Linda Cutillo, Maggie Hoye, Chantelle Mansfield, Kristann Montague, Karen Feldman McCracken, Chris Clay, Mary Clay, Charlene Gunnells, Ruth Chamberlain, Lisa Kiplinger and Lisa Hitt for brainstorming, reading, commenting and not rolling their eyes at me (much).

- Grace Morgan for her dogged determination (and Janet Chapman for introducing us).

- Wendy McCurdy and Allison Brandau for the BEST editing suggestions.

- And last but not least: All my friends and family who've always supported me in what sometimes seemed like an impossible dream. We did it! Woo hoo!

# 1

KENDALL FALLS POLICE DETECTIVE CHASE MANNING steered his SUV into the muddy parking lot of the construction site for McKays' Tennis Center. He would have preferred to avoid this case like a bad sunburn, but he couldn't *not* respond when it involved Kylie McKay, the woman he loved more than life before she walked out on him. As if Mother Nature shared his mood, lightning flashed against the backdrop of ominous dark clouds on the horizon.

Shoving bad memories out of his brain, he stepped out of the truck to the low rumble of distant thunder. His partner, Sam Hawkins, was talking to a group of four or five construction workers near a mobile home, so Chase headed in that direction.

The construction site was in the beginning stages of development. Freshly felled trees dotted the sandy dirt landscape. Two yellow, mud-caked earthmovers sat silent, as did a huge dump truck filled with tree branches and other debris. A chain-link fence with intermittent KEEP OUT signs surrounded it all.

His stride faltered when he saw her talking to another construction worker. She nodded at the man, her eyes shielded by sunglasses and her mouth set in a grim line. In red shorts, a white tank top and sneakers, and her long dark hair caught in a ponytail that shed curls around her face, she still looked every bit the professional tennis player: lithe, tan and toned.

His gaze locked momentarily on the black knee brace that extended from midcalf to midthigh, a harsh reminder of the violent and bloody assault that tore them apart ten years ago.

When dark rage boiled up inside him, he clenched one fist and looked away to see Sam striding toward him. His partner of five years looked rock solid as always, biceps and thighs bulging in a navy polo shirt and khaki slacks. A prematurely gray crew cut topped his heavy brow, making him look dangerous. Very few people messed with Sam.

"What have we got?" Chase asked.

"Maybe it's best if you let me handle this one."

"What have we got?" Chase repeated, his voice hard.

Sam hooked his thumbs in his belt and rolled his massive shoulders. "Construction worker found a bat."

"As in baseball bat?"

"Kylie ID'd it as the one used to take out her knee."

Chase couldn't respond for a moment. Holy shit. Holy *shit*. Unable to stop himself, he glanced in her direction. She'd just looked upon the weapon that two unknown assailants had used to shatter her dreams, and yet she chatted with the construction worker as if they discussed nothing more major than the impending storm. Her calm facade eerily mirrored the aftermath of the brutal attack, he realized. But she'd been in shock then, pale and hollow-eyed, disoriented from pain medication and spinning from endless talk of surgeries and physical rehabilitation . . . and no more competitive tennis.

"Chase."

He blinked and looked at his partner. "What?"

"You sure about this? I can take it from here, you know."

"Like hell. This case has been cold for ten years."

"Yeah, I know, and you've been itching for a reason to

open it back up, and now you've got it. But there's a major conflict of interest here."

"I'll be fine, Sam. Kylie and I have been over for a long time."

"That was easier to buy when she lived on the other side of the country. She's back now, and you've been wound way too tight ever since."

"That's bullshit—"

"Just let me handle it, Chase."

Chase started to knead the back of his neck, where tension always settled into a giant, throbbing knot. Sam was right. He couldn't possibly be objective on this. Not when the mere act of looking at her stirred up a maelstrom of contradictory emotions. Anger. Grief. Anger. Resentment. Loss. Christ, the anger, after all this time. "Fine. We'll play it by ear."

Sam rolled his eyes at the vague surrender but said nothing as they walked over to Kylie, where Sam extended his hand. "Hello, Miss McKay. Detective Sam Hawkins, Kendall Falls Police."

She clasped his hand and gave him a perfunctory nod. "Detective."

Sam gestured toward Chase. "You know my partner."

She glanced at him, her eyes unreadable behind the sunglasses. "Chase," she said, both her tone and expression neutral.

"Kylie."

So incredibly poised, cold even, as if meeting a competitor before a career-changing match. Coach Daddy had trained her well.

She gestured to the construction worker beside her, a balding man with a deep tan and a small gut pooching out over the waistband of his faded jeans. "This is the foreman," Kylie said. "Robert Arnold."

The men shook hands all around before Sam said to the foreman, "You're the one who found the bat?"

Robert nodded. "Dug it up this morning while we were cleaning out the trees. It was wrapped in a dirty T-shirt and a

garbage bag. I set it aside for my kid and didn't think anything of it until one of the other guys said it looked like the
one . . ." He trailed off as he shot an apologetic glance at
Kylie. "Kind of makes all the other stuff that's been happening a bit more significant, in my opinion."

Her expression remained unchanged, but her shoulders
tensed. "I don't think—"

"What other stuff?" Chase cut in, narrowing his eyes at
her.

"Nothing that—"

"Vandalism started about two weeks ago," Robert said.
"Sugar in the gas tanks of the earthmovers. Sabotaged en-
gines. Stolen materials. More annoying than serious, but
definitely suspicious."

"Why didn't you call the police?" Chase directed the
question at Kylie.

"I didn't see a need. Like Robert said, the incidents were
more annoying than serious."

"But escalating," Robert pointed out. "Whoever's behind
it is getting bolder. I don't—" The ringing cell phone on his
belt cut him off. "Excuse me, folks," he said and stepped
away.

Chase moved in on Kylie, deliberately invading her space.
"Someone's trying to scare you off, and you're not doing
anything about it?"

"Chase . . ."

He ignored Sam's warning tone. Screw the conflict of interest. Kylie was being threatened. "You should have called
the police, Ky."

"You're here now." Cool and solid, not a flicker of emotion.

"That's not the point," Chase said. "Escalating vandalism
can quickly turn into violence. You should have—"

"We need to stay on track here," Sam said.

Chase took a breath to check his temper. Figures. *Her* past
had just risen up to take a swing at her, and *he* was the one
on the verge of losing control. Being near her could make
him so irrational. "Where is it?" he asked, teeth gritted.

She gestured with a rock-steady hand toward the off-white trailer that served as the foreman's office. A metallic blue aluminum baseball bat with red lettering sat propped under one of the shadeless windows. On the dirty yellow tape wrapped around the grip, one word had been scrawled in black marker: KILLER.

Chase's stomach flipped. *Jesus*, that was the bat that demolished her knee to the point where only the fast work of one doctor saved her leg. Saved her *life*.

He realized now that she must have locked everything inside her down. No way could she look at that thing and not feel *something*. So she'd done what she could: kept her eye on the ball with the same laser focus that won her the Australian Open at seventeen, launching her into tennis stardom mere weeks before two barbaric bastards held her down on a deserted path and viciously destroyed her.

He swallowed as the same old helpless rage welled inside him. He'd been head over heels in love with her, and all he could do after the attack was stand there, powerless and lost and pissed off, while her world imploded. She lost everything that day, in the course of one or two bloody minutes. Her future. Her sense of security. Her innocence. Her very identity.

When he was feeling rational, he couldn't blame her for running away from Kendall Falls. She'd landed on center stage, under a glaring spotlight, at the most vulnerable time of her life. It was like being assaulted twice.

A flash of lightning, closer now, jolted him out of his thoughts, and as he looked away from the bat, he realized Sam watched him with a warning in his gaze. *Keep it together, man.*

Chase cleared his throat. No problem. Do the job. "Where are the shirt and bag?"

"Foreman said he tossed them before he knew what he had," Sam said.

"Tossed them where?" Chase asked.

"Dumpster." Sam jerked his thumb toward the back of the site.

"We'll have to go through it," Chase said.

"Is that all you need from me for now?" Kylie asked.

So stoic and controlled and, God, still so achingly beautiful. When she cocked her head, waiting for his response, he had to swallow against the tightness of his throat, sure she had no idea what was coming.

Thunder crashed, and Chase noticed everyone except Kylie glanced up at the furious clouds. Her focus had zeroed in on him and his next words.

"Construction has to be shut down," he said. Blunt, to the point. Like ripping off a Band-Aid.

Nothing in her expression changed, her eye obviously still on the ball. "Completely? Delays have already put us behind schedule."

"It's only temporary, until we can determine that this is indeed the weapon used in your attack."

"Of *course* it's the weapon. It's exactly the same. How many bats have you seen with 'killer' written on the grip like that?"

So matter-of-fact and unemotional. How did she do that? But he knew. As her training partner so long ago, he'd helped make her the player she'd been, the woman she seemed to be now. Cool, focused, driven.

"It still has to be tested," he said. "Your description of it was common knowledge back then. Someone could have, well, made one based on that."

"Like some kind of joke?"

The crack in her voice hit Chase like a soft blow to the gut, and suddenly he hoped like hell she'd get her game face back and fast. She'd been broken ten years ago, but he'd never *seen* her broken. He suspected no one had.

"The whole site is a crime scene," he said. "It has to be off-limits to everyone but the crime scene investigators."

"How long is this going to take?"

Steady again. He almost let out a sigh of relief. "If we don't find any evidence on the bat or shirt that connects them to your attack, we're looking at a day."

"And if you do?"

"We'll have to search the site for more evidence. Best-case scenario: a couple of weeks."

Nothing in her face moved, but the set of her shoulders firmed. "A couple of weeks" was not a good answer. "Worst case?" she asked.

"A couple of months."

She looked away for a moment, a muscle flexing at her temple. "I can't afford that much of a delay."

"Don't you want to know who did that to you?" He gestured none too smoothly at her braced knee.

She looked at him, eyes well hidden behind dark shades, but he sensed their narrowing. "Finding out who did it won't change anything."

"Might be nice if the bastards paid for what they did." Nice was a major understatement. He wanted blood. A shit-load of blood. And some screams for mercy.

"We're getting ahead of ourselves here," Sam said. "Kylie, can you at least shut things down for a day while we test the evidence? We'll go from there."

Chase had to give him credit for making it sound like she had a choice.

She nodded reluctantly. "I'll let the foreman know."

"Thank you," Sam said. "We'll be in touch."

She'd taken only a few steps when Chase went after her. "Wait."

She faced him, and he saw from the angle of her head that she darted a glance after Sam, as if she'd lost her buffer. "Yes?"

"Are you okay?" So lame, he thought. Of course she wasn't okay. Why was he asking anyway? They hadn't parted as friends, and every time they'd run into each other since she'd returned, they'd danced around each other as gracefully as newborn colts.

She gave him a thin smile. "I'm fine. Great, really. Couldn't be better."

Before he could snap back with something equally sarcastic, she blew out a huff of air as a small, contrite smile softened her features. "Wow, that was bitchy."

The stiffness in his shoulders eased some, and he smiled back. "I won't argue with that."

"I'm sorry. I've had . . . well, this day . . ." She trailed off, eyebrows cinching together above the rims of her sunglasses.

"It can't be easy."

The splash of puddles in the parking lot had them both looking in that direction. As a news van parked next to Chase's SUV, she sighed. "Terrific."

"Media hell all over again, huh?"

She nodded without looking at him. "It never seems to end around here."

"So you're taking off soon then?"

He knew it was a dig, and part of him, the ugly, still-ticked part, meant it as one. When the going got tough, and the spotlight switched on, Kylie got packing. Why would now be any different than ten years ago? And, really, who could blame her? She had a past the press loved to rehash. Nothing sold newspapers like blood and guts and brutalized, pretty women.

She glanced at him, her smile hard now, forced. "I'm staying. Dad wanted a tennis center in Kendall Falls with the family name on it, so that's what I'm doing. Sabotage didn't chase me away. And neither will a ten-year-old baseball bat and endless media attention. Any other questions?"

He was glad she couldn't tell by looking at him that the determination in her voice had sparked awake something long asleep inside him. He'd always been so turned on by her competitive spirit. He'd missed that since she'd gone. Hell, he'd missed it before she took off.

"I think that about covers it," he said, unable to stop the quirk to his lips. "Have a nice day." If he'd worn a hat, he would have touched the brim with a muttered "ma'am" and a nod.

"You, too," she said stiffly before she turned and walked away.

He watched her go, appreciating the slight sway of her slim hips. As a teen, she'd had a compact, athletic body trained for lightning speed and power serves. But the tomboy had grown up, and toughness and strength were now tempered by soft curves that were way too sexy for the guy in him to ignore.

The black knee brace, so stark against the tanned skin of her leg, cooled the heat in his gut, though. That brace was part of the reason he'd become a cop. He'd vowed to make the people who did that to her pay.

As the wind picked up and lightning cracked, almost immediately followed by a crash of thunder, he thought that maybe now he'd get the chance.

# 2

KYLIE TOSSED THE TENNIS BALL INTO THE AIR AND slammed it with a satisfying *thwack*. At the height of her career, when she won her first, and only, Grand Slam tournament, she could knock the ball into the service court at a hundred miles per hour. That was ten years, eight knee surgeries and a full year of physical rehabilitation ago.

Lately, when she punished the innocent little yellow ball, she did it to show her college tennis team the proper form. Most of the time. She also did it to work out her issues. Of which she seemed to have many, especially since quitting her coaching job at UCLA to return to her hometown with the idea of reclaiming the life she'd abandoned.

She hadn't planned on running into Chase Manning so regularly, though. It didn't help that he didn't sport a huge gut and flabby arms. No, he was even more gorgeous than when she'd embraced her inner coward and left him. Tall, imposing, muscular in the perfect kind of way that was sculpted but not bulky. Green eyes the color of the deep forest and capable of being just as dark and intimidating. He smelled the same, too—like tropical sunscreen.

Leaving him . . . no, "leaving" wasn't strong enough.

Running away, that's what she'd done. Run and run and run, as fast and as far as she could. By the time the reality check smacked her in the forehead that she'd abandoned and hurt the one person who could get her through losing her dreams, losing her way, he'd had a ring on his finger and a kid on the way.

Drawing in a long, pulse-slowing breath, she bounced a tennis ball several times and tried to get her focus back. Punish the ball. Work it out.

But, God, he'd called her Ky this afternoon. Hearing her name in that radio-ready voice—like expensive brandy: smooth with just a hint of fire—conjured memories of breathless whispers and naked, sweat-slicked bodies that fit, and moved, together so perfectly.

Cheeks heating, she angled her head to pop the tension out of her neck. Right. It's not too warm out here at all. Focus, damn it. Hit the ball into the next galaxy.

"So, bad time?"

She whirled at the voice behind her, heart rate spiking into the fight-or-flight zone. She'd already yanked her racket up, ready to defend herself, when she recognized her best friend easing through the gate in the fence surrounding the lighted court. Trisha's arms were loaded with a couple of bottles of blue Gatorade and two takeout Chinese boxes.

Feeling foolish, yet grateful that Trisha appeared oblivious to her overreaction, Kylie jogged over to help her with her bounty.

In khaki shorts and an orange and teal Dolphins T-shirt, Trisha Young looked the same as she had in high school. Freckles still crowded her otherwise fair complexion, and her short, curly auburn hair still frizzed in the Florida humidity. She'd gained a few pounds in recent years, but she liked to joke that the pounds landed in prime locations: her boobs and her butt.

Trisha started laughing as she bobbled a chilled bottle of Gatorade right into Kylie's waiting hands. "Good catch."

"Let me guess who loaded you up with all this stuff. Jane?"

"Quinn, too. They're worried about you."

"I know. They've been hovering all night."

"Can't say I blame them," Trisha said lightly.

Kylie twisted open a bottle and quenched a thirst she'd been too stubborn to deal with half an hour ago. Doing so would have required going inside where her overly concerned siblings lingered. Much as she appreciated their concern, she couldn't cope with their constant questions.

Are you all right?

Do you need anything?

Want to talk about it?

Yes, no, double no and please, *please* go away.

"What have you got?" she asked Trisha, nodding toward the takeout boxes. Starving didn't begin to cover the gnawing in her belly. And it had nothing, absolutely nothing, to do with Chase Manning. This was good old plain hunger. Beefcake wouldn't satisfy it. Right? Right.

"They couldn't agree on your favorite," Trisha said, "so they had me pick up Singapore rice noodles and Mongolian beef. So which is it?"

"Singapore rice noodles, hold the shrimp."

Trisha grinned and held out one of the boxes and a plastic fork. "Quinn wins."

Kylie grinned back. "He usually does."

They both plopped down on the court with their backs to the fence and tore open their respective containers.

Trisha already had a mouthful when she said, "It's so nice out here. Quiet and peaceful."

Kylie nodded as she glanced around at the private tennis court. A short walk away, through a small forest of palm and pine trees, sat the home she'd rented when she returned to the area. The house itself—a modest fifteen hundred square feet with two bedrooms, two baths and an open layout—was nothing special. But it sat on the beach, surrounded by thick, green vegetation that provided the kind of privacy rarely seen in newer beachfront property.

She'd furnished it with some of her father's belongings, but living with his things, without him, had been difficult the past six months. Everything still smelled like Irish Spring . . . and the past. In fact, everything about Kendall Falls, from the salty gulf air to Chase's sunscreen, smelled like the past. And it wasn't all good.

"I hope you plan to share," Trisha said, eyeing Kylie's takeout container. "I love me some Mongolian beef, but I'm a sucker for the noodles."

Kylie nodded as she swirled her fork among the thin curried noodles. "Always happy to share."

"Except when it comes to feelings," Trisha pointed out before launching into a mournful, off-key version of the old standard. "Whoa, whoa, whoa, feelinnnnngs."

Kylie laughed. "Please stop, I'll talk. I'll talk!"

Trisha quieted, expectant eyebrows arched as she forked up a large piece of beef and chewed.

Kylie captured some noodles and savored the silence. And missed Los Angeles, where she did her job and lived quite happily in the present and never had to talk about the past. Every once in a while, a new friend would ask, but after a couple of vague answers and deliberate changes of subject, she always managed to wiggle off the hook. Not so here in Kendall Falls, where the world still seemed to revolve around the blackest day of her life.

"You're not talking," Trisha said, her words muffled by food.

Kylie smiled. Trisha hadn't paid much attention to manners as a teenager, and the years hadn't changed that about her. She'd changed in other ways, though. She no longer skirted the tough topics. Her blunt questions drilled right to the heart of the matter without fear of offense or hurt or stirring up bad memories. Kylie hadn't quite figured out how to duck and dodge this new aspect of her friend when they were face to face. On the phone long-distance, it was easy enough to say she had to go and end the conversation. E-mail was even easier: She just didn't respond to the parts she didn't want to.

"How about I get you started," Trisha said. "I'll start a statement, and you can finish it. Ready?"

"I don't—"

"I really hate, or love, reality TV because . . ."

Kylie was too relieved by the reprieve to laugh. "It's addictive."

"Hate it or love it?"

"Both, for the same reason."

"Fair enough. Here's another: If I could rule the world, I'd . . ."

Grinning, Kylie drank some Gatorade before answering. "Make daily naps in the workplace mandatory."

"Good one," Trisha said, nodding. She held out her Chinese container. "Trade?"

Kylie made the swap and dug into the Mongolian beef. Maybe she could handle this little game after all.

Trisha cleared her throat. "When I saw that baseball bat this afternoon, I wanted to . . ."

Damn. Damn. Damn it.

"Take your time," Trisha said, casual as she sucked a twirl of noodles off her fork.

The beef that tasted fabulous a moment ago became flavorless in Kylie's mouth, and she had to force herself to swallow it. No longer hungry, she set aside the takeout box and rolled her shoulders in the night air. Humidity made everything feel sticky and thick and uncomfortable, and she thought for the millionth time of standing in front of Chase Manning while he'd stared at the bat, his face flushing red. The air had been sticky and thick and uncomfortable then, too. And it had taken every instant of competitive training over the years to stand there, shoulders squared and face still, while her world shifted off its foundation.

When Trisha cleared her throat, calling attention to the lengthening silence, Kylie felt she had no choice but to say *something*. "It might not be the bat."

"What if it is?"

Shrugging, Kylie retrieved the box of noodles from Trisha's hand and dug back in. "I'll deal."

"Too easy. What if it is?"

"I'd rather jump off that bridge when I come to it."

"Hmm, I wonder what Dr. Jane would say about talk of bridge-jumping."

Kylie grinned at her. "Nothing. Psychiatrists aren't allowed to treat family members."

Trisha, for once, didn't grin back, her expression dead serious. "Quit dodging and talk to me. This thing, this bat being found . . . it's huge."

"It isn't huge until they prove it's the weapon."

"You know it is or you wouldn't be out here alone at ten at night smacking the stuffing out of tennis balls."

"Tennis balls don't have stuffing."

Trisha's reddish brown eyes narrowed. "Now you're starting to irk me."

"I'm not trying to. I just . . ." Frustrated, she set aside the container. "I just can't, okay?"

Trisha turned her attention to hunting around in the other takeout box for any beef she'd missed. "You know I had to try, right? It's my duty as your best friend."

"I appreciate it. I really do. And I'm fine. I promise."

Trisha cast her the sure-you-are eye, but before she could dive into another touchy subject, Kylie asked, "So how's Roger?"

Trisha gave a little shrug. "Eh."

"That doesn't sound good."

"He really isn't my type, anyway. Hey, I heard Chase Manning is on the reopened investigation."

Damn. Cornered again. Kylie managed a casual nod. "He's one of the detectives on the case. I think we went to school with his partner, Sam Hawkins. He seems familiar."

Trisha nodded. "He was a year behind us. He asked Patti out once. Remember?"

Kylie didn't, but whatever. She'd managed to change the subject. "Do you still talk to Patti?" When she'd left, she'd lost touch with all of her friends except Trisha.

"Occasionally. She's a nurse in Tampa now. Last time she came to Kendall Falls, we got together, but it wasn't the same without the rest of the gang. We should plan something now that you're back."

Kylie gave a noncommittal nod, but before she could respond, Trisha said, "Maybe you and Chase will, you know, work out your differences."

Kylie had to force herself not to stiffen. "We don't have any differences to work out. He became a father nine months after I left. There's not a much more decisive way to say he got over me in record time."

With that, she pushed to her feet and started gathering the trash from their dinner. "Shall we go in before Jane and Quinn come looking for us?"

Trisha rose, too, and brushed at the seat of her khakis. "Interesting. You'd rather face the hovercrafts than talk about Chase."

"There's nothing to talk about. It was a teen romance that ended the instant I went away to college. End of story."

"A gross oversimplification if I ever heard one. You'd still be together if—"

"How about some Rocky Road? Jane said she picked some up on the way over. She thinks it's my favorite, but I'm sure Quinn could tell her it's Moose Tracks."

Trisha sighed as she fell into step beside her. "Okay, okay. Hint taken. You win."

Kylie draped an arm around Trisha's shoulders and hugged her. "Finally!"

# 3

CHASE SAT WITH THE SPORTS SECTION SPREAD BE-
fore him on the kitchen table, his coffee cooling near his
right hand. The scores didn't have his attention, though. No,
that was focused on Kylie McKay. The woman was so very
different from the girl he remembered. The attack changed
the warm, outgoing, fun-loving girl he'd adored into a
guarded, contained woman bent on not feeling anything—or
at least pretending she didn't feel anything. Somewhere
along the way, she'd begun applying the strategies of the
game to life. Don't show emotion. Out-thinking opponents is
as important as out-playing them.

And he'd somehow become an opponent. Probably
around the time he tried to get her to open up and talk to him
about what happened to her on that path. He'd expected tears
and anger. He'd thought maybe she'd rage around, maybe
throw a few things, hopefully not at his head. Instead, she'd
packed her bags and took off, using college as an excuse to
break it off with him. She hadn't wanted a "long-distance
relationship." Like hell. She hadn't wanted a *relationship*,
period. That would have required feeling and wanting and
coping—all the things she'd stopped doing the moment her

doctors said she could no longer play competitive tennis. Frustrating as hell, but what could he have done then except let her go to find her new way?

Not that he'd had a choice. He'd begged to go with her, shameful as that was. But he'd been a kid then, a teenage boy struck dumb by the grace and beauty of a girl he'd seen for the first time across a net. Pussy that he'd been, he would have chucked everything for her. Though a crappy childhood—with a mother who wussed out on her only child and a father who punctuated his every irrational point with brutal fists—wasn't much to chuck, really. But still.

And when he'd pleaded, she'd crushed him with one simple word: No.

She needed time, she'd said, completely dry-eyed and stone-faced as she'd spouted her bullshit. She needed time to find her "new identity." That one still made him wince. Amazing, really, after all this time. She'd wanted a new identity, separate from him, separate from everything they'd shared. As if he'd somehow become a third assailant.

Not fair. So *incredibly* not fair.

Well, he wasn't going to let her twist him into knots again. Unlike her, he'd dealt with his demons, left them dead and buried shortly after she walked out on him. No way in hell did he plan to get caught up in her drama, or lack of it, again. If she wanted to dry up into an emotionless husk of a woman, that was her problem.

He did, by God, plan to find out who tried to cripple her so long ago.

First, though, he needed to focus on the escalating vandalism at the construction site. Someone didn't want Kylie building that tennis center, and she'd made it clear that sabotage wouldn't chase her away. So far, the incidents had been directed at stalling the actual work, but it wouldn't take long for the perp, or perps, to realize that to make an impression they needed to get personal. On top of all that, the sabotage and the bat could be related—probably *were* related, considering their concurrence. Which raised the possibility that one or both of her attackers from ten years ago were messing with her now.

He'd already asked for an unmarked car outside her house, especially at night when she was home alone. She'd hate that, but she didn't have to know. She was most likely safe while at work, considering other people were around and no one had made any overt threats toward her.

Pushing back from the table, he got up and carried his coffee cup to the sink. He desperately needed a pick-me-up, so he reached for the phone and called his daughter.

"Hi, Dad."

At the sound of Maddy's voice, his smile felt like it would split his face. "Hey. You've got that caller ID thing down, huh?"

Maddy giggled in her nine-year-old way. "That's what Mom does. Then sometimes she answers like she doesn't know who it is. Not when you call, though."

He chuckled. "Are you ready for school yet?"

"I'm eating scrambled eggs. Scott made them, with cheese and bacon."

"Hey, save some for me."

Chase liked the man who'd married his ex-wife. Scott was totally devoted to Rhonda, and he was good to Maddy. Maybe that made Chase a dork, but he didn't care. He wanted his ex-wife and daughter to be happy, and Rhonda had decided long ago that he wasn't up to the task. He hadn't been able to argue with her, not when he'd married her because he'd knocked her up rather than because he'd fallen for her. And, frankly, a divorce relieved him of the fear that he would become like his father, trapped in a loveless marriage and so angry about it that he brutalized those closest to him.

When Maddy stopped giggling, he said, "I was thinking we could do some mini-putting next week."

"Oh, you know what I want to do?"

"Hit me," he said, grinning like a clown. She made his heart so full.

"There's this new go-kart place."

"Oh, sure. Over on Lakewood. I busted some kids for speeding over there last night."

Her laugh was sweet and innocent and the best thing he'd heard in days. "Really?"

"Yeah, they must have been doing ten, fifteen miles an hour on the track. Way over the limit."

"That doesn't sound very fast."

"Trust me, it was way too fast. So I was thinking I'd swing by and give you a ride to school this morning."

"Cool."

"Think your mom would mind?"

"She never minds."

"Want to check with her for me?"

While Maddy covered the mouthpiece and carried on a muffled conversation, Chase dumped the contents of his cold coffee into the sink. Everyone should have a kid to call when shit got them down.

# 4

Kylie, coffee cup gripped in both hands and the morning newspaper on her lap, sat on the deck and watched the gently rolling waves of the Gulf of Mexico as they slid ashore and retreated. A haze of humidity hung thick over the water, seemed to cling to everything with a cloying determination that made her long for California. Especially now that the bat had turned up.

She should have stayed there, in LA, safely ensconced in her peaceful world of churning out the best college tennis players she could. Racking up wins and losses and even a few NCAA championships along the way. Nobody watching her or asking leading questions. No one expecting, or even wanting, her to crack open and spill her guts at their feet.

She couldn't help but want to run away again. Screw Kendall Falls. Screw the past. Screw . . . everything. She could even leave knowing she'd given rebuilding her life here a shot, and it hadn't worked. Too much pain, too much emotion, too much . . . Chase Manning. God, that man. He could turn her inside out with a look, something she totally didn't need right now. They'd both moved on, so why did he have to be in her face *now*?

Hearing the glass door behind her slide open, she angled her head back, glad to see her brother, a welcome distraction, stepping outside with a coffee cup in one hand. Quinn was tall—topping out at six-three—and slim, though he worked hard to counter the lankiness with avid workouts that made his arms and legs ropy with muscles.

"Hey," he said, dropping onto the weathered, wooden Adirondack chair facing hers. His wavy blond hair—in need of a comb and a haircut—hung in brown eyes that were so dark they were almost black.

"Hey," she replied, smiling at his sleepy expression.

He gave her a crooked smile and stretched his back. "That sofa isn't long enough for an adult to stretch out on."

"You could have let Jane talk you into taking the guest room, and she could have slept on the sofa."

"But then she would have won the martyrdom contest."

Kylie laughed. She might have had a different mother than Jane and Quinn, but all three had inherited their father's gene for competition. "You guys really didn't have to stay last night. Especially both of you. I was fine."

Settling back in the chair, Quinn sipped his coffee and grimaced at its heat. "Dr. Jane begs to differ."

"Dr. Jane isn't my therapist."

"Want to talk about how that makes you feel?"

She threw the newspaper at him, and he caught it, grinning. As he unfolded it, his levity faded with a low whistle. "Look at that."

She already had. The headline had leapt out at her from the front page: *Bat That Ended Mac's Career Found?*

A file photo of her hoisting the Australian Open trophy in triumph accompanied the story that covered the highlights of yesterday's find: Construction on McKays' Tennis Center was on hold while the police awaited test results on the bat. Local experts speculated that it was unlikely that after all this time the bat would yield evidence, such as fingerprints, that could be used to identify her attackers.

"Maybe you should think about taking a vacation," Quinn said without lifting his gaze from the paper.

"What would that accomplish?"

"I'm just saying, maybe it'd be good for you to get out of town until this stuff blows over. Maybe you and Wade could go somewhere."

Kylie shifted at the mention of the doctor who'd treated her knee ten years ago. Shortly after she'd returned to Kendall Falls, they'd gone on their first date. Six weeks later, they went on their last date. "Wade and I aren't seeing each other anymore."

"When did that happen? You and Dr. Bell were like two peas since you moved back."

She tried to shrug it off. "The pod was . . . overanalyzed." Before he could respond or do any overanalyzing himself, she said, "And I'm not going anywhere. Once the case gets solved, we can all put it behind us. It's been ten *years*. I, for one, am sick of thinking about it."

When Quinn's eyebrows shot up, she realized she'd overdone the vehemence, but before she could backpedal, his gaze shifted to the door beyond her shoulder. "You might want to put a lid on the stress. Here comes Dr. Jane."

Kylie turned to greet her sister with a sunny smile as she slid open the door. "Good morning, Jane. Did you find the coffee?"

"You know I don't drink coffee," Jane said, wrinkling her perfect nose in distaste. "Aren't you hot out here? It's so humid."

Jane was already showered and dressed in a pastel yellow dress that hugged the angles of her slim frame. With her delicate stature, pearl jewelry, golden blond hair, dark brown eyes, flowery perfume and high-heeled shoes, Jane was the epitome of priss. Kylie often thought she and her sister couldn't possibly have been more different. Kylie was all athlete, and Jane was all princess.

Pushing herself to her feet, Kylie said, "As it turns out, I was just coming inside for a bagel." With Jane, it was easier to give in than disagree.

Quinn hopped up. "Me, too."

In the kitchen, Kylie separated a bagel and dropped the

two halves into the toaster, while her sister hovered in the background and her brother topped off his coffee.

"What are your plans for the day?" Jane asked.

"The usual," Kylie said. "I've got my class of third graders in less than an hour." She'd started the classes shortly after she'd moved back as a way to build an eager audience for the upcoming tennis center. Plus, she loved working with kids. They still knew how to have fun, whereas college students tended to take the game way too seriously.

"You didn't cancel your classes today?" Jane cast an exasperated glance at Quinn. "Tell her she should cancel her classes. Better yet, you're her boss: You can cancel them for her."

"Whoa, ho, ho," Quinn protested with a big belly laugh. "I'm not Kylie's boss."

"You manage the health club, so doesn't that put you in charge of who runs the tennis classes there?"

Kylie grinned at her squirming brother. "She's got a point."

He raised his hands in a gesture of surrender. "I plead the fifth."

"Quinn, come on," Jane said. "Stop horsing around and be useful for a change."

"And that's my cue to fly," he said, and turned to address Kylie. "While you're eating that bagel, do I have time for a shower?"

She nodded. "Save me some hot water."

He brushed a quick kiss over her cheek. "Good luck," he whispered.

"Bailer," she whispered back.

He flashed her a grin before he sauntered out of the kitchen.

At the pantry, Kylie withdrew a jar of peanut butter and a box of teabags. "Isn't this the kind of tea you like?"

Jane took the box and reached for the red tea kettle on the stove. "Why don't you sit? I can make my own tea. When your bagel's done toasting, I'll bring it over."

Kylie let her hands fall to her sides. Here we go. "Jane."

Her sister, filling the kettle with water, glanced over her shoulder. "What?"

"I appreciate you being here, but, really, you don't have to take care of me."

Jane set the kettle on the stove and twisted on the burner, then leaned against the counter and folded her arms under her breasts. "All right. Since you're so fine, let's quit dancing around the issue. Are you prepared for what's going to happen if it turns out that that bat is the one those boys used on you?"

Kylie suppressed a sigh. Oh, to have a conversation about the weather.

Jane was already shaking her head, as if Kylie's silence were answer enough. "I'm serious about this. You would have never walked into a tennis match without being mentally prepared."

Kylie slathered peanut butter on her bagel a bit too vigorously. "This isn't a tennis match."

If it were, she'd know exactly how to respond. But this she had no training for, no point of reference. And, frankly, all she wanted to do was run as fast as she could. Just forget Kendall Falls and her family and the tennis center and Chase Manning, and go back to that safe place in California where no one cared how she felt or what she thought or whether she worked the day after a vital piece of her past resurfaced. Safety in anonymity.

Realizing that Jane hadn't tossed out one of her insightful, snappy comebacks, Kylie glanced over and found her sister watching her like a therapist observing a patient trying to wriggle out of a straitjacket. She had a knowing smile on her porcelain-doll face.

Putting aside the peanut butter–smeared knife, Kylie decided to ignore her. Not that that ever worked.

Jane hummed a little as she cranked the flame higher under the tea kettle. "I find it . . . interesting who's involved in solving the case."

"It's not interesting. It's his job."

"Technically, he shouldn't be involved. It could be considered a conflict of interest because of your past together."

"Sort of like psychoanalyzing your sister?"

Jane's peach-tinted lips tightened. "All I'm trying to do is help you."

Jane meant well, but that didn't change the fact that Kylie had the childish urge to push her face into the wall. Sisterly love at its best.

Deliberately loosening the set of her jaw, Kylie started toward the hall, bagel clasped in one hand. "As much as I'm enjoying this session, I'm running late."

Jane called after her, "I'd say you're running right on time."

# 5

QUINN MCKAY STARED DOWN AT THE SCHEDULES
spread across his desk. Two of the personal trainers had already bitched that they should have been posted on the health
club's bulletin board yesterday. He'd promised he'd get them
up right after lunch, which was right now, but he couldn't
focus, couldn't think. All he could do was worry.

He scrubbed his hands over his face. Christ, why did that
fucking bat have to turn up now, after all this time? Damn it,
he'd known when Kylie picked that particular parcel of land
for the new tennis center that it was a terrible idea. He'd tried
to tell her so.

"Why not there?" she'd asked. "It's perfect. It's in our old
neighborhood, which, in case you haven't noticed, looks like
hell these days. A new tennis center would give the kids a
place where they can be safe."

He supposed, too, that she'd wanted to recapture some of
her own unjaded happiness from those times.

"I just think that something on the newer side of town
would be more appropriate," he'd said. "You'd get a better—
richer—clientele, and in the winter, there'd be tourist traffic."

But again she'd shaken her head. "That's not the point. The old neighborhood is falling apart. There were beer cans and cigarette butts all over the lot when I toured it. The Bat Cave isn't what it used to be."

He'd chuckled at that. The Bat Cave referred to the abandoned house that had stood on the lot. With concrete walls on the outside and nothing but the wooden frames of walls inside, the house had been a stand-alone cave on two acres of Florida foliage. One of their friends had dubbed it the Bat Cave during a childhood game. Interesting how people's memories were so different. Where Kylie fondly remembered fun and games at the Bat Cave, Quinn recalled hours of getting drunk, feeling sorry for himself and resenting the hell out of her.

He'd tried again to dissuade her. "You probably won't even be able to get the people who own it to sell. They've let it sit there for years."

"I've already had the title search done and contacted the owner. She told me the history of the place and, Quinn, it's just heartbreaking. She and her husband were living in Chicago and building their dream house on that lot, but then her husband died in a car accident, and she abandoned the project. She didn't want to finish it or sell it."

"Christ, that's sad," Quinn said, relieved at the same time. "So it's going to be a tough sell to get her to part with the land."

"It *was* a tough sell." Kylie was beaming. "Turns out she's a tennis fan. When I told her what I wanted to do with the tennis center, she caved. Pun intended."

Quinn had given her his best fake smile and a warm hug. "Congratulations."

How ironic that the start of something new and good for her, the tennis center, had flicked the spotlight back on on the darkest part of her life.

A knock at his office door brought his head up. "Yes?"

Detective Sam Hawkins walked in, looking as serious as a tornado warning.

Quinn, his heart racing, could already sense the howling wind whipping into a destructive frenzy. "What can I do for you, Detective?"

Sam fixed him with a cold, dark stare. "We need to talk."

# — 6

KYLIE NAILED NOTHING BUT AIR AS SHE SWUNG her racket at the ball.

"Keep your eye on the ball!"

She looked across the net at the lanky, dark-haired fourteen-year-old on the other end of the court and laughed. "That's my line."

T.J. Ritchie shook his head in mock disgust. "Not when you're missing shots I could have gotten with my eyes closed."

She gave an apologetic shrug as she slipped a ball out of the pocket of her shorts. They were ninety minutes into a sixty-minute lesson under the hot sun. But she didn't mind. He was, by far, the most promising kid she worked with. Wiry and well on his way to six feet tall, T.J. had an easy grace that made him unbelievably swift on his feet, a winner at the net or running the baseline. The more time she could get with him, the better.

Besides, she sensed something troubling him today. He'd been slamming the ball back at her harder than ever.

"I'm a little off," she said. Maybe he'd respond that he was, too, opening the door to a conversation.

"No shit?"

She fell out of her serving stance and cast him a chastising glance. "Watch your mouth, kid."

He bounced from one foot to the other, racket grasped in both hands before him, ready to return her serve and grinning like a fool. "What are you going to do about it? Kick my ass?"

"Uh, yeah. Ever occur to you that I've been taking it easy on you because you're a kid?" She enjoyed their trash talk, having discovered early on that she could tweak his form by firing him up. Her dad had often done the same to her.

T.J. rolled his eyes. "So, just now, when you whiffed on that ball, that was your way of taking it easy on me, huh?"

"You were looking winded."

"Yeah, right. More like *you* were winded."

She loved how easy and relaxed he was with her. "You are so not ready for what I've got."

"Yeah? Show me."

She tossed the ball up, but instead of firing it across the net, she caught it and arched her brows at him. "Sure you're ready? 'Cause I've been holding back."

"I can handle whatever you've got."

"That's what you think."

"I think you're trying to psych me out."

"Ah, so you have been listening."

"Half of the game is mental. Blah, blah, blah. Are you going to serve or what?"

"Blah, blah, blah? That's what my age-old wisdom is to you?"

"Emphasis on the 'age-old' part."

She hammered the ball past him before he'd finished laughing at his own joke.

"Hey! I wasn't ready."

She slipped another ball out of her pocket. "You're not going to cry, are you?"

He dropped into his ready posture, eyes slits. Competitive to a fault. "Let's see you do it again when I'm not distracted by your yapping."

He sounded just like Chase, and for a moment, she let herself miss the days they'd spent together on the court, training for the next big match. He'd made drills fun. Teasing and flirting and, with perspiration gleaming on his arms and too-long hair flopping on his forehead with every shot, he'd looked . . . so . . . so . . . breathtaking. It had never occurred to her that he could so easily replace what they had. And it still hurt. God, it hurt.

Shaking off the memories, she called, "One more and we're done. Match point, Ace."

She powered a serve at T.J.'s feet, pouring every ounce of past hurt into it. He managed a weak return that she slammed back so swiftly it bounced right past him.

She chuckled at his eye-blinking shock. "Don't worry about it, kid. You'll get there."

His shoulders drooping, he strolled to the side of the court to retrieve his water bottle. Before she could regret putting him away so easily, she remembered that he wasn't given to pouting when he lost. Something big was on his mind.

Uncapping her own water bottle, she waited for him to join her by the tall, chain-link fence that enclosed the four tennis courts behind the Kendall Falls Health Club. They were the only players at the moment, thanks to the almost-daily thunderstorm brewing in the distance.

"What's with the long face?" she asked.

"Nothing." He shrugged with one shoulder, then said, "Oh, I almost forgot." Shoving his hand into the front pocket of his shorts, he withdrew a wad of damp bills. "I know it's not what I owe."

Kylie looked from the money to his sweat-streaked face, but he avoided her gaze.

When she made no move to accept the cash, he thrust it at her, his pink cheeks reddening. "I know my mom hasn't been paying."

Ah. Now they were getting somewhere. The boy had major mother issues, and as far as Kylie could tell, not one of them was his fault. "That's between your mom and the club."

"Well, it's between the club and me now." When still she hesitated, he scowled. "I'm not a charity case."

She released an indelicate snort. "Of course you're not. You're my friend, and I play tennis with my friends because I like to, not because they pay me."

The suggestion of a smile touched his eyes, and he pocketed the money. Angling his chin to indicate something over her shoulder, he said, "That guy's been watching us awhile."

She glanced around to see Chase Manning sitting casually in the metal risers next to the courts. An unexpected shiver ran through her, and she shook it off. Don't be an idiot.

"Do you know him?" T.J. asked.

She forced a smile at the teen. "Yes."

"Looks like a cop."

The distaste in his tone surprised her. "You don't like cops?"

He shrugged. "Don't think about them one way or another." He swallowed some water and recapped his bottle. "Same time tomorrow?"

"You bet."

He gestured at the ball-littered court. "I'll clean up before I go."

"Thanks."

As T.J. retrieved the hopper and began collecting tennis balls, Kylie slid her racket into its case, conscious of Chase's steady gaze on her. The fit of the brace on her knee felt more snug than usual, and she resisted the urge to adjust it. She couldn't help the self-consciousness. The scars underneath represented everything that had gone wrong with her life back then, with *them*.

Easing through the gate, she took advantage of her sunshaded eyes to study him as she approached. He had changed so much over the years. He wasn't "cute" anymore, not like when he'd been her training partner. He'd been boyish then, and quick to smile only for her, and tease. Now, his jaw seemed made of granite, untempered by the nearly black hair that the wind feathered over his forehead.

She paused at the bottom riser of the bleachers and took

off her sunglasses, determined to show him, and herself, that she didn't feel the need to hide behind them.

Chase's lips curved, but the smile didn't touch his emerald-hard eyes. "Looked to me like you were a little hard on the kid."

The deep pitch of his voice washed over her like a caress, so sensual that she imagined his lips near her ear, his warm breath against her sensitized skin. Her pulse kicked into a higher gear, and she swallowed against the tightening in her throat.

And what the hell did he mean by that anyway? Training was about challenge. He knew that better than anyone. He'd challenged her all over the court, until she was ready to drop from exhaustion, and still he'd pushed her. He'd been like that making love, too, when they'd finally taken that step, never fully satisfied until she was so sated she could barely move.

Gazing at him now, unsure of how she should respond to his comment, she watched his smile become knowing, as though he knew exactly where her head had gone.

Heat flushed into her face, and she set her teeth. "Can I help you with something?"

"You were always merciless on the court, but I figured you'd mellowed by now."

"So you're here to critique the way I give lessons?"

"That forehand is still a killer. The kid never saw it coming."

"The 'kid's' name is T.J. Ritchie. And, as you well know, he'll be a top-notch player because of the way I challenge him."

A muscle in his temple contracted. "Not as good as you, though, is he? You just made sure he knew that."

She wished she'd left her damn sunglasses on. Then she could have looked away and he wouldn't have known, but now she had no choice but to hold his gaze and not blink. The ebb and flow of his anger washed over her like a gulf wave eroding the beach, and she wondered why, after so many years, he still held so tightly to it. She wasn't the one who'd gotten someone pregnant mere days after they'd split. Hell, maybe it hadn't even been days. Maybe he'd knocked that girl up *before* she left.

Okay, she could deal with this. Eye on the ball.

"You stopped by for a reason?" she asked, pleased at her neutral tone.

His expression didn't change as he rose and stepped over the first row of bleacher benches, agile as a cat with none of the cuddly attributes. When he stood beside her, taller by at least six inches with shoulders twice as broad, he pulled a notebook out of his back pocket and flipped it open with professional precision. Game on.

"The bat didn't yield any evidence," he said. "Looks like it was wiped clean before it was buried."

The knot in her stomach muscles loosened. Maybe she could avoid the media nightmare after all. Everyone could stop asking her if she was okay. She could get on with the tennis center, with rebuilding her life in Kendall Falls. Everyone could move on . . .

Except Chase's manner didn't say, "It's over. The case is cold again." He couldn't have looked more serious if he'd been aiming a gun at her, his finger on the trigger.

His features softened, anger yielding to the expression a cop made when he was about to tell you a loved one had just died in a car accident. "Maybe you should sit down."

Every cell in her body went on high alert, and she squared her shoulders, raised her chin. "I'm good, thanks."

He glanced down at his notes for a moment, and when he raised his gaze, his brow furrowed. "The crime scene guys found the shirt your foreman mentioned. Looks like it was used to clean the bat before both were wrapped in a garbage bag and buried. The bag protected them from the elements."

"Lucky break," she said, not feeling lucky at all. Trapped was more like it. Imprisoned by the past with no hope of escape.

Chase rubbed the back of his neck. "Our forensics team found blood on the shirt. If you could stop by the lab later to provide a blood sample, they can determine if it's yours."

"Okay." She heard herself say it, heard her own voice, clear and steady and strong, while inside, she wanted to scream. What good would it do to know if the blood on that shirt belonged to her? They had no fingerprints, no DNA from the attackers. It wasn't like they had to prove *she* was at the scene of the crime. She started to say that when she realized Chase watched her with an intense focus that made her heart skip. He wasn't done with what he'd come to share. And whatever it was, it was bad.

She felt sick for a moment, dizzy. If she hadn't been a trained athlete, taught to run to the net to take control of the game, she might have decided to sit down after all.

Instead, she met the intensity of his green eyes and gave him her game face. Nothing shakes me. Go ahead, aim at my head and see what happens. "Just tell me."

"The shirt . . . it's a gym shirt from Kendall Falls High. It belonged to your brother."

# 7

CHASE WANTED TO LOOK AWAY, BUT LIKE A RUBBER-necker at the scene of a horrific accident, he kept his gaze on Kylie, waiting for her to buckle. She couldn't possibly *not* react to this news.

He thought of how she'd looked when he'd arrived. A fine film of healthy perspiration had glistened on her arms and legs, toned muscles flexing as she fired tennis balls at the kid like rockets. She'd chided and teased and taunted the boy with such affection, and just like that, she was there, the girl he'd fallen for so many years ago. Right *there*.

With someone else.

Ladies and gentlemen, meet Chase Manning, jealous of a damn kid.

How stupid and immature could he get? But she did it to him. Kylie. The woman who ripped his heart out and stomped all over it all the way to the other side of the country. As if she couldn't get far enough away from him.

"How do you know the shirt is Quinn's?" she asked, her steady voice breaking into his thoughts.

He focused on her, on her blue gray eyes so level on his. She hadn't even flinched at what he'd said about the shirt.

She'd absorbed it, thought about it and come back with a logical question. No shock brimmed in those steel eyes. No denial. No anxiety. No nothing. What the fuck?

Shaking his head, he consulted his notes even though he didn't need to. He did need, however, to remind himself that he was there as a cop, not a jilted lover.

"His initials are on the label," he said. "There was only one Q.M. at Kendall Falls High back then. Maybe ever."

"So I suppose this means construction stays shut down," she said. Even, steady, unshakeable. Incredible.

He cleared his throat. "Until we can do a search for more evidence, yes."

"I've probably got a week of wiggle room financially. That's it."

"I can't promise we can get it done in a week. It's a large area to cover, but we'll work as fast as we can."

She nodded, not a smidge of slippage in her expression. "Okay then. Is that all?"

He almost gaped at her. *Is that all?* For a moment, he thought she hadn't gotten it, that maybe he should spell out what finding Quinn's shirt meant. But, no, even the queen of denial couldn't dodge the facts.

"No, that's not all," he said. "I have some questions about Quinn."

"You should probably talk to him, then. Last time I saw him, he was in his office."

"My partner is talking to him now."

"Then what do you need from me?"

"Do you remember where Quinn was at the time of your attack?"

"I assume he was home. At least, he was when I left for my workout." Ruthless control. Not even an eye-twitch of emotion.

"Did you talk to him before you went?" Chase asked.

"This is a waste of time."

"Humor me."

"Yes, I talked to him. He was supposed to go running with me but changed his mind at the last minute."

"Why?"

"I don't know."

"I think you do. You two didn't have the best relationship, as I recall. Did you have a fight?"

"As I'm sure you can imagine, everything that happened that day before I went running is somewhat of a blur."

"Then let's talk about what happened *after* you went running."

Her eyes narrowed for the briefest of moments before she clamped down on the flare of alarm. "I went over that with the police back then. I'm sure they kept notes."

He ignored the sarcasm. "I need you to go over it with me now. I'm new to the case."

She clenched her jaw so hard he should have heard teeth grinding. "What are you trying to do here?"

"My job."

"You were there."

His confusion must have shown on his face, because she repeated it. "You were there, with me, afterward. I shouldn't have to tell you about it."

Oh. He swallowed hard, remembering in high-definition sitting by her bedside when she woke from that first, emergency surgery. She'd been so beautifully out of it, disoriented from the pain medication as she groped for his hand with a loopy smile, telling him she liked the way he smelled. Like coconuts, she'd said. Rough and hard on the outside, soft and sweet on the inside. Like you.

He wasn't feeling so soft and sweet on the inside at the moment. More like the middle of a compost heap. "I'm not talking about the aftermath," he said tightly.

"So, let me get this straight. You're still bent out of shape that I wouldn't open up to you about it back then, so you're using your job as an excuse to force it out of me now. Is that it?"

"If that's the way you want to look at it. Either way, you need to tell me. From the beginning. In detail."

She didn't respond for a long moment, as though debating her options. But he already knew she wouldn't walk away.

He'd issued a challenge that her competitive spirit, her drive to prove that she was A-OK, wouldn't allow her to rebuff.

Finally, she gestured toward the empty, paved track that circled the health club. "Can we walk?"

He nodded and fell in step beside her, catching her scent on a shift in the wind. Cocoa butter and vanilla. It sparked a memory of being sprawled on the beach with her. The water had lapped at the sand near their bare feet. They'd been relaxed and happy, curling easily against each other. He hadn't felt like that, like he'd been home, since. The very next day, while he sat in English class at Kendall Falls Community College, two fuckwads took her down with a blue aluminum baseball bat.

She didn't speak until they'd reached the first curve in the track, until the change in direction and the approaching thunderheads provided a cooling breeze. "You already know the basics. I was out for a run. Usual time. Usual place, on the path through the wooded area behind the Bat Cave."

He remembered that path like it led through his own back yard. They'd run it together a million times. He'd run it a million times since, catching himself still looking for clues, stopping sometimes to catch his breath at *the spot*. He remembered vividly what the area looked like after the attack—the plants, dead leaves and pine needles inside the circle of yellow crime-scene tape trampled flat and spattered with blood. *Kylie's* blood.

His own blood had ended up on the trunk of a nearby tree, which he'd mindlessly hammered with his fists the day she'd walked away from him.

He glanced sideways as she put her sunglasses on, despite the growing darkness of impending rain. Tension bled off her like waves of heat, and his need to hear, in her words, what happened wavered. But he had to do his job.

"Ky?"

Her chin inched up, and her shoulders squared. An ingrained response. "There were two of them," she said. "Both slim and wiry. Most likely teenage boys."

"Wearing?"

"Blue jeans. Both of them. Ratty, with holes in the knees. The one . . . the leader wore a black T-shirt with some kind of red band insignia on it. Aerosmith, I think. The other one had on a gray T-shirt that had 'XXL' on the front, like a generic gym shirt." She glanced quickly at him. "Not a Kendall Falls High shirt. Those are red and white."

He acknowledged that with a nod. "Neither was wearing the shirt we found with the bat. What else?"

"Black ski masks. That was my first clue that I was in trouble. Funny, really. You'd think my first clue would have been the bat. The one in the black shirt was slapping it against his palm like . . ."

Chase waited her out like a cop was supposed to.

"When I turned to run the other way," she continued, voice still strong, "the second guy was behind me, blocking me. I ran off the path, into the woods, but it was muddy and slippery. Maybe if I'd stayed on the path, I could have outrun them. I probably could have gotten past the second guy. He was smaller than the first, weaker."

Amazing, Chase thought. Monday-morning quarterbacking her own attack.

"They caught me easily. The one without the bat seemed reluctant, like he thought it was a joke at first. He kept saying, 'I can't.' He sounded like he was crying, like he—" She stopped as her voice cracked for the first time.

Chase curled his right hand into a tight fist. A crack in Kylie McKay's voice was the equivalent of a screaming sob from any other woman. Instead of responding to it, he tried to nudge her along. "Did you recognize anything about their voices?"

Shaking her head, she cleared her throat. "Just that they sounded like boys. The leader bullied the other one."

Chase's steps faltered. This was new. "Bullied him how?"

"He kept yelling at him, calling him names. Pussy and dickweed. He seemed kind of over the top with it, actually. Giddy one minute and mean the next, like he was high."

This also was new. He wrote "high" in his notebook and put two question marks next to it. "So the leader was aggres-

sive toward his partner," he said, more to prod her along than
to clarify.

She nodded. "He threatened to kick his ass if he didn't
hand him the bat."

"Wait, I thought the leader had the bat."

"He dropped it when he hit me."

"He hit you?" That sure as shit wasn't in the case file, and
he had to fight the swell of hot rage that started in his gut and
blazed to the top of his head. The attack as he'd understood it
from the report had been bad enough, and that had been
without punches being thrown.

"He was trying to subdue me, and I kicked him. In the
shin, I think, and it made him angry. It was more of a slap
than a punch."

She had the unemotional tone down to an art.

"And after he slapped you?"

"I started screaming my head off, so he put his hand over
my mouth. It smelled like peanut butter and gasoline, like
he'd put gas in his car before he had a sandwich."

Chase's stomach turned, and it took all his cop training to
stay on track. "And then?"

"I bit him."

He almost smiled. He hoped she'd drawn blood.

"Dumb move," she said. "*Really* dumb, actually. He hit
me again, with his fist this time, and I almost blacked out."

Bastard. Fucking bastard. And why the hell wasn't any
of this in the file? Had the cops not questioned her closely?
"Keep going," he prodded, his tone as level as hers. Main-
taining that tone, and his distance, was getting harder,
though.

"He yelled at the other one to hand him the bat. The
weaker one gave it to him, and that's when I saw it the most
clearly. It had 'killer' written in big capital letters in black
marker on the grip. The one guy was crying by then, and the
leader called him a fucking moron and told him to snap out
of it and help him."

*Jesus.* "And then?"

She compressed her lips into a grim line, her jaw tight.

"I need you to tell me what happened next, Ky."

She stopped walking and faced him, pulling her sunglasses off at the same time. Gray blue eyes that flashed with silvery light under the darkening clouds clashed with his. "The weaker one held me down for what seemed like minutes, but it was probably only a second or two before he let me go and ran away. I thought it was over, and just as I started to roll over to crawl away, the leader hit me with the bat. I heard the crunch before I felt the pain, and then it was like my leg had caught on fire. The second time he swung the bat, I lost consciousness."

Chase stared into her eyes, floored by the unwavering way she stared back. Sick didn't begin to describe the greasy feeling in his gut as the images in his head spun out. She'd been alone out there, bleeding and unconscious for who knew how long. Vulnerable and unable to defend herself from further harm.

"Any other questions?"

He blinked, surprised at her terse voice, her straight-on gaze. He'd helped train her, had witnessed her father's coaching, and neither of them had had such ironclad focus or expected it.

When one eyebrow ticked up, indicating the wane of her patience, he cleared his throat. "Do you remember how you got to the ER?"

"The police think the one who ran away called 911. I suppose I should be grateful. I could have lost my leg."

Or bled to death. His rage returned, and it wasn't the first time he understood why certain people sought vengeance.

As the first roll of thunder rumbled in the distance, Kylie slid her sunglasses back into place with a hand that was steadier than Chase's whole body. When she spoke again, her voice held no tremor, no doubt. "There's no way my brother had anything to do with that."

# 8

CHASE TAPPED HIS THUMBS ON THE STEERING wheel while he waited for his partner to finish talking to Quinn McKay. The rain had started, and it flooded down the windshield in torrents. Thunder boomed so violently that the truck shook.

He couldn't get the damn ache out of his throat, and he knew exactly what caused it: The woman he fell in love with was gone, probably forever. He couldn't even reconcile the woman he'd just talked to with the woman he'd made love to for the first time. That Kylie had been open and trusting, easygoing and relaxed. Being that close to her, connecting with her in a way that no one else ever had, had been incredible, mind-blowing. He remembered how good she'd felt around him, so tight and hot and wet, and how he'd climaxed too fast. He'd regretted that, being so greedy for his own release that he hadn't made it just as memorable for her. Luckily, she'd let him make it up to her later.

The passenger-side door jerked open, startling him as Sam all but dived into the SUV to escape the slashing rain.

It took Chase a moment to shake the memories, to refocus on work. "How'd it go with Quinn?" he asked.

"Didn't get much."

"Not surprising. The game face must be a McKay gene. What'd he say about the shirt?"

"Said it rained that day, and he got wet. Took it off while he was hanging out at the abandoned house—"

"The Bat Cave," Chase said.

"Right, the Bat Cave. Anyway, says he forgot it when he left."

"So whoever buried the bat could have grabbed the shirt when he needed something to clean it up. Can anyone vouch for him leaving the shirt?"

"Says he was there alone."

Of course he was. Chase started the SUV, and the windshield wipers began to flap. As he steered into slow-moving traffic, he asked, "Where did he say he was when Kylie was attacked?"

"In their parents' garage getting drunk."

Chase's brain seemed to give a little jerk as he thought about the note he'd made when Kylie mentioned the giddiness of the lead assailant. Could he have been drunk rather than high, as she assumed? "Was he drinking with anyone?"

"Nope. Says he was all by his lonesome."

"Figures."

Sam flipped through his own small notebook. "Quinn was in my high school class," he said as he scanned his notes and absently rubbed at the side of his hand like he had an itch. "Weird to think we all went to the same school."

Chase didn't even remember Sam from high school, probably because Chase was a senior when Sam and Quinn were freshmen. And he had other things on his mind as a senior, such as behaving himself as Kylie's three-years-older training partner, at least until her dad wouldn't be inclined to kill him once he found out they'd fallen for each other.

Chase shook the memories out of his head. Useless to go there now. "You remember anything in particular about Quinn?" he asked.

"You probably know more about him than I did, considering you were dating his sister."

"Tell me anyway. I was biased."

"He struck me as one of those angry guys," Sam said. "Quick to throw a punch."

A punch? Chase remembered strong words and attitude, but no punches. "You saw this in person?"

"A couple times. Nothing major. You have any insight?"

Chase shrugged. "The McKays weren't your typical family."

"That's what happens when you've got a star athlete at home, huh? The siblings get resentful."

"It wasn't just that. The family dynamic was . . . off."

"Off how?"

"Most people don't even know this, but Lara McKay isn't Kylie's biological mother."

"No kidding? She calls her mom, doesn't she?"

"Yeah, but Ky's real mom died when she was a baby. Her dad, Nolan, remarried fairly quickly, though, so Lara's the only mother she's ever known."

"So Quinn and Jane are actually Kylie's half siblings."

"A technicality most of the time," Chase said.

"But Quinn liked to poke at her about it?"

"When he was at his surliest, he'd tell her their mom didn't love her as much as she loved him and Jane. Bullshit, of course. I saw Lara in action, and she loved her stepdaughter just as much as her own kids."

"Did Quinn ever get physical with Kylie?"

"Not that I saw. I mean, I wanted to punch his lights out more than once for the way he talked to her. Kylie shrugged it off, for the most part. I know it hurt her, but she wasn't afraid of him. Not that she ever indicated, anyway. More often than not, she defended Quinn. Her dad didn't pay enough attention to him, she'd say. That's all he wants: attention."

"I have to say all this puts a disturbing spin on the shirt," Sam said.

Chase reluctantly agreed.

"So what do you think?" Sam prodded. "You like him for the attack?"

"What would be the motive?" Chase had his own ideas but wanted to hear Sam's unbiased opinion first.

"Jealousy," Sam said.

Check.

"Resentment."

Check.

"Sibling rivalry."

Check. Same page, all the way.

"You want to bring him in?" Sam asked.

"I think we should wait until the results come back on the shirt. If that blood isn't Kylie's, we'll be at a dead end all over again."

Sam nodded. "Works for me."

"In the meantime, who else have we got?"

"According to the case file, cops looked at the usual suspects, mostly competitors, considering the nature of the attack. But they didn't come up with anything."

"They talked to me," Chase said. And he'd had a hell of a time answering questions when all he could think about was getting back to the hospital. At one point, he'd leapt out of his chair, ready to take the cop's head off when he suggested Chase might have resented the fact that Kylie was a better tennis player, that maybe his ego couldn't take it and he'd lashed out.

"I saw the transcript," Sam said. "It pissed me off."

Chase cast a tight smile at his partner. "Thanks."

"You're lucky you didn't ditch classes that day."

"Yeah." He'd considered doing just that until Kylie chided him into going. Otherwise, he might have been on that trail with her, and maybe none of it would have happened. As it was, she'd said Quinn had promised to run with her, and she'd wanted the time with her brother.

Which meant that when Quinn backed out on her, he'd known when and where she was going. Shit.

"Mind if I throw out a bit of advice?" Sam asked.

"I need some advice?"

"You're about to rip the steering wheel out of the dash with your bare hands."

Chase relaxed his grip and flexed his fingers. "Okay, sure, give me some advice."

"You shouldn't be on this case, and you know it. You're too close."

"You're wrong if you think Kylie and I are close," Chase said. "We couldn't be further from close."

"You know what I mean. The boss would understand, considering. In fact, he's already asked me to try to talk some sense into you."

"He's afraid to try it himself?"

"He just figures that as your friend, I'd have a better shot at getting you to see reason."

Chase angled his head forward, hearing the pops as taut tendons readjusted. No way was he walking away from this. Not when he might actually get the chance to nail those two fuckers to the wall for what they did to Kylie.

"I get what you're saying," Chase said, "but Kylie and I will be fine."

# 9

JANE MCKAY CHECKED HER REFLECTION ONE MORE time in the hand mirror from her desk drawer, irritated at her brother's tardiness. If he didn't show up soon, she was heading over to Macy's to check out their one-day shoe sale before her next appointment. Rubbing a smudge of lipstick off her teeth, she wondered again why Quinn insisted they meet at her office instead of at a restaurant or one of their respective homes, but she had a feeling she knew what he wanted to talk about.

The phone rang, and she glanced at the caller ID display, her heart doing a dance of anticipation when she saw who it was. She took a breath and let it out before snatching up the phone.

"Hi, Tiger," she said, pleased at how breathy she'd managed to sound.

"We should talk."

Shoulders slumping at his lack of reaction to her "take me" voice, she leaned back in her black leather chair and swiveled so that she faced the floor-to-ceiling window overlooking Kendall Falls' premier boulevard lined with towering palm trees.

"What do you want to talk about?" she asked.

"You know. When Kylie finds out—"

"You mean 'if.' "

"What?"

"*If* she finds out. Not when."

"Either way," he said, "she's not going to be happy."

"She's not happy anyway."

"Jane."

She blew out a frustrated breath. "Fine, what do you propose we do?"

"I propose you tell her."

"Why should I tell her? What about you?"

"You're her sister. It should come from you."

Figures. Men were such cowards.

"Jane, seriously." He sighed into the phone. "She needs to know. The sooner the better, for all of us."

The buzzer that signaled Quinn's arrival brought her head up. "I have to go."

"Wait. Will you meet me later?"

She smiled in spite of her irritation. "Maybe."

"No maybe. I want you." He paused. "Again."

"All right then. I'll see you later."

When she opened the door to the waiting room, Quinn turned from the window.

"You're late," she said before she registered the circles under his eyes and the curved, vertical lines that flanked the grim set of his mouth. Uh-oh.

She gestured him into her office.

The soles of Quinn's shoes squeaked on the pristine, ceramic tile floor as he walked by, and Jane glanced down, noting that their footwear mirrored the sharp contrast in their careers. Her brother wore simple black loafers that had been well used, while Jane strode back to her desk in a brand-new pair of strappy sandals that had probably cost more than Quinn's monthly car payment.

Jane settled behind her mahogany desk, satisfied as always by the leathery crunch and crackle of her chair, while

Quinn sank into the overstuffed easy chair provided for patients.

"Thanks for agreeing to meet like this," he said.

"You're lucky I had a cancellation this afternoon. So what do you want to talk about that we couldn't discuss at home or in public?"

The horizontal lines of anxiety that seemed permanently etched into his forehead tightened like a squeezed accordion. "You know exactly why I'm here. And I didn't want Kylie to see us. She'd get suspicious."

Jane picked up a pen and tapped it against the yellow legal pad awaiting her notes. "Okay, let's talk. You go first."

# 10

KYLIE WALKED TO THE HEALTH CLUB'S BACK PARK-
ing lot in the humid, airless afternoon. The sun glared down
from a cloudless sky, turning the scattered puddles from the
earlier thunderstorm into steaming pools.

Several hours after the encounter with Chase, she still felt
hollowed out and raw, memories so close to the surface that
the air surrounding her seemed to vibrate with her own
screams for help. The remembered scent of wet earth clung
to her senses, and her fingers vividly recalled the squish of
mud between them as she'd tried to claw her way away, to
safety, before solid aluminum smashed her safe, beautiful
world into a million jagged pieces.

She'd pulled herself back together on the other coast, built
a new passion—for coaching and teaching—and pretended
the past didn't exist. It didn't hurt there, and life was easy.
No sisters or brothers or friends hammering at her to open
up.

Talk, talk, talk. That's all they ever wanted to do here. As
if talking could fix everything that had gone wrong. Didn't
they realize that, more than anything, *not* talking helped? All
the bad stuff faded away when she could focus on planning

the tennis center. She loved shaping a place where kids who didn't have rich parents would be able to learn the game and play.

Like T.J. Ritchie. When she watched him play, she understood exactly why her father had pushed her the way he had, always demanding more, always pressuring her to play harder, play better, play smarter. T.J. had star power, and he improved every day on the court, increasing her anticipation of the moment when he realized he was destined to win. A lot.

Time with him, time with the tennis center, had made all the other stuff fade into the background, had made it bearable to see the looks of concern—*unnecessary* concern, damn it—from those she loved. Eventually, she'd figured, the looks would fade, just like the nightmares and physical pain and bitter disappointment of dreams lost.

Sighing, she thumbed the remote on her key ring to unlock the doors on her royal blue Jeep Liberty. After stowing her racket and bag behind the driver's seat, she slid behind the wheel and hoped that a relaxing ride home with some fun Sheryl Crow blaring from the speakers would lighten her mood.

Movement out of the corner of her right eye had her twisting toward it with a gasp as a black-clad figure rushed the passenger side of the Jeep. Before Kylie could draw breath for a scream, something smashed, hard and violent, into the windshield. She jerked back, arms flying up to protect her head, and scooted her butt down in the seat. Hunkered down, eyes tightly closed and heart thudding, she braced for the next blow that would no doubt shower glass all over her. And then he'd be in . . . and he'd . . . he'd . . .

It took her several terrified moments to grasp that the only sound in the Jeep was her own harsh breathing. Outside, tree leaves rustled in the wind and a distant motorcycle engine roared to life.

She opened her eyes and looked around just in time to catch a glimpse of a slim, all-in-black shape disappearing into the wooded area at the back of the parking lot.

Hands shaking, she dug for her cell phone to call 911, taking in the cracks that spread across the windshield like spider-webbed fault lines. Safety glass, she realized. But, holy God, it took a massive blow to bow it inward like that.

Her stomach jittered, and she fumbled with the door handle, suddenly frantic to get out. It took both hands to get the door open.

Eye on the ball, McKay. Focus. Eye on the ball.

As if that would help.

Outside, she stood on trembling legs, hanging onto the Jeep's door for support. She felt dizzy, outside herself.

"Nine-one-one emergency."

The voice focused her. "I . . . uh . . . I'm in the back parking lot of Kendall Falls Health Club. A man just smashed my windshield and ran away."

"Are you hurt?"

"No, no, I'm fine."

"Are you certain he ran away? He could still harm you."

"Yes. I saw him."

"I'm dispatching police officers to your location right now. Who am I speaking to?"

"Kylie McKay."

"And you're sure you're not hurt, Kylie?"

"I'm fine."

"Can you describe the person? I'll alert police to search for him."

"I just had a glimpse. He wore black. That's all I saw. I'm sorry."

"That's okay, Kylie. The police will be there soon. Are you alone?"

"I can . . . I can go inside. My brother—" She broke off, choking up at the thought of facing Quinn right now, shaky and freaked out.

"That's a good idea. I'll let the officers know where you are. Can you hang on for a moment?"

"Yes." She waited for what seemed like an eternity, and as her equilibrium began to return, she cursed herself for being such a coward. How the hell did closed eyes protect her from an attack, for God's sake? She should have locked the Jeep instead of cowering. Should have laid on the horn. Should have grabbed her cell phone and dialed 911 right then. Should have done *something*.

She'd vowed never to be caught unprepared again, and what did she do at the first sign of a threat? Act like a scared rabbit: If I don't see you, you won't see me. Fool. *Stupid* fool.

Right that minute, she should have been walking back into the safety of the health club instead of standing there like a quivering mass of gelatin, waiting for the windshield-smasher to come back and take a swing at *her* this time.

Pressing trembling fingers to her lips, she started to pace toward the front of the Jeep. She just needed a minute to get it together, and then she'd seek out Quinn.

Eye on the ball. Focus. Breathe.

She'd just turned to pace back the other way when a gruff voice assaulted her ear. "Kylie, it's Chase. Where are you?"

She stopped in midstep. Chase? He must have heard the chatter about her 911 call on his police radio and asked the operator to transfer her to his cell. She closed her eyes and rubbed at her forehead. She couldn't think. "Uh, I'm by my car—"

"Go inside. Do you hear me? I'm on my way, but I want you to go inside."

She nodded without speaking, her stomach surging again at his urgent tone. Oh God, oh God.

"Are you listening to me?"

"Yes," she croaked.

"Go. *Right now*."

The infuriated, demanding growl brought her head up. "Okay. I'm—"

She broke off as she saw what lay on the pavement on the passenger side of the Jeep.

A blue aluminum baseball bat.

# 11

KYLIE ROSE FROM WHERE SHE SAT ON THE CURB AS Chase's Explorer tore into the parking lot, a red light flashing on its roof. Tires squealed the SUV to a stop, and an instant later, two car doors slammed. While Sam did a wide circle around the Jeep, surveying the damage, Chase strode to Kylie's side and shocked her by taking her arm a bit too aggressively.

"Are you okay?" He looked her over as if he expected to find gaping wounds.

She couldn't respond at first, thrown by the intensity of his inspection as much as the pressure of his fingers around her upper arm. She hadn't felt his touch in years, and all the blood in her brain seemed to rush to the point of contact, swirling the scent of his tropical sunscreen through her head. Oh, God, it was staggering.

"Kylie?"

The alarm in his voice snapped her back, and she took a quick step away from him, forcing him to release her. Breathe, breathe. "I'm fine. My Jeep, on the other hand . . ."

His narrowed eyes took in the vandalism. "Damn."

Kylie said nothing, her mind's eye focusing again on the

thing on the ground on the other side of the Jeep. The smashed windshield was bad enough, but the bat. *That* bat, just like the one . . .

Sam joined them, his features tense. "Kylie."

"Detective." She tried to smile at him as she chafed her arms with the palms of her hands. It wasn't cold out, but she'd started to shiver.

"Notice how she did what I told her to do and waited inside," Chase grumbled.

His anger, apparently at *her*, caught her by surprise, but before she could respond, Sam said, "Are you okay? You're awfully pale."

Concern. God, she hated concern. It made her feel so weak. Taking a breath, she held it for a moment—steady, steady—and let it out. "I'm okay. Shaken, of course."

"Perfectly understandable," Sam said.

Chase paced over to the Jeep to check it out, looking pissed and tense in faded jeans and a tucked-in navy polo shirt that emphasized the ridged plane of his abdomen. His fists clenched at his sides, bulging the muscles in his biceps and cording the veins in his forearms. Just looking at him, taking in the flush of his anger, the energy in his stride as he stalked around the Jeep, sharp gaze scanning first the pavement and then the trees at the back of the parking lot—everything about him made her heart hitch and stutter into a higher gear. The distraction helped break the choke hold that fear had on her throat . . . until he glanced over at her, his eyes spitting fire.

When he strode over to rejoin her and Sam, he stopped too close and glared down at her from his cringe-inducing height. "Tell me what happened."

He was so close she felt she couldn't draw a decent breath. Why was he trying so hard to intimidate her? "He came out of nowhere, hit the windshield and ran away."

"Wearing?"

"Black."

"Can you be more specific?"

"Black pants, black shirt, black hat . . . or ski mask, I guess. Black gloves."

"Gloves?"

"Yes, he had on gloves. It didn't register at first, but he was definitely wearing gloves. I can't even tell you if he was black or white."

"Build?"

"Tall and thin."

"How do you know it was a guy?"

"I assumed, I guess, because he was strong enough to break the windshield."

"Any ideas who would want to scare you?"

"No."

"Anything else suspicious happen lately? Other than the sabotage at the construction site."

"No."

"Weird phone calls? Hang ups? E-mails?" He fired the questions at her so quickly they seemed to whirl around her.

"No."

"Have you had a falling out with anyone since you returned?" He leaned closer, as though trying to blast the truth out of her with his laser vision.

"No," she said steadily. Breathe, breathe.

When he turned to squint up at the stucco walls of the health club, she felt as though the air-conditioning had just kicked in on a steaming hot day. As her shoulders relaxed and she managed a full breath, the spinning sensation in her head leveled.

"This place have security cameras aimed at the parking lots?" Chase asked.

Sam shifted to peer at the building, too. "Looks like there's one at the east corner. I don't see any others."

"Quinn would know about that," Kylie said.

"Is he here?" Sam asked.

"Yes, in his office."

"I'll check with him," Sam said, and took off.

As soon as they were alone, Chase rounded on Kylie. "Why didn't you go inside like I told you to do?" he demanded.

"If whoever did this wanted to hurt me, he had ample op-portunity."

"Which brings up another point. Why the hell are you parking in a back lot that's virtually empty?"

"Safety has never been a problem here."

He took a jerky step toward her and made a furious ges-ture at her SUV. "You don't call *that* a problem?"

This time, she couldn't check her urge to take a step back, and the heel of her tennis shoe caught on the curb. Chase's hand shot out, wrapping hard and firm around her upper arm to keep her from stumbling.

"Careful," he said.

The timbre of his voice had shifted lower, and suddenly they were standing close enough that his cool breath feath-ered over her cheek. Before she could fortify her guard, his heat invaded her space, enveloped her, and she stilled, over-whelmed by the desire to lean against his strength.

As if he knew what she was thinking, he lifted his free hand to tuck stray hair from her ponytail behind her ear.

The gesture, so tender and caring, completely disarmed her. She could have melted right against him, let his strong arms enfold her. So easy and what a relief to—

"Ky," he said.

The sigh in his voice had the same effect as if he'd placed a chisel on the crack in her defenses and tapped with a ham-mer. Alarmed, she tried to pull away, but his grip tightened, and the bare skin of her arm started to burn where his long fingers almost completely encircled it.

"Let go," she said.

Her cheeks heated at how she'd sounded. Like she was choking. Oh, God, she was so close to losing it. Right in front of him. But that . . . thing, it was just like the one that shattered her dreams. And someone, some twisted *bastard*, was using it against her. Why? Why the hell . . . *why*? And Chase . . . God, Chase, was right here. Watching her every move, her every expression and reaction, analyzing and scru-tinizing. What the hell was he looking for anyway?

Chase dropped his hand to his side, and the tight muscles in his face visibly relaxed. "I'm not trying to upset you, Ky."

He used the even, conciliatory tone of a cop dealing with a hostile witness, and it hit her like a slap that he was trying to *manage* her. As she snapped her spine straight, she bit back the urge to snipe at him. It wouldn't accomplish anything but make her feel bitchy. And none of this was his fault. He was just there to do his job.

"So what do we do now?" she asked. "Do you have to gather evidence before I call someone to come fix my windshield or what?"

His expression gave nothing away as he pulled out his cell phone. "I'll call in the crime scene unit."

# 12

QUINN JOGGED TOWARD KYLIE, WHO STOOD ON
the sidewalk facing her SUV, arms wrapped around her middle as though chilled. An official-looking black woman with
glossy, close-cropped hair and gold hoop earrings snapped
pictures of Kylie's Liberty from all angles. Chase Manning,
down on one knee at the head of the truck, scribbled on what
looked like a sandwich-size Ziploc bag. Several other small
Ziplocs littered the asphalt around him.

Quinn's stomach seized at the sight of the truck's windshield. Sam had told him what had happened, but knowing
didn't blunt the shock of seeing.

"Hey," he called to Kylie when he was still several feet
away. She could be so jumpy, and he didn't want to startle her.

She turned to greet him with a smile he recognized as
plastered on only because he'd seen her give that same smile
to the well-wishers at their father's funeral. Not too big as to
look fake, not too small as to look forced. Christ, she was so
good at it that it scared him sometimes.

When he spotted the aluminum bat on the ground, his gut
flipped. He hadn't quite believed Sam, but there it was, the
sun shooting blinding blue sparks off it.

Kylie's voice broke through his shock. "They're gathering evidence." She indicated the woman with the camera. "That's Sylvia Jensen, a forensics expert."

He glanced sharply at his sister. She sounded as though they were at a party, for Christ's sake—hey, that's my buddy Sylvia over there; you'd like her—when a normal person would have been huddled on the curb shaking her ass off. Hell, *he* was shaking, and he hadn't been attacked.

Guilt added to the queasiness in his stomach. He should have gotten his butt out here as soon as Sam told him, but the detective had had a bunch of questions about the video surveillance, and then Quinn had had to set him up with the equipment so Sam could find what he was looking for. Meanwhile, his sister had stood in the hot sun with who knows what kind of crap circling in her head.

He gently grasped her elbow, felt tension instantly infuse her already rigid muscles. She didn't pull away, though, and he didn't know if that was a good sign or a bad sign. "Why don't you come in while they finish up?" he said. "It's too hot out here."

She relented without a word, and he led her inside and down the cool hallway to his office without speaking. While she sat in the lone, metal-framed visitor's chair, he popped open the mini fridge in the corner and retrieved a bottle of water. After twisting off the cap, he handed her the bottle, glad when she drank without being prodded.

He hated that he had no idea what to say. He hadn't known what to say for years and berated himself for not dogging her more. But she'd been so far away, physically and emotionally, that he hadn't known where to start. Letting her work it out on her own had been easier. He'd had his own issues to focus on, after all.

"You might want to think about replacing this chair," she said. "It feels rickety."

His throat closed. Leave it to Kylie to focus on something that had nothing to do with the blue aluminum symbol for her shattered sense of identity.

"Funny word," she murmured. "Rickety."

"Kylie—"

"Unless that's the idea. Most of the people who use this chair are probably employees in trouble. You wouldn't want them to be too comfortable while you rip into them."

"Kylie, come on. Don't you want—"

"Can we just sit here and not say anything? Just for a few minutes?"

Quinn sighed. Agreeing to be quiet, for her sake, was easy. It always had been.

# 13

WHILE FORENSICS EXPERT SYLVIA JENSEN FINISHED cataloging the evidence, Chase went looking for Kylie. He hadn't been to the fitness center before, but he'd heard about its state-of-the-art equipment and Olympic-size swimming pool. He would have joined if the monthly fee had been slightly less than astronomical, but the place clearly targeted rich retirees and the Fortune 500 executives whose vacation homes dotted Kendall Falls' beaches.

Not for the first time, he felt a nudge of admiration for Kylie's choice of location for her own facility. She planned to cater to the less-well-to-do portion of the population on the other side of town, something few entrepreneurs in the area ever did.

Chase stopped a young woman wearing the health club's uniform of white polo shirt and navy shorts. "Can you tell me where I might find Kylie McKay?"

She gave him a big, flirtatious smile as she gestured down the hall. "Just saw her in Quinn's office, on the left."

"Thank you."

"Hey," she called after him. "I'm a personal trainer. If, you know, you ever want a one-on-one workout."

He waved over his shoulder without acknowledging her wink. "I'll keep that in mind, thanks."

A few strides later, he spotted an office door bearing a plaque that read QUINN MCKAY, MANAGER. Through the half-open door, he saw Kylie sitting with her unbraced leg crossed over the other, her focus intense as she peeled the label off an empty water bottle. The flush that had stained her cheeks while they'd argued was gone, and she'd tidied up the curls that had earlier escaped her ponytail. The Tennis Pony, she'd called it way back when, because that's how she wore her hair when she played.

With concentration creasing her forehead, she looked older. And tired. Jesus, she looked tired.

He lightly rapped on the door before stepping into the tiny office that held a simple desk and the two occupied chairs.

"Are you done already?" Quinn asked, elbows on the desk, hands clasped tightly in front of him.

"Just about. Sylvia's bagging up the last of the evidence."

He glanced at Kylie and found her watching him with the calm, quiet look of someone who'd popped a Xanax. If he hadn't known her so well, he would have assumed she had. But Kylie McKay didn't do tranquilizers. She chanted shit in her head, like "eye on the ball" and "breathe." Mind over matter, that was her motto.

Looking away, he leaned against the wall to wait for Sam. He'd asked her everything he could about the incident, and the bat through the windshield sounded like a scare tactic. The perp had had the perfect chance to harm her—defenseless woman alone in a deserted parking lot—but he'd attacked only the Jeep and immediately fled into the woods. Chase figured someone didn't want her building the tennis center. Sabotage hadn't worked, so the perp had tried a more personal approach, just as Chase had feared.

Hearing familiar footsteps, he glanced out into the hall to see his partner striding their way. "Hey," Sam said with a nod.

Chase gestured him into the office and shut the door. The restricted space would have been close with two people. With

four, it was claustrophobic. When Chase sat on the edge of
Quinn's desk, his knee accidentally brushed Kylie's, and she
quickly shifted to avoid further contact. He pretended not to
notice, or care. But he did notice. And care. Against his better
judgment.

"Any luck with the security camera?" he asked Sam.

"Nope. There's nothing on the feed for today but snow,
and I don't mean the cold and slippery kind."

"You're kidding," Quinn said. "That can't be right."

"Afraid so," Sam said.

"Crap," Chase said under his breath.

"So what was the point?" Quinn asked, his face pale.

Sam cocked his head. "Point?"

"Of smashing her windshield with a bat that looks like
the . . . other one."

"Someone's trying to scare me," Kylie said.

Hearing her say it in that soft, inflection-free voice made
Chase's insides clench. She might as well have been a robot.

"But why?" Quinn gave Chase an imploring look. "I don't
understand why."

Before Chase could respond, Sam said, "Maybe Sylvia
will turn up something useful from the evidence around the
Jeep."

Quinn didn't look appeased. "What about protection? If
someone's trying to hurt my sister—"

"No one tried to *hurt* me," Kylie cut in. "He could have,
easily, and he didn't."

"Still," Quinn said. "I don't want you staying home alone,
and I'm working late tonight. Maybe Jane can—"

"I don't need a babysitter, Quinn."

His face reddened. "I'm not trying—"

"Hold on," Chase said, raising his hands to placate both
before tension could rise further. "We'll put an officer in a
car in Kylie's driveway. Does that satisfy everyone?" It was
happening regardless, but he liked to be diplomatic when he
could.

Kylie nodded. "I can live with that."

"Okay," Quinn said, shoulders sagging with relief.

"Are we done then?" Kylie asked as she got to her feet.

"Actually," Chase said, "I want to talk to you about something."

Chase sensed rather than saw Sam furrow his brow at him, but he cast his partner a glance that said everything would be fine. Kylie, in the meantime, nodded at Quinn as if to tell her brother it was okay.

Sam indicated the door with his thumb. "I'll go check on Sylvia's progress."

Quinn squeezed Kylie's arm on the way out. "I can give you a ride home when you're done."

Once Quinn and Sam slipped out the door, Chase closed it after them, then resumed his position leaning against the front edge of the desk while Kylie sat back down. Less than a foot separated them, and now that they were alone in such close quarters, he noticed the scent of vanilla that clung to her. It struck him then that vanilla was such a delicate contrast to her tough shell.

"You have more questions?" she asked.

Her raspy voice sent a shudder up his spine before he could squelch it. Easy there. But, damn, that voice did it to him every time. Low like that, it reminded him of nights together on a blanket on the beach. Trying to be quiet but giggling like fools while they'd grappled with each other's clothing, stilling and shushing each other at every suspicious scuff of sand. The sound of waves caressed the beach in time with the stroke of his hand on her skin, her breath catching each time his fingers glided over a particularly sensitive spot. She'd let him know what pleased her, what drove her wild, and she hadn't hesitated to do the same for him, that low, sexy voice laughing at his groans and pleas for her to slow down, to let him catch up. She'd been so responsive then, so open and trusting.

And it hadn't just been when they made love. She'd been like that all the time, whether they were working out, talking over lunch or traveling to or from the next tournament. Open, so open. And now she was closed. Shut down to everyone, it seemed.

"Hello?"

Snapping his focus to her, he cleared his throat. "I wanted to ask if you'd stopped by the lab to provide a blood sample."

"Not yet. Is tomorrow okay?"

"How about now? I can get Sylvia to take care of it right here." Before she could shoot him down, he added, "It's even more important now that there are two bats."

She arched her eyebrows. "Could they both be fakes?"

"It's possible."

"But why would anyone do that?"

"There's got to be a reason they're trying to scare you. Maybe they're trying to distract you or chase you away."

"Because I'm building the tennis center?"

"Maybe."

"But why? I'm not stepping on anyone's toes."

"The owners of this health club might disagree. Your place will be a direct competitor. Brand new and a lot more affordable. And there are the usual suspects: someone who has similar plans but was slower on the trigger with their proposal or whose same idea was shot down by the zoning board. Even environmentalists."

"I already had an environmental study done. The site was cleared."

"Doesn't mean someone out there doesn't agree."

"So what you're saying is that it's possible that the bat found at the construction site might not be the one from ten years ago."

"Once we ID the blood on the T-shirt found with it, we'll know more. So, may I go get Sylvia?"

She nodded, and for just a flash of a moment, she looked tired again. Exhausted, really.

"Are you sleeping?" he asked before he could rethink the wisdom of asking.

Her shoulders tightened, the lines in her forehead smoothing out as completely as if she'd run a steaming iron over them. "I'm fine."

"That's not what I asked."

Blue gray eyes met his, colder now, challenging. "I'm fine."

Annoyed at how quickly she swatted down his concern, he cocked his head and let anger take the wheel. "Oh, you're more than fine, aren't you? You've got that game face honed to perfection."

He hadn't thought she could get any stiffer, but somehow she managed as she stood up and eased by him toward the door, careful to avoid all contact. "While you're getting Sylvia, I'm going to—"

"Run away?"

She faltered, her hand on the doorknob. For a moment, her shoulders curved inward, as though he'd landed a blow square in the chest. Then, without a word or even a glare tossed over her shoulder, she walked out and gently closed the door behind her.

Biting back a groan of frustration, Chase shoved away from the desk.

God, she could make him act like such an ass.

# 14

"DAMN!" KYLIE TOSSED THE REMAINS OF A CHARRED bagel into the sink and sucked the tip of the finger she'd burned on the toaster. Time for pizza instead. Snagging the cordless off the wall, she dialed the memorized number for Pizza Outlet and was waiting for an answer when her doorbell sounded. She shouldered the handset to check the peephole.

What the hell?

Her pulse speeding, she clicked off the call and pulled the door open.

Chase Manning stood on her porch, hands in his back pockets, his dark hair mussed by the wind. He wore the casual attire of a man who'd taken a long walk on the beach—khaki shorts, navy T-shirt and sand-caked Nikes that had been abused for years. He smelled fresh and salty, like gulf air and beach. A light beard shadowed his jaw, and she remembered that after a particularly passionate kiss so long ago, he'd trailed a fingertip over her stinging cheek and joked that he'd have to start shaving twice a day to spare her skin. So sweet.

He hadn't been sweet this afternoon when he'd asked her if she planned to run away. But, then, she supposed she deserved the dig. She *had* run away.

"Hey," he said, and gave her a tentative smile.

"Hello."

"May I come in?" he asked.

She considered saying no. They had nothing to talk about anyway. But maybe he was here about the afternoon's incident. Maybe the police had caught the guy or at least had a lead.

"Please?" he said.

She stepped back and gestured him in. As he crossed her threshold, his body stirred the air in front of her. Wind and sea and . . . sunscreen. Longing speared through her, and she suppressed it. The want was about the past anyway, not him. "Did you catch a break in the case?" she asked.

The skin around his extraordinary green eyes crinkled. "You must be an *NYPD Blue* fan."

The unexpected teasing sent her back to all the times he'd given her that grin in the past, and she automatically slipped into banter mode. "Depends on whether you're here to squeeze my shoes," she said, borrowing an infamous phrase from the old cop show.

He glanced, ever so briefly, at her chest, and she tried not to react as she remembered she wasn't wearing a bra. Her body had other ideas, and while her traitorous nipples began to harden, Chase's eyes narrowed speculatively.

"I'm not here to squeeze your shoes," he replied, his voice rougher than before.

"What a relief." Blood rushing in her ears now, she shut the door with a soft, uneasy laugh.

They stood there, staring at each other, and Kylie shifted when his gaze began to scan her features. She ended up staring at the dark blue cotton stretched taut over his chest. So close, so available for her to run her palm over all those yummy contours of muscle. The scent of his sunscreen, combined with the salty air, reminded her of the hours they'd spent on the beach. Watching the waves, holding hands, talking about anything and everything. Touching and kissing, tasting. God, his mouth on hers, his tongue . . .

She realized her breath had quickened and struggled to control it and the steamy images quickly taking over in her head. "I'm assuming you stopped by for a reason."

"I . . . can we sit outside and talk?"

"Uh, sure. Do you want something to drink? I've got water, iced tea, beer."

"Beer would be great."

She swept a hand toward the sliding-glass doors that led to the deck. "I'll meet you out there."

In the kitchen, she opened the refrigerator and stood in the cool breeze, damp palms pressed to cheeks that felt feverish. She shouldn't have let that grin disarm her, shouldn't have brought up squeezing anything. She was a detriment to her own sense of control, which she had to get back before she went out there to talk to him.

She began to play an imaginary tennis game in her head. Forehand, backhand, go to the net, fire the ball at the feet of her opponent. Yes! Right on the line. Break point and she was back in control.

She opened two bottles of Sam Adams and set them on the counter, then retrieved a denim shirt from the back of a kitchen chair and drew it over her T-shirt and shorts. Any future nipple erections would be safely obscured.

Outside, Chase had settled into an Adirondack chair, propping his sneakered feet on the wooden table before him. His legs were hairy and tanned, calf muscles telling of long jogs on the beach, or perhaps hours on the tennis court. So very nicely shaped, just like the rest of him . . .

Throw the ball high into the air, slam it into the service court. Ace!

She handed him one of the amber beer bottles.

"Thanks," he said, and immediately drained a large gulp.

She settled onto the chair next to him, wishing the July air weren't quite so thick with humidity. Maybe she wouldn't have had to concentrate so much on breathing evenly. Focusing on the horizon, where water met pale blue sky that reddened with the arrival of sunset, she tried to let the sound of the waves rolling ashore relax her.

Chase lowered his feet and leaned forward to rest his elbows on his knees. "I'm sorry. About this afternoon. What I said was . . . inappropriate."

She swallowed some beer before nodding. "Okay."

One side of his mouth lifted in an unhappy quirk. "Don't do that."

"Do what?"

"Don't put on your game face."

"I don't have a game face anymore."

His gaze strayed to her right knee, and she realized belatedly that it was bare, scars front and center that were usually hidden beneath the brace she wore while coaching. She itched to move her hand over them, to protect them from his gaze, but doing so would tip him off that his eyes on them bothered her. So she stayed still and drained another too-big gulp of beer, knowing she was drinking too quickly on an empty stomach but too unnerved to stop.

"I thought you would come back," he said softly.

She cocked her head. Come back? Huh? "I did. Three months ago."

"Sooner," he said, and sat back, rolling his shoulders as though tense. "I thought you'd come back sooner. When you were done with school."

Ah. That's what he wants to talk about. The past. Always the ever-loving, godforsaken *past*. Shrugging, she locked her gaze on his. "What would I have come back for?"

His head jerked back as though she'd struck him. "Are you serious?"

Why did he look so damn shocked? "I hadn't even made it through one semester when I learned from Trisha that you were engaged. That pretty much told me all I needed to know about where we stood."

"Rhonda was pregnant. What was I supposed to do?"

"Exactly what you did, of course."

"It was a mistake. We made a mistake."

"When you got her pregnant, you mean. How long after I left?"

"*You* left *me*." He dared her to look away.

Game on, she thought, and returned his stare without blinking. "And how many days later did you knock someone up? Couldn't have been too many. Your little girl's birth notice showed up in the paper nine months after I was gone."

"Maybe that should tell you something then. I was pissed off and hurt. I sought solace."

"Unprotected solace, apparently."

He broke their locked gazes, and if she hadn't felt so hollow, she might have smiled. She'd always been the victor when they'd played chicken. Nerves of steel, he'd said. But instead of celebrating the win, she closed her eyes and clamped down on the building, squeezing pressure in the center of her chest. It shouldn't hurt so much. Why did it still hurt so much? He was right. *She* left *him*. She had no right to be irked about what he did after she bailed. She just hadn't expected him to turn around and . . . do what he did so soon.

He sighed. "Fuck."

Yeah, fuck. Fuck you for fucking some other fucking woman. But she kept the angry words to herself. God, they couldn't even yell at each other. He'd been raised in a house filled with furious shouts and decided long ago that he wouldn't fight that way. She'd been trained to direct her anger at a little yellow ball. No shouting here.

"You know I loved you, Ky," he said, sounding more tired than he had a right to. "You know I did."

She tightened her grip on the cold beer bottle in her lap. She wanted to throw it. Just chuck it as hard and as far as she could. Even better if it shattered against a wall into thousands of satisfying pieces. But, no, that wouldn't solve anything, except make her look foolish. She'd already taken care of that quite well.

She realized he was waiting for her to respond. She didn't want to. Didn't want to do anything except take all the anger and hurt and heave them into the gulf. Instead, she pushed herself out of the low-slung chair and set aside the bottle before she could fling it at his head. When she spoke, she chose her words carefully.

"I'm sorry I hurt you the way I did by running away. What happened wasn't your fault, and you shouldn't have gotten caught in the aftermath. But you didn't have any trouble replacing me, so I don't see why we should have a problem now."

"You ran away. That's the problem."

"*Ten years ago*. We were barely adults. And I think it's pretty clear that we've both moved on."

He rolled to his feet, the sudden move driven by frustration, but when she took a step back from him, he crossed instead to the railing, where he took a long drink of beer before setting the bottle on the railing and facing her, his face in shadow. "So did you find what you were looking for out there?"

Calm again. He was fighting for control as fiercely as she was.

"I got an education, yes. And then, as you know, I got a job coaching the UCLA women's tennis team. We've done well the past few years. NCAA champs two years running."

He picked up his beer and took a generous swallow, his throat working jerkily, then set the bottle down with a hollow clunk. "See, when you left, and wouldn't let me come with you, you told me you had to find out who you were apart from tennis. Two NCAA tennis championships doesn't sound like a tennis-free identity to me."

"I didn't know where I would end up."

"No, you just knew you'd end up somewhere without me."

"I didn't plan it that way."

"Yes, you *did*. You left me, Kylie. Not Kendall Falls. Not tennis. Not your family. You left *me*."

"That wasn't what I intended, but you were a part of my identity then. And that revolved around tennis."

"I thought I was a part of *you*."

She closed her eyes as that arrow hit its mark. Ouch, ouch and double ouch. And while part of her winced, another part got stubborn and pissed off, and she opened her eyes to spear him. "What do you want me to say? I'm sorry? Fine, I'm sorry I hurt your little-boy feelings ten *freaking* years ago. I was a bitch, as cold and self-centered and selfish as a girl can possibly get. Does that soothe your wounded ego enough?"

He took a step toward her. "That's not—"

She backed off, raising her hands to keep him from touching her. "Or maybe you'd like to hear me admit that I made the mistake of my life when I walked out on you. By the time I figured it out, though, you'd already gone out and snagged yourself a fiancée."

His face flushed red. "I didn't go out and snag—"

"I don't get where this attitude is coming from. You're the one who got married and had a kid. Do you see any rings on my finger? No. You know why? Because I'm so messed up that by the time a guy starts to get to know me, he realizes that I'm more trouble than I'm worth and heads for the hills. How about that? Does that make you happy? While you were bouncing a beautiful baby girl on your knee and talking baby talk, I was sitting home alone with a book and a bottle of wine and several decades of loneliness stretching before me."

She stopped and turned away, fists clenched at her sides. Damn it, she'd let him prod her into a tirade. This was exactly what he wanted, and she'd handed it to him on a heaping platter of self-pity and bitterness. Good job keeping your eye on the ball, Ace.

Tears, the ultimate disgrace, welled into her eyes. Before they could overflow, she strode to the sliding door and pulled it open. "I want you to go now."

He didn't move, his face still but his eyes dark and watching her. "I'd rather not."

He thought he could wait her out until she started blubbering. Screw that. She didn't cry for anyone. "You did what you came here to do, now please go."

"What do you think I came here to do?"

"I admitted I was wrong. What more do you want from me? Tears? You won't get them."

"You think I'm that shallow."

"You're still whining about what happened when we were little more than kids, aren't you?"

"Whining?" He stared at her, dumbfounded. "We lost something, something *incredible*, and you think I'm *whining*?"

Incredible? Oh, God. "Yes," she said, "and it's way past time to get over it. Now please go."

Shaking his head, he stepped past her and walked through the door without a second glance.

Kylie slid it closed behind him and paced away, felt control begin to slip free of its moorings. Stupid, stupid, *stupid*. She let him get to her, had vowed he wouldn't, then let him rip her apart piece by piece.

At the railing, she snatched up his empty beer bottle and hurled it at the door.

# 15

Chase was in Kylie's living room, striding back toward the kitchen after doing an about-face at the front door. Walking away mad wasn't the answer. He let that happen ten years ago, and look how long it had taken to get to this point of hashing it all out. No, they needed to talk through all the anger and bitterness and hurt. They needed to find a way to resolve their issues so they could start fresh. He refused to be a child this time, refused to let her be a child.

He'd made it back to the kitchen doorway, bracing himself to confront her again, to somehow reach her, when the explosion of glass froze him in midstep, and he watched in disbelief as a glittering shower rained down on the ceramic tile. It took him a few beats to get that the sliding door had exploded inward.

His heart in his throat, he dove for what was left of the door. His Nikes skidded through shards of glass, and he caught glimpses of brown among the jagged pieces. Blood?

"Kylie!"

He stopped dead when he saw her on the deck, staring at what was left of the door.

Cop instincts kicked in, and he lunged forward and

grabbed her, nearly yanking her off her feet as he dragged her into the shelter of the kitchen and away from the vulnerability of the shattered door.

Pressing her against the wall, covering her with his body, he peered over his shoulder toward the door, scanning what he could see of the beach. His brain was racing, latching onto and discarding scenarios in split seconds.

A bomb? No smoke.

A gunman? But only one shot, and he'd missed.

A rock? He glanced at the floor, saw the brown again, like blood but solid with jagged edges. Not blood. Glass. *Beer-bottle* glass.

What the hell?

He shifted to look down at her, to ask her what the hell happened. But the way she stared up at him, her expression so open and broken, wiped his brain clean. Her eyes, swimming with tears that threatened to spill but didn't, looked bluer than ever. The slight tremble in her chin nearly undid him.

He released her and stepped back, raising his hands to placate. Oh, Jesus, if she cried . . .

His back-off move must have surprised her, because her eyes widened further, and then, like that, the aching vulnerability vanished. She lifted her chin, a furrow of concentration appearing above the bridge of her nose.

"I thought you left," she said, her voice as flat and emotionless as her expression.

The fucking game face. It was like a kick to the gut. He would never win with her. *They* would never win. "I decided it was a mistake to leave angry," he said, just as flat, just as emotionless.

Her eyes narrowed, flickered, then she pushed hair off her face with both hands. "I appreciate the concern, but I'm fine."

"Yeah, I see that."

He deliberately swept his gaze over the shattered remains of the door before meeting her eyes again. She didn't look away, but he could see in the way her jaw muscles tightened that it cost her. She was grinding her teeth to dust. Jesus, she never gave up. That's exactly how she'd played tennis, never giving up on even one point. The media called her the Mac Attack, a warrior on the court, mercilessly taking down enemy after enemy like a soldier with a tennis racket as her weapon. Until those bastards had used a bat to destroy her ability to fight.

He wanted to save her. He wanted to jerk her out of her emotionless shell and remind her what it was like to live. To *love*.

But she stood there, watching him with curtained eyes, tension coiled in her center as she tried to anticipate his next move and how she might counter it. A competitor to the end. A beautiful competitor with flawless skin and blue gray eyes he could drown in.

He didn't think, he just reached out.

She stepped back on a quick intake of breath, but the wall at her back stopped her short. He took advantage and slid his hands into her soft, silky hair before capturing her warm, moist lips with his.

She tensed, brought her hands up to curl around his forearms, but he tightened his grip, preventing retreat, and let himself fall into her taste. God, oh, God, she tasted like beer and want and everything he'd craved since the day she walked out of his life.

When she moaned out a protest, pushing at his arms and shoulders with clenched fists, he resisted letting her go even as his head told him he had to. Instead, he deepened the kiss, telling her with his lips and tongue and teeth how much he wanted her after all this time, after all the hurt. She moaned again, but this time she melted against him, her fists unfurling to clutch at his shoulders, her lips parting, inviting him in. The sweep of her glorious tongue against his stole his breath and sent blood rushing to the too-long-denied part of his anatomy.

He moved in, pressed her against the wall as he nudged his thigh between hers—Jesus, skin on skin and so close to her heat, it was . . . it was . . . too much.

He fought the need to come up for air. He didn't want air. He just wanted this. He just wanted her. He couldn't get enough, couldn't go deep enough, couldn't taste enough or feel enough.

And then, just like that, as if someone threw a switch, he lost her.

She stiffened against him and jerked her head back so quickly it rapped against the wall. Her hands shoved at his chest, and a weird choking sound came from her throat.

He backed off fast, hands off her and raised. "What? What did I do?" Did he misread something? Did he go too far too fast? What?

She struggled to get control of her breathing, one hand held before her as if she didn't trust him to stay back. "You have to go."

Go? *Now?* They were just getting started. "Ky, come on—"

"Don't call me that!" She squeezed her eyes shut. "Don't . . . God, just don't call me that anymore."

He saw the tremor in her hand then, and the shock made his head spin. Kylie "There's No Need to Worry" McKay was *trembling*. Sympathy overrode his disbelief. "Jesus, Ky, you're—"

She lunged forward and shoved him back a full step. "Leave!"

He snapped his mouth shut and debated his options. Leave, obviously. Or stay and piss her off so much maybe they'd never recover. But, Jesus, she looked like a prime candidate for spontaneous combustion, her cheeks flushed, her eyes flashing daggers in silver and blue.

His body, clearly not the least bit intimidated, responded to all that angry energy, egged on by memories of truly fantastic sex after harrowing knock-down-drag-outs on the court with her. He didn't want to leave, damn it. He wanted to bury his need, bury it in her. He wanted to fuck away the past and move on. Together.

Before he could think of the right words to say—maybe there weren't any—she pushed past him and headed for the living room.

"Where are you going?" he called after her.

"You won't leave, so I will."

The front door slammed so violently the house shook.

Squeezing the back of his neck with one hand, Chase sur-
veyed the glass scattered across the kitchen tile and, against
his better judgment, began to grin. He'd made Kylie, the ice
queen, slip on her own cool. He'd made her tremble, with
rage or desire—did it matter? The fact remained: He'd gotten
to her. He'd broken through her defenses. Hell, he'd made
her throw a beer bottle through one door and slam another so
hard they probably heard it across the gulf in Texas.

Okay, so the encounter hadn't ended as well as it could
have. In fact, it hadn't ended well at all, considering the
throbbing discomfort in Chase Jr.'s neighborhood. But, damn,
he'd still made her tremble. And moan. Don't forget that.
There'd been some pretty heavy duty, heady moans before
she'd flipped out on him.

The trembling, though. That was the main thing. He could
still make her shake for him.

Maybe there was hope for them yet.

# 16

KYLIE WANDERED HER STEPMOTHER'S LIVING ROOM, picking up knickknacks and studying them. Not because she'd never seen them before, but because she needed something to do with her restless hands. Because of last night.

Chase. God, Chase. She'd made such a fool of herself. Throwing beer bottles and slamming doors. By the time she'd returned home from a two-hour walk on the beach—more of a stalk, really—he'd swept up the broken glass and secured plastic sheeting over the sliding doors in the kitchen. He must have made a run to Home Depot for the plastic, even. God, he could make her feel so small.

And restless. She hadn't slept all night, didn't think she'd ever sleep again, at least not without seeing that frustrating look of pity transform his face. She must have looked and sounded truly pathetic for him to go so quickly from I'm-going-to-fuck-you-against-the-wall to I-feel-so-damn-sorry-for-you.

Her throat tightened at the memory, and she closed her eyes to contain the sting of tears.

"Are you going to rearrange my bric-a-brac all day or sit down and welcome me home?"

Kylie replaced the clay pot she'd been examining and faced her stepmother with a self-conscious laugh. "Guess I'm distracted."

"I hadn't noticed," Lara said, crossing her legs where she sat on the white leather sofa.

She was an older version of Jane. Her long, dark blond hair was twisted into an artful knot at the nape of her delicate neck. Her makeup looked as if an artist had applied it, making her appear years younger than she was. Even her clothing, a soft yellow, short-sleeved sweater with a V-neck atop tailored white slacks, looked like something her daughter would wear. And so much more stylish than the faded blue jeans and red T-shirt Kylie had thrown on this morning.

As Kylie settled in the leather chair next to the sofa, she picked up the raspberry iced tea Lara had poured for her. When her hand shook, she braced the glass on her denim-clad thigh and swallowed hard. She hadn't stopped shaking since he'd touched her. But it couldn't be because of him. No, it had to be exhaustion. She hadn't slept since the bat was found. Hadn't eaten much, either. So, exhaustion and low blood sugar. Not Chase. Never Chase. What a relief.

Realizing her stepmother's shrewd gaze tracked her every move, Kylie forced a smile that couldn't have looked all that sincere. Eye on the ball, McKay.

"How was Paris?" Kylie asked.

Lara sipped her own tea, watching Kylie over the rim of her glass. "Fabulous, as always. I'm sure Rome will be as wonderful in a few days."

Kylie nodded, envious suddenly of the woman who'd become a globe-trotter after she divorced Kylie's father. Paris on Monday, Rome on Wednesday, Berlin on Friday. No danger of anyone getting too close when you did that.

Lara cocked her head, appraising. "Jane told me about what's going on at the construction site. How are you holding up?"

Oh, that. Long lost bats and bloody T-shirts. Besides

Chase Manning, it was all she could think about. A shaft of anxiety caught her off guard. Keeping her eye on the ball was impossible when it was nowhere in sight.

"I'm holding up great." Her voice cracked, and unable to sit still for another second under that watchful gaze, she set aside her glass and rose to pace behind the chair. Moving helped. As did barriers. She always liked something to hide behind.

Lara's eyes, a dark velvet brown, traveled her features then dropped to where Kylie had clamped her hands on the chair's back. "I think you need to sit back down and talk to your mother."

Kylie stared down at her white-knuckled hands. Talk. Right. She'd rather run a marathon without training. Or try to teach a cranky four-year-old how to serve for twelve hours straight. Or play soccer with a thriving bee hive. Or stand without her knee brace in front of roving, curious eyes.

"Here."

She glanced up, surprised to see Lara holding out a rocks glass that contained what looked like two shots of amber liquid. She hadn't even heard her stepmother move. "I don't—"

"It's whiskey," Lara interrupted. "Drink it."

She accepted the glass with a soft laugh, glad it didn't have ice cubes that could knock against each other and give away how shaky she really was.

Lara resumed her position on the sofa, legs crossed and hands clasped on her knees, and waited for Kylie to do as she was told.

"Cheers," Kylie said, toasting her stepmother before swallowing the fiery liquid in one gulp. The burn on the way down into her empty stomach reminded her of Chase's lips tracking the side of her neck to the top of her shoulder, the heat of his fingers on the sensitive skin just beneath the hem of her T-shirt. He knew how to touch, knew how to stroke, knew exactly how to make her want. Clearly, he knew too much.

Lara started to smile. "Well, I see some color in your cheeks, so Mr. Johnny Walker must be doing his job."

Kylie squinted her watering eyes and nodded. Yep, it's Johnny Walker all the way. "Thank you."

Lara tilted her head to one side, but when Kylie said nothing more, she sat back. "Let me guess: You don't want to talk about it. Not that I had to guess. Jane filled me in on that part, too."

"I figured she would."

"She's just worried—"

"I know. God, I know." She looked down into her empty glass. A refill would have been nice.

Lara pursed her neatly lined and lipsticked lips. "I hate to say it, but you're even more tense than usual. Sit down, look me in the eye and talk to me." She smiled in a sweet way that had defy-me-and-die undertones. "Please."

Kylie obeyed, at least on the first and third requests. "I'm not trying to avoid—"

"Yes, you are."

"But it's not because—"

"Yes, it is."

Kylie blew out a sigh and sank back against the chair cushion's squishy, sink-into-me comfort. "I'm a mess."

"Yes, you are."

Kylie met her stepmother's unperturbed gaze and had to laugh. "So now that that's settled, can we talk about Paris?"

Lara's smile turned tight. "No, we cannot." Sitting forward, she looked Kylie straight in the eye, her gaze warm but imploring. "Is Chase why you and Wade stopped dating?"

It took Kylie a moment to catch up. Number one: She'd never mentioned to Lara that she and Wade Bell stopped seeing each other. Jane must have taken care of that when she'd filled her in on all the other gossip. Number two: She hadn't thought much at all about Wade since . . . well, crap, since she'd stood next to Chase staring at the "killer" bat.

"It wasn't because of Chase," she said. A lie, though. Every time it didn't work out with a guy, it was because of Chase.

"Do you think you gave Wade a fair chance?" Lara asked. "You went out for such a short time."

"It was enough to know."

"But he's such a nice man, and a doctor."

"So I've heard."

Lara cocked her head. "Yes, I know you of all people know that. I'm just saying . . ." She trailed off with a shrug. "Handsome, smart, orthopedic doctor with regular hours, a sharp dresser and a full head of hair. What more could a girl want?"

Passion? Connection? Chase? Yes, Dr. Wade Bell had worked the miracle that saved her leg after the attack, and they'd developed a warm friendship in the years afterward that he'd suggested they escalate into romance when she returned from LA. But . . . but damn it, nothing happened when he kissed her. *Nothing*.

Kylie searched for the right words. "We didn't connect on that level. He was right to break it off."

"I'm sure that was a difficult decision for him."

"We dated for six weeks, Mom. It wasn't that difficult."

"I got the impression that he waited for you for ten years."

The idea amazed Kylie, and she laughed. "No, he didn't. He was married twice. And the idea of dating didn't even come up until we got together for dinner after I returned."

"I don't know. He was very devoted to you before you left for California."

"I was his patient."

"A patient he liked very much."

"Regardless, it's not going anywhere. We're friends, period."

Lara, obviously unsatisfied with that response, got up and crossed to the bar, where she poured a glass of whiskey for herself. Kylie watched her posture-perfect back, trying to figure out what was up. Lara had never been one to push or express disapproval. She let her kids do their thing and offered constructive guidance when she thought it necessary.

When Lara returned to the sofa, she wore a forced smile,

further alerting Kylie that something big was bothering her.

Kylie reached out and put her hand on her stepmother's knee. "What's on your mind, Mom?"

Lara patted the back of Kylie's hand then grasped her fingers and squeezed. "Your father would be so happy that you're home. You know that, right?"

Thrown by the tears in Lara's eyes, Kylie nodded. "Sure, of course." She couldn't stop the spear of guilt, though. She should have returned *before* he died. But no one had known he was sick, and he'd died so unexpectedly . . .

"He always wanted to start a tennis center," Lara said, "but he didn't want to do it without you. He also didn't want to pressure you to return."

"I know."

"I'm sure the construction delays are taking a toll on your finances."

Kylie gave a noncommittal shrug. "Hopefully everything will clear up soon."

"How long have you got, do you think?"

Kylie didn't want to go into the specifics—or say that she didn't have long at all before the bank got antsy and rescinded her credit line. "Don't worry. I'm sure it will be fine."

"He'd want you to keep going on it, not to honor his memory, but because he believed it would make you happy."

"I plan to, Mom. Where's this—" She withdrew her hand and glanced away as it hit her. Well, damn. No one, not even her stepmother, expected her to stick around for long. It was official: She had a rep. When adversity mounted the front porch steps, she crept out the back door. Incredible how much that made her feel like a slug. Dirty and slimy and not someone anyone who loved her could count on. Biting back the hurt, she said, "So you think that if Wade and I stayed an item and as long as I had the tennis center, I'd be less likely to leave again."

Lara's velvety eyes filled with tears again, and she pressed her lips together for a moment. "I'd understand. We all would. It's painful for you to—"

"Mom, come on. I'm not going to—"

The front door opening cut her off. "Mom?" Jane called from the foyer. "You here?"

"In here, Janie," Lara responded, casting Kylie an apologetic glance. "We'll finish this later."

Jane strode into the living room, a plastic-wrapped newspaper clasped in one hand like she wanted to hit somebody with it. "You haven't opened your paper yet today," Jane said in an accusing tone.

Lara smiled at her youngest daughter. "Hello to you, too, Janie. Paris was wonderful, thanks for asking. How are you?"

Jane ripped the plastic bag off the paper with lethal-looking, manicured nails and held it up. "This is how I am."

Kylie's heart dropped straight into her stomach as she read the headline: *Mac's Brother a Suspect in Attack.*

"*This*," Jane gave the paper an angry shake, "says the police found a T-shirt that belongs to Quinn wrapped around the bat from the construction site."

Lara took the paper and sank down onto the sofa to read. "That can't be right," she murmured.

Jane whirled toward Kylie, dark eyes flashing. "Did you know about this?"

Kylie couldn't respond as her thought process arrived at the jarring realization of what this would do to Quinn. He already knew about the shirt, but everyone else knowing—and jumping to the conclusion that he was a monster—would devastate him. She needed to get to him, needed to make sure he was okay.

Realizing that Jane waited for an answer, Kylie nodded. "Yes, I knew."

"But this can't be right," Lara said, shaking her head. "The story must be wrong."

"It's not wrong, Mom," Jane said without looking away

from Kylie. "Kylie has the details. She just didn't bother to share them with us." She folded her arms and cocked her head. "As usual."

Attitude. Perfect. "They're running tests on the shirt," Kylie said. "I'm sure they'll clear Quinn."

"But the damage is done," Jane replied. "He's already been destroyed in the press. Once again, this family is being dragged through the mud because of poor, pitiful you."

"Janie!"

Ignoring the shock in her stepmother's voice and the bitter anger in her sister's, Kylie crossed to the phone and picked it up. When her hand trembled—damn it—she turned her back to the other two women and started dialing Quinn.

Everything would be fine. All she had to do was talk to him, assure him that nothing had changed, that an old gym shirt didn't make her think for a second that he'd done anything to her. He'd be fine. They'd be fine together.

"I've already tried that," Jane said. "He's not answering at home, work or his cell."

Kylie replaced the phone in its cradle. "Then I'll go over there."

"The media's camped out in front of his house," Jane said. "And he's not answering the door. I tried that, too."

Kylie nodded. No problem. She had a key to his house. "I'll give it a shot anyway."

"And you think he'll open the door to you instead of me because . . ."

"I don't know," Kylie said, fighting for an even tone. "Maybe he's no longer in the shower?"

"You think I didn't try hard enough, is that it? You think you're the only one he talks to? Who do you think he talked to while you were on the other side of the country pretending none of us existed?"

"Janie—"

"This isn't helping Quinn," Kylie said to Jane, then looked at her stepmother and gave her a gentle smile. "I'll let you know as soon as I talk to him. I'm sure he's fine."

Lara nodded, tears glittering in her eyes. "I want to come with you, but maybe it's best if you . . ."

Kylie grasped Lara's hand, then decided that wasn't enough and gave her a tight hug. "Don't worry. I'll have him call you."

# 17

CHASE STOOD NEXT TO THE EXPLORER PARKED AT the edge of the site of the future McKays' Tennis Center, his eyes narrowed against the morning sun. The bustling activity of construction workers had been replaced with the quiet, careful work of a small forensics team combing two acres of dirt for ten-year-old evidence.

Sylvia Jensen, in jeans and an untucked, dirt-smudged, white T-shirt, waved from several yards away and started toward him. Chase waited for her, knowing better than to tread on the land that had been sectioned off by twine to organize the search. There wasn't much his feet could disturb after construction crews had already worked over the land, knocking down trees and leveling the minor hills and valleys, but he still respected the rules of forensics.

Sylvia, large hoop earrings swinging and sunglasses hooked in the collar of her shirt, stepped over a puddle to join him. As always, he was struck by the absolute beauty of her light hazel eyes against the backdrop of dark chocolate skin.

"Anything?" he asked.

"Nothing concrete, but we have discovered something

a bit strange. It appears that someone has been digging around."

"Digging around?"

"At the back of the site, where the land butts up against the wooded area there," she said, gesturing at the ragged line of unkempt trees that marked the edge of the property. Chase remembered cutting through that wooded area many a time to meet up with friends at the hollowed-out house they'd called the Bat Cave.

"We've found several areas where the soil's no longer compact," she said. "Someone's been digging holes, then filling them back in. Recently."

"How recently?"

"They broke ground on the project last month, so it could be since then. Can't tell specifically because of all the rain."

"Could it be related to the construction? Utilities? Cables?"

"Already checked with the foreman. The positioning is off."

"So you think someone's been looking for something?"

"Thought it could be the baseball bat," she said. "Maybe whoever buried it found out the land was being developed and went to work trying to find it."

"Or maybe our culprit is looking for something else he buried here in addition to the bat, such as the masks that were worn during the attack."

"Possible. He also might have already found what he was looking for."

"Are you saying that you think this is a waste of time?"

"Not at all. I'm just giving you the heads up that we might spend weeks out here and not find anything."

"Let's hope that's not the case," he said. Kylie had a lot invested, financially and emotionally, and he didn't want to see her robbed of another dream. "Did you find anything among the evidence you collected near Kylie's Jeep?"

"Nope. Sorry," she said. "Should get a report on the prints tomorrow morning. I planned to have it today, but we've been swamped."

"I'll be surprised if you get anything. Kylie said the guy was wearing gloves."

"He might have handled the bat before he put them on."

Chase was doubtful, but he'd known other thugs to be as stupid. "That'd be a lucky break, but I'm not holding my breath."

Sylvia tugged at an earring, an unconscious gesture that Chase recognized as a signal that she was about to switch gears on him. "Shame about the story in the paper today," she said.

Chase gave her a sharp look. He'd overslept this morning after a restless night and hadn't had a chance to open the newspaper before he'd rushed out the door to meet Sylvia here. "What story?"

"About Quinn McKay's shirt being found with the bat."

"Ah, hell," he breathed. "That's not supposed to be public knowledge."

"Uh-oh." She frowned. "You can rest assured that no one in my office leaked that information. They know I'd rip them bald."

Chase smiled at the very Sylvia-like expression. "Yeah, I know." He wondered what he should do, if anything. Kylie had to be tied up in knots over this, but seeing him would just tie her up even more.

"Just curious here," Sylvia said, "but where you do stand on Quinn McKay? To an outsider like me, he and Kylie seem pretty close. When you see them together in public, they're more like good friends than siblings."

"They are now, but that wasn't the case back then."

"Ah. I wasn't living here yet. I knew the attack was big news, though. People still talked about it when I got here, what, five years ago."

Chase nodded. "It was huge."

"So Kylie and Quinn weren't best buddies back then, huh? Was it your typical brother-sister animosity or more than that?"

Chase met her striking eyes. She wasn't just curious. She had a specific point to make. Not that he minded. She had a sharp mind that he'd taken advantage of plenty over the years. "You're going somewhere with this," he said.

She shrugged. "Well, I have to admit I'm a wee bit curious about why you haven't arrested him."

"We don't have enough evidence."

"You've got means, motive, opportunity and his shirt buried with the weapon. I assume you also have a theory."

Chase stretched his neck from side to side, wincing as guitar-string-tight tendons protested. Jesus, he hated being put on the spot, especially when the other person meant well—and was right.

"So let's hear it," Sylvia prodded. "Let's hear this theory you're keeping to yourself."

He took a breath then blew it out. Okay, it wouldn't hurt to run it by an objective professional. "Quinn ended his sister's career because he was jealous of the attention she got. He dumped the bat and shirt here, then he was so guilt-ridden, he turned himself around. When she picked this place for the tennis center, he started the sabotage to slow down construction hoping he could find the bat and shirt before anyone else did."

Sylvia nodded, forehead lined with concentration. "So why haven't you arrested him?"

"We're waiting on the results on the shirt. If that's not Kylie's blood—"

"Mind if I share an opinion?"

"I'd appreciate it, actually."

"If your gut is telling you her brother took out her knee, make the arrest. By the time the grand jury takes a look at the case, you'll have the results on the shirt. Simple."

"I wish it were that simple."

"Let me put it to you this way, Chase. Go look at the pictures of what was done to her and ask yourself if you're willing to risk that happening again. If her brother did it, he's probably desperate to avoid getting caught. For all you know, he's the one who took the bat to her windshield. He knew where to find her alone and when. He had proximity, and he, as well as anyone, knows best what's going to freak her out the most. Didn't you say the video surveillance of that parking lot was blank? He knew how to deal with that, too."

Chase's gut felt like he'd swallowed rocks. He hadn't even *considered* Quinn for the windshield. What the *hell* was wrong with him? What Sylvia said made perfect sense. But Quinn had looked more shaken than Kylie had. Not that that was a good comparison, considering Kylie's game face. "I just can't imagine he'd—"

"He might," Sylvia cut in. "That's all I'm saying. If he's the guy, he's already proven once that he can take a whack at her with a weapon. A bum knee could end up being the least of her problems."

# 18

KYLIE WAS HALFWAY TO QUINN'S WHEN HER CELL
phone rang. Relief—it had to be Quinn, because she'd left him
three messages already—made her fumble the phone before
she was able to hit the right button to answer it.

"Quinn?"

"It's Chase."

The sandpaper sound of his voice sent a chill through her,
and she hit the rental car's brakes harder than necessary to
stop for a traffic light. What could he possibly want? "I'm
kind of busy at the moment."

"The story in the paper didn't come from the police department."

"Where else would it have come from?" she asked, glad
he couldn't see the flush that heated her cheeks. He hadn't
said one sexy word, yet her insides fluttered and clenched as
if he'd whispered something erotic into her ear.

"I honestly don't know."

"The police are the only ones who know about it."

"The construction workers—"

"Didn't know the shirt was Quinn's," she cut in.

He sighed before he tried again. "Quinn knew he was a

suspect because Sam talked to him, so none of this is news to him."

There was that annoying this-is-how-cops-respond-to-hostility tone again. It made her want to scream. "All of Kendall Falls didn't know," she snapped back, not caring how bitchy she sounded. This was *Quinn* they were talking about. "Can you seriously not grasp that this could destroy him? He's not just a face in an LA crowd. He has a life here, a history."

"And I'm sure that whatever happens, he'll deal with it. He's not completely innocent, you know."

"What the hell does that mean? Of course he's innocent. He didn't—"

"I'm not talking about your attack, Ky."

She stiffened at the nickname. Damn it. Why did that throw her off every damn time? "Then what are you talking about?"

"He hasn't always been the brother you know now."

"Oh, for God's sake. Teenagers are unpleasant. You had your unpleasant moments, as I recall."

"I never had a hate-on for my sister."

"You don't have a sister. And, besides, Quinn did not *hate* me."

Silence.

She knew he was waiting her out, using his lack of response to try to rattle her and make her talk. To say what, she wasn't sure. To implicate Quinn? Fat chance. She clamped her lips together and thought about hanging up on him. But, no, he'd consider that a win. So, as the light turned green and she resumed the drive to Quinn's, she tried to take control of the game.

"If resenting me back then is all the evidence it takes," she said evenly, "then you should look at Jane. If anyone *hated* me, it was my little sister. I got all of our father's attention, and she got nothing. Once, the newspaper referred to her as Kylie McKay's gangly, coltish sister who would probably never grow into her sister's grace. If anyone had reason to take me out of the game, it was Jane."

"Ky—"

"And don't forget my stepmother's issues. She and Dad had blow-the-roof-off-the-house fights about how he spent every moment of every day obsessing over my tennis career. It's why they got divorced. So, hey, you know what that means? Everyone in the family's got a motive now. Maybe all three of them got together and ambushed me. But, no, there were only two attackers. Oh, wait, I know. Mom was the mastermind, and she sent Quinn and Jane to do her dirty work. That makes perfect sense. I bet they even—"

"Kylie, stop."

She squinted her eyes against the burn behind them. No crying. *No* crying. "I have to go. I'm almost at my brother's."

He sighed into her ear. "Will you call me if you need me?"

Yeah, right. "Sure, okay."

"I mean it, Ky."

"Thanks." She cut off the call and tossed the phone into the passenger seat. Bastard. Son of a bitch. Jerk.

Tears again stung her eyes, and she angrily swiped at them. Eye on the fucking ball.

She didn't even know why she felt like crying. She'd lost nothing. There'd been nothing to lose.

As she turned into Quinn's neighborhood, she saw three TV news vans parked along the street's sandy shoulders. Sharply dressed, perfectly coiffed broadcast journalists milled around, chatting and peering at Quinn's small, light blue stucco house with dark blue shutters and terra-cotta roof tiles. With the blinds drawn, the house looked uninhabited, but Quinn's beige Accord sat under the carport.

Her heart began to drum in her ears, her palms growing slick, as she parked in the driveway. Watching the journalists in the rearview mirror as they raced up the drive to converge on her, she steeled herself to get out. Memories of the claustrophobic crush of bodies, microphones and shouting voices filled the silence of the car. She recalled hobbling out of the hospital on crutches, wobbly and uncertain but grateful that the nurse had let her leave the wheelchair behind once they'd reached the lobby.

She'd wanted to slip out a back door, but her father had insisted that the media—and, therefore, the world—had to see her walk out on her own. If she avoided the cameras, rumors would fly. She hadn't really cared one way or the other, but then Chase had made the best argument of all: If you hide, they'll keep coming after you. Smile for the cameras, stop for a brief chat. Give them what they want, and maybe they'll go away.

So Kylie had walked out into the Florida sunshine, smiling and nodding because waving was impossible with both hands occupied by crutches. While Chase stayed by her side, Quinn had run interference like a defensive lineman. She'd been surprised at that, surprised at his sudden attentiveness. As if the violent end to her career had somehow awakened him from his resentful stupor. He'd become a different person overnight. Even after she'd moved away, he'd kept up the phone calls and e-mails, always light and airy and funny.

And this was how he got repaid, she thought bitterly. Accused of being responsible. The unfairness felt like a razor-sharp spear through her heart.

Eye on the ball.

Oh, fuck the damn ball. Why did she even bother chanting that? It didn't work.

Taking a deep breath, she let it out in a long stream, then slipped on her sunglasses and shoved open the car door. As one, the mob stepped back to let her out, then moved forward again, shouting the nickname the media assigned to her long ago. "Mac! Mac!"

Keeping her head down, she aimed for Quinn's front porch. Screw the smiling and chatting. She knew this routine just as well, had had to employ it for several days after she'd made the announcement that there would be no more Grand Slam victories in her future. Leaving all of this behind had been such an incredible relief.

"Just a word, Mac!"

"How do you feel about your brother being a suspect?"

"The paper said construction of the tennis center is de-layed indefinitely. Is the project in any danger of folding?"

She kept moving without acknowledging that she'd heard any of them. She'd almost reached the porch when one of them blocked her path. He was tall, blond and good-looking in that TV reporter kind of way.

"Come on, Mac, give us a break," he said with a toothy, saccharine grin.

Smooth, crafty, fake. Just like the ones who'd stalked her every limp ten years ago. Tension stiffened her back, and she clenched a fist at her side, wanting to ram it into his oily smile. "You're on private property," she said in a low voice.

His grin didn't falter as he thrust a microphone at her chin. "Do you think he did it? Be honest."

A beat went by in which she considered letting her fist have its way with the bastard's face. But then the whine of a siren and the play of flashing red and blue lights bouncing off the sea of suits in Florida pastel told her the police had ar-rived.

Oh, goody. Maybe she could have some of the media wolves ticketed for trespassing. But then another thought struck her. Had the blood tests come back on the shirt? Was Quinn about to be arrested? Oh, no. Oh, crap.

She made a break for the front door. Maybe she could barricade it once she got inside and keep everyone, including the cops, away from her brother, much the way he had pro-tected her when she'd left the hospital that first time.

Her steps faltered, though, when she heard a familiar, raised voice.

"Unless you want to get arrested for trespassing, I'd sug-gest you move off of Mr. McKay's property."

She turned to see Chase striding up the driveway toward her, a charming smile belying the sternness of his words. The way his faded jeans formed to his body, molding the muscles in his thighs, bulging at the crotch like there was something in there that wanted out, made her mouth go dry. God, he looked good in jeans. In fact, even his simple white polo made something flutter deep inside her, with the way the sleeves stretched to accommodate his biceps, the ribbed material clinging to abdominals ridged with the hills and valleys of ruthlessly developed muscles.

He was absolutely, unbelievably beautiful, the perfect manifestation of affable authority. Strong, capable, sexy.

By the time he joined her on the porch, she had her hormones under control and whispered, "What are you doing here?"

He continued to smile as the newshounds moseyed over to the other side of the road. "I thought you might need some reinforcements."

So he was being helpful. For some reason, all that did was irk her. Fending off this unreasonable yearning for him would have been so much easier if the guy were a jerk.

Mindful of the watching reporters, she forced herself to smile pleasantly up at him. "Meanwhile, they're going to report that the cops were called to my brother's house for reasons unknown."

"If you'd like to take a swing at me to give them something else to report, go ahead." He said this while nodding at the TV news people, his genial expression firmly in place.

Checking her scowl, she turned and pushed the doorbell. She didn't expect Quinn to answer, but she didn't want to walk in without some warning. When she tried to jam Quinn's house key into the lock, her hand shook so much she missed.

"Damn it," she muttered, irritated that her nerves were so visible. She was already anxious about what she would find when she got to Quinn. Add Chase to the mix, and she was a wreck. If she hadn't let him provoke her, and kiss the daylights out of her last night, she would have been fine. The guard she'd reinforced for more than a decade would have been perfectly intact.

When she fumbled the key the third time, Chase's palm, big and warm, slid over the back of her hand, and he eased the key ring from her fingers. "Let me do that."

She held her breath as he stepped closer to maneuver the

key into the lock. When she began to feel lightheaded from lack of air, she drew in the light tang of sweat mixed with tropical sunscreen. Longing immediately followed. She had a weak body, a traitorous heart.

"Are we going in or what?"

She opened her eyes, wondering when she'd closed them, and felt the heat of a blush race into her cheeks. Ignoring his knowing look, she brushed by him and into Quinn's living room.

"Quinn?"

The closed blinds made the room semidark but not so dark that she didn't see the uncapped bottle of tequila on the coffee table. An empty glass with an abused wedge of lime in the bottom sat next to the bottle. The *Kendall Falls News* lay crumpled on the floor next to the gray sofa, as if Quinn had angrily balled it up after reading the front-page story.

"Quinn?" she called, louder this time.

The air-conditioning kicked in, adding a low hum to the silence and stirring air that carried the unmistakable odor of booze.

"You stay here while I check the rest of the house," Chase said.

Kylie watched him move quickly toward the hallway that led to two bedrooms and a bathroom, fear prickling at the back of her neck. Unable to just stand there and wait, she walked into the kitchen. Nothing seemed amiss, though an empty Absolut bottle, a half-full bottle of vermouth and a jar of olives littered the white countertop of the center island. Quinn had either started with martinis and moved on to tequila or vice versa.

She went to the sliding-glass doors that led to the back-yard and twisted the plastic wand that opened the vertical blinds. She had to narrow her eyes against the harsh sunlight that poured through the glass.

"Ow."

She jerked in surprise and turned to see Quinn sitting on the floor between the island and the white refrigerator, his hand up in front of his eyes to block the light. He looked as if he'd been sleeping—or passed out—propped against the fridge door. His navy T-shirt and white shorts were wrinkled, and a beer bottle rested on the floor between the knees of his outstretched legs.

"Owwww," he repeated, drawing it out.

Kylie quickly closed the blinds, her legs watery with relief. He was okay. Drunk off his ass. But okay.

"I was worried about you." Determined to play this cool, she went to the coffeemaker and flipped up the top before rummaging in the cupboard for a fresh filter. "How long have you been drinking?" she asked, glancing over her shoulder at him.

He checked his wrist, but it was bare, so he shrugged. "Couple of days."

She scooped coffee into the filter. "I just saw you yesterday, ya dope."

"Couple of hours," he amended.

At the sink, she filled the glass carafe, focusing intently on the bubbles that formed on the water's surface. Chase had had plenty of time to check the rest of the house by now, so she assumed he stood in the hall outside the kitchen, analyzing their conversation for clues to Quinn's guilt. Well, she damn well was not going to give him anything he could use.

"That story is crap, you know," she said to Quinn.

"What about it is crap?" he asked, his words slurred. "I'm a suspect. The cops think I could have . . . done that to you."

"And we both know that's bullshit." She faced him, the carafe grasped in both hands, and considered dumping the cold water over his head.

He gave her a loopy grin. "You said bullshit."

A soft, relieved laugh escaped her. So he wasn't going to fall apart on her.

"It'd be funnier to hear Janie say it," he said. "She's so much more proper."

Kylie turned to pour the water into the coffeemaker, knowing now how to snap him into sobriety. "Speaking of our sister, you'd better get straightened out before she shows."

He sat up, knocking the beer bottle between his knees askew and fumbling to catch it before it fell over. "Did you call her?" he asked, the demand faintly accusing.

"Nope, but she knows about the story. She said she's going to stop by." She checked her watch. "I figure you've got about ten minutes before she's banging on your door."

Quinn pushed himself to his feet and wavered, slapping a hand onto the island for balance. "Damn. Think I'm seriously trashed."

She had to laugh at the note of amazement in his tone. "Go take a cold shower. I'll bring you some coffee and make you breakfast."

"Thanks." He gave her an exaggerated nod. "You're too good to me."

The way his voice cracked set her on edge. "And don't you forget it," she said, determined to keep it light.

He hung his head, still gripping the counter. "I've been a terrible brother, Kylie."

Her heart rose into her throat. What did he mean by that? The alarm grew double-edged as she pictured Chase, the cop on the hunt for evidence, listening on the other side of the door. "Go take a shower," she said. "You're drunk."

He gave his head a vigorous shake, deep lines furrowing his forehead as he stared at his feet. "It's all my fault. All of it. I should never have—"

"Quinn."

He raised his head at the sharpness of her tone and made a visible effort to focus on her face.

Putting her hand on top of his on the counter, she squeezed. "Think about the grief Jane is going to give you if she gets here while you're like this."

He straightened his shoulders. The fear of Jane was greater than the fear of God. "Right. Shower."

"Long and cold," she called after him as he swayed his way out of the kitchen.

Alone, waiting for Chase to show himself, she capped the olives and put them in the fridge. Her hands began to tremble as she threw the empty Absolut bottle in the recycling bin and stashed the vermouth under the sink, Quinn's words echoing inside her head.

*I'm a terrible brother.*

*It's all my fault.*

What could he possibly mean by that?

# 19

CHASE PAUSED IN THE KITCHEN DOORWAY TO watch Kylie vigorously wipe the island countertop clean. She looked beyond tired, and her ponytail was falling apart, yet she was so stunning that his breath clogged in his lungs. It didn't help that her red T-shirt hugged her slim curves, the short sleeves conforming to the toned shape of her upper arms. It *really* didn't help that her nipples were poking against the cotton of her shirt, yet it wasn't even close to being chilly in the kitchen. In fact, in his opinion, it was too damn warm.

His body started to react to the sheer physical appeal of this woman he'd kissed to within an inch of his sanity just yesterday. Jesus, he wanted her. And not just to sink into her heat and lose himself in her body, her rhythm, her life force. He wanted to heal her and love her and cherish her. He wanted to make her so dizzy with need that she leaned on him, and only him, for support.

Dragging a hand through his hair—it was good to have fantasies—he took a mental cold shower. "Guess you don't need me here anymore."

She turned to drop the sponge onto the edge of the sink. "Thanks for coming. I appreciate it."

He should have turned and left. But at least a little bit of blood had returned to his brain, so he decided that now was a good time to ask her some questions about the conversation she'd just had with Quinn. Cop, first. Horny guy, second.

Chase went to the blinds and opened them. "I'd be happy to make Quinn some breakfast before I go," he said. "One of my killer omelets would help soak up the booze in his blood."

When she didn't respond, he glanced over to find her staring at him as if he'd just double-faulted on match point. "What?" he asked.

"You want to make an omelet for a suspect in your case?"

He pocketed his hands, figuring that was the only way to avoid grabbing her and wiping all the frosty anger out of her with a mood-altering kiss. No, better to flee while they were still friends. Sort of.

"Guess I'll be on my way then," he said, walking to the door. "Call me if you need me."

"I won't need you."

He paused to look back at her. She returned his gaze with a defiance that didn't surprise him in the least. She didn't *need* him? They'd see about that.

He pivoted toward her, darkly satisfied at the way she drew back into the corner where the counter took a turn.

She raised a hand to hold him off. "Look, I don't know what you're—"

She broke off when he paused with his chest pressed against her palm, and he couldn't stop the triumph that swelled in his chest at how wide her eyes had gotten. She didn't know what to do, how to react. She wasn't slapping him, so clearly she wasn't going to make a big squealy deal out of this, probably for fear of making him think he had power over her. Little did she know.

Reaching up, he grasped the wrist of the hand she'd planted against his shirt, but instead of drawing her to him, he stepped forward, fencing her in.

"This isn't—"

"Shut up, Ky," he drawled.

Letting go of her wrist, he braced his hands on the counter on either side of her and went in for the kill. She turned her head to the side, avoiding his lips by a scant inch. The move put his nose at the crook of her neck, and he breathed in her vanilla scent, enjoyed the lazy spin of his senses. After letting his slow exhalation caress the side of her neck, he tried to kiss her again, only to have her turn her head to the other side. Since she had yet to try to push him away, he angled his head forward, lightly brushing the tip of his nose over the surface of her cheek.

"I don't want this," she said softly.

Yet, he noted, her breathing had gone shallow and choppy. Oh, yeah. "I think you do want this," he murmured, and nipped at her earlobe with his teeth.

She breathed in sharply. "Stop."

"I don't think so." He tried a third time—it's the charm after all—and nearly groaned out loud when her lips finally met his.

Heat flared instantly, and it was the kind that sucked all the air out of his lungs. His plan to thaw her, to prove how much she was kidding herself, flew out of his head the minute her tongue stroked against his. When her hands slid into his hair, and she pressed fully against him, making a small, helpless sound in the back of her throat, he lost complete control of the kiss.

He surged against her, wanting more, needing more. He'd meant only to kiss, to make a point, that no matter how cold she pretended to be, he knew just how to set her on fire. But it wasn't enough. With her, a kiss was never enough. He wanted so much more. He wanted everything.

And then she shoved him back, her formerly stroking hands planted firmly against his chest. He blinked away the blinding desire to focus on her face, saw the glitter in her eyes, the icy set of her jaw. A smile that didn't come close to touching her eyes played at the corners of her mouth.

"You really should think these things through," she said.

The realization that she'd played him struck like a ringing slap. He should have known better than to challenge her competitive nature, to play dirty. She'd always come out swinging. Game, set, match.

He raised his hands in a gesture of surrender. "Clearly, I'm out of my league."

He thought he saw a flash of doubt, or maybe hurt, in her eyes as he turned away. But he didn't turn back. He had his own hurt and doubt to deal with.

He walked out of the house, his steps sure and probably a bit too stompy, not pausing or looking back. Next to the SUV, he stopped, squinting against the harsh sunlight and trying to ram his brain back into work mode.

Things had changed. He'd heard with his own ears as Quinn had tried to confess something to Kylie, and she'd shut him down. To protect him. She believed he was innocent, fine. But Chase's doubts were growing, and Sylvia Jensen was right. If Quinn did indeed attack Kylie with a bat, he could easily do it again.

In a matter of minutes, he was on his cell, outlining the case to Assistant District Attorney Rebecca Morgan. "I've got means, motive, opportunity. His shirt links him to the probable weapon. His alibi is weak. Drunk and alone."

"Are there other suspects?"

"Not at the moment. I'm waiting on some test results on the shirt that could add to the case."

"For now, though, you do realize that this case is circumstantial," she said.

"My gut tells me he's one of the guys."

"Your gut carries a lot of weight with this office, but I'd need more to make a strong case."

"My plan is to get a confession."

"So just bring him in for questioning."

"My partner questioned him already and didn't get anything. I need him in cuffs and intimidated if I'm going to get anywhere with him."

"Okay. I'll get a warrant issued, and we'll see what happens. We can present the case to the grand jury, and if they don't bite, kick it."

"Done. Thanks, Rebecca."

"Good luck."

Disconnecting the call, Chase pushed the speed dial button for Sam.

"Hawkins," Sam answered.

"How soon can you meet me?"

"Half an hour, forty minutes. What's up?"

"I just talked to the prosecutors' office. It's time to make an arrest."

"Who are we arresting?"

"Quinn McKay."

# 20

KYLIE USED A PAPER TOWEL TO WIPE UP WATER drops around the sink. Her lips still throbbed from Chase's kiss. Hell, her whole body throbbed. Especially her heart. She should have been feeling victorious: He'd tried to show her how weak she was, and she'd flipped the game on him. She couldn't have asked for a more satisfying win. Except it didn't feel like a win. It felt like a loss. Empty.

The phone rang, and she snagged the receiver off its cradle.

"Hello?"

"So he *did* let you in," Jane said. "I won't bother to ask you why, since it's hardly important." Which was her way of saying it was totally important—to her. "How is he?"

Kylie snugged the phone between her ear and shoulder as she tore another section of paper towel off the roll. "Fine. He's in the shower."

"Fine? He can't possibly be fine." Jane released a sigh, the one that said "I'm surrounded by incompetents." "When he gets out, will you let him know that I'm on my way over?"

"You really don't have to do that. I've already talked to him."

"I'm sure your idea of talking included an extended discussion about the weather."

Kylie bristled. So what if she and Quinn didn't have a deep, dark conversation about how there were evil bastards in the world and sometimes they hurt innocent people? Maybe all he needed at the moment was a fresh pot of coffee. "You'll be happy to know that our discussion got a little heated when I said it was partly cloudy and he insisted that one big cloud that covers the entire sky means it's mostly cloudy."

"What is it with you two? You have to make everything a joke. Well, this situation is not a joke. Our brother could go to prison."

Kylie turned as Quinn walked in wearing a clean T-shirt and shorts, his hair wet and combed back. He looked like total, haggard crap as he raised a questioning brow.

"He's not going to prison, Jane," Kylie said. "He didn't do anything."

Rolling his eyes, he strolled barefoot over to the coffeemaker.

"Innocent people go to prison all the time," Jane said. "And don't think that just because your high school sweetheart is on the case that he'll give Quinn a break. He has a job to do, and he's going to do it no matter what it does to you."

Kylie turned her back to her brother and walked toward the deck doors. "For the record, I trust that Chase will do the right thing, and the right thing is not putting Quinn in prison for something he didn't do."

Jane made a sound that would have been a snort if she hadn't managed to make it so delicate. "I don't know why I bother to argue with you. I never win."

"Funny, that's how I feel."

"You're too defensive. When did you get so defensive?"

Her voice had shifted smoothly into professional gear. Kylie's cue to bolt. "Quinn just got out of the shower. I'll tell him you're on your way."

"This is a difficult time for you, Kylie. You shouldn't keep it all bottled up inside."

"I'll work on it. But I think Quinn needs your attention more than I do right now."

"Wench," Quinn growled behind her.

She shot him a wicked grin over her shoulder. "When shall I tell him you'll be here?"

"An hour. I have to clear my schedule."

"Drive safely."

She clicked off the call and faced her brother, taking in his pallor and the puffiness around his eyes. More than drunk, he looked unhealthy, stressed.

He set down his cup with a grimace. "This coffee is terrible."

"I made it the way I do every day."

"Why do you think Jane always wants tea?"

Kylie wished things could stay like this. Easy and bantering. "You're just bitter because I ruined your morning as a happy drunk."

Groaning, he plopped onto a stool at the end of the island. "Christ, I can't believe you sicced her on me."

"She'd whipped out the legal pad that has my name at the top. No way was I in the mood to be analyzed." Especially after that kiss with Chase. Her lips still vibrated. To occupy her restless hands, she retrieved a cup from the cupboard above the coffeemaker and filled it.

"Ever wonder what that legal pad says about you?" Quinn asked.

It took her a moment to remember what they'd been talking about. "I imagine lots of doodles of tennis players with rackets broken over their heads. What does yours say?"

"I don't even want to think about it," he said.

She tore open a pink packet of sweetener and dumped the contents into her coffee. After retrieving the milk from the fridge, she dribbled enough into her cup to turn her coffee the color of light caramel then gingerly took a sip. "There's nothing wrong with this coffee. It's fine."

"That's because you put all that crap in it. Once you're done messing with it, it's milk and saccharine with a tablespoon of coffee for color."

She gave him a benign smile. "Now you're just being mean."

Pushing off the stool, he crossed to the fridge and jerked it open. "I'm ruined, you know. People are never going to forget this."

"The people who know you know better than that, Quinn."

"Maybe it'd be okay if we lived in a big town, like Miami or even Tampa. But Kendall Falls—"

"Is filled with people who care about you."

He slammed the door shut with a rattle of glass bottles and faced her, his eyes dark with misery. "I don't know how you can even look at me."

"Trust me, you're much easier to look at now that you've had a shower."

"I'm serious, Kylie. My *shirt* was found with the bat."

"Did you hit me with that bat?" she asked, her tone deliberately sharp.

He flinched back, and something that looked like pain contorted his features before his Adam's apple bobbed. "No. I didn't."

"All right then."

"It's really that easy for you?"

She took a breath. Nothing was ever easy, or black and white. She believed him when he said he didn't do it, but his behavior—*I've been a terrible brother*—confused the hell out of her. Still, he needed her to sound sure, so she gave him a firm, convincing nod. "Yes. It's really that easy for me."

He turned away—she thought she caught a glimpse of tears—and reopened the fridge to peer inside as if searching for something to eat.

She walked over and stood beside him. "Are you going to be okay?" she asked softly.

He nodded without looking at her. "Yeah." But his voice sounded constricted.

"I've got a student in fifteen, but I can postpone."

"I'm fine, Kylie. I promise."

"Do me a favor?"

"What?" He glanced at her reluctantly.

She grinned. "Say hi to Dr. Jane for me."

Laughing, he swatted at her ponytail as she walked away.

AS SHE CLOSED QUINN'S FRONT DOOR BEHIND her, Kylie paused on the front stoop. Chase was leaning against the front fender of his SUV, looking formidable and unfairly sexy in those soft, faded jeans. When she noticed his stony expression, trepidation congealed inside her.

"What are you still doing here?" she asked.

"I'm waiting for Sam."

"Why?"

He straightened away from the truck. "I don't have a choice, Kylie. I'm a cop."

Her heart started to pound in her ears. No way. He wouldn't. But she could see by the look on his face, the resigned hardness in his eyes, that he would.

"If he's indicted," he went on, "he'll have a trial. If he's innocent—"

"*If* he's innocent? Of course he is. He didn't do it."

"That's not for you to decide."

"But I'm the one who was attacked. Don't I get a say?"

"You're not objective."

"And you are?"

"Hell, no. If I were, Quinn would have been sitting in a cell a long time ago. My job is to look at the evidence and make an informed decision. It's up to the grand jury to look at the same evidence and decide whether charges should be filed."

"Evidence that you're going to continue to collect."

"Ky, please. I'm not doing this to hurt you. But I have a job to do, and I'm going to do it. End of discussion."

# 21

CHASE STRODE INTO THE INTERVIEW ROOM, YANKED
a chair out from the table and sat across from Kylie's brother.
He felt Quinn's wary gaze on him but didn't acknowledge
him just yet, instead taking in his body language without
being blatant about it. Quinn sat with his elbows on the table,
his hands clasped before him. The pads of his thumbs were
pressed together and moving back and forth in a nervous
dance. His swept-back hair revealed a glimmering sheen of
sweat on his forehead. The guy was clearly on edge.

"Let's start with where you were the day Kylie was attacked."

"How is she? Is she freaking?" Quinn's dark eyes were
bleary with booze and distress.

"That's not an answer to my question."

"As I told Sam the other day, I was getting drunk in the
garage." Quinn kept up the steady, back-and-forth rhythm of
his thumbs.

"Alone?"

"Yes."

"Why alone? Why not with friends?"

"Wasn't in the mood."

An alarm sounded in Chase's head. Quinn's speech pattern had just changed. He'd been answering questions with "I" as the subject, and suddenly he'd dropped the pronoun. Could be a classic liar's mistake or just a coincidence. "How did you find out about what happened to your sister?"

Quinn paused the thumb boogie but didn't respond.

"You have to think about it?" Chase asked.

"I was drunk off my ass at the time."

"I would expect you'd remember clearly where you were when you found out something so big."

"I'm sure most people would," Quinn said slowly, enunciating each word, "but I was loaded."

Chase switched gears. "Let's talk about the bat."

Quinn dropped his hands apart and sat back. "What about it? I've never seen it."

"You saw it yesterday next to her Jeep."

"That was a fake, wasn't it?"

"How would you know that?"

"I assumed, like everyone else. Didn't you? Does that make *you* a suspect?"

Chase didn't react. "What about your shirt at the scene? How do you explain that?"

"I already told Sam. It rained, and I got wet. I took off the shirt, and I forgot it when I left. Don't you two communicate?"

Chase sat forward, looked Quinn dead in the eye. "You're not helping yourself here."

Quinn stared at him for a long moment, his expression maddeningly blank. Kylie blank. "You only want answers that incriminate me."

"You incriminated yourself. Otherwise, your shirt wouldn't have been buried with the bat used to tear up your sister's knee and you'd have an alibi other than 'I was in the garage getting drunk *all by myself.*'"

Quinn's red-rimmed eyes went flinty.

"No matter what I say, you're going to see me as the guy who attacked my sister. And you know what? I don't think you're all that objective."

"I'm probably the only cop in this town who *wants* you to be innocent. It scares the shit out of me what it'll do to your sister if it turns out that you're the guy who hit her with that bat."

Quinn's lips thinned, and his chin actually trembled. "I didn't do it. I couldn't have done it."

"Prove it."

"Don't you think I would if I could?" Quinn shoved back his chair. He began to pace with all the pent-up frustration of a wild animal in a too-small cage.

"Tell me what you meant this morning," Chase said.

Quinn whirled back toward him. "What I meant about what?"

"When you told Kylie that you'd been a terrible brother."

He looked confused for another moment, and then the blood drained from his face. "Christ, you heard that? And, what, you immediately jumped to the conclusion that I meant because I destroyed her knee?" Turning away, he scrubbed his hands over his face and groaned aloud. "I am so fucking fucked."

"What did you want to tell her, Quinn? You're obviously desperate to get it off your chest."

"Fuck that. I want a lawyer."

Chase winced inwardly. Damn it, he'd pushed too hard. "Kylie believes you're innocent. If it turns out that you're not, I'm personally going to make you a very miserable man."

# 22

KYLIE HAD PACED THE LOBBY OF THE KENDALL
Falls Public Safety Building for so long that the woman at
the front desk, a redhead with radiant blue eyes, had started
smiling at her like they were old friends. After the first two
hours of watching Kylie trying to wear a path in the black-
and-white tile floor, the woman had even offered to get her
some coffee or water.

Her cell phone rang, and Kylie flinched. Her hands shook
while she fished it out of her bag. "Hello?"

"Do you know where Quinn is?"

"Jane. I tried to call you earlier, but you'd already left and
your cell was off."

"I'm at his house," Jane plowed ahead. "Didn't you say
he'd be here?"

"Yes. It's just . . ." She had no clue how to say it.

"I've got a lot on my plate today," Jane snapped. "I canceled several appointments so I could be here."

Kylie bit down on the urge to bark back at her impatient
sister. Instead, she was blunt. "He was arrested. We're at the
police department."

Silence.

"Jane?"

"Arrested for what?"

Kylie had to take a breath before she could say it. "My attack."

"Oh my God. Oh my God. Not *Quinn*."

"He didn't do it," Kylie said quickly.

"Of course he didn't. I was just thinking of how awful it must be for him."

"That's why I'm here. I'll post his bail and take him home, make sure he's okay." Kylie sank onto a chair. "Chase won't listen to me. I was there, Jane. I was on that path. I would have known if my own brother had . . . hurt me like that."

"I don't know much about the law, but the evidence is circumstantial, and really, Kylie, what are we talking about here? No one was killed. You recovered fine. The chances of Quinn going to jail even if he were convicted are slim."

"You must not have read the entire story in the paper. It said a conviction for assault with a deadly weapon could carry a five-year prison term."

Jane didn't do anything more than breathe for several seconds. "Have you called a lawyer?" she finally asked, her voice thin now from stress.

"Yes, of course."

"Good. I'm on my way."

"Maybe we should wait until Quinn's been released before we tell Mom?"

"Definitely," Jane said. "She wouldn't take it well."

Finally, she and Jane agreed on something. "See you in a bit."

Kylie cut off the call and looked up to see Chase standing several feet away watching her. Her breath caught as her gaze met his. He looked both sad and angry, as if he knew something she didn't and he dreaded the moment she found out. Jane would say she was projecting, that the look on his face was basically indecipherable and she assigned her own meaning to it, a meaning that she feared.

Taking a fortifying breath, she asked, "Are you done with him?"

"He lawyered up."

"Just now? You've had him in there for more than an hour."

"Well, I had to get in a few good punches before I started questioning him."

Sarcasm. Just what they needed. She bit back her own snarky response and let the ball stay in his court. One of them had to be the adult.

He took a step toward her, lowered his voice. "Your brother just lied to me about where he was and what he was doing when you were getting the living shit knocked out of you ten years ago."

His words stunned her, and for a moment she could only stare at him in silence. Quinn wouldn't lie. He had no reason to lie. The answer was simple: "You're wrong," she said.

Sighing, Chase took her arm. "Let's continue this conversation somewhere more private."

She forced herself not to stiffen at the feel of his fingers on her skin and let him lead her to the squad's break room. While he poured coffee, she sat automatically at the wooden table, barely taking note of the ancient avocado refrigerator and shiny new coffeemaker.

Chase had to be wrong. *Why* would Quinn lie?

Chase set a cup of caramel-colored coffee in front of her. "Be careful, it's hot."

She looked up at him. "What makes you think he's lying?"

He sat across from her, loosely linking his hands on the table. The circles under his eyes and the lines in his face spoke of exhaustion, yet she reminded herself that his fatigue shouldn't concern her. Only Quinn concerned her.

"He made the mistakes that liars make," Chase said. "His body language was off, and his speech pattern changed. I've been trained to watch for that kind of stuff."

"What stuff, specifically?"

"He hesitated when I asked him where he was when he found out about your attack."

"Why is that so significant?"

"Because it's human nature to remember details of where you were, what song was playing, what you were wearing, et cetera, when you find out something . . . emotional."

She thought about when her stepmother had called to tell her that a stroke had killed her father. She'd been wearing a purple T-shirt and white shorts when the phone rang, sifting a scoop of freshly ground hazelnut coffee into the coffeemaker. Ever since, the scent of anything hazelnut made her feel sick.

"I'd just come home from class," Chase said, drawing her out of her memories. "Got an A on my English paper about how weather metaphors throughout *Jane Eyre* paralleled the seasons of her life. Dad was passed out on the sofa, in boxers and a white shirt, reeking of the usual. A *Frasier* rerun was on too loud on the TV. Mom was in the kitchen making dinner. She had on a pretty sundress. Light orange with butterflies on it. One of her favorites. She'd been crying, so I knew right away they'd had a fight. I said something sarcastic, like, 'When are you going to leave that asshole?' And she made excuses for him that I no longer heard. I went to my bedroom and slammed the door. Picked up the phone to call you and got no answer. So I started changing out of jeans and a blue Cubs T-shirt Dad picked up while in Chicago for something or other. I figured I'd just go over to your place and practice my serve until you returned from wherever you were. We could play some tennis, have some dinner. Talk. I really just wanted to talk. We were good at that then."

She swallowed against the thickening at the back of her throat. "I get the point."

"Not yet, you don't. So I'm walking out the door, almost to my car, when Mom comes running out of the house. She tells me your mom is on the phone and needs to talk to me. I knew, right then, that something terrible had happened to you. I ran into the house, and your mom tells me, in this weak, cracking voice, that there's been an accident. She tells me you're going to need me and could I come."

She closed her eyes. She *so* didn't want to hear this. "Chase—"

"Let me finish."

Sitting back, she waited for him to say what he needed to say and get it over with.

"I don't remember the drive to the hospital," he went on. "I don't remember parking or running inside. I don't remember anything after the moment when I heard your mother's voice until I was at your side and watching you wake up. But before all that, before the ax fell, I remember the damn butterflies on my mother's dress. Yet Quinn can't remember where he was or what he was doing when he found out."

She took a steadying breath. She could see the logical explanation even if he couldn't. "People are different. And you're not taking into account that he'd been drinking."

"A ready excuse, it seems. He was drunk this morning when he tried to tell you something and you shut him up."

"Drunk people say stupid stuff sometimes."

"You knew I was listening."

"I'm not protecting him."

"Then why did you shut him up?"

"I didn't know what he was going to say. He could have said something innocent that sounded incriminating, and the next thing I know, you're hauling him off in handcuffs. In fact, that's exactly what happened."

"What do you think he meant by what he said?"

*It's all my fault. All of it.* Doubt crept in on her all over again. What *had* he meant? But she shoved the uncertainty away. She trusted her brother. "I have no idea."

"What are you afraid of?" Chase asked softly.

The shift threw her, and when she met his scrutinizing gaze, her stomach flipped. God, why couldn't he be a stranger, someone who knew nothing about her, had no history with her? "I'm not afraid of anything."

"You're scared to death, Ky. I can see it in your eyes."

She shoved back from the table. "I'm going to wait for Quinn's lawyer out front."

Chase followed her to the door, and when she would have opened it and slipped out, he placed his palm against the wood to hold it closed. Trapped between his body and the door, Kylie felt his warm breath on her hair, felt his nose nudge forward just enough, as he inhaled.

She quickly faced him, ignoring the way his sunscreen scent filled her head, swirled tantalizingly through her senses.

"What are you doing?" she asked, hating how breathless she sounded. His heat was overwhelming, just like it had been this morning. But she'd been stronger then, focused. Now, her pulse was all over the place, lunging like a cat that had spotted a helpless mouse. She was sure he would see its heavy throb at the base of her throat.

He leaned in closer, until they were all but nose to nose. "None of this is about persecuting your brother. This is about finding the truth. That's what I do. And you know what you do?"

His breath caressed her lips, and she almost closed her eyes but somehow managed to keep them steady on his. "I'm sure you're going to tell me."

"You put so much effort into keeping the people around you at arm's length that you've managed to convince yourself and everyone else that that's what you want. So they all tiptoe around you, avoiding the tough topics at all costs. And you know what the really sad thing is?"

She stayed silent, braced against the door, trapped by his heat, his scent. This was a game, and he was trying to break her serve. Fat chance.

He angled his head, making her heart leap when it seemed he was going to kiss her, only to back off an inch. "You're not living," he breathed, his voice so low she felt its vibrations slide up her spine.

She raised her chin a notch. Stop it, she thought. Stop *feeling* him.

"You're just going through the motions," he said.

"Maybe I like the motions."

"Why not? They're safe. I remember a time when you had passion. Remember that? Remember what it was like to win?"

Something strong and ruthless tugged at her heart. "I can't play like that anymore."

"Not tennis. But what about life? Just because you've got a bum knee, you're not allowed to be passionate about anything ever again?"

She wanted to shout at him. She *was* passionate! She was passionate about the tennis center, which his investigation had brought to a grinding halt. She was passionate about rebuilding her life here, reconnecting with her family, which his investigation was going to destroy. And she was passionate about Quinn's innocence, which Chase was trying to shred.

Chase, Chase, everywhere. She wanted to scream.

But then he cocked his head in the other direction and moved in closer, forcing her to press the back of her head against the door to maintain an inch between them.

"Let me help you," he said, his voice soft, almost a caress. "Let me find out who took out your knee and why. Let me help you deal with why it happened and who did it so you can move on. Can you do that? Not for me, but for yourself."

She tried to breathe evenly, fighting the urge to shove him back. But, no, that would give him the advantage, let him know he was getting to her. He wasn't, she thought. *He wasn't.*

"I'd like to go," she said, coolly.

He didn't budge. He just stood there, trapping her without touching her, his laser-beam gaze considering, speculating. The flaring heat in his eyes was her only warning before his mouth was on hers.

She would have gasped if the taste of him hadn't flooded her senses. It wasn't a sweet, tender kiss. It was a grinding, I've-got-something-to-prove kiss. Nonetheless, she responded because she had no choice. She never seemed to have a choice with him. With a moan, she pressed her fists against his muscled chest.

But instead of letting her go, he captured her face in his palms and gentled the kiss. Her knees went weak, and she would have melted against him if he hadn't leaned into her first, trapping her hands between them. His knee nudged between hers, and she felt his arousal against her belly. A sharp ache speared through her middle.

Then she twisted her head to the side, breaking the embrace. "I can't do this," she said, embarrassed that she was panting.

His breath, fast and urgent, was warm against her skin as he nuzzled her cheek with his nose. So tender, so loving.

"I have to go," she choked.

He released her and stepped back, making a point of looking down. She followed his gaze to the bulge in his jeans and felt her cheeks flame along with a renewed flare of desire. God, she wanted him inside her so much she could have begged.

"Honey, if you stare much longer, you're going to drool."

She raised her gaze to the smug satisfaction on his face, perplexed by the shift in his attitude.

He ran his knuckles down her cheek. "If I'm an asshole," he said, "then it's easier for you to hate me, isn't it? And that's what your friends and family do. Make things easier for you."

She slapped his hand away. "Don't do me any favors."

He sank his hand into her hair and cupped the back of her rigid neck, drawing her close but not making contact in any other way. "One of these days, Ky, I'm going to make you cut loose in a way you've never cut loose before. And I'm going to enjoy the hell out of watching you come apart in my arms."

She swallowed against the rush of lust that nearly buckled her knees. "Is that a challenge?"

His eyes glittered like hard emeralds. "Sure. Why not?"

"Well, what do you know? It worked."

The grim set of his lips twitched. "What worked?"

"Your ploy to be an asshole."

She shoved him back a step and fled.

# 23

QUINN RESTED HIS HEAD AGAINST THE CONCRETE wall behind him and stared at the wall's twin six feet across from him. The thin, bare mattress under him reeked of body odor, but with six cellmates, there was nowhere else to sit.

So this was jail. Just as noisy and stinky and overcrowded and scary as he'd expected.

"What're you in for?"

He glanced sideways at the cellmate sharing the mattress, a scrawny white guy with a bald head and a blond mustache. He looked like he hadn't eaten a full meal in a year.

"Doesn't matter," Quinn said. "I didn't do it."

The guy grinned, showing a darkened front tooth that needed to be pulled. "Yeah, me neither. The other guys in here? They didn't do anything, either. Same goes for the shitheads in the cell next door."

Quinn closed his eyes. Christ, he was fucked.

And he deserved it. If he hadn't been such an immature butthead ten years ago, this wouldn't be happening now. But he'd been filled with bitter resentment then, blaming his older sister, the tennis star who was everything he wasn't, for his own unhappiness. As if Kylie had anything to do with his teenage desire to do nothing but skip school and hide out in the garage with whatever booze he'd swiped from their clueless parents' liquor cabinet.

He'd thought the alcohol helped. He'd thought it numbed the pain, back when he didn't even know what true pain meant. He could sit on the cold concrete in the garage with his back against the wall and swallow shot after shot, raising the bottle for toasts like a drunken idiot.

Here's a toast to failing American history.

Here's a toast to skipping English class. Over and over and over.

Here's a toast to being denied his driver's license because Dad caught him watering down his favorite bottle of Jack.

Here's a toast to being so desperate for a mind-numbing drink that he suffered through his mother's sugary favorites: root beer schnapps and crème de menthe.

Here's a toast to getting only half the tennis-playing genes that it took to please a demanding, driven father.

Here's a toast to being sidelined as his sister's training partner because he was no longer good enough to challenge her.

Here's a toast to life, at sixteen, already sucking more than he could ever imagine.

And on that day ten years ago, drowning his lame sorrows in the cheapest crap he could afford, bought at the only liquor store in town that sold to minors, he'd blown off the sister he couldn't stand. He'd told her, "Bite me, go to hell, fuck off. Take your pick."

She'd walked away without saying a word, heading into a workout on her own.

He'd raised his bottle in one final toast: "Drop dead, gorgeous."

That one had made him giggle. Loaded, toasted, smashed, blasted, wasted—whatever he was, it had felt pretty fucking good. While under the influence, he hadn't felt bad about anything. He'd just felt good. Great, really. Fucking great.

The world, especially his father and his tennis-prodigy sister, could have kissed his ass.

He'd flipped the universe the bird that day. And now the universe was flipping it back.

# 24

CHASE PACED HIS TINY KITCHEN. HE HADN'T HAD any coffee this morning, yet his heart raced as if he'd drained three supersized cups. Who needed caffeine when they'd had no sleep and carried around enough nerves for three football players the night before the Super Bowl?

He'd called Steve Burnett, the officer sitting in front of Kylie's, every couple of hours, and every time the report had been the same: All's quiet on the driveway front.

Chase had delivered the requisite chuckle at his co-worker's effort to lighten his surly mood, but he hadn't felt like laughing. He felt like beating something with his fists. Not that that would solve anything, but it would bleed off some of this restless energy.

Sex would help, too.

Groaning, he stopped pacing and braced his hands on the edge of the counter.

Kylie brought out the pieces of himself he couldn't stand: his propensity for violence—how many times had he pummeled inanimate objects after she'd walked out on him?—and his blinding, driving need when he was around her.

He wasn't a just-out-of-his-teens adult anymore, eager to

get his rocks off with a hot girl. He was a grown man perfectly capable of controlling himself. Yet, from the moment they'd kissed in her kitchen, glass glittering on the floor all around them, he'd felt . . . edgy and out of control. Quality time in the shower, while thoughts of Kylie naked and moaning danced in his head, hadn't helped. He'd simply dried off with a bigger need growing inside him, a need that his hand and a fantasy wouldn't satisfy.

And it pissed him off. He'd vowed not to let her twist him into knots, yet that's exactly what happened. And instead of focusing on the case, working the angles and theories and suspects, he was pacing the kitchen like a caged panther, frustrated and wanting.

Sam was right, he thought. He should have let his partner handle the case. He should have walked away, from the case and Kylie, and everything would have been fine. The status quo. How he loved the status quo.

Which was bullshit. He'd fooled himself into thinking that for the past ten years in order to get through. But the truth was, the status fucking quo *happened* to him when he wasn't looking. He became a father by accident. He got married because that was the right thing to do. He got divorced because that was the right thing to do. He became a cop because he didn't know what else to do, and his father had been such a lousy one that he'd wanted to show the bastard how it was done. Plus, that would gain him access to the biggest cold case in Kendall Falls history: Who destroyed Kylie McKay's knee? Not that he'd made any more progress than the cops at the time had. Until now.

And that put him at a crossroads. He wanted two opposing things.

He wanted Kylie.

He wanted to find the bastards who tore her apart, and one of them might be her brother.

He couldn't very well build a case against Quinn McKay while rebuilding a relationship with the guy's sister.

He had to choose. Kylie or justice? And if he chose Kylie, would she choose him?

The phone rang, jolting him, and he snatched it up without checking the caller ID. "Manning."

"Chase, Sylvia Jensen here." He turned to lean back against the counter as the crime scene analyst kept talking. "I pulled a clear set of prints off the bat used on Kylie's windshield."

He straightened away from the counter. "Excellent."

"That depends on how you look at it."

AS KYLIE STIRRED SWEETENER AND CREAMER INTO her coffee, her back to her plastic-covered deck doors, she worried about Quinn. He hadn't been in good shape when she and Jane had dropped him at home after bailing him out of jail yesterday. When they'd offered to stay the night with him, he'd brushed them off with the excuse that he needed some alone time. Kylie feared that meant he planned to try to drink his troubles away again. He'd gone through a stage like that in his teens, but he'd managed to kick the habit before it became a problem he couldn't deal with without intervention. Now, she wasn't so sure.

But when Jane didn't push to smother him with her usual sisterly assistance, Kylie backed off, too. Her sister knew, better than anyone, how to deal with someone in Quinn's state of mind. "Let him cool off," Jane had said. "We won't get anywhere with him until he's had some time to process what's happening."

Still, Kylie had to fight the urge to reach for the phone and check on him. Or maybe it'd be better to go by his house and do it in person. Except maybe not enough time had passed. Should she call Jane first?

Sighing, she picked up her coffee and sipped, wondering if this was how her siblings felt when they wanted to reach out to her. Not knowing what to do sucked. And not doing anything seemed wrong.

The shoe was on the other foot, and it pinched.

Deciding not to hover, at least until she'd talked it over

with Jane, she carried her coffee to the table and stared down at the bold newspaper headline that had her heart pounding double-time all over again.

*Mac's Brother Arrested in Career-Ending Attack.*

Apparently, there was no bigger news happening in Kendall Falls.

She thought of Chase, so determined to pin the attack on Quinn. He had nothing else to go on, no other evidence, so he went gung-ho after her brother. How could she make him understand that Quinn hadn't hurt her? She would have *known*.

Meanwhile, Chase seemed just as driven to pick at her. Like he had something to prove. Like he thought he could back her against the wall and kiss the past away and none of it would matter.

But it *did* matter. It did. He replaced her in a heartbeat. Less than a heartbeat. True love shouldn't be so easy to discard. She certainly hadn't been able to. If she had, she wouldn't be resigned to an eternity alone and unloved. She'd have fallen for Dr. Wade Bell, like a normal woman. Yet, she'd botched that, and every other relationship attempt over the years.

She'd thought she'd done everything right with Wade, until the day he looked her in the eye and said, "You're here, but you're not *here*."

And instead of trying to fix it, of trying to be *here*, she'd let him walk away.

The story of her life.

And then there was Chase.

*I'm going to enjoy the hell out of watching you come apart in my arms.*

Just thinking about him saying that, his voice low and sexy as he held her so close that his heat surrounded her, made her shudder.

The phone rang, startling her, and she picked it up off the table and walked into the living room for a change of scenery. The caller ID didn't look familiar, and she hoped like

hell it wasn't another reporter. She'd have preferred to silence the ringer last night but had feared she'd miss a call
from Quinn.

"Hello?"

"Hi. It's T.J."

Shoulders relaxing, she turned toward the bay window
and, for the first time since the cop car had parked in the
driveway, she didn't feel like scowling, or hiding, when she
saw it. Maybe T.J. was calling to ask for some extra tennis-
court time. That'd be a welcome distraction. "Hey, T.J."

"I need to talk to you. I . . . I'm . . . I need to talk to you."

At the anxiety in his voice, she stiffened again. She'd
never heard him sound so distressed. "What's wrong? Are
you all right?"

"I think I'm in big trouble."

"Where are you?"

"Will you . . . I need . . ." His voice wavered as he trailed
off.

"Let's start with where you are, T.J. I'll be right there."

"Will you meet me at the health club?"

"You're at the health club?"

"No, I'm at home, but I—"

"I'll come there then. Just give me your address."

"No!" He sounded panicked. Worse, he sniffled, like he'd
been crying. "I'm . . . fine. I just . . . I just want to . . . I have
to tell you something, okay? At the health club."

"You're not all right, T.J. I can tell."

"Can you be there in an hour and forty-five minutes?"

She knew it took him an hour to get to the club by bus.
The extra forty-five minutes must take into account the bus
schedule. "Let me pick you up."

"Just, please, can you meet me there? Okay? Is that
okay?"

"Sure, of course. In an hour and forty-five minutes."

He released a sigh. "Thank you."

"Whatever's going on, it's going to be okay, all right? I'll
help you figure it out."

He sniffled again, and when he said, "Okay," it sounded choked. "Bye."

The line clicked in her ear.

CHASE STOOD ON KYLIE'S FRONT PORCH AND RANG the bell. Last time he'd done this, they'd ended up pressed against the wall, about to board the F Train to paradise. He figured the only train they'd board this time would be the Go-to-Hell Train, and he'd be riding it solo.

When Kylie pulled open the door and cocked her dark head, Chase immediately noticed the flat expression and bored eyes. The game face in all its maddening glory. Yet it didn't distract from how sexy she looked in bare feet and a black, form-fitting T-shirt that didn't reach past the waistband of her faded jeans. She had her long hair pulled back in a Tennis Pony, and other than tired, she looked . . . God, she just looked *good*.

"Is this stopping-by-unannounced thing going to become a habit?" she asked.

He didn't waste time with a comeback. He had a job to do. "I need the address of your student, T.J. Ritchie."

Her eyes flickered with something—surprise, yes, and something else—but her full, tempting lips remained set in a straight, uncompromising line. "Why?"

"I need to ask him some questions."

"What kind of questions?"

"I'm not at liberty to say."

She folded her arms under her breasts. "Then I'm not at liberty to give you his address."

"It's police business, Kylie."

"What business could the police possibly have with a fourteen-year-old?"

"That isn't for me to tell you."

"Well, you're going to have to if you want information about him from me."

"Damn it, Kylie—"

"Why don't you just get what you want from some police database?"

"His correct address isn't in the database."

"Hmm, well, that's too bad for you, then, isn't it?"

Okay, if that's the way she wanted to play it. "We got a hit on fingerprints found on the bat used to break your windshield. They belong to T.J."

Shock parted her lips, and her eyes went wide. "That's not possible."

"Fingerprints don't lie. So if you don't mind, I'll take that address now."

She straightened her shoulders, lifted her chin. "I don't have it."

"Kylie—"

"I can't give it to you if I don't have it."

She was lying. He couldn't see any clues, but he knew she was organized and methodical. She'd have records on all of her students, especially her favorite. "This isn't the time to be stubborn."

"If you'd like, I can make one up." She smiled, but it didn't come close to reaching her still eyes.

He tried another tack. "What about a phone number?"

"I'm sorry, but no."

"How do you reach him when you have to cancel a tennis lesson?"

"I've never canceled a lesson."

He almost groaned aloud. "Of course you haven't."

"Is there anything else? I have a lot on my plate today, what with my brother going to jail yesterday and all."

"Ky, come on. You know I had no—"

"Nothing else then? Great. You have a nice day screwing over someone else's innocent brother."

She slammed the door in his face.


KYLIE LEANED BACK AGAINST THE DOOR, HER HEART racing. T.J. had shattered her windshield? She couldn't—*wouldn't*—believe it. Something big was going on with him, and no way was she letting someone who didn't care about him have first crack at questioning him about it. But she didn't want to wait until meeting him at the club. She needed to talk to him now, before Chase tracked him down.

She checked the window to make sure Chase had left. He stood beside the police cruiser in her driveway, chatting away with the officer inside. Terrific. How the hell was she supposed to get to T.J.'s without either one, or both, following her?

First things first. She dug her BlackBerry out of her bag and retrieved T.J.'s phone number from her contacts list. When she called, though, she discovered the line had been disconnected. So she retrieved his address and went online to get directions. As she jotted them down, she decided she could slip out the back, hike up the beach a ways and call a cab to pick her up at the first access road.

If she was lucky, she could catch T.J. at home before he left to catch the bus.

# 25

WITHIN HALF AN HOUR, KYLIE WAS SEEING WHERE
T.J. lived for the first time. She'd cut it close on the timing,
but she'd spotted the bus stop only a few blocks away. A few
people waited, but T.J. hadn't been among them.

As she walked up the sidewalk, she took in the rundown
house, weedy yard and rusted metal lawn furniture on the
sagging front porch. The smell of fried food seemed to add
weight to the moisture-laden air. There was no doorbell or
screen door, so she rapped her knuckles on the door and lis-
tened for movement behind it.

Nothing.

Had she missed him?

Turning to survey the neighborhood, she tried to decide
what to do.

Sirens shrieked in the distance, and an argument in the
front lawn of a house two doors down was growing more
heated. Somewhere nearby, she heard glass breaking. A shudder went through her. This was T.J.'s home. She didn't feel
safe here, yet this is where he *lived*.

Another scent filled the humid air, growing steadily

stronger. It reminded her at first of roasted marshmallows on a campfire but quickly turned acrid.

Something was burning.

Turning back to the door, she raised her hand to knock again. That's when she saw the flicker through the narrow, rectangular window in the door.

Flames.

And something else: T.J.

Sprawled on the floor next to a sofa that looked like it'd been rescued from the curb on trash day.

"T.J.!" Kylie started pounding on the door. "T.J.!"

No movement. She couldn't tell through that tiny little window whether he was breathing, but the flickering was getting worse, and she saw flames licking up a wall far to the left of where the teen lay.

Frantic, she tried the doorknob. Locked.

Fumbling out her cell phone, she thumbed 911 as she raced around the side of the house toward the back. When the emergency operator answered, she rattled off the address, already coughing from the smoke billowing through a broken window.

The back door was unlocked, and she swung it open before jerking the hem of her T-shirt up to cover her nose and mouth and plunging into roiling, black smoke. "T.J.!"

She couldn't see jack through her stinging, watering eyes. Too much smoke. Couldn't see. Couldn't breathe. Where was the living room? She couldn't even tell where she was. Kitchen? Family room? All she knew was that she was surrounded by smoke, and there was tile underfoot. Must be the kitchen.

"T.J.!" She kept calling his name, hoping to rouse him. If anything, the sound of his voice could lead her to him.

She heard sirens and thought, thank God, help. But she didn't have time to wait. She had to move fast, before the whole house went up in flames. The smoke was getting thicker, searing her throat, burning her lungs. She moved blindly forward, toward the front of the house, running her hand along a wall, seeking an opening that would lead to the living room and T.J.

Focus, McKay. Find T.J. Get out. Much easier than winning in the final of the Australian Open.

The wall under her hand disappeared. The door.

She stumbled forward, dizzy and disoriented, felt the heat of flames nearby and recoiled. She tried to call T.J.'s name, but the only sound that came from her throat was a desperate wheezing. She started to cough harder.

Fear built when she saw the flames consuming the wall at the other end of the room, rolling and tumbling toward the ceiling like waves on a beach. Based on what she saw earlier, this had to be the living room.

She dropped to her knees, wincing at the sharp pain that flared through the right one, and crawled forward, sweeping the floor with her hands to feel her way through the smoke. Her fingertips grazed something . . . a shoe, and she surged forward. "T.J.?"

Please, please, *please*.

Soft, warm, slight. Yes.

She leaned over him, close to his face, felt his breath against her cheek, and shook him. "T.J., wake up."

He didn't stir.

She moved behind him and shoved him up into a floppy, sitting position. The kid couldn't weigh much more than a hundred pounds, but she could barely budge his dead weight.

Hooking her arms under his armpits, she locked her hands across his chest and heaved him backward, across the carpet, toward the kitchen and the way out. Skin-melting heat seemed to surround her, and the back door was miles away.

She couldn't breathe. Couldn't . . . breathe.

Without warning, her legs buckled, and she went down, the world swirling with black and red spots as she struggled to get air between the strangled coughs.

A loud crash came from somewhere, the sound of wood cracking and splintering. Oh, God, the ceiling. It was going to come down on their heads.

She fought to get her legs under her, dizzy and light-headed, no longer aware of which way was up or down. All she knew was that she had to get T.J. out *now*.

Eye on the ball, McKay. Get your eye on the ball.

She used the last of her strength to haul the boy through the kitchen door. When his dragging butt hit the tile, his body slid faster than she'd expected, and she tumbled backward, ending up with his limp form draped across her legs.

Coughing, tears streaming, she wriggled out from under him, grabbed one of his wrists and towed him the rest of the way across the kitchen to the back door. She shoved through, out into what should have been fresh air, except it was thick with smoke, too. Staggering down the two porch steps, conscious that poor T.J.'s body bounced down behind her, she collapsed onto her hands and knees in the grass, the spinning world darkening around her.

She sensed rather than saw a bulky shape rush forward but didn't have the strength to panic before she recognized him as a firefighter in full fire gear. When he grabbed her arm and tried to help her to her feet, she waved him away. "No! Get T.J. first. He's—"

"My buddy's getting him," he shouted.

The fireman hooked one of her arms around his neck and hauled her to her feet. She stumbled along beside him, conscious that he was doing most of the work but not caring. She'd done what she needed to do. T.J. was out.

The fireman lowered her to the grass, well away from the burning house, where a paramedic ran over to meet them and slipped an oxygen mask over her head. As cool, fresh air filled her lungs, making her cough even more, she kept an eye on T.J. stretched out on the grass nearby, looking pale and small with a female paramedic hunkered over him. The woman wasn't frantic as she checked his vitals. A good sign.

Feeling a hand on her wrist, she turned her head to see the paramedic tending her wrapping a blood-pressure cuff around her arm.

"He's going to be okay," he told her, nodding toward T.J. "You got him out in time."

Grateful and relieved, she dropped her head forward and coughed until every muscle ached.

# 26

CHASE BARRELED INTO THE ER LIKE A FREIGHT train, nothing in his head but white noise and the stomach-turning refrain: Kylie had been in a fire. The fellow officer who'd called to give him the heads up said she was okay, but he wouldn't believe it until he saw her with his own eyes, whole and breathing and unharmed.

Sam followed close behind. "Burnett said she must have slipped out the back. He didn't even know she was gone."

Chase didn't respond. He didn't give a shit how she ditched the cop in her driveway. He just wanted to see her.

"While you find Kylie," Sam called from behind him, "I'll get some info from the guys on the scene."

Chase blew by the information desk. He knew this ER, knew the doctors and nurses and orderlies, so he shoved right through the double swinging doors into the treatment area. A doctor, chart and pen in hand, intercepted him before he'd taken three steps.

"Detective Manning, hello. How can I help you?"

"Kylie McKay," he croaked. "Where is she?"

"She's in trauma one. I'm—"

He didn't hear anything beyond that. Trauma one? That

was the area reserved for critical patients. Which meant she *wasn't* okay. She couldn't be okay and be in trauma one.

Heart jolting, he just about ran over a nurse on the way and, mumbling a "sorry," pushed by her despite the big smile that curved her lips. "Chase, hi. Long time no—"

He plowed through the door into trauma one and stopped dead just as Kylie jumped to her feet, a hand at her throat and her eyes wide.

He'd startled her, and now he felt like an oaf, a relieved-beyond-belief oaf, because she did indeed look unharmed. Another body occupied the gurney, an oxygen mask obscuring the face. Still, he gave her a thorough once-over just to be sure. Her rosy cheeks made her eyes more blue than gray, and soot marked every inch of exposed skin—arms, hands, face, neck.

The acrid odor of smoke clung to her, but even in dirty jeans and an ash-smudged black T-shirt, dark hair tumbling around her shoulders in disheveled waves, she'd never looked more beautiful. It took all his strength not to grab her to him and hug her close.

Instead, he stayed where he was and tried to act normal. Nothing to see here. No one coming unraveled at the thought of losing the woman he'd already lost once. Not that she was his to lose, but still.

He cleared the lump out of his throat. "You okay?"

She nodded. "Mostly." Her already-low voice sounded like she'd gargled with gravel, and there was a faint wheeze when she breathed.

Thinking she probably should go back to sitting down, he indicated the chair she'd occupied. She lowered herself to it without comment, her movements as careful as someone who'd had too much to drink. Her fingers lightly but briefly massaged her right knee but stopped when she saw him watching.

He glanced at the gurney and took in the thin arm bearing an IV.

"It's T.J.," she said softly.

His gut flinched at the exhaustion underlying the words. "What happened?"

"I went to see him. He was unconscious on the floor, and the house was . . . on fire." She rubbed at her eyes, seemingly unaware of the filth on her hands. "I didn't even think to check to see if his mom was home."

"She wasn't," Sam said as he joined them. "No one else was in the house. The fire guys said you saved the kid's life. They wouldn't have gotten to him in time."

Relief dropped her shoulders, or perhaps that was fatigue. Chase wondered whether she'd slept at all since the construction workers had unearthed the bat.

"How's the kid?" Sam asked.

Chase realized he'd been so focused on Kylie's condition that he hadn't asked her about T.J.'s.

"Smoke inhalation," she said, "and a mild concussion."

"Concussion?" Chase asked, surprised.

"Doctor said he must have fallen when he tried to get out," Kylie said.

Chase exchanged a glance with Sam, who angled his head toward the door. As much as he didn't want to leave Kylie alone, Chase got the hint that his partner wanted to talk privately.

"We're going to step outside for a bit," he told her.

She nodded without looking at him, her tired and worried gaze fixed on the unconscious boy.

Out in the waiting room, Chase faced his partner, anger seeping in behind the fear. A fire that almost killed her the day after some son of a bitch planted a baseball bat in her windshield? It couldn't be a coincidence.

"What've you got?" he asked Sam.

"The fire was deliberate. Firefighters thought at first it was caused by candles. The kid was using them for light. But then they found the source of the fire in one of the bedrooms. Glass bottle filled with gasoline, stuffed with a rag and set on fire. It was pitched through the window."

"A Molotov cocktail? Jesus." Chase rubbed at his forehead until his skin protested. "Did someone follow her there and try to kill her? Does that make any damn sense at all?"

"Her presence could have been a coincidence. The house has been on the market for nearly a year with no takers, and the sellers are desperate. Could be insurance fraud."

"That's just a bit too convenient, don't you think, when someone's been terrorizing Kylie?"

"I'm just telling you what I was told."

"So what's T.J.'s story? Have you gotten that far?"

"A couple of our guys talked to neighbors. T.J. and his mother were the last residents of the house. Evicted about six months ago, though T.J. showed up again a couple of months ago."

"So he's a squatter. Where's the mother now?"

"No one's seen her since T.J. turned up," Sam said. "Neighbors said she's split on him before, but she's always come back within a month or two."

"She abandoned her kid?"

Sam nodded. "Sick, isn't it? Some people don't deserve to be parents."

"Hell," Chase breathed.

"She's an addict of some kind. Neighbors try to keep an eye on the boy, but they say he's pretty resourceful on his own. Does yard work and other odd jobs for cash. Even gets himself to school regularly."

And his fingerprints were on the bat used on Kylie's Jeep. What the hell? "So why's he smashing Kylie's windshield?"

"There's something else."

Chase tensed further at the dead-serious tone of Sam's voice. "What is it?"

"I asked the doctor if it was possible T.J. got that concussion from being knocked over the head rather than a fall."

When Chase stared at his partner without speaking, Sam nodded gravely. "Someone knocked him unconscious before they set the place on fire. We're looking at attempted murder here."

"Attempted murder?"

Chase whirled to see Kylie standing a few feet away. Ah,

shit. She'd heard, and now she looked like she'd keel over any second. He took a step toward her, but she backed away, hands raised to hold him off. In the next instant, her shoulders firmed and her chin inched up, the moment of shocked weakness under control. Even exhausted, she kept her head in the game.

"Who would try to kill T.J.?" she asked. "He's just a child."

"We don't know anything more than you do," Chase said, doing his best not to sound placating. "But we'll find out."

"We'll know more once we've had a chance to talk to him," Sam said.

She gestured toward the door to trauma one. "He's awake. The doctor . . . he's checking him out again. He said you can probably talk to T.J. when he's done."

"Excellent," Sam said.

She grimaced as she ran steady fingers through her tangled hair. "I'm going to get cleaned up a little," she said.

When she started to step by them, Chase rested his hand at the crook of her elbow to stop her. Her muscles tensed under the contact, but he didn't let go, too grateful that her skin was so warm and alive. "You told me you didn't know where he lives."

Sam cleared his throat. "I'll just . . ." He made a walking-away gesture with his fingers.

When they were alone, Kylie shifted so that her back was no longer to the wall. Previous . . . incidents had made her wary of letting him trap her. "I wanted to talk to him before you scared the crap out of him," she replied.

"That's called obstruction of justice, Ky."

Her lips thinned, eyes flashing silver. "Are you going to arrest *me* now?"

Not a bad idea, actually. He wouldn't have to worry about her safety then. Of course, she'd never forgive him for that. He let it go and moved on to the second point he wanted to make. "Running into a burning house? Not the smartest thing to do."

"If I hadn't, T.J. could be dead."

He couldn't argue with that, but all he could think was that *she* could be dead. "Just don't do it again," he said, unable to manage a demand-free tone.

She stiffened, but her taut expression remained unaltered. "Are we done here?"

"Did you know T.J.'s mother abandoned him?"

Her lips parted, and her eyebrows drew together. "God, no."

Finally, some honest emotion. "He's been living in that house alone for a couple of months."

"I knew something was up, but I didn't realize it was that serious." She shook her head, looking more drawn than before. It seemed her ability to remain aloof weakened the more tired and stressed she got. "I should have paid more attention."

Sighing, he rubbed the back of his neck. Damn it, he hadn't meant for her to blame herself. "Kids like him, they're experts at pretending everything's good when it's all falling apart." The boy had a lot in common with the woman standing before him, in fact.

"What will happen to him now?" she asked.

"Foster care. He's been in and out a couple of times already."

Her forehead creased further, and she paced away, arms wrapping her middle. "I had no idea. I mean, I met his mother once when she brought him for his first lesson, and she seemed good with him. Attentive and loving."

"Some of the worst parents know how to act the part when they're in front of other people."

She rubbed her eyes again, apparently unaware that she was allowing her fatigue to show in front of him. "So foster care . . . is that how you identified his fingerprints?"

He hesitated. "You should go get cleaned up."

"Chase, tell me."

He met her eyes, surprised to hear his name in her raspy voice. Was that the first time she'd addressed him by name in ten years?

"Chase, come on," she prodded, impatient.

He drew in a silent breath, chastising himself for letting such a simple thing catch him off guard. But it seemed significant. Wasn't it? She *never* called him by name. Okay, man, do your job and move on.

"He's got an arrest record, Ky."

# 27

KYLIE SAT ON THE SIDE OF T.J.'S BED IN THE curtained-off ER cubicle where he'd been relocated. The teenager looked so young, his shoulders narrow, his brown eyes big and dark. She never thought of him as a child when they faced off across the net, probably because he could be so intimidating, pounding shots at her that she increasingly had to scramble to return. But that's exactly what he was: a child. And right now he looked so miserable and scared that she had to fight the urge to pull him against her and hug him. She wasn't sure how he would respond to that, so instead, she patted his forearm.

"How's it going?" she asked.

One side of his mouth quirked up. "Everything's aces," he said, and began to cough.

She reached for the water a nurse had brought and held the straw for him. His eyes watered while he sucked down half of the cup's contents. Then he sat back and swiped at his face, his cheeks glowing as though the tears embarrassed him. "How about you?"

She shrugged. "I've had better days."

They both laughed a little, which led to some synchronized coughing.

When they'd settled down and breathed easier, Kylie said, "A police detective is going to be here soon to talk to you."

"About the fire?"

"And a few other things." Chase had given her explicit instructions not to question the boy about her windshield or the fire.

"Oh." Fear shadowed his eyes.

"You don't have to worry, though. He just wants to help you. I promise."

When the fear in his expression didn't fade, she wondered again what lay in his past that had led to his arrest. There had to be a logical explanation. She knew this boy, and he wasn't a delinquent. "Seriously, as long as you tell the truth, you'll be fine, okay?"

He gave her a reluctant nod, blinking back tears.

She swallowed and suppressed a wince at the rawness of her throat. Her heart had felt just as raw, guilt a clenched fist in the pit of her stomach, since Chase had told her what Sam had learned from T.J.'s neighbors. She'd let this child down, so wrapped up in her own issues that she hadn't responded appropriately when she'd sensed something was off.

"Do you know where your mother is?" she asked gently.

His gaze shifted away, and he shook his head.

"How long has she been gone?"

He lifted one shoulder and let it drop.

Chase ducked through a gap in the curtains. His presence seemed to make the close space even closer, and Kylie resisted the instinctual desire to tense. This was about T.J., not her and Chase.

"Hi, T.J.," he said. "I'm Detective Chase Manning, Kendall Falls Police."

Kylie watched them shake hands, struck by how Chase's large hand engulfed the boy's.

"I have some questions for you, if you're up to it," Chase said.

T.J. cast an uncertain, panicked glance at Kylie. She wasn't sure what to make of it, but then she remembered her windshield. Maybe he didn't want her there while he talked to the police. She started to get up. "How about I let you two talk alone."

"No!" T.J. grabbed her hand. "Don't go. Please?"

She settled back down, tears stinging her eyes at his desperation, and gave him a reassuring nod. He smiled with shaky relief but held tight to her hand.

Chase took out a small notebook and flipped it open. "Let's start with the fire, T.J. Do you have any idea why anyone would want to hurt you?"

T.J.'s grip on her hand tightened. "No."

Chase watched the boy carefully but without looking intimidating. "Are you sure?"

T.J. nodded, though Kylie thought it wasn't very convincing.

"It's okay to tell the truth, T.J.," she said.

"No one's going to be mad," Chase added, his voice surprisingly gentle.

T.J. looked from her to Chase and back again. "I don't know. I don't."

"Okay." Chase flipped to a new page in his notebook. "Let's talk about Kylie's Jeep."

T.J. stiffened and let go of her hand, but he didn't deny anything or pretend he didn't know what Chase meant. The fist in her stomach clenched into apprehension.

"Your fingerprints are on the bat used to smash the windshield," Chase said, intent on T.J.'s face. "Explain."

T.J. glanced at Kylie before darting fearful eyes away. "I . . ."

"Just tell the truth," she said. "We'll work it out."

"I, um . . ." He trailed off again.

"You're among friends here," Chase said. "You know that, right? No one here wants to hurt you." Patient yet firm, authoritative yet kind.

"This guy . . . he tried to give me two hundred bucks to break it." Once he started talking, it poured out of him. "He handed me the bat, but I gave it back to him and said no way."

"This was at the health club?" Chase asked.

"No. He was waiting on the path I take home, off the back parking lot at the club."

Kylie's breath stalled as visions of another deserted path unspooled in her head. She pushed off the bed and paced away, snugging her arms around her midsection. But, God, it was more than just painful memories. A mysterious man had approached a vulnerable child because he wanted to freak *her* out. T.J. could have been hurt. Because of *her*.

"Kylie?"

She turned at the tremor in T.J.'s voice, found him watching her with wide, dark eyes. "You believe me, don't you?"

Oh, God, the poor kid. Giving him a reassuring smile, she retook her spot on the side of the bed. "Of course, I believe you." She captured his cold, clammy hand and clasped it between both of hers. "Don't worry, okay? Everything will be fine."

She glanced at Chase. He also watched her, and she could tell by the compassion in his expression that he knew exactly where her head had just gone. For once, that empathy didn't make her want to throw something at his head, though she wasn't sure why. Maybe because he understood but said nothing. He just shared a long, supportive look with her, his slightly curving lips spreading warmth through her stomach.

He glanced away first and cleared his throat. "Can you describe the guy?" he asked T.J. "Tall? Short? Young? Old?"

"Young, I guess, but older than me." Now that no one had yelled at him, he regained some confidence. "Tall, like you. Skinny. He wore a baseball cap. And he had blue eyes. Creepy blue. Really light."

Chase jotted notes. "Think you'd recognize a photo?"

T.J. tensed. "Um . . ."

Chase reached over and patted the boy's knee. "You're safe now. He can't hurt you. But you need to help me find him so I can make sure he doesn't hurt anyone else. Okay?"

T.J. nodded.

"Do you think you'd recognize him if you saw a picture?"

"I think so."

"That's good. Once you're released, we'll go down to the police station so you can look at some mug-shot books. Okay with you?"

T.J. glanced at Kylie. "Will you come?"

"Of course."

"Great," Chase said. "So can you tell me how you left things with this man?"

"He got mad because I wouldn't do what he wanted. I said I was going to go to the cops, but he said he'd come after me if I didn't keep quiet." His fingers clamped around Kylie's so hard she fought back a wince.

"He was in the house," he blurted at Kylie. "After I called you from my neighbor's, I went home and he was there. He said he couldn't trust me to keep my mouth shut. I don't remember anything after that. I'm sorry. I should have told you before, but . . . I'm scared. What if he comes back?"

"It's okay, kiddo," she said. "You're safe now. No one's going to hurt you again. Chase and I both will make sure of it."

When he relaxed back against his pillow, Kylie stroked his cheek with the back of her hand and smiled. "I'm going to step outside for just a minute, okay? I'll be right back, though. I promise."

He nodded.

She didn't look at Chase as she eased through the gap in the curtains and headed out into the nearest hallway. There, alone, she braced one hand on the painted concrete wall as the rush of blood in her ears grew to a roar, and dizzy comprehension spun through her senses.

T.J. had almost died because of *her*. He was in a hospital bed now, suffering from a head injury and smoke inhalation, scared to death of a man with creepy blue eyes, because of *her*.

A shudder rolled through her, accompanied by a cold

sweat, and she closed her eyes and leaned her forehead against the cool wall, not sure what her body planned to do next. Throw up? Pass out? Sink to the floor and shake to pieces?

Hang on, McKay. You've got to hang on. For T.J.'s sake. Don't be a drama queen.

Feeling a hand on her back, she jerked her head up, surprised to find that Chase stood beside her. His palm, warm and reassuring, rested in the center of her back, and as she met his eyes, deep and dark and green, that strong hand gently stroked once, twice.

Her balance returned in a rush almost as dizzying as the horror, and she pulled in a trembling breath. She wanted to move away from him, away from his touch, but it'd be so easy to lean against him, to let those strong arms enfold her and ward off all the demons.

"Okay now?" Chase asked, voice soft and low.

She nodded but didn't look at him. "Yes. We should get back to T.J. He shouldn't be alone."

"Just give yourself a minute," he said. "I think you need it."

She swallowed hard against the lump in her throat. He could be so sweet it made her ache down to her bones. She bet he was a wonderful father. He had the kindest heart she'd ever known. And she'd pitched it away like it didn't matter.

Focus on T.J.

Raising her chin, she stepped away from Chase and nodded. "I'm fine now."

She heard him sigh as he followed her back into T.J.'s cubicle. As she took up position next to the bed, Chase said, "We need to reach your mother, T.J. Do you have any idea how to do that?"

"I don't know where she is." He looked at Kylie with an intensity she'd seen in him only on the tennis court, and his chin began to tremble. "I won't go back to foster care. I *won't*."

Kylie's heart broke. The poor kid desperately needed

someone to look out for him. "Don't worry," she said, and offered him sanctuary without a second thought. "You can stay with me, okay?"

She glanced at Chase just in time to see him scowl.

# 28

"SO," SAM SAID, "WHAT DO YOU THINK THE ODDS are the kid'll be able to pick the guy out of the mug books?"

"Sounds like he got a good look at him," Chase said, leaning back in his screechy chair while he massaged the knot at the base of his neck. It felt good to be back in their grungy office after the antiseptic hospital.

Sam began to tap a ballpoint pen against his desk blotter. "So you believe this kid?"

"He doesn't appear to be lying."

"Have you forgotten that we're talking about a kid who's been busted twice in the past?"

"For shoplifting food, Sam. Come on. His mother deserted him, and he didn't have enough to eat."

"All I'm saying is that you're placing an awful lot of trust in someone who might be a little con artist. You don't know this kid."

"Kylie knows him."

"She knows her brother, too, and he's not looking so innocent."

Chase grimaced. Sam made a good point. But he also trusted his gut, and his gut told him T.J. was a good kid in a bad situation. His gut hadn't made up its mind yet about Quinn.

"What're we going to do if he comes up empty with the mug books?" Sam asked.

Chase studied his partner, surprised by the hard glint in his eyes and the way he rubbed at the scar on his hand that itched when he got antsy. Funny how they both had their quirks. Chase kneaded his neck when he got stressed, and Sam massaged a scar.

"You have a suggestion?" Chase asked.

"We arrest him for vandalism and teach him a lesson."

"What lesson would that be?"

"I'm just saying, we let him off the hook and he goes out and gets into more trouble. We put the fear of God into him, and he'll walk a straight line."

"He's doing the best he can under the circumstances," Chase said. "Maybe what he really needs is a break."

Sam grunted and began clicking the tip of the pen in and out. Another quirk. "So where's Kylie?"

"Out in the lobby."

"Does she know she's not taking him home with her? Someone should tip her off to the way the system works."

With a sigh, Chase scooted his chair back with a loud shriek of wheels. "I'll take care of it."

He found her pacing in the lobby, and he paused to watch her before she saw him.

She'd washed the soot from her face and arms and tidied her hair. Her black T-shirt, still splotchy with ash, fell short of the threadbare waistband of her jeans by about an inch, revealing a tantalizing strip of pale skin. His mouth went dry, and blood threatened to rush straight to his groin, so he lifted his eyes higher. But then he was gazing at the dark hair that fell in soft waves around her shoulders and remembering how silky soft it had felt twined around his fingers so many years ago. They'd had everything then. The world before them and each other. He hadn't felt so happy, so excited about the future since. He blamed the loss of that anticipation on getting older, on becoming jaded by life and his job. But he wondered sometimes if all it took to get it back would be to wake up every day next to the woman who made him whole.

As if sensing him, Kylie turned toward him, and for once, she didn't immediately raise the barriers. Sure, she wasn't open and trusting and smiling, but she didn't look like she wanted to slam a ball at his head, either. Unfortunately, he knew the game face would be back in all its stony splendor in about a minute. What he wouldn't give to take it away from her and lock it somewhere where she could never get at it again.

"Can we talk?" he asked.

She walked with him to the cramped room that he and his fellow officers used for breaks. He'd never noticed how pathetic it was until he saw through the eyes of a visitor the battered, avocado-green refrigerator and the gray wooden table with thick square legs surrounded by three folding chairs. The saving grace of the inhospitable space: a new coffeemaker.

"Coffee?" he asked as Kylie lowered herself onto one of the folding chairs.

"No, thanks. I just want to get T.J. and go."

"Actually, that's what I wanted to talk to you about."

Sitting back in the chair, she watched him without speaking, her features drawn. Her hand rested on her right knee, fingers working at the denim of her jeans as though the joint underneath ached.

He'd been about to sit but changed his mind and went for the coffee. Coward, he thought. But he didn't want to look at her while he pissed all over her expectations.

He took a breath as he filled a cup. "You're not going to be allowed to take him home," he said.

Silence answered him, and as he turned to face her, he braced for the usual. But instead of blank tolerance, she just looked confused. "Why not?" she asked.

He swallowed. This was harder than he'd expected, and it

didn't help that she wasn't playing this like a competitive point for a change. "You're not a relative, and you're not his guardian."

"How do I get that arranged?"

"Becoming a foster parent takes months. You can fill out the paperwork, but there are hoops to jump through, including several hours of training and counseling. Until you're approved, he'll be placed with another foster family."

"I promised him he could stay with me. You were standing right there."

His chest muscles clutched at the weary resignation that made her smoke-roughened voice raspier than usual. They both remembered the anxiety in T.J.'s eyes when he'd said he wouldn't go back into the system. But, damn it, there wasn't anything Chase could do about it. The law was the law.

"So that's it?" she asked, voice cracking until she cleared her throat and firmed her jaw. "I'm supposed to just walk away after I made him a promise?"

"It's not my call, Ky. I'm sorry."

"He's scared, Chase. He's obviously had a tough time in foster care before."

"I understand that, but frankly, it's probably not safe for him to stay with you anyway. You're the reason he's—" Damn, that hadn't come out right. And he could tell from her swift intake of breath that he'd started to say something she'd already thought. Fuck. Why did being around her make him such a bonehead?

Pushing back from the table, she stood. "Okay, then. I should go tell him. The sooner he finds out, the better."

He followed her to the door and caught her arm before she could walk out. "What happened to him wasn't your fault," he said.

She lowered her head but didn't try to pull away. "That's not what you were going to say."

"You can't blame yourself. You're not responsible for what bad people do."

She closed her eyes. "Right."

He felt the tremor in her muscles and drew his hand back,

shocked that she hadn't distanced herself first. Either she'd decided he wasn't the enemy, or she was too worn down to reinforce her defenses. Most likely the latter, and that concerned the hell out of him. Kylie McKay didn't succumb to defeat. Ever.

"I'll do what I can for him, okay?" he said. "I need you to trust me on this."

She glanced back at him and nodded, eyes shadowed and sad. "Okay."

Guilt and regret settled on his chest like ten-pound weights. He couldn't give her what she wanted, what she needed. He never could. And it shouldn't have made him feel like such a worthless failure. But it did. Jesus, it did. And the hell of it was he wasn't done making her miserable.

"Look, we need to talk about putting you in a safe house."

She turned and leaned back against the door, arms wrapped tight around her middle as she focused on something over his left shoulder. "I'm thinking maybe I should . . . just go."

"Go? Go where?"

"Back to LA."

He didn't move, but in his head, he threw a punch at the nearest wall. Son of a *bitch*. Was that her answer to everything? He'd thought they were getting somewhere working together to help T.J. Two steps forward, thirty-two steps back.

Outwardly, he kept his cool. "Leaving town isn't going to solve anything. This guy can follow you wherever you go."

"But maybe all he wants is for me to leave town. I mean, all this started with the tennis center. When it was sabotage, I could take it. But if this guy is willing to kill to keep it from being built, fine."

"I don't think that's the point. It's gotten too personal for that."

"Then what is the point? What's the point of attacking a young boy and setting his home on fire? Clearly, my presence here is a danger to people I care about."

He put his hands on her arms, ignoring the way she

tensed. "Ky, listen to me. Running away won't solve anything. It never does. Don't you know that by now?"

"I ran away ten years ago to protect *myself*, Chase. This time, it's not about me."

Suppressing the urge to shake her, he released her and turned away. "So, what, is that the new excuse then? Since you're being heroic about it, it's okay to run away?"

"What do you want me to do?"

He faced her and fought to keep his voice level. "I want you to let me take you to a safe house. I want you to stick around this time and let me help you."

"I don't think I can do that. I . . ." She trailed off and swallowed, shaking her head and looking away. "I'm . . . tired."

He stepped forward, and before she could dodge him, he cupped her face in his palms and kissed her. Gentle and tender, expecting her to shove him away in the next instant and not really knowing what he was trying to prove anyway, except maybe remind her of what she'd be walking away from if she left again.

When her lips trembled open under his, he forgot to go slow and deepened the kiss, nothing in his head but her taste and the feel of her soft, warm skin. He stroked his fingers over her temples, her jaw and back into her hair. God, her hair. Her mouth. Her skin. Her . . . tongue. It stroked against his, and he lost his breath, lost his place in the universe.

She moaned into his mouth, but instead of melting against him, she stiffened and pushed him away, turning her head to the side to break the embrace. "I can't do this," she breathed. "Quinn . . ."

Chase grasped her head and forced her to meet his eyes. Hers looked fever bright and tormented. "Quinn has nothing to do with *us*," he said.

"He has *everything* to do with us."

"Not if he's innocent."

She went still in surprise. "You believe he's innocent?"

"I believe in your instincts, Ky. I need you to believe in mine." He smoothed his thumbs over the arches of her cheekbones, reveled in the satiny texture of her skin. "Can you do that?"

She watched him, brow furrowed, uncertain and confused.

He kissed her forehead, nuzzled her temple, breathing in the scent of burnt wood and soap and Kylie's skin. "Trust me, okay? That's all you have to do."

Slowly, ever so slowly, the rigidity of her body eased. She didn't lean against him, as he would have preferred, but she relaxed enough for him to decide she wouldn't bolt the instant he let her go.

It felt like victory after a six-hour tennis match in the blazing sun.

# 29

JANE SANK ONTO THE SOFA, THE PHONE CRADLED between her chin and shoulder. "So you're not going to be able to make it back?"

"I can make it, but I'm going to be late."

"But we made plans for this afternoon. I'm cooking for you, remember?"

"I know, but duty calls. How about a late dinner? Say, eightish?"

"You sound weird. Are you okay?"

"It's been a rough day. So I'll see you later? We can eat then."

She glanced around at the dozens of candles she'd arranged around his living room. It had taken her half an hour just to light them all. And in the kitchen, homemade pesto was so fresh it was still in the food processor.

"Jane? Are you there?"

"I'm here."

"I'll make it up to you. I promise." He laughed so low and sexy that it tickled her ear. "Think hot fudge and whipped cream."

She giggled. Had she ever giggled over a man? "Don't make the fudge too hot."

"It'll be just right."

"I'm sensing a Goldilocks fantasy."

"And you can analyze what it means about me all night long."

By the time she hung up, she was laughing. She wandered around, blowing out candles and making plans to relight them later. Even thinking about how Kylie would react when she found out didn't steal her joy.

# 30

CHASE SLOWED FOR A STOPLIGHT AND CHECKED the rearview mirror. Traffic made it impossible to tell whether anyone followed the Explorer. He would have preferred to skip going over to Kylie's so she could pack some things, but he understood her need for clean clothes after the fire.

He glanced over at her, noting that she kept massaging her right knee. Had she hurt it in the fire, or was it a nervous gesture? That'd be something, he thought. Kylie McKay with a nervous gesture.

As he turned onto a side street that would take them to her house without using the main thoroughfares, he did another mirror check. No other vehicles followed.

He'd just begun to relax when he spotted the silver BMW convertible in front of her house. The sun reflecting in the Beemer's wheel rims nearly blinded him as he stomped on the brake. "Whose car is that?"

"Wade's," she said.

He looked at her. "Wade who?"

"Wade Bell."

The name clicked. The doctor who repaired her knee ten

years ago. He remembered not liking the guy back then, but his skills had paid off for Kylie. "What's he—"

Movement at the side of the house snatched his attention, and Chase tensed.

"That's him," Kylie said, as though sensing his high-alert status.

"What's he doing here?"

"I don't know. He probably came by to check on me."

"Why would he do that?" He glanced at her, noting her expression had become maddeningly impassive. "Are you having a problem with your knee?"

"No. My knee is fine."

"Then why would he check on you?"

She sighed. "Would you just chill? He's a friend."

The way she said "friend" set his teeth on edge, and Chase watched the man striding toward the SUV, disliking him all over again. He was tall and lean in black slacks and a prissy pink polo, his eyes shielded from the sun by fancy sunglasses that probably cost more than Chase made in a week.

When the doctor spotted Kylie in the truck, his deeply tanned face broke into a broad smile, as if the sun had come out after the rain and shot rainbows all over the fucking place. Friend, my ass, Chase thought. That guy was head over heels for her.

Opening her door, Kylie got out of the truck to greet him.

Chase's resentment of the doctor faltered when he noticed she favored her right leg. Her knee was *not* fine. She must have hurt it when she'd pulled T.J. out of the burning house. Why the hell hadn't she said anything?

His blood pressure only spiked further when the doctor met her at the front of the SUV and folded her into his arms, the embrace more intimate than any man had a right to give a woman he wasn't sleeping with.

Chase got out of the truck and slammed the door harder than necessary, but it didn't help to ease his growing agitation.

Wade drew back from Kylie, but his hands stayed on her

arms. "I hope you don't mind that I stopped by to check on you. I went around back to see if maybe you were on the deck."

Kylie gestured at Chase. "You probably remember Chase Manning, Wade. He's a detective now, working on the reopened case."

Wade drew off his sunglasses and extended his hand. "Of course I remember. It's been a long time, though."

Forcing a civil expression, Chase gave the doctor's hand a firm pump.

"Easy there, detective, I need that hand."

Chase let go, feeling childish but satisfied nonetheless. The scrawny son of a bitch probably couldn't take a punch, either. "Good to see you again, doctor."

Wade turned back to Kylie, and his pearly white smile faded as he looked her over, taking in the smudged shirt and dirty jeans. "What happened? Were you in an accident?"

"Just a little mishap," she said.

Chase almost snorted. A little mishap indeed. Who the hell did she think she was kidding? Well, she was going to hate him for sure in about a second. "Maybe he could take a look at your knee."

Kylie flashed him an I'm-going-to-kill-you look as Wade glanced down. "Is it bothering you?" the doctor asked.

She shook her head. "I just need to rest it."

"He's here," Chase said. "You might as well let him take a look."

"I'd prefer it," Wade said. "You don't want to mess around with that knee."

"Fine," she said, rolling her eyes, and led the way to the house.

Chase's triumph lasted only until he noticed how the other guy's gaze slid down her back and over her ass. Yeah, she had a good, cuppable butt, but where were the doctor's manners? He had at least fifteen years on Kylie, yet he looked her over like a man taking measurements for a wedding gown.

In the house, Wade took in Kylie's jeans and said, "Hmm, well . . ."

"I'll go put on some shorts," Kylie said. As she walked by Chase, she muttered, "You'd better not hurt him while I'm gone."

He leaned against the wall and folded his arms. The thought had crossed his mind.

Alone with the doctor, Chase said nothing. He had nothing *to* say.

"Chase Manning," Wade said, cocking his head. "You were Kylie's—"

"Yes," Chase snapped. "What about you?"

"What about me?"

"You have a thing for her." It wasn't a question.

A small smile twitched at Wade's lips. "A thing? What is this, high school?"

Chase straightened away from the wall, but before he could do anything stupid and immature, like take a swing at the guy, Kylie returned, wearing a clean white T-shirt and navy shorts with double white stripes up the sides. She was barefoot, and her legs, Chase noticed, were toned and tan except for the startling paleness of her skin where she wore the knee brace during lessons. A sun-kissed circle of tanned skin in the center of her knee resembled a target.

Sensing her gaze on him, he looked up to see her shooting him a squinty-eyed, go-the-hell-away look. Jesus, why had she gotten so tense again?

Wade gestured at the khaki easy chair adjacent to the matching sofa. "Have a seat, and I'll check you out."

Wade moved aside the wicker chest that served as a coffee table and knelt before her. He lifted her bare foot onto his thigh, then slid his pale, manicured hands over her calf and to the back of her knee, gentle as a groom divesting his new bride of her garter belt. The intimacy of the gesture hit Chase like a blow to the temple. That wasn't the impersonal touch of a doctor.

Wade's voice cut through the growing buzz in Chase's head. "You've got a lot more muscle tone than you should. Makes me think that perhaps you've been playing harder than you're supposed to."

Chase's hands formed fists. If he didn't turn away, he was going to grab the guy and hurl him against the wall.

Kylie met his gaze again, and one brow ticked up ever so slightly, her steel-blue eyes seeming to ask him what his problem was.

He turned abruptly and walked into the kitchen.

# 31

KYLIE'S HEART HITCHED AND SPUTTERED AS SHE
watched Chase's retreating back. On one hand, she was relieved to be free of his intense scrutiny. On the other, she
feared her scars repulsed him or made him feel sorry for her.
She couldn't stand it if he felt sorry for her. It shouldn't matter, but it did. Maybe because she was so incredibly tired.

"Kylie?"

She focused on Wade. "I'm sorry?"

"I was wondering if you've been playing tennis harder
than you're supposed to."

"Oh. Maybe. I fell earlier. I'm sure that's why it's bothering me."

"Where's the pain on a scale of one to ten?"

"Maybe a three."

"Which means it's more like a six." He sat back on his
heels with a knowing smile. "Other than some swelling, everything looks good structurally. As far as I can tell without
an X-ray, anyway. Are you good with ibuprofen or do you
want a prescription for something stronger?"

"Ibuprofen is fine."

Rising, he held out a hand to help her up. She took it, but when she stood in front of him, he didn't release her. His thumb slid over the back of her hand, and she looked up, surprised at the caress. He leaned toward her, and before she realized his intent, he captured her mouth in a seeking kiss.

She didn't react at first, taken by surprise, and then she jerked back so quickly, the backs of her legs hit the chair behind her.

As Wade grabbed her by the arms to prevent her from falling, his cheeks reddened. "I'm sorry. I . . . that was an impulse. I'm sorry."

Before she could respond, she heard the kitchen door slide open then slam shut hard enough to shake the house. Well, the broken doors had obviously been fixed, but one more slam like that and she'd have to have them replaced again.

Wade's mouth lifted at one corner in a sheepish smile. "Oops. I think someone's jealous."

Kylie sighed. What an incredibly crappy day.

"Let's not make more of this than it is," Wade said. "I wasn't thinking. Seriously. I know you don't . . . love me."

She wanted to ask him how he knew she didn't love him. She thought she'd done everything she was supposed to. She'd laughed at his jokes, returned his smiles, liked it when he held her hand, responded to his kisses. Of course, they hadn't been like Chase's kisses. Hot and wild and breathtaking.

"I just miss you, Ky," Wade said. "I miss you a lot."

Ky. Her heart didn't skip when he called her that. Didn't even pause. Only one man could do that to her.

"Ky?"

She raised her gaze to Wade's, tried to recall what he'd said. Oh, yes, he missed her. "I miss you, too."

His lips pressed into a thin line, as though to say, "Sure, you do."

Sighing, he moved the wicker chest back into position in front of the sofa and chair, then headed for the door. "Take it easy on the knee. Technically, you shouldn't be playing tennis at all, and the swelling won't go down if you keep abusing it."

He shut the door without looking back, and Kylie stood there and felt like a jerk. The guy cared enough to stop by to check on her, and all she'd done was make him feel bad. She couldn't win with anyone.

Alone, she sank into the squishy cushion of the chair, laid her head back and shut out the world.

# 32

CHASE CALLED TO THE DOCTOR BEFORE HE COULD get to his shiny new Beemer. "Dr. Bell."

Wade turned, his look quizzical as he propped his sunglasses on his head. "Yes, detective?"

"I have a few questions for you, if you've got a minute."

"A few questions about what?"

"Just bear with me," Chase said, flipping open his notebook and jotting the doctor's name at the top of a page. His pulse was just now slowing since he'd stood at the spot where kitchen tile met carpet and watched the doctor lay a kiss on Kylie's ready and waiting lips. He hadn't waited for the embrace to end, just about-faced and stalked outside, where he'd braced his hands on the deck railing and heaved in deep, calming breaths, fighting the urge to rip the railing from the deck and snap it like a twig, preferably over the doctor's skull. Instead, he'd stared out at the gulf waves rolling ashore, concentrating on the ebb and flow until he could notch his brain into work gear.

That was when he decided that Wade Bell might be someone worth questioning.

Jealous bastard? Sure, why not? Cop with a job? Even better.

"Where were you this morning?" Chase asked.

The doctor's blond brows shot straight up. "Why?"

"Just answer the question."

Wade hesitated. "I'd like to know what this is about first."

"I'd like an answer first."

"I was with someone."

"That someone have a name?"

"I answered your question, now you can answer mine."

Chase took a step closer. "Who exactly do you think is in charge of this conversation?"

"You are, but wouldn't it be easier if you gave a little instead of being a total asshole?"

Smiling, Chase backed off. So the doctor wasn't easily intimidated. He could deal. "Kylie's had a little trouble lately."

"Yes, I know. I read the newspaper."

"Not everything that happens to her ends up in the paper. Someone smashed her windshield with a bat yesterday, just like the one used to destroy her knee. And this morning, she got caught in a deliberately set fire."

Wade paled beneath his tan. "Holy Christ. I had no idea." Then, as it clicked why Chase was questioning him, his shoulders went rigid. "Wait a minute. You think I had something to do with that?"

"I'm just covering all the bases."

"Why would I do anything to hurt her?"

"You used to be a couple, didn't you?" Chase asked.

"So?"

"Who instigated the split?"

"I don't see what this has to do with—"

"Just answer the question."

Wade rolled his eyes. "Maybe you'll find this hard to believe, but I did."

He was right. Chase didn't believe him. "Why?"

Wade leaned back against the car and folded his arms. "I

wanted all of her, and she wasn't ready for that kind of commitment."

Chase didn't find that hard to believe. "What was the tone of the breakup?"

"Amicable, of course. Did you see her tell me to get the hell away from her when you two got here earlier?"

Chase didn't respond at first as the image of that kiss seared through his frontal lobe. "I'm just wondering if you're one of those guys who tries to win over a woman by scaring the shit out of her."

Wade jerked his keys out of his pocket. "I'm leaving before one of us gets punched."

Chase couldn't help the tight smile. "I wouldn't recommend assaulting a police officer, doctor. Why don't you tell me your whereabouts this morning?"

Grabbing the sunglasses off his head, Wade folded them and shoved them into his shirt pocket. "Like I said, I was with someone. I'd rather not say who."

A secret. Now they were getting somewhere. "I can be discreet, Dr. Bell."

"I appreciate that, but no."

"Let me put it to you this way: Answer the question here or we take this downtown."

"You're going to arrest me because I won't tell you who I spent the morning with?"

"No. But I will take you in for questioning."

Wade's chin jutted out. "I hate to have to mention this, but the mayor is a personal friend of mine."

"Did you spend the morning screwing the mayor?"

Wade barked out a laugh. "No."

"Then I don't give a shit how friendly you two are. Now answer the question or I'm hauling you in. I can make it painfully public, if you'd like."

"Jane," Wade blurted. "I was with Jane McKay."

Chase almost failed to school his shock. "And Jane will confirm?"

"I really don't want Kylie to—"

"Jane will confirm?" Chase repeated.

"I don't know. She doesn't want Kylie to know about us."

"Really. I wonder why that could be."

"I trust you'll be discreet, like you said."

Letting the statement dangle, Chase moved on. Let the shifty son of a bitch sweat. "One other question." He flipped to a new page in his notebook. "How is it that you ended up being the surgeon who worked on Kylie's knee ten years ago?"

"What the hell does that have to do with anything?"

Chase waited for a response.

Wade's complexion turned a fiery red as he curled his hands into fists. "I was already in the ER for another case when she was brought in."

"And the case you were originally there for? What was that?"

"It's unrealistic to expect that I would recall."

"But if I were to go back and check the ER records, there'd be another patient with your name on their file?"

Wade, seeming to have gotten control of his anger, cocked his head. "What exactly do you think I did? I'm in the mood for a good laugh."

Easy, Chase thought. Don't blow it. "You were in the ER when Kylie arrived, were you not?"

"You make it sound like I was waiting for her at the door."

"Were you?"

"No, damn it. She was in a trauma room when a nurse came to get me for a consult. And she was damn lucky I was there. If I hadn't been, she'd have a stump instead of a knee."

Chase took a steadying breath against sudden vertigo. "Certainly you acknowledge that was some good fortune for you, too. A star athlete with a terrible knee injury that you fixed. She's a walking billboard for your good work, not to mention an attractive woman who'd make someone like you a kickass trophy wife."

"So what do you think happened, detective? You think I arranged the attack on her so I could fix her up and woo her?"

"You're forgetting. I was there," Chase said. "I saw the way you looked at her back then."

"And I saw the way *you* looked at her. I had no intention of getting in the way of that."

"Yeah? Why do I have a hard time believing that a guy who puts the moves on two sisters at the same time is the upstanding kind?"

Wade took a step toward him, his fury palpable. "Listen to me, you son of a bitch. I work in Florida, the retirement capital of the fucking world. I'm up to my eyeballs in knee and hip replacements. I don't need to go around looking for work, and I certainly wouldn't sic two fucks with a baseball bat on a defenseless girl alone in the woods."

Satisfied, Chase put away his notebook. As much as he wanted to go after Wade for the attacks past and present, it didn't fit. If Wade were truly twisted, Kylie would have had trouble with him a long time ago. "If I have any other questions, I'll call you."

Wade got into the BMW and took off with a squeal of tires.

Good riddance, Chase thought as he opened the front door and stepped into Kylie's living room. He paused when he saw her with her head lolled back against the chair cushion, her eyes closed. He thought she was sleeping soundly, thank God, but then noticed the fine film of perspiration that dampened her brow.

Her whimper shot his heart into his throat, and he took a step toward her just as she shifted restlessly, flinging an arm out that crashed into the lamp on the table beside her. She started awake with a sharp gasp and frantically looked around.

When she saw him, she pushed herself straighter, the fearful expression on her face smoothing into blank indifference. How quickly she managed it floored him. Maybe they hadn't made any progress after all.

"Why didn't you wake me?" she asked, groggy.

"You obviously needed the rest."

Pushing to her feet, she folded the blanket and replaced it

on the back of the sofa. Other than trembling hands, she looked as steady and poised as ever. "It won't take me long to pack."

He watched her walk away and wondered what it would take to rip away her game face for good.

# 33

THEY DIDN'T SPEAK TO EACH OTHER ON THE WAY
to the safe house located about an hour from Kendall Falls,
though Kylie used Chase's cell phone to call Trisha to ask
her best friend to check in on Quinn for her. After that, Kylie
could have used meaningless conversation as a distraction
from the persistent images in her head that had started with
the nightmare. Blue aluminum baseball bats, merciless attackers in ski masks, smashed windshields. She desperately
wanted it to stop. All of it. Even if just for a few minutes.
God, she was so tired. She just wanted to curl up and lapse
into unconsciousness for a few days.

Chase steered the SUV off a two-lane Fort Myers street
flanked by palm trees into a middle-class neighborhood. In
the middle of the first block, he pulled into the driveway of a
small, white stucco house with a tidy front yard and a large
banyan tree arching over the terra-cotta roof.

"It's nothing fancy," he said, "but it's safe."

They walked up the front walk together, Chase toting her
overnight bag. They could have been a married couple returning from a Caribbean cruise or walking into their new
home for the first time. Inevitably, she thought of the kiss

back at the police station. Nothing at all like Wade's kiss, and Wade was a pretty damn good kisser. Yet his mouth on hers didn't shoot her senses over the rainbow. Not like Chase's did.

"Are you hungry?" Chase asked as he slid the key into the lock and turned it.

"Starving." It came out with more enthusiasm than she'd intended, with guttural overtones, thanks to the clenching of her insides, and she gave him a sheepish smile. "I can't remember the last time I ate."

He grinned at her. "Then that will be one of our first priorities."

He gestured for her to precede him through the door and hit a light switch. As she walked in, pleasant, lemon-scented air greeted her. The décor was simple: relatively new beige carpet, a used but decent overstuffed sofa in a generic teal-and-peach pattern, midsize TV and a glass and wrought iron coffee table piled with magazines. The day's *Kendall Falls News* had been left amid the magazines, next to a half-full cup of coffee, as if whoever had cleaned had paused for a break with the newspaper before taking off.

Chase set her bag down inside the door. "Looks like Sam was able to get someone to prepare the place. That means there are groceries. I'm thinking pasta, if that sounds palatable."

She nodded, but she wanted a shower first. The pungent odor of smoke clung to every skin cell.

"The shower's down the hall," he said. "And you can have your choice of bedrooms."

She picked up her bag and headed in that direction, grateful that he'd read her mind.

The tiny bathroom probably hadn't been renovated since the house had been built in the seventies, considering the aqua blue bathtub, sink and toilet. But it had a shower, hot water and clean towels—all that she needed. She stripped and stepped in and sighed as clean water splashed over her face. Thinking nothing but "lather, rinse, repeat," she washed away the aftermath of the fire.

Afterward, she wrapped herself in a thin towel that hit her at midthigh and ventured into the nearest bedroom, where she dropped her bag on the floor by the bed. The small room had the look of a middle-of-the-road hotel: cheaply decorated with a palm tree print bedspread and a lamp with a square shade on the bedside table. A white wicker chair sporting a flowery cushion sat in the corner.

Sinking down onto the side of the bed, Kylie closed her eyes—just for a minute—and then she'd pull on some clean clothes and go check on the progress of dinner. Her stomach growled at the thought, and she tried to decide which she wanted more. Food . . . sleep . . . food . . . sleep . . .

Curling up on her side—just for a minute—she thought groggily about what she wanted more.

Food . . . sleep . . . Chase . . .

CHASE MOVED AROUND THE SMALL KITCHEN, IM-pressed that the house had fairly new white appliances and decent blond-wood cabinets. It was a typical rental property, though: clearly lived in by people who hadn't cherished their surroundings because they didn't own them.

The timer went off to signal the pasta was done, and he dumped the noodles into a strainer in the sink. Steam rose to the light overhead, and as he watched it, he thought about how normal it seemed to make dinner while Kylie showered. They'd never had a chance to do anything normal like cook together, always either training, attending their respective classes or traveling to the next tournament. Whenever they could snag free time together, they spent it far away from either of their families, and therefore not near any kitchens.

Once he'd pulled the garlic bread out of the oven, he went looking for Kylie. He suspected she'd fallen asleep, but he wanted her to eat something. She'd gotten pale and thinner over the past few days, so he suspected she was eating as much as she was sleeping.

Sure enough, he found her zonked out on the bed, curled on her side and still wearing the towel from her shower, wet hair soaking the pillow. The scent of vanilla soap floated on the air as he took a moment to appreciate how peaceful and relaxed she looked. She must have been sleeping so soundly she didn't hear him walk in, because she didn't move, and her breathing remained deep and even.

He hated to wake her, but he hated more how prominent her collarbones looked under her skin. She had to have been running on fumes since the discovery of the bat at the construction site.

Perching on the side of the bed, he stroked a gentle hand over her upper arm. "Kylie."

Nothing. Not even a shift in her breathing.

He leaned down, careful not to jostle her. He'd seen how easily she startled, and he didn't want to alarm her now. "Kylie," he said, a bit louder than before.

She didn't move, though a small smile curved her lips.

He stopped before saying her name again, surprised by the smile. What was that about? An unconscious reaction to the sound of his voice? That'd be cool.

Smiling himself now, he grazed his fingers over the dark strands of hair at her temple. "Kyylieee," he whispered, sing-songy now.

She stirred under his hand, shifting onto her back with a deep sigh. "Chase?"

"Dinner's ready," he said, voice still soft. "You said you were starving."

"Hmm."

His smile grew. He loved her soft and sleepy and out of it. Maybe it was sad, but that was when she was most like she'd been when he'd fallen in love with her the first time.

Shaking his head, he caressed the back of her hand draped over her stomach. "I made spaghetti," he said. "And garlic bread. You love garlic bread."

"Mmm. Garlic bread."

He laughed at the sensual moan, but it caught in his throat when she ran a loose hand back through her damp hair and breathed his name through barely parted lips. "Chase."

His heart stuttered, and he held his breath, watching her

and waiting. This was a bad idea, sitting on the edge of her bed while she was half asleep and gloriously naked under that towel, smelling of soap and shampoo and everything that turned him on. He should get up and leave right now. Right. Now.

But then the hand she'd sifted through her hair dropped onto his thigh, and she bent one knee, shifting her legs slightly apart under the towel and canting her hips up just a tiny bit.

He couldn't move, riveted by the sight of that terry cloth sliding ever so slowly upward, revealing more of the most gorgeously toned thighs he'd ever seen. Perfect thighs for wrapping around his hips and—

Okay, he'd leave in a minute.

Closing his eyes, he savored the heat of her fingers through his jeans. Not a thing sexual about it—she was still out of it, not knowing what she'd done—but his body seemed to think it was the sexiest thing ever. He held back his response, concentrating on breathing evenly, until her breath hitched, and her head arched back into the pillow, her lips parting on a soft moan.

Oh, Jesus, she was having a sexy dream.

Blood rushed straight to his groin, tightening his jeans to the point of discomfort.

Lowering his head and swallowing, he drew in a slow, steadying breath and started to count backward from twenty . . . no, wait, that wouldn't do it. A hundred might work.

Around thirty-four, the throb began to ease.

That's it. Time for Chase Jr. to go back into storage.

Except Chase Jr. *really* didn't want to go. Chase Jr. wanted some attention. *Needed* some attention. And just thinking about the kind of attention he wanted—needed—the kind Kylie was getting in her dream, made Chase's jeans too tight all over again. Tighter than before. *Damn it all to hell.*

"Later," he muttered through his teeth.

"Chase?"

He snapped his eyes open to find Kylie blinking and

bleary. The fingers resting on his thigh moved to rub at her eyes, and he breathed an inward sigh of relief. That would help.

"What time is it?" she asked as she pushed up onto one elbow and peered at him with sleepy eyes.

"Dinner time," he said, rolling to his feet and aiming for the door. Jesus, he sounded like someone had used sandpaper on his vocal cords. Thank God, he could keep his back to her. No need for her to see what a fucking teenager he was. "I'm sorry I insisted on waking you up, but you really need to eat."

"Okay," she murmured.

He glanced back to see her ease back down. "Kylie."

She opened one squinty eye but didn't otherwise move. And, hell, she looked so fantastic in that white towel, the cinched ends emphasizing cleavage that begged for a tongue dip.

He cleared his throat. "Seriously. You need to eat. Half an hour, and you can crash again."

He left her alone and returned to the kitchen, not sure she would actually get up, but he figured it was up to her now. She knew best what she needed more.

Meanwhile, he checked the cupboards for something alcoholic to take the edge off his own need.

# 34

QUINN RAISED HIS HEAD AND BLINKED SEVERAL times, trying to figure out what had awakened him. A noise of some kind. Thunder? Yeah, that must have been it.

He dropped his head back to the couch cushion and ran both hands through his grungy hair. He hadn't had a shower or changed clothes since going to jail and still had no desire to do either. Or eat, even. The thought of food turned his stomach. The thought of *living* turned his stomach. It'd be easier for everyone if he took a page from Kylie's playbook and fled the state. He'd have to leave the country, though. And how far would be far enough? Australia perhaps. Had to be Australia. They spoke English there. It'd take time getting used to the flipped seasons, but he could live with it. Everyone would be happier that way.

Another round of pounding snapped his head up again. That wasn't thunder. Someone was at the door.

Groaning, he pushed himself up into a sitting position, placing his feet flat on the floor, and considered blowing off whoever it was. He looked and smelled like crap. Well, not crap literally, but close. He couldn't remember the last time he brushed his teeth.

He figured it wasn't reporters. They'd stopped bugging him around the time the cops had cited two or three for trespassing. Chase Manning's doing, probably. Not that it mattered. That guy'd throw him in a dungeon in a heartbeat if he could get away with it. And Quinn couldn't blame him. He would have thrown himself in a dungeon if he could find one in Florida.

More pounding, followed by a woman's voice: "Quinn? It's Trisha. I know you're here."

Trisha? Trisha *Young*? Kylie's friend? What did she want?

Going to the door, he pulled it open to frizzy auburn curls and freckles that he'd begun to think were pretty cute the last few years, not that he'd ever mentioned that to either of his sisters. Standing in the doorway, he didn't say anything, just arched an eyebrow at Trisha.

She gave him a tentative smile that looked as fake as plastic palm trees. "Hi," she said, a little breathless and awkward. "I . . . Kylie asked me to check on you."

Quinn leaned a shoulder against the door jamb and cocked his head. "Why?"

"She's worried about you."

"Yeah? Then why isn't she checking on me?" He had to admit it hurt that Kylie hadn't been the one pounding on his door by now.

"I . . ." Trisha moistened her lips. "She didn't say."

"Ah." He couldn't stop the bitter twist to his lips. He'd wondered how long his older sister would stick by him after he'd been arrested for her attack. She talked a good game, but when it came right down to it, she was only human.

"You know she'd be here if she could be," Trisha said.

"Maybe she's on her way back to LaLa Land. I get the impression she prefers it there. No messy baggage to deal with."

Trisha pursed her full lips as she looked him up and down. "She'd probably be able to smell you there, though."

He glanced down at his wrinkled shorts and stinky shirt, and felt like a pig. A pitiful, headed-for-slaughter pig. "This is my new look," he said, and glanced up with a wry grin. "You don't think it works?"

She shook her head, curls bouncing. "It really doesn't for someone who's having company."

"I'm not having company."

"Oh. I guess that means you're not inviting me in for dinner?"

He paused, surprised. "Uh . . ."

Trisha smiled, blue eyes starting to sparkle with lights he'd never noticed before. "Hey, I know. How about you go take a shower, and I make *you* dinner?"

He snapped out of his shock. Was he really so sad and pathetic that Kylie had sent a friend over to babysit him? "That's not necessary. But thanks."

She pushed past him into the house as if he'd shouted, "Sure, come on in!"

"Wow, it's dark in here," she said, and went to the front windows to roll open the blinds to let in some meager light from the fading day.

"Storm's brewing," she said, peering out between the blinds as if she hadn't just come from outside. "Looks like it's going to be a doozy, too."

Quinn watched her, noting that she filled out her khaki slacks more fully than either of his sisters did, and he liked that. More to grab onto during . . . okay, where the hell did *that* come from? Not cool, thinking about sex while appreciating the butt of his sister's best friend. Of course, they were all adults here and Kylie had hinted more than once that he and Trisha would make a good pair . . .

Trisha flashed a smile over her shoulder. "You know, the longer it takes you to get cleaned up, the longer it's going to be before we can eat. I don't know about you, but I'm starved."

He stayed where he was, considering his options. Ask her to leave and continue his downward spiral or . . . well, he hadn't eaten a decent meal in several days.

He gave her a sloppy salute and headed down the hall toward the bathroom, where he took the fastest shower he'd ever taken, complete with razor and toothbrush. While he was towel-drying his hair, he heard the doorbell. Damn, that better not be Jane, he thought. Nothing like his youngest sister to analyze all the potential fun out of a situation.

After throwing on a clean T-shirt and shorts, he padded barefoot to the kitchen. Something smelled heavenly, like pizza . . . no, Chinese food . . . no, pizza . . .

Either way, his stomach growled even as he wondered what on earth Trisha could have whipped up so quickly with what he had in his fridge: beer, cheese, mustard and perhaps some butter.

He paused in the kitchen doorway and chuckled. Domino's and China Express had both paid a visit.

Trisha looked up from where she was setting plates and silverware on the table. "I wasn't sure which you'd want, so I ordered both. Pepperoni okay?"

"Happens to be one of my favorites."

"And I remember you said you liked moo shu chicken."

His mouth started to water. "Perfect."

Trisha pulled out a chair and plopped down. "Dig in. I'm about to expire."

"How about some wine?" Quinn asked, opening the fridge. "I think I've got a bottle of pinot in here."

"Water for me," Trisha said before she sank her teeth into a thick slice of pizza. "You should have water, too. You're probably dehydrated."

He figured she was right and figured, too, that she'd steered him away from the alcohol on purpose. Surprisingly, he didn't mind. After filling two glasses with ice and water, he settled at the table and helped himself to some pizza.

"So how much prison time are you looking at?" Trisha asked.

Quinn stopped with the slice half an inch from his mouth. "What?"

Trisha shrugged as she reached for her water. "You're acting like it's a done deal, so I just wondered how much time you think you'll get."

He lowered the pizza back to his plate, no longer hungry as nausea churned through his gut. "I didn't do it."

Trisha's forehead wrinkled as if that shocked her. "Really?

Because holing up with the blinds closed, drinking yourself into oblivion and letting yourself waste away clearly says to the world, 'I'm innocent.'"

"What am I supposed to do?"

"Hell if I know. What *can* you do? I mean, the whole town's already decided you're the monster who tried to maim his own sister. What is there to do?"

He picked a piece of pepperoni off his pizza and dropped it on his plate without eating it. "I'm thinking of leaving."

Trisha gave an exaggerated nod. "Oh, that's the perfect solution. Definitely. Because then you'd be, what, a fugitive? That wouldn't make you look guiltier at all."

Sitting back, he wished he'd broken out the bottle of wine after all. He wished, too, that he'd let Trisha keep banging on the door instead of opening it and letting her in. Deep down, he supposed he was still an optimist. That wouldn't last. "What would you do?"

She looked at her plate as she finished chewing, then washed it down with a drink of water. When she spoke again, she met his eyes with a sympathetic expression and an apologetic shrug. "I really don't know," she said softly. "I'm just trying to, you know, buck you up. How am I doing?"

He pushed back from the table and went to the fridge to retrieve the wine. To hell with it. A nice buzz would mute the frustrated voice screaming in his head. He returned to the table with the bottle, two wineglasses and a corkscrew.

Trisha watched him as he dispensed with the cork and splashed wine into both glasses. "That isn't the answer," she said.

"It is for now."

She reached out and covered his hand before he could pick up his glass. "Kylie knows you didn't do it."

Amazingly, his eyes began to burn. What was it about another person's touch that could jerk the emotion right out of you? "She's not here, though, is she?"

"She sounded stressed when she called. I didn't ask questions."

He drew his hand away and sat back but left the glass on the table. "What do you think of Australia?"

"I think it's a long way away, mate."

He grinned at her joke as he picked up his pizza and took a bite. A few bites later, the constant throb in his temples began to ease.

"You're not really going to run, are you?" Trisha asked as she reached for the boxes of moo shu.

He shrugged. "I'm thinking about it."

"What would it accomplish?"

"Everyone would be happier. Especially Kylie."

Trisha cocked her head. "You think Kylie would be happier thinking you ran because you were guilty? Did you let the booze soak all the common sense out of your brain?"

"A trial would destroy her," he said, his throat threatening to close up on him. "She'd have to relive all of it, in detail, in public."

"And she'd do it in a heartbeat, every damn day for the rest of her life, if it meant proving you innocent."

He smiled slightly. "You like to overstate things."

She grinned and nodded. "To make a point, yeah. Especially one that needs to be made because the person I'm making it to is too dim to get it on his own."

His smile broadened. "Did Kylie know you'd talk to me like this when she sent you over?"

"I have no doubt. She knows what a hardass I can be."

"Yeah, you're a real hardass." He pushed aside the wine bottle and snagged a box of moo shu. "Do you talk to her like this?"

"Are you kidding? Any time I try, she shuts me down with that look. You know that look, right?"

"Oh, yeah. The look that says, 'One more word and you're toast.'"

"That's the one." Trisha made an exclamation point in the air with her fork. "One more word and life as you know it will cease to exist."

Quinn chuckled. "One more word and I'll break my

racket over your head and wrap the handle around your neck."

"I don't think I've seen that one," Trisha said. "She must reserve that one for pesky brothers."

"I was *never* pesky."

Grinning, Trisha waggled her finger at the white takeout box near his elbow. "I think the pancakes and plum sauce are in there."

He handed it over, sobering when their fingers brushed and heat flushed up his arm. "Thank you," he said, his voice lower than before. "I needed this."

She smiled. "Pizza and Chinese food fix everything."

"Yep," he said with a nod. "It's the food."

# 35

KYLIE OPENED HER EYES AND YAWNED. GOD, IT felt so good to just lay there and drift. She considered continuing to do just that when she scented garlic in the air. Had Chase mentioned garlic bread? Oh, yeah, and spaghetti.

Stomach rumbling, she sat up and started to scoot off the bed. That was when she realized, holy crap, that she still wore the towel from her shower. Not one of those big, fancy bath towels that covered a lot of acreage, either. This one barely reached from the tops of her breasts to midthigh. And she had an impression of Chase sitting on the side of the bed talking to her, coaxing her to wake up in a low, sexy voice.

While she'd lain there in nothing but a thin towel.

Her heart thudded in her ears, and her cheeks heated as she remembered the images flitting through her mind as she'd drifted. Chase, shirtless and filmed with perspiration as he'd fired tennis shots at her under the hot sun. Chase, muscles and tanned skin streaming with seawater as he rose out of the surf, swim trunks clinging to the part of him that made her throb with want. Chase kissing the side of her neck, the underside of her jaw, teeth nibbling at the pulse in her throat, hands and fingers stroking and soothing and, oh, yeah,

venturing slowly and agonizingly into dark, weeping places
that ached for attention. The best part had been building
when she woke up and found Chase right there, watching her
with an intensity that speared right through her.

Could he have known? He'd certainly seemed rattled
when he went to the door. Rattled and in a hurry to get out.

Sitting on the side of the bed like that, he could so easily
have kissed her, and she would have wrapped herself around
him in a heartbeat. But he hadn't kissed her. He hadn't made
any move at all. Maybe he'd decided she was too much work.
She wouldn't have blamed him. She *was* too much work.

Groaning with frustration, she forced herself out of bed,
ignoring the unsatisfied ache that clutched between her
thighs, making her want to squirm to somehow relieve the
growing need. Squirming, however, would do no good. Unless
Chase had his hands, lips or tongue on the throb.

Oh, *God*.

Fifteen minutes later, in clean clothes and with damp hair
curling around her shoulders, she walked down the hall to the
dining room, where the table was set for two. Two tapered
candles, flames flickering, graced the center of the table. A
romantic dinner? Really?

When Chase walked out of the kitchen, wiping his hands
on a white dish towel, her breath stopped. He'd rolled his
sleeves up, revealing hairy forearms corded with veins and
muscle. Incredibly sexy arms, the kind you could lose yourself in. She wanted to lose herself in them again, had wanted
to lose herself in them for the past ten years. But she'd been
an idiot and walked away. The biggest idiot ever.

He paused in midstep and cocked his head with a questioning expression. "What?"

She blinked her gaze up to his and smiled, hoping her
self-recriminations didn't show in her face. "Need any help?"

"Sure. You can pour the wine." He nodded at the bottle of
red breathing on the table next to two wineglasses.

When he disappeared back into the kitchen, she was glad,
because her hand shook as she poured the wine. Too tired,

she rationalized. Tired and punchy and apparently horny.
Once she got some sleep, that would fade, and she would be
back in total control.

Hearing the rumble of thunder in the distance, she
glanced toward the large bay window in the living room and
noted the limbs of the banyan tree swaying in the wind.
Weak lightning flared, the storm several miles away yet.

Chase returned, carrying a plate of steaming spaghetti in
one hand and holding a basket of garlic bread in the other. As
he set them on the table, he nodded at one of the chairs.
"What are you waiting for? You've got to be about to gnaw
off a limb."

She laughed softly as she sat. "This all looks really good."

"I slaved over it for hours," he said with a smirk as he
plopped down in the chair adjacent to hers and reached for
her plate. He piled noodles and sauce on it until she protested
then piled it higher before handing it over. "There's more
when you're done with that."

She picked up her fork and dug in with one hand, diving
for a piece of garlic bread with the other.

They ate in a silence punctuated by occasional soft rolls
of thunder, and by the second glass of wine, Kylie began to
enjoy the soft, warm glow that spread upward from her
belly.

"You're a good cook," she said as she set down her glass.

He flashed her a grin. "Ragu's a good cook."

"But you added stuff to it, didn't you? It's not usually this
good."

"Must be the company. Or the fact that you really were
starving."

She smiled as she finished off her third piece of garlic
bread. "Thanks for insisting I get my butt out of bed to eat. I
feel much better now."

"Any time." He clinked his glass against hers and finished
the last of his wine. "If you want to crawl back in, I won't be
offended. You're pretty exhausted."

Shaking her head, she pushed her empty plate back and

rested her elbows on the table. She was awake now, and she didn't want to waste this pleasant buzz. "What's she like?"

He met her eyes, one eyebrow arched in question. God, it was sexy when he did that.

"Your daughter," she supplied. "She's, what, nine?"

He nodded, and his eyes began to glimmer like dark emeralds. "She's incredibly complicated for a nine-year-old. Smart as a whip. And, my God, the sarcasm."

"She's sarcastic? Really?"

"She got that from her mother."

"Ah."

He glanced at her quickly, as if to check to make sure he hadn't said something he shouldn't have, but Kylie sipped wine, wondering if the glowy, dizzy feeling in her head was official confirmation that she was drunk. Thunder, closer now, gave the house a mild shake.

"So," Chase said, drawing it out as he stirred his fork through the sauced pasta still on his plate. "Wade Bell?"

She smiled at him over the rim of her glass, for once not a bit unnerved by the intensity of his stare. So, so drunk. In about a minute, she'd be singing Irish drinking songs. "Wade's a good guy."

"He's hung up on you."

She shrugged. Okay, that's a bit of a buzzkill. "He'll get over it."

"You think you're that easy to get over?"

She held his gaze, unblinking, earlier giddiness fading fast as rain began to lash the windows. "You didn't have any trouble."

"Is that what you think?" he asked, incredulous.

"I don't have to think it. There's evidence."

"As much as I don't like labeling my child a mistake, that's technically what she was."

"The best mistake, though. You can't deny that."

"I'm not denying it. But I am denying that you were easy to get over. I met her mother in a bar—"

He broke off when she sat back abruptly and set her glass down with an ungraceful clunk. "I don't need to—"

"I think you do." He kept his gaze level with hers. "And even if you think you don't, I'd like to tell you."

"Why? So you can feel better about it?" Great, from buzzed to bitchy in three-point-two seconds. Gotta be a record.

"No," Chase said. "So you can."

"It's not about me."

"See, that's where you're very wrong."

"I'm sure your ex-wife would appreciate hearing you say that."

"She knew. Rhonda's one of the smartest people on the planet. Otherwise, we'd still be married and miserable."

She cocked her head, struck by the realization that he spoke about his ex-wife with sincere affection. "You like her."

Melancholy tinged his smile. "I like her a lot. I liked her the first time I met her."

"In a bar," she said wryly and took a drink of wine that was more gulp than sip.

He nodded. "The night you left."

She closed her eyes. Great. Fan-*freaking*-tastic. Even the crash of thunder, so close and violent it sounded as though a boulder slammed into the side of the house, didn't alleviate her growing anxiety. She didn't want to talk about this. Ever.

"I drank myself into oblivion," he said anyway. "Though I don't remember much of it. Woke up the next morning in Rhonda's bed, sick as a dog."

"How romantic."

He went on as if she hadn't spoken. "She made me breakfast and lectured me about drinking and driving. She's the one who took my keys away from me."

Kylie swallowed against the tension in her throat. He could have totaled himself that night. *Because of her.* And suddenly she was grateful that someone with a brain had been there to look out for him.

"We went our separate ways, and three months later, she showed up at my door."

"Pregnant." The word stuck in her throat like a popcorn husk.

"She didn't want anything from me. Said she just wanted me to know, because I had a right. I showed up at her door a few weeks later. It didn't seem right to let a child come into this world without a father."

He was so honorable it made her heart ache.

"We did okay for a while. Not great, but it wasn't horrible, either. The main problem was we never fell in love. After a while, it's not enough to just be good friends."

"It all sounds very mature," she mused, looking into her empty glass and wishing for more wine.

"If mature is a synonym for passionless, then yes, it was very mature."

Her heart began to thud as she remembered holding tight to him, sweaty and naked and mindless, as he'd pumped himself furiously into her, his body shaking with need, his moans as incoherent as hers. Passion? Oh, yeah, *they'd* had passion. Nothing passionless about them. She almost smiled, and the buzz made a comeback.

The storm was backing off already, thunder still growling but no longer as violent, as he gave her a self-conscious smile. "So you and Wade . . . how was that?"

She tipped her head to one side, her gaze on his, and pursed her lips as she ran her finger around the rim of her glass. "Exceedingly mature."

His smile turned into a full-blown grin. "I'm sorry to hear that."

Leaning her elbows on the table, feeling lighter than she had in days . . . years, she asked, "What's your daughter's name?"

"Maddy. Well, Madeline, actually."

"After your mother. I bet she loved that." She reached over and touched the back of his hand. "I was so sorry when I heard . . ."

He turned his hand and grasped her fingers for a fleeting moment. "The flowers you sent were nice."

"I wanted to come for her funeral, but . . . well, it didn't seem appropriate."

"It would have been fine."

"How long does it take?" she asked.

"How long does what take?"

"It's been six months since Dad . . . but it doesn't seem real. I mean, I'm here in Kendall Falls, and he's not, and I've never been here without him, but it just . . . doesn't seem real." She rubbed at her eyes, embarrassed that she'd started to babble. "Think I'm drunk."

Chase captured one of her hands, and when he stroked his thumb over her palm, she couldn't suppress an answering shudder. She had to blink to get herself to focus on his face. And what a beautiful, beautiful face it was. All angles and stubble and stunning green eyes. It'd be so easy to fall into them, fall into him, all over again.

"It gets easier," he said softly.

When tears stung her eyes, catching her off guard, she pulled her hand free of Chase's and sat back. Drunk and emotional. What the hell was she doing? Acting like nothing had changed in ten years, like they'd never exchanged angry words or hurt each other. Stupid, really, to try to reclaim the past, as if it were as easy as sharing a bottle of wine, a meal and a heart-to-heart.

Chase cleared his throat, drawing her attention outward. "I talked to T.J.'s foster mother while I was working on dinner. He's getting settled in."

She smiled, both relieved for T.J. and overwhelmed at how caring Chase had been with the boy. "That's good."

"I'm sure you'd like to see him as soon as possible, but we should probably give him a chance to get acclimated."

She nodded, swallowing against a renewed surge of emotion. "That makes sense. I . . ." Her voice cut out, and she paused to draw in a breath, struck by the shift of something inside her chest. What the hell was that? Affection? Desire? Regret? All three and then some? Or a warning that it was time to flee before things got complicated again?

Forcing a smile, she set her napkin on the table and scooted her chair back. "Think I need to go to bed before I fall face-first into my plate."

He nodded, face clouding as though she'd disappointed him. Or maybe he'd just wanted to talk more. Or something else. "I'll clean up here," he said.

She hesitated in the doorway, rain a constant drone outside, and turned back as he rose and picked up the empty bread basket. "Thank you," she said. "For dinner and taking care of T.J."

"It was my pleasure."

And he smiled, all white teeth and crinkling eyes.

A wave of dizzy need swirled through her. She wanted him. She'd never wanted anyone as much as she wanted him.

She swallowed jerkily at the tug of inner muscles making a heated demand. And as he cocked his head, silently asking her what she wanted, she stopped thinking and strode over to him, grabbed the front of his shirt and pulled him toward her.

He dropped the bread basket and met her halfway, his mouth just as eager as hers. Somehow, her back hit a wall, and he pressed fully against her, his thick, muscled thigh slipping between her legs while his big hands gripped the sides of her head and his tongue stroked against hers, sensuous and hot.

Everything about him was consuming: his garlic–pinot noir taste, his sunscreen scent, the scrape of his razor stubble against her skin, the way he couldn't seem to get enough of kissing her, going deeper and longer and wetter every time their lips met. Without leaving her mouth, he slid a hand under her shirt, his fingertips feathery against skin that jittered at first contact then warmed under his caress. She gasped into his mouth when his fingers stroked over her bra then began to knead and tease until her nipple was so hard and sensitive that each gentle touch and tweak weakened her knees and sent a spear of need straight to her center. He started on the other breast, and she arched her head back against the wall, breathless and aching, exactly where she wanted to be, mindless and doing nothing but feeling.

He took advantage of the unconscious invitation and trailed kisses over her throat, down to the hollow of her collarbone, his tongue setting off firecrackers of pleasure everywhere it touched. She couldn't take much more. She needed him inside her. *Now*.

"Bedroom," she gasped.

The world went dizzy and spinning as he lifted her, and she clamped her legs around his hips and held tight as he carried her down the hall.

And then they were discarding clothes as fast as they could, panting and desperate. As she yanked her shirt over her head, she watched him shuck his jeans down his legs, saw his erection spring free. Her breath left her, and she stared at him in silent fascination. He was built like a god. His long, sculpted torso tapered down to a flat belly and narrow hips. She couldn't wait to get her hands on all that muscle, to take his hard, hot flesh inside her and ride.

Catching her watching him, he grinned and dropped his last sock on the floor. Naked and glorious, he advanced on her with a predatory glint in his eyes. He took her down to the bed and braced himself above her without giving her his weight. She grasped his hips, arching her own toward him, but he held back and instead took her mouth in another deep, wet kiss that wiped her mind clean.

She moaned as he skimmed his hand up the inside of her thigh, let her head drop back, closing her eyes. Yes, yes, *yes*. This was what she needed. Chase, Chase and more Chase.

He slid a finger inside her heat, and she arched, gasped, then felt him smile against her lips. "You're already wet for me," he murmured.

"Please," she whispered. "Now."

He obliged, sinking into her with a long, drawn-out groan. The pleasure of the slide stunned her, and she opened her eyes to find his gaze locked on hers. Sensation spiked at the intense connection, and he began to move, slowly, in and out, sinking in deeper with each long thrust, his hot, glittering gaze steady on hers, his jaw clenched.

The knot of pleasure tightened, began to build, and her

breathing went more ragged. Oh, God, oh, yeah, that's it, that's exactly it. She tried to quicken the pace, to race to the finish line, but he suddenly pinned her hips to the mattress, stilled her.

"Don't stop," she gasped, frustrated and digging her nails into his back.

But he did. He kept her immobilized while he breathed slowly, as if battling back from the edge. She wanted release, needed it, was so close that the pulse of it throbbed inside her, beating, beating, beating, now, now, now.

But he had other ideas, another pace, and he lowered his head and kissed her, his tongue sweeping inside her mouth, the tip glancing off the underside of her top lip, setting off sparks. Her heart, already hammering, tripped and stuttered at the intimacy, the tenderness. With his eyes on hers, he moved his head down to roll his tongue over her nipple, then gave it a gentle tug with his teeth, his gaze never leaving hers. He resumed thrusting, grinding forward and sliding back, forward and back, deepening each stroke with an extra, subtle jerk of his hips.

She bowed back, her heart about to explode out of her chest.

He took her hands and raised them above her head, trapped her wrists there with one hand while he gripped her hip with his other and thrust and thrust, harder and faster, grunting now and groaning, straining for the peak, sweat sliding between their bodies, sticking them together in wet delight. The whole time, his eyes stayed intent on hers, not letting her look away, not even blinking, his jaw tight, his teeth clenched, his neck corded with muscles and tendons and strain, pumping into her, ruthless and hard and oh so wonderful.

Her body rose to meet his, little mindless whimpers of pleasure catching in her throat, trying to explode out of her each time his hard, hot flesh hit her in just the right spot. She tried to free her hands, to touch him, to roam, but he held fast while the pleasure built, rode her like a piston, faster and faster, higher and higher, impossibly higher still, until the wave she rode bucked her off, and she soared, her body taut and singing, screaming its release in long, hitching, uncontrollable jerks and shudders.

For long moments, she couldn't breathe, couldn't think, could feel only the ecstasy repeatedly stretching her muscles as tight as guitar strings, the music of orgasm flooding her heart, her soul, again and again, blinding her to everything but the explosion of feeling that blossomed from her center out to the rest of her body in a reckless, bucking cacophony.

His thrusts became almost frantic, and he released her wrists, grabbing her hips with both hands, lifting her, angling her so he could drive deeper still, and then he was jerking against her, his open mouth on her neck, his teeth grazing her skin, nipping, biting, a harsh, agonized groan ripping out of his throat, his fingers digging desperately into her hips. She slid her hands around to his tight butt and held him close, pressing as tightly against his heat as she could, riding out his pleasure, rewarded with an extra fluttery sensation as he came in an endless, hot gush.

And then they were still, their breathing harsh and synchronized. His hand, hot and damp, stroked her thigh, her ribs, his fingers gentle, almost tickling.

Holy crap, she thought vaguely. He'd just fucked her all the way to heaven.

An odd sound came from the other side of the room, and she lifted her head, surprised when it spun. "What's that?" she asked, then wondered if the words had sounded as slurred to him as they did to her. Yep, she was drunk. Drunk on wine and incredible, incredible, *fucking* incredible sex.

He chuckled, the sound low and lazy, vibrating his body under her. That was when she realized that somehow she'd ended up on top of him, that she was sprawled across his chest, her hair cascading over them both, her breasts pressed against his muscled chest. He was still nestled firmly inside her. Her nipples instantly hardened, and she sighed, closed her eyes, head taking a slow, lazy spin.

"Cell phone," he murmured.

"Oh." She pressed her hands against his chest, started to push herself up, too lazy to pull her hair back and out of her face, but he easily flipped them, pinning her to the bed, and kissed her on the mouth, his tongue briefly touching hers. She welcomed the kiss, reluctant to let him go, reluctant to break the moment. She didn't want this to end. It was too good. It was like coming home after being out of the country, living with people who didn't speak the same language, for too long.

"Let it ring," he said as he raised his head and brushed a kiss over her forehead. "Am I too heavy?"

She closed her eyes and smiled. She couldn't seem to catch her breath. "You feel good." He felt right. He'd always felt right.

"God, your smile," he breathed. "I've missed that. I've missed *you*. So much."

She opened her eyes, her heart skipping at how intensely he stared into her. Then he sighed, caressing her cheek with the back of his hand, before he tucked a wayward strand of hair behind her ear. "I'm sorry, you know. For everything."

She nodded and swallowed against the sudden lump in her throat. "Me, too. I was such an idiot to leave."

His smile spread into a grin. "Kind of, yeah."

"It was never you. It was me."

"That's what women say when they want to dump a guy."

"But in this case, it's true. I couldn't . . . deal."

He kissed her, gentle, tender, reverent. "I know. I wish I knew how to help."

"There wasn't anything you *could* do. It was up to me to get over it."

His brow furrowed. "You can't just get over what happened to you, Ky. It's part of who you are."

"I just want it all to be over."

He started to respond, but his cell phone rang again. "Damn," he said, dropping his head to nuzzle her cheek.

"Maybe you should get it," she murmured as she rubbed her fingers through the soft hair behind his right ear.

"Probably should."

He kissed her one last time. "When I'm done, we can pick up where we left off."

"You've got a date."

# 36

CHASE, GRINNING LIKE A FOOL, GRABBED HIS CELL out of his pants on the floor and walked stark naked into the living room. Rain continued to fall outside, and he wondered vaguely whether there'd be flooding issues in Kendall Falls.

"Manning."

"Sylvia Jensen here, Chase. I've got the test results on the shirt that was buried with the baseball bat."

Chase stopped in midstep, fingers freezing where they'd started to give himself a satisfied belly-scratch. "Okay."

"It's definitely Kylie's blood."

Chase shoved a hand through his hair. Damn. He'd hoped against hope that it wasn't. "You're sure?"

"Positive. That bat was the weapon used in her attack. No doubt about it."

Ah, hell, he thought. Things weren't looking good for Quinn, innocent or not.

"There's something else," Sylvia said. "Another type of blood on the same shirt."

Chase turned to look down the hall toward the bedroom.

Kylie was in there, naked and waiting. He wanted her again already. "Whose?"

"I'll run the DNA through the system first thing tomorrow to see if there's a hit. This could be what you need to identify at least one of the attackers."

"Or it could just be Quinn's blood, since it's his shirt. And that wouldn't tell us anything we don't already know."

"I can tell you right now that, based on the DNA in the sample Kylie gave us, it's not Quinn's. Whoever's it is isn't related to the McKays. But we could get a hit in the DNA database."

"Okay. Let me know as soon as you get anything."

"You bet."

"Thanks, Sylvia."

He cut off the call and stared down at the floor, tapping the edge of the phone against his chin. Just because Kylie's blood was on Quinn's shirt didn't mean Quinn did anything to her. It could have happened just as Quinn said. He'd gotten wet and left the shirt at the Bat Cave, and the attackers used it to clean up the bat before they buried it. But would a grand jury see it that way? Especially considering Quinn's reputation for being a jealous, resentful brother? Not to mention his lack of alibi and love of booze.

"Are you coming back to bed?" Kylie called from the bedroom.

Drawing in a deep breath, Chase headed in that direction. She was going to hate this, but he had to tell her. They'd just found each other again, and he wasn't about to risk it by keeping secrets.

She sat up the second he walked into the bedroom, the playful expression on her face falling away. "What's wrong? Who was that?"

"Sylvia Jensen, the—"

"Forensics expert, sure. I remember."

"The tests on Quinn's gym shirt came back. It is your blood."

"Oh." Her eyebrows cinched together as she processed that. "So that was the bat, then."

He nodded as he sat on the edge of the bed and brushed his fingers over the back of her hand. "This won't be good for Quinn, Ky."

Her widened eyes met his. "But you said you believe—"

"I *do* believe you, Ky. But I also have to follow the evidence, and the evidence is pointing very confidently at your brother."

"He didn't do it, Chase. He couldn't have."

"I'll do my best to prove that, but it isn't up to me to decide."

"So in the meantime, you'll be building a case against him."

"I'm a cop, Ky. That's what I do."

She sat back against the pillow. "I see."

He sensed the shutdown in her emotions before he saw it in her expression. "Ky, come on. You know I'll do everything I—"

He broke off as she shoved aside the covers and slid out of bed. She was beautifully naked as she walked to the door, but he didn't get to appreciate it as the game face slammed him in the temple in all its Kylie McKay glory. Anger quickly followed. Thirty minutes after talking out the past and fucking each other into a stupor, and she whipped out the game strategy the instant they hit a bump in the road? What the fuck?

"Ky," he said, struggling to control his tone. "Don't walk out on me."

She paused at the door and turned, crossing her arms over her breasts. "Don't railroad my brother."

"I don't *railroad* anybody."

"You know what I mean."

"Do you think I'm a bad cop?"

"What does that have to do with anything?"

"Just answer the question. Do. You. Think. I'm a bad cop?" So much for keeping his voice from betraying his anger.

She narrowed her eyes. "I don't know what kind of cop you are."

That hurt. It shouldn't have, because she was just lobbing shots, but it still hurt more than it should have. "Good cops don't put innocent people in jail without a damn good reason. I've got three damn good reasons to throw your brother's ass in jail. They're called means, motive and opportunity. I've got his shirt with your blood on it connecting him to the weapon. He has no alibi for the time of the attack. If you weren't his sister, you'd be shaking your head and tsking right now about how that boy's going to spend the next five at Everglades Correctional Institution. So don't give me that railroading crap."

Turning away, he jammed a hand through his hair and shook his head. Shit. He shouldn't have gone off on her like that. But, hell, she should *know* he would do the right thing. Where the hell was the trust?

"Are you finished?"

At the soft question, he glanced over his shoulder at her and nearly groaned aloud at the flat expression and dead eyes. Was it possible that she was even colder than before or did it just seem that way because of the heat they'd just shared? Two steps forward, thirty-two steps back? Hell, with Kylie, it was more like a hundred and thirty-two steps back.

"Yeah," he sighed. "I'm finished."

"Thank you for dinner."

Surprised, he turned fully as she walked out, shutting the door quietly behind her.

He picked up the nearest object—a pillow—and whipped it at the door.

THREE HOURS LATER, WHILE ANOTHER THUNDER-ing storm shook the small house, Chase tossed fitfully, unable to get Kylie out of his head, naked and bucking under him, clamped around him, so hot and tight and open. In thirty minutes or less, like a damn pizza delivery, she'd shut him down and walked out on him—again—and now he couldn't decide what he was more: angry, hurt or disappointed.

But the more he thought about it, the more he began to wonder how open she had really been. Sure, they'd talked about the past. They'd apologized to each other, and all seemed like water under the bridge. Yet, their exchange just before his phone rang began to bother him.

*"It was never you. It was me."*

*"That's what women say when they want to dump a guy."*

*"But in this case, it's true. I couldn't . . . deal."*

*"I know. I wish I knew how to help."*

*"There wasn't anything you could do. It was up to me to get over it."*

*"You can't just get over what happened to you, Ky. It's part of who you are."*

*"I just want it all to be over."*

When you got right down to it, she hadn't said much of anything in that conversation. She was *still* saying what was expected of her, *still* holding everything at bay. He'd thought they'd shared a breakthrough, but all they'd really shared was platitudes and sex. Maybe that worked for other people, but it ticked *him* off. He didn't want platitudes. He wanted Kylie, naked in more ways than one, sharing what she really felt rather than what she wanted everyone to *think* she felt.

Groaning, he scrubbed his hands over his face. Christ, his fucking divorce hadn't been this much work or hurt nearly as much. He didn't know what to do anymore. Didn't know what to say, how to act. Should he corner her or leave her alone? Should he walk away and never look back? Could he? Had he even tried hard enough yet? Or the right way?

Frustration made his head begin to throb. He needed a plan, a different approach. Maybe it was ironic, but he needed a strategy to strip away *her* strategy. If she wanted to play life like it was a game, then he had to figure out a way to outplay her until she had no defenses.

And in the meantime, he needed to solve the damn case.

Maybe if he did that, closure would help drag her out of her emotional quicksand. Or, considering how guilty Quinn looked and acted, it could drag her under . . .

He needed other suspects.

He knew the police at the time interviewed fellow tennis competitors, amateur and professional, but hadn't come up with anyone viable. Maybe she'd had an obsessive fan no one knew about. Except obsessed fans didn't work in twos. Hell, maybe the attack had had nothing to do with tennis. Maybe she'd had a rival at school, someone whose boyfriend decided he had a crush on Kylie instead. Maybe she'd blown the curve on a chemistry exam. Maybe she'd spurned the advances of a boy. Any one of those scenarios could have led to a teen boy, or girl, employing the help of a friend to teach her a lesson. But surely she would have remembered something like that and brought it up after the attack. Unless she hadn't realized anything like that had happened.

And finding anyone who looked as logical as a suspect as Quinn depended heavily on several key variables coming together. Whoever did it knew when and where to catch Kylie alone. That meant they had to know her workout schedule and her workout path. Considering how often Chase trained with her, they also had to know *his* schedule and that on that day at that particular time, he would be occupied by English class at Kendall Falls Community College.

And then a truly awful thought struck him. What if the attack had been about *him*? Some twisted kid got angry at *him* for some perceived slight and took it out on his girlfriend. And, fuck, that line of thinking opened up a whole new slew of possibilities. He hadn't been the only one close to Kylie. Someone pissed at Quinn or Jane or either of her parents could have cornered her. And that didn't take into account the group of girls she'd hung around with. Kylie was known for sticking up for her friends. Had she ticked off someone that way?

Jesus, the list was endless. It didn't help that T.J. had

struck out with the mug books. Having a suspect in the present would sure help in trying to figure out the past.

All he could hope was that Sylvia got a hit on the other blood on Quinn's shirt that sent him in a workable, new direction.

# 37

JANE STEERED HER LEXUS THROUGH THE GATED
entrance of her neighborhood, appreciating, even in the rain,
the majesty of the towering palm trees that lined both sides
of the street at precise intervals. Her cell phone began to ring,
and she checked the caller ID screen before eagerly flipping
it open. "Hi, Tiger."

"I need to see you now."

The urgency in his voice sent a rush of pleasure flowing
over her. "I thought you wanted a late dinner."

"No. I need to see you now."

Realizing she'd mistaken anxiety for urgency, she frowned.
"What is it?"

"Just . . . where are you?"

"I'm almost home."

"I'll meet you there in ten minutes."

"Wait! Do you think that's a good idea?" But he'd already
hung up.

Determined to not let concern put creases in her brow just
yet, Jane pressed the button that opened the door of her two-
car garage and pulled in.

In the house, she deposited her briefcase and bag in her

office then continued on into her bedroom, unbuttoning her dress along the way. The three-month-old house was cool and smelled like a meadow, the quiet disturbed only by the low hum of the air filter next to her bed.

She changed into a pink sundress and let her hair down before walking barefoot into the kitchen and pouring herself a glass of iced tea. By the time Wade's BMW pulled into her driveway, she was standing in the living room waiting for him, her toes sinking into plush new carpet while the ceiling fan spun lazily above her head. Sipping tea, she watched him get out of the car and run for the door as if the rain would melt him. He was frowning so hard that lines appeared engraved on either side of his mouth.

She'd never seen him angry before, and a thrill of anticipation zipped through her. Maybe he would earn his tiger stripes, so to speak, in bed later. It shocked her that she could want him again so soon after their morning together. Kylie had been an absolute fool to let this man go. Well, Jane thought, one woman's trash was another woman's pleasure.

She opened the front door before he rang the bell, and instead of the smile he'd been giving her lately when he saw her, he brushed by her into the foyer.

"Well, hello to you, too," Jane said wryly.

"She's going to find out," he said.

Jane knew who he meant, and what, and struggled to keep her expression from reflecting the sudden wild pounding of her heart. "How? We've been discreet. Well, before you parked in my driveway just now, anyway." She tried to smile to temper the criticism.

He didn't seem to notice. "Detective Chase Manning questioned me."

Her attempt to smile turned to bafflement. "About what?"

He walked into the living room, raking a hand through damp, normally perfect hair. Jane followed, refraining from asking him to remove his shoes. What he'd said was more upsetting than the thought of a dirty carpet anyway.

"He thinks I could have had something to do with Kylie's attack," Wade said.

Jane stopped, stunned. "What? That's impossible."

"Chase Manning doesn't seem to think so. Can you imagine what it would do to my practice if the newspaper gets a hold of such bullshit? I'd be ruined."

"I don't understand where this is coming from. What could possibly have given him the idea you had anything to do with something that happened ten years ago?"

Wade dropped onto the yellow floral loveseat. "He doesn't buy that it was a coincidence that I was in the ER when she was brought in." He cradled his head in his hands briefly before looking up at her with red-rimmed eyes. "Hell, for Kylie, it was pure *luck* that I was there. Those idiots had no clue what they were dealing with."

Jane eased down next to him on the loveseat. "You didn't do anything wrong, Wade. He can't prove anything."

"You said your brother didn't do anything wrong and look what's happening to him. If my name gets dragged through the news like his has, I'm fucked." He lowered his head and rubbed at his eyes. "Goddammit, Jane."

She massaged his back with one hand, trying to figure out how to diplomatically steer him back to the thing that had alarmed her initially. "You mentioned that Kylie is going to find out about us."

Wade sighed. "Manning wanted to know where I was this morning."

She stopped caressing him, her whole body flashing cold. "And you told him?"

"What was I supposed to do? Lie to a cop?"

"That was an option, yes." She removed her hand from his back and settled it in her lap, no longer so interested in soothing him. The idiot had screwed them both.

"Right," he said sarcastically, "and then when I get busted for that, I look guilty on the other stuff. Forget it. I told him the truth. And, frankly, if we'd been honest with Kylie from the start, it wouldn't be such a big deal now."

Maybe not to him. But Jane wasn't keen on the idea of owning up to making a move on Kylie's ex. She already had enough issues with her hard-headed, emotionally stunted sister.

Beside her, Wade's shoulders seemed to slump even more. "There's something else I have to tell you."

Wonderful, she thought. His body language told her everything she needed to know: He was about to blow a great big puff at the one joker holding up her house of cards.

He squared his shoulders, as though bracing himself. "I stopped by to check on Kylie."

Jane sat back and closed her eyes. She already knew where this was going, and she wanted to smack him upside the head. He was so bloody weak, so bloody in love with a woman who'd never wanted him, while the woman who did love him was sitting right here.

He hurried on. "I know you told me she was doing okay, with everything, but I wanted to see for myself. This has all got to be so hard on her."

Jane stayed silent, her jaw aching from being clenched. He was going to break her heart no matter what she said or did, so she simply sat there and let him do it at his own pace.

He took a ragged breath and held it for a moment. "I kissed her."

As much as Jane had thought she'd prepared herself, it still hurt. Like someone had taken a tennis racket and slammed its edge square against her chest. Pushing up from the loveseat, she paced away. At the window, she stared outside, vaguely noting the romantic flicker of the faux–gas lamp in her front yard.

She'd thought he might be the one. He made her stomach flutter, her head go light. He was *supposed* to be the one. Yet, during all the times he'd been naked and sweating with her, he'd no doubt been thinking about her sister. She pressed a hand to her belly, hoping to suppress the nausea that churned inside. It would never end. After all this time, all these years, she would never escape her sister's shadow. She would always be a poor substitute for the real thing.

"Please say something," Wade whispered.

"Do you love her?" she asked, so softly that maybe he couldn't hear her.

He didn't respond for a long moment, and she hoped to God he hadn't heard her. That would be easier than this awful, telling hesitation.

"Jane—"

She turned to face him, resigned now, knowing what needed to be done. "I'd like you to leave."

His eyes widened and he brought his hands up to reach for her, but when she flinched back, he dropped them. "Jane, please."

She walked to the door on stiff, shaky legs and opened it.

Wade vigorously shook his head. "Jane, no, we need to talk about this."

"I'm done talking." I'm done with *you*, she silently added.

"Just because I kissed her? Come on."

"No, you idiot. Because you slept with me when you love *her*. Now get the hell out of my house."

# 38

THE SCENT OF COFFEE TEASED KYLIE AWAKE, AND she rolled over, surprised that she'd managed to sleep at all. On top of a steady rain outside her bedroom window, she heard the shower come on and imagined Chase with water streaming in rivulets over all the angles and valleys and ridges of his beautifully sculpted chest. Imagined what it would be like to slip into the shower with him and . . .

*Stop it.*

Sitting up, she pulled the hair back from her face with one hand and peered at the clock on the bedside table: 7:34 A.M. She'd managed to sleep like the dead for a full eight hours.

Now that she wasn't absolutely exhausted, all the emotions she'd kept at bay started filtering in. She was raw, empty and frustrated. All thanks to Chase. Why couldn't he just leave her alone? Everyone else did, and everything worked out just fine. The past ten years, in fact, had been about as drama-free as watching an ice cube melt on a hot day. Slow and easy, and after it was gone, no mess. She liked it that way. People trapped in the rat race would trade everything they owned for such a stress-free existence.

Chase was just going to have to get over it and move on.
Like she had. Well, okay, like she *planned* to. As soon as
Quinn was cleared. As soon as the tennis center got back on
track. As soon as the case closed and she didn't have to deal
with Chase in her face every three seconds, harping on her
about passion and living and going through the motions. She
*liked* the motions, damn it. Consistent and safe and predict-
able. Everyone should be so lucky.

Besides, she needed to focus on Quinn right now. She
needed to find a way, some way, to help prove he didn't take
a baseball bat to her knee. She didn't have time to deal with
Chase and his demands. Quinn was in crisis. Quinn had to be
her focus. And, by God, he *would* be.

After pulling on a pair of jeans and a loose-fitting white
blouse, she secured her hair in a tight, smooth ponytail before going in search of coffee.

In the kitchen, she found coffee already made and began
pouring a cup when she heard Chase approach from the hall.
She almost expected him to come up behind her, to feel his
hands settle on her shoulders, stroke down her arms. When
he didn't touch her, or brush against her, she had to swallow
against the returning depression. She had to remind herself
that she didn't want that anyway. Being with him would
make her weak, and she refused to be weak.

"Good morning," he said.

She opened her mouth to echo the greeting, but words
failed her when she turned and found him standing close
behind her, still damp from his shower . . . and gorgeously
shirtless. Naked to the waist, with the top button of his jeans
undone, he was all sharply honed muscles and soft, baby-fine
hair. Undeniably, magnificently masculine. She had to concentrate to keep from leaning forward to nuzzle her nose
against the ridged planes of his torso.

He softly cleared his throat, and her gaze flew up to
see him cock his head, one eyebrow arched as he stared back
at her, his stunning green eyes more than a bit knowing. His
hair fell over his forehead, as though he'd towel-dried it then
combed it with only his fingers.

"Good morning," she replied. Her traitorous voice sounded even lower than usual.

He grinned a little as he took the coffee cup she thrust toward him. "How'd you know that's what I wanted?"

She turned away to pour herself another cup, glad he couldn't see the blush staining her heated cheeks. Brain-wiping, heart-thumping lust had a name. It was Chase Manning without his shirt, smelling of soap and talking about what he *wanted*. She knew what *she* wanted. It was hot and it was dark and it wasn't coffee. And, damn him, he knew it and was teasing her, tempting her . . . *daring* her to deny it.

She took her time opening a packet of sweetener, willing her hands steady as she stirred it into her cup. It didn't help that he didn't budge from where he'd invaded her personal space, less than a full step behind her. The longer she stalled, the longer he stood there, his body heat seeming to reach across the space between them and soak into her back. Apparently, he wasn't going anywhere.

She picked up her cup and turned, planning to slip by him with her head down and her gaze averted, but he shifted almost imperceptibly to block her. She raised her head in surprise, starting to ask him what the hell he was doing, but the question died on her lips when he reached out and stroked the back of his hand over her cheek.

"Did you sleep okay?" he asked.

She caught the inside of her bottom lip between her teeth as the cheek he'd so tenderly caressed heated, as did other places that should have been well sated after last night. "I slept like a rock."

He smiled, eyes soft as new grass, but he said nothing.

She would have stepped back if she'd had anywhere to go. As it was, she was pressed so hard against the counter that its edge dug into her back. What was it with him always trying to trap her? She needed a distraction. "So how's this going to work today?" she asked.

His gaze shifted from her eyes down to her mouth. The tip of his tongue edged along his lower lip before he glanced back up again. "What do you mean?"

God, what was he doing? The man had "I want to fuck you" written all over him. She probably did by now, too. Hadn't he learned by now that no matter how hard they tried, how good they fit together, they were doomed?

She swallowed hard, resisted the urge to clear her throat again. "I mean, you've got work to do," she said, pleased at the steadiness of her voice. Set the ball up and serve. Clean, easy, just right. "I've also got work to do on the tennis center plans. I'm smart enough to know that your hero complex is so massive that you're not going to let me go about my day as if nothing is off. So am I stuck here for the duration or what?"

His full lips, still moist from the stroke of his tongue, quirked. "Hero complex, huh?"

"Isn't that a cop thing?"

"In my case, it's a you thing."

She narrowed her eyes, thrown. He threw her even more by setting aside his coffee cup then taking hers and doing the same, before bracing his hands on either side of her.

Fully trapped, her hard-won control took a header. She pressed her wrists to her sides to keep her hands from doing the natural thing and resting against the smooth, bare skin of his chest. "What are you doing?"

"I'm cornering you." He smiled slowly, his arched brow asking her, "What're you going to do about it?"

She knew what she wanted to do. Shove him back and flee into the living room, or better yet, to the next continent.

"You hate being cornered," he said, leaning in briefly so that his nose hovered a hair's breadth from where the curve of her neck met her shoulder. His breath, warm and moist, fluttered against her skin, making her shiver. But instead of touching her with his lips, the way she anticipated being touched, he drew back and met her eyes again. "In fact," he drawled, "you hate it more than most people. And you know what happens?"

"You're going to tell me," she said, unable to block the weariness from her tone, "so why don't you just get it over with?"

"I've thought long and hard about this, Ky. Studied all the angles, trying to find the thing that we've all been doing wrong, the thing that's keeping us all from reconnecting with you in a meaningful way. And you know what? I think I've nailed it."

She lifted her chin a notch. He thought he had her all figured out. Like she was some kind of defective puzzle he could take apart, shake up the pieces and put back together the way it was supposed to be, fixed. Like it was easy. "Just say what you mean and get it over with."

"No one challenges you, Ky. You say, 'Back off,' and that's what we do. You say, 'Leave me alone,' and that's what we do. Everyone has done it. Quinn, Jane, Lara, your father, me. So what happens?"

She would have crossed her arms over her chest, but he was standing so close that she didn't dare move. Standing there facing him while he deconstructed her was hard enough without risking contact.

"What happens?" he prodded. "We all do what you want, and then what?"

She didn't respond, didn't want to continue this. It could only lead to disaster.

"What, Ky? Tell me what happens when we do what you want."

"Everybody's happy," she said softly, her lips barely moving.

"Wrong. *Nobody's* happy. You're not sparing us. You're just making us worry about you all the more."

"There's no reason to worry. I'm fine."

"Right. After ten years of holding yourself in firm check, you're fine. Eventually, you're going to snap."

Snap? Hell, no. She'd made it through ten years without snapping. Three months in Kendall Falls would *not* undo everything she'd worked so hard to overcome. She was *fine*. Just because Chase didn't think so didn't mean she wasn't. So she kept her eyes level on his, defiant and challenging. He wasn't in control here. *She* was.

Chase leaned in so that he was nose to nose with her, so that his chest with its hard, firm muscles pressed against her palms. "Go ahead, Ky. *Snap*."

His nearness, the expectant intensity of his eyes shifted something inside her. What if he was right? What if all it took to lift this elephant-like weight off her chest was letting go?

No. *No*. She was letting him get to her, letting him make her doubt everything. She knew herself, knew what worked. It had worked for *ten years*. So she dug for the strength she'd drawn on when fighting for the winning point in a long, tiring rally and decided she had to shift the direction of this conversation, turn it back on him in some way. But how?

He nodded, his smile almost feral. "That's it. Figure all the angles."

The smug tone jerked her out of the uncertain spiral, and she realized she was overthinking this. She'd already mastered the strategy that drove him nuts.

Looking up at him, meeting his gaze without blinking, she let the muscles in her face relax.

"Oh, no you don't," Chase growled and yanked her forward.

He buried his mouth against hers, and she suppressed a shocked gasp when his hands skimmed down to cup her buttocks and pressed her forward against the hard ridge of his erection. Oh, God, that felt good. *He* felt good.

But she couldn't do this. She needed distance.

She put a hand on his chest, to push him back, acutely conscious of his heart thundering under her palm. She started to say, "Don't," but his mouth stole the word and her air, and then he was lifting her against him, turning with her in his arms.

She didn't want this.

She couldn't want this.

Oh, God, she wanted this.

With a broken moan, she wrapped her legs around his waist and her arms around his head and lowered her mouth to his. His tongue met hers, eager and welcoming, and she closed her eyes, losing herself in his kiss. He tasted like heaven, like hot, rich coffee, melting chocolate, thick, sensuous caramel.

He suddenly tipped forward, and they fell together. Her back hit the softness of a bed—when had he carried her to the bedroom?—and he landed on top of her, nestled firmly between her legs. She arched against his heat, sucking in a harsh breath when his hardness ground against her center. It wouldn't take much to send her flying off the edge, and oh, God, she couldn't wait.

Some small, coherent part of her mind whispered protests, but she ignored them as she slid her hands down over his hips, wanting to caress him through his jeans, eager to take in that hot, silken part of him. She wanted his fullness to fill the void inside her, to drive out the emptiness like he had last night.

But he shifted, angling his hips to the side, away from the juncture of her thighs, and trailed his lips over her throat, his tongue doing a teasing dance against her skin while he unbuttoned her blouse and laid it open. Next, he undid the clasp of her bra, spread the cups aside and skimmed his hand down between her breasts and over her flat, quivering stomach.

"So soft," he murmured, surprising her as he lazily cupped her right breast in his warm hand, gently kneading, caressing his thumb over the nipple. "So pretty."

Her heart kicked at the reverence in his voice, in his eyes. And she started thinking again. She needed to make him stop, needed to push him away. No, she needed *this*. But, God, he wanted more from her than she could give.

When he lowered his head to suck the nipple into his mouth, all thoughts flew out of her head, and her eyes drifted closed in pure pleasure. She sank her fingers into his hair, grasped his head between her hands, fighting the conflicting needs to make him stop and urge him on. But, God, he felt so good, so right.

While he sucked and laved, nipping with his teeth, a different kind of tension began to mount inside her. This was too . . . intimate. It was never just sex with him, but this time he seemed especially focused on forging a connection she would be too weak to break.

"Relax," he whispered as he moved to her other breast and rolled the nipple between his tongue and upper lip. "Just relax and let me love you."

He left her breasts, their tips hard and wet, and trailed hot, open-mouthed kisses down the valley between her ribs, his hands stroking, soothing, before his fingers worked open the button on her jeans and eased down the zipper.

She released an involuntary moan, her heart racing now, her breath starting to hitch. Stop, please, stop. But the words refused to come out.

"You smell so good," he said, burying his nose against the skin of her lower abdomen and breathing in deeply. "Like the sun." He caught the lacy edge of her underwear in his teeth and let it go with a small snap before dipping his tongue underneath.

She arched, and he chuckled darkly as he skimmed his hands inside her jeans and began to draw them down her legs. "You're going to come for me, Ky."

She closed her eyes tight, trying to calm the uneven, gasping breaths rasping out of her throat. Don't lose control. Eye on the ball. Focus. Don't lose . . . don't lose . . .

"You're not going to just come," he murmured as he discarded her jeans and panties then moved over her, above her. "You're going to come *for me* and *only* me."

Her pulse stumbled. "No," she moaned. "No, stop." She couldn't do this. She couldn't let him in, couldn't let him shatter her control . . .

His hands, gentle as they slipped between her thighs, urged her to relax her tensed legs. "Come on, Ky, open for me."

She resisted, biting into her bottom lip as she fought against what her body so desperately wanted. "Stop."

Shifting, he slid his hands up her ribs to her breasts, where he massaged and kneaded, his thumbs stroking repeatedly over aching, ultrasensitive nipples. "Stop this?" he asked, then lowered his head and sucked one between his lips, his tongue pressing it against his teeth then letting it go with a small, back-bowing pop. "Stop this?"

His mouth settled on hers again, his tongue gentle but insistent as his fingers danced over her ribs and belly, caressing and wearing down her resistance, clouding her mind with a need so intense she couldn't remember why she tried to defy it. This was good. This was *Chase*.

Her legs drifted open, and in the next instant, his hand was there, touching her, worshipping her with his fingers. She arched into the spear of sensation, a small cry escaping before she could suppress it.

"That's it," he murmured, firming his caress. "That's it. Just let me in."

His teeth nipped at her earlobe, then the muscles that corded along the side of her neck. The whole time, his fingers stroked, caressed, probed.

At the first involuntary buck of her hips, he withdrew his fingers, and she thought, yes, yes, ready for the next part, always ready for that. But instead of stripping off his jeans, he began kissing his way down, over her breasts, down her flat belly, until his mouth hovered above the aching, throbbing part of her that wept for him. He used his hands to nudge her legs farther apart, blew gently against her sensitized flesh. As she arched her head back against the pillow, surrendering to him with a helpless moan, he lowered his mouth. And became merciless.

She dug her fingers into the sheets, biting her lip to try to stop the whimpers catching in her throat as she strained against the stroke and dart of his tongue, the caress of his lips, the gentle bite of his teeth, while the building passion tensed her muscles to the point of pain. Her breathing grew harsh and ragged, and he sank his fingers into her hips, lifted them to still her restless movements. Oh, God, right there, right *there*.

Her body snapped taut as pleasure burst inside her, waves and waves of it rolling through her like convulsions. Then he braced over her on one hand, kissing her again, using his tongue on her mouth the way he had between her thighs moments before, his free hand caressing her breasts until pleasure spun through her all over again.

"Tell me what you want," he whispered, tenderly kissing her jaw, the side of her neck, his tongue glancing off the frantic pulse in her throat.

She tried to breathe, to think. Every nerve in her body throbbed, and there was more. She knew there was so much more, and she wanted it. She wanted it all. With Chase. Forever.

"Tell me," he said, his lips barely touching the corner of her mouth.

She swallowed, her body humming, vibrating as his hand stroked down her ribs in a feathery caress. "I want you," she breathed. "I want you inside me."

His lips curved, and he moved to shed his clothes then settled against her so that he rested hot and hard at her entrance. He stroked her first, and she lifted her hips, inviting, wanting, and sighed as he guided himself to her. Braced above her, with only one thrust separating them from being joined, he paused and breathed deeply, then kissed her, his tongue stroking against hers and retreating, all the while holding himself back from her.

She grasped his hips, tried to take him in on her own, but he angled his hips back, denying her what she so desperately wanted.

"Please," she whispered, mindless and not caring that she was begging. "Please. I need you."

He looked into her eyes. "Say my name."

She didn't hesitate. "Chase," she said. "Chase."

He smiled and rewarded her with a long, slow thrust. Her breath hitched at how good it felt, how good he felt. Her answering moan turned into a strangled gasp as he eased almost entirely out and slid back in, maddeningly slow.

"Oh, Christ, you're so tight, so hot," he growled.

She sank her nails into his lower back, arching under him, trying to quicken the pace. She was already . . . so . . . close.

But he seemed intent on tormenting her with slow, easy

strokes, each thrust grinding his hard length against flesh so sensitive that a mini flare of fireworks went off inside her. She dropped her head back, her breath fast and desperate. Another orgasm was building in glorious waves, and she felt her body tense around him in preparation. Oh, yes.

But then, abruptly, he stopped moving, his breathing rough as he pinned her hips to the mattress, stilling her restless, frantic movement with his superior weight. Drawing her hands from around his waist, he trapped her wrists on either side of her head and kissed the corner of her mouth, her temple, her forehead.

She strained against him, nearly sobbing with frustration. She was so close, and yet he refused to move, to shoot her to the stars. "Please, Chase. I can't take it."

His breath, his lips, caressed her face. "Look at me."

She opened her eyes, focused on his glittering green gaze. What more could he want? She was giving him everything she had, letting him destroy her with every mind-blowing stroke.

His mouth curved, and she heard him swallow. She tugged at her wrists, wanting to run her hands over the muscles bunched in his back, over his smooth, tight butt. If he didn't let her come soon, she was going to scream.

"I love you, Ky."

She stopped breathing, stared up into his eyes. Her racing heart skipped several beats before continuing at an even faster pace. What? *What?*

He dropped his forehead against hers, his breathing ragged and uneven. He shifted a little, kissing her gently at the same moment that the movement wrung a small gasp from her. "I love you. More than anything, Ky, more than life." He gave another mind-spinning, neck-arching thrust only to stop again, to pin her motionless. "But you can't live like life's a tennis match you have to win at all costs. It's okay to lose, Ky. And it's okay to lose control." He swallowed hard, obviously struggling against his own body's demands. "Right now, you're out of control, and it feels

good. It feels right. That's how it's going to be with us. I'm
going to make sure of it. Because I love you."

He began to move again, more firmly now, gathering her
against him and holding her as he pumped into her, again and
again, faster and harder, until the world exploded into frac-
tured prisms of light. He followed immediately, his body
jerking against hers as a long, harsh groan escaped through
his clenched teeth.

He collapsed against her and rolled so that she lay across
his chest. They were both panting, gasping. Every so often,
she felt a small, breath-stealing jolt where he was still inside
her. As her senses returned, the lump in her throat caught her
off guard, and she swallowed against it. Like the orgasm,
uncontrollable emotion was building in a wave.

Chase loved her. *Chase loved her.*

Oh, God, she was going to lose it.

She pushed at his chest but was dismayed to realize that
he had his arms wrapped securely around her, his fingers idly
stroking the damp skin of her back. His touch was so reverent, so loving, that it tipped her world the rest of the way on
its side.

"Let go," she said, appalled at the jagged-glass sound of
her own voice.

His hands stilled. "Ky—"

He broke off as she scrambled away from him—giving
him no choice but to release her—and off the bed. Her wobbly knees almost buckled, and she caught herself with a hand
on the mattress before bending to grab her shirt off the floor.
She needed to get out, get away. Now.

She jammed her arms into it and looked around for her
underwear. Finding it, she jerked it on while he shifted onto
his side and propped his head in his hand, watching her with
a speculative expression, as if this were exactly what he'd
expected.

Seizing her jeans, she ignored him and pulled them on.
She was done with these mind games, done with everything.
As soon as Quinn was cleared, she'd move back to LA, pick

up where she left off. Blessed peace. That's all she wanted. Peace.

"I love you," Chase said softly.

Her heart banged against her ribs like a wild, frightened animal, and she closed her eyes. "Stop it."

"Stop loving you? Not going to happen. I tried that. It didn't work."

She shook her head, fought for balance. "This is . . . this is . . ."

"What? Come on, Ky, spit it out. Tell me what this is. Tell me how I'm wrong. Tell me you don't love me. Tell me to fuck the hell off."

Whatever control she'd managed to regain spun out of her grasp as she grabbed a pillow that had ended up on the floor and hurled it at his head. "Fuck the hell off!"

He caught the pillow, a huge smile curving his lips. "Excellent."

She stared at him in open-mouthed shock. He was smiling, beyond pleased with himself. "Are you seriously *enjoying* fucking with my head?"

His smile scaled back, and he cocked his head. "No, actually. I'm not. But if this is what it takes to get to you, I'll do it. Because I love you."

A hard surge of helpless anger and despair surged into her throat. "You *know* we won't work."

"And why the hell not?" He snapped it out, his easygoing smile gone as he shoved off the bed and took a step toward her. When she flinched almost violently back, he backed off, hurt softening his features. But then they hardened again, with anger, with frustration, and he turned away to snag his jeans from the foot of the bed.

"This is about you, Kylie," he said as he yanked them on. "What *you* want. What *you're* doing. You're the only one saying it won't work. Why? Why are you fighting me? Fighting *this*?"

"I can't be who you want me to be!" she shouted at him, shocking them both. "I can't be this person, this . . . this *emo-*

*tional* person. I can't do it. I can't." Sinking down onto the bed, she covered her face with her hands, horrified when a dry sob burst out of her throat. "I'm not worth all this . . . *effort*. You're wasting your time."

"Oh, God, baby, that's not true." He knelt at her feet, grasped her head in both of his large hands and urged her to raise her chin, to look at him. She kept her eyes closed, unable to bear seeing herself reflected in his eyes.

"I love you," he said, his guttural voice fracturing with emotion.

She squeezed her eyes more tightly closed. "I don't know how to do this. I never did."

"It doesn't matter. Just let it out." He tightened his grip on her head, leaning forward to nuzzle her cheek with the tip of his nose, then the line of her brow before pressing whisper-soft kisses on her eyelids. And then his lips settled on hers, tentative at first, then growing more demanding, more aggressive, until she opened her mouth on a helpless moan, powerless to resist him. His tongue met hers, stealing her breath, her heart.

"I love you," he murmured against her lips, drawing her off the bed and gathering her onto his lap on the floor, holding her close, secure.

He loved her. God, he loved her. And it made her feel so full, full to bursting. She'd missed him, missed this, and now she couldn't remember why she'd tried so hard to deny it, deny him. Always so stupid and stubborn and . . . determined to not let anyone in. But this, his arms around her, holding her together as she fell apart, this felt right. Maybe she *could* do this. As long as Chase was there.

Except Quinn . . . oh, God, Quinn. Chase had a job to do, and her brother would pay the price. How could she . . . how could she . . . it was too much, too much.

As she began to shudder, she felt a single tear trickle down her cheek only to be stopped by Chase's warm lips. His thumb, warm and gentle, grazed the shell of her ear, her jaw, the side of her neck, and settled into a steady caress over the throbbing pulse in her throat. More tears began to fall, tears she'd held back for so long and could no longer suppress.

He rested his forehead against hers, and she felt his warm, moist breath against her cheek, followed by the feather brush of his lips. "It's okay. I'm here. You can let go."

# 39

CHASE TIGHTENED HIS ARMS AROUND HER AS SHE began to weep, the violent hitches in her breath clawing at him. She cried the way she played tennis, all-out, go-for-broke fury, as ten years of grief and frustration poured out of her in a hot, gasping rush. He stroked her hair, her arm, her hip, his cheek pressed to the top of her head while her tears drenched his skin. And the whole time, relief hummed through him. She'd surrendered. Everything would be okay now. *They* would be okay.

She quieted after only a few minutes, too soon in his opinion, considering everything she'd been suppressing for so long. He kept holding her, stroking her, until she eased away from him and wiped at the moisture on her reddened cheeks. She avoided his eyes, but that was okay, he thought. Baby steps. He could wait for her to tell him what she needed. No matter what it was, he vowed, he'd give it to her.

When she spoke, her voice was hoarse. "I think someone else should protect me."

He went still. No way in hell was he giving her *that*, not when the thought of losing her made everything inside him go black and silent.

"That's not an option," he croaked. No fucking way was it an option.

Fresh tears welled into her eyes, making them bluer than Caribbean ocean water. "I can't do this anymore. I can't handle ... this ... with you at the same time that Quinn ... I just ... can't." She closed her eyes, and a lone tear dropped down her right cheek. "I'm tired. I'm so tired."

His heart wrenched inside his chest. Love, *his love*, should have made her stronger, not weaker. Why couldn't she see that?

She opened her eyes, looked into his. "I can't choose, Chase. I can't choose between you and Quinn."

His throat clogged, and he clenched his fists at his sides. He wanted to grab her, shake her, make her understand that without her, he was nothing. And, without him, she was empty. He could fill her up, make her whole, if only she'd let him.

"I'm not asking you to choose," he replied, fighting to keep his tone steady.

"If Quinn goes to trial, you'll be gathering evidence. You might even get on the stand and testify about how you think he's a monster. And if I'm with you ..." She trailed off, as if for a moment she couldn't make herself say the words. "If we're together," she continued, stronger now, "it will look like I believe it, too."

He curled his hands into fists, desperate to reach out to her, to pull her to him and hold her until this insanity went away. "I don't understand, Kylie. Make me understand."

Her eyes were still damp, but her tears had stopped falling, and her gaze had become unwavering. "He's my brother."

The twisting in his chest returned, only this time it was accompanied by anger. She said she couldn't choose, but she had.

She got to her feet, and he rose, too, unable to stop himself from advancing on her. He ignored her surprised expression, the way she backed away, and grabbed her by the arms, hauling her forward until her fists were pressed against his chest and her red-rimmed eyes were wide with surprise. He wanted to hurl angry words at her like stones, wanted to kiss her until she was pliant and yielding, until she surrendered to him all over again. He wanted her weeping and broken in his arms, not stoic and unflinching, denying his love and begging him to let her go.

But he couldn't, damn it. He couldn't let her go, not again, not when they'd been so close, when she'd been so open.

And then her faint wince, the flicker of her eyes, broke through his fury, and he realized how tightly he held her, realized his fingers would leave bruises. He released her and backed off. Turning away, he jammed a hand through his hair while shame merged with his frustration. It would take years for a trial to play out, years before Quinn would be declared innocent or guilty. Fucking *years*.

"Chase, please," she said, her voice shaking. "I'm sorry—"

"Don't." He faced her, and his features felt stiff, not his. He tried to give her the game face, the one she used so well on him, but he wasn't certain he managed it, not when everything inside him burned. Love hurts? Yeah, it hurt like hell. He felt like an idiot at how much it hurt, how much he wanted her to hurt right along with him.

"I thought you were strong," he said. "But you're not. You're a fool."

She took a startled step back, as if he'd raised a hand to strike her.

Unable to look at her, to watch the wounds his words caused, he snatched his shirt off the floor. "Weak people run away from love," he said, shoving his arms into the sleeves and shooting the first button through its tiny hole. "*Weak* people. You did it ten years ago, and you're doing it again now."

He looked at her then, strong enough now in his self-righteous anger to see the effects of his arrow-tipped words. All the emotion, and color, had drained out of her face. Her eyes, her lovely, blue gray eyes, so big and vulnerable and damp earlier, had gone flat, as expressionless as cool steel.

He wanted to take it all back, hold her until all the hurt went away. He moved toward her, ready to babble out an apology. He'd say anything to bring the shining light back into her eyes. But she edged back.

"You're right," she said, her voice low and trembling. "I should have been stronger."

He closed his eyes, lowered his chin. God, he was a dick. And he couldn't take it, couldn't stand having her look at him with that blank expression. He'd thought earlier that he'd finally won, that she'd surrendered to him, to love. But he'd been wrong. Match fucking point. She'd won again.

He walked out of the bedroom without looking back.

# 40

AS RAIN CONTINUED ITS DELUGE OUTSIDE THE kitchen window above the sink, Chase jerkily washed up the dishes from the night before. He didn't realize how violent his actions were until the stem of the wineglass he was washing snapped in two in his hands. As he watched his blood swirl down the drain—just like everything he wanted with the woman he loved—his cell phone started to ring on the counter beside him.

Wrapping a dish towel around his hand—luckily, the wound wasn't deep—he snatched up the phone and flipped it open. "Manning."

"Chase, it's Sylvia Jensen." She sounded as if she'd called from inside a hurricane zone.

He turned away from the sound of rain thrashing the window on his end and covered one ear to hear her better. "Where are you?"

"At the tennis center site."

"In the rain?"

"The rain's caused some trouble over here."

"What kind of trouble?"

"There's been some major flooding that ... well, it's turned up a body."

"What? A *body*?"

"Wrapped in a tarp," she said, "so it's been mostly protected from the elements, though everything has gotten pretty wet. I can't do anything with it in this weather, so it's being transported to the morgue."

His head was still spinning. "A body? Are you kidding me?"

"I'm thinking it could be what our saboteur has been looking for."

"Holy shit." He turned to stare into the living room at the rain washing down the bay window.

"Hang on. I need to tell you something else." A slamming sound on Sylvia's end of the call was followed by a cessation of much of her background noise. She must have gotten into her car. "I ran that DNA from the shirt through the database right before I got summoned out here, so I didn't have time to call you about that. I'm sorry, but I didn't get any hits."

Chase's brain was still stuck on the body found at the tennis center site. So all that had happened to Kylie might have been about a murder, not her attack ... unless they were related. Shit, he thought. *Shit*.

"So you'll meet me at the morgue?" Sylvia asked.

He shook his head to focus his attention. "Of course. I'll give Sam a call and have him meet us there, too."

Sylvia sighed. "I have a feeling it's going to be a long day."

AN HOUR LATER, AFTER GETTING FELLOW COP Steve Burnett to stay at the safe house with Kylie, Chase arrived at the morgue in the basement of Kendall Falls General. The tropical décor—colorful fish, sea horses and starfish painted on ocean-blue walls—always caught him off guard, as if whoever designed the hospital decided the morgue should be extra cheerful to counter the cold grimness of corpses. It didn't help. The place was still cold as a freezer with an ambience that was just as stark.

He spotted Sam talking in hushed tones to Sylvia in a glass-enclosed office. They were both dressed in jeans and T-shirts, as if they'd thrown on whatever was available when their respective summonses had come.

As Chase approached, he glanced toward the room where he knew the body from the construction site would be laid out for examination. A tech was hunched over a mud-slathered pile of what looked like garbage on a metal table, meticulously scraping at something. Chase saw the young woman's breath in the chilled air, and he shivered as he continued on into the adjacent office.

"What have we got?" Chase asked as Sam and Sylvia greeted him.

Sylvia, trademark hoop earrings swinging, said, "Lucky break. The body still had ID on it."

Sam, who looked as if he had slept less than Chase had in the past several days, indicated a deteriorating wallet and its damp contents spread over a metal tray on the desk. "Driver's license and school ID."

Chase squinted his eyes, but the big type on the school ID struck him first and hardest: Kendall Falls High School.

"Name's Mark Hanson," Sylvia said. "Date of birth on his driver's license indicates he would have been twenty-seven this year."

Chase snapped a glance at Sam. "Ten years ago, he would have been in your high school class."

Sam nodded, his expression grave. "I didn't know him, but Quinn McKay might have."

Chase rubbed at the back of his aching neck. Great, just what the case needed. Another connection to Kylie's brother. "We'll have to bring him in and ask him."

"There's more," Sylvia said, nodding at Sam.

Chase looked at his partner, who consulted his notebook. "Missing-persons report was filed on Mark Hanson, age seventeen, about a week after Kylie's attack. According to the case file, the police never found him. Apparently, he'd run away a few times before, so no one suspected foul play."

"Who reported him missing? Parents?"

"Mother. Sheila Hanson."

"She still live in Kendall Falls?"

"According to her Department of Motor Vehicles' file, she's residing at the same address."

Chase nodded and closed his eyes. "We'll have to tell her we've found her son."

"That's not all," Sylvia said, her voice low and tense.

Chase swung his attention back to her.

"The medical examiner did a cursory examination of the body," she said. "The side of the skull has been crushed by blunt force trauma. We'll have to do more tests, but it looks like the weapon could have been a baseball bat."

# 41

KYLIE RAISED HER HEAD AND BLINKED AGAINST the light coming through the window, surprised to discover that she'd been sleeping on the floor with her back against the wall and her head on her knees. She felt disoriented and fuzzy, unsure at first where she was or what had awakened her. Then she remembered. Safe house. With Chase.

His angry words—*weak people run away from love*—rang in her ears, and she scrubbed her hands over her face with a long groan.

He was right, of course. She was weak. *He* made her weak. Weak and scared and pathetic. Everything she vowed she didn't want to be when she fled Kendall Falls ten years ago.

But what was she supposed to do about Quinn? He was her brother. She couldn't possibly betray him by allowing herself to love the man who would help put him on trial. She might not know anything about love, how to love, how to be loved, but she knew all about loyalty. Quinn was going to need hers, especially when the glare of the spotlight turned relentless.

She should have stayed in LA. If she'd known what awaited her at home, she wouldn't have done it. She'd have stayed where she was, head firmly buried in Venice Beach sand. But, no, she'd followed her heart. She'd thought she could fill up the emptiness inside her by reconnecting with her family, by reclaiming the life she lost when she left Kendall Falls. She'd known she would run into Chase, but she'd figured she could deal with it, especially if it were only an occasional thing.

Tired of her circling, no-win thoughts, she pushed herself to her feet, determined to rise above it all and carry on, and headed for the bathroom. A shower would clear her head, wash away the distracting, mesmerizing scent of Chase on her body and perhaps soothe the ache between her thighs that reminded her of what they'd done, what they did so well. What they could never do again.

He loved her.

She closed her eyes, pausing in the bathroom doorway and putting her hand out to steady herself. She was so tired, weary to the bone. Too much fighting, too much emotion. She needed her defenses, needed the strength that enabled her to shove it all away and ignore it. She was good at that. Not love. She'd never been good at love. She was good at tennis, competing. She was built for the game, for chasing down a ball and slamming it over a net, for strategizing how to defeat any opponent, for landing shots exactly where they needed to land. Love had nothing to do with it, other than a losing score. Neither did emotion. Just strategy and winning. She was, after all, what her father, her coach, made her.

In the bathroom, she stripped and stepped into the shower. As the water sluiced over her, anger, disappointment in herself, frustration with the ironies of life—all of it expanded in her chest, welled into her throat, spilling fresh tears down her cheeks. And that just annoyed her even more. Now that she'd started crying, she couldn't seem to stop.

Just as she'd feared. She'd let the dam break and now she

couldn't focus. Couldn't keep her eye on the ball. Couldn't breathe through the pain.

Thanks to Chase.

Who loved her.

She buried her face in her hands.

He loved her, and she'd hurt him. The memory of his face when she'd said she had to choose Quinn over him . . .

Seeing it again caused the ache in her chest to sharpen.

*"I thought you were strong. But you're not. You're a fool."*

A fool to think they could go back. A fool to think they could ever get it right. A fool to think she could handle the intensity of his love and passion.

He wanted too much, expected too much. She'd made a lifetime career out of suppressing and dodging and pretending. Changing those habits would be like winning a Grand Slam tennis tournament barefoot and with a broken racket.

Yet . . . he made it sound so easy.

*"Trust me."*

*"Let me help you."*

*"I love you."*

How could she just walk away from that? From him?

Was she really that big of a fool?

She pictured life after Quinn's innocence was proved. She'd have a new tennis center, assuming the bank didn't get cold feet with her credit line. She'd have her family to continue reconnecting with: Lara, Quinn and Jane. She'd hopefully have a long coaching career with T.J. Ritchie, if he'd have her.

And who would she share it all with?

And what would happen when she saw Chase with another woman? A woman capable of letting down her guard and loving him and giving him what he wanted. A woman who bore his babies and adored him as much as he deserved to be adored. A woman who wasn't her.

Reaching for the faucet, she yanked the water off and stood there, dripping and shivering, her arms wrapped around her middle.

No, that wouldn't work. That . . . that . . . wouldn't work *at all*. Not in a million years.

And she realized how completely she'd been kidding herself.

No way could she stay in Kendall Falls.

# 42

CHASE STRODE UP THE WALK TO THE MODEST peach stucco house, Sam trailing silently in his wake. Chase figured his partner dreaded telling this woman her missing son had been found dead as much as he did. Not that he could blame him. He hated this part of the job. Hated it almost as much as he hated that he'd left Kylie in the care of another cop when he could have let Sam handle this. But he hadn't felt like he could stay in that small house with her and not try to corner her all over again. That would just lead to more disaster, and he'd had about all he could take when it came to his bruised heart. For now, he needed to buck up and be a cop.

"Jesus, it's humid," Sam muttered behind him.

Chase nodded without glancing back. The tropical-like rainstorm had left stickier-than-usual moisture behind, making it feel as though they moved through thick steam.

On the porch, with Sam hanging out a few feet back, Chase pulled open the screen door to rap on the door with his knuckles. As he waited for an answer, he glanced around. The older neighborhood was one of the more popular areas in Kendall Falls to live. It had no sidewalks, and the uncurbed streets were narrow and overhung with banyan trees. But each house had its own, distinct character. Stately two-stories with two-car garages and fancy landscaping resided right next to low-to-the-ground one-levels with carports.

It was a stark contrast to the opposite side of town, where a dozen houses shaped by the same cookie cutter popped up in a week, all arranged neatly around the perimeter of a brand-new golf course.

A woman who looked about fifty opened the door and peered at him through the screen. The extra pounds she carried didn't detract from her pretty face, though her skin looked blotchy without makeup. Her short, light brown hair was parted on the side and had been recently highlighted. She wore blue stretch pants and an untucked, loose-fitting lavender blouse.

Chase held up his badge. "Detectives Chase Manning and Sam Hawkins, Kendall Falls Police Department. Are you Sheila Hanson?"

Her wary eyes settled on the badge for a moment before they tracked behind him to Sam and then back to meet Chase's gaze. "What can I do for you, detectives?"

"May we come in and talk to you?"

She opened the screen door and stepped back.

The inside of the house was cool and orderly, quiet except for the distant sound of a television tuned to a talk show, perhaps *Oprah*.

Chase didn't stall with small talk. "Ten years ago, you filed a missing-persons report on your son, Mark."

She nodded, her expression grave. "Yes. I . . . Have you found him?"

"I'm sorry to have to tell you this, ma'am, but Mark is dead."

She jolted as if he'd pinched her, and the color washed out of her cheeks. "Oh."

Chase reached out to give her shoulder a comforting squeeze. "I'm so sorry."

"How did he . . . I mean, how—"

"I'm afraid that it appears he was the victim of homicide."

Her hand flew up to cover her mouth, and her eyes immediately brimmed with horrified tears. "Oh my Lord."

Chase took her arm and gently steered her down a short hallway toward the living room. "I know it's a shock, Mrs. Hanson. Let's sit down, okay?"

As she perched on the edge of the sofa facing the TV, she picked up the remote control with a badly shaking hand and muted *Oprah*.

The living room was comfortable and free of clutter, the air scented with lemon furniture polish. As Sam hovered in the hall, studying a montage of framed family photos on the wall, Chase sat on a solid blue recliner adjacent to the matching sofa.

Pressing her lips into an emotion-stifling line, Sheila asked, "Would you boys like something to drink?"

"No, ma'am, thank you." Chase's heart went out to her. She'd just found out her son was murdered, and she still offered them drinks. Denial, maybe. Or just an ingrained urge to always be polite no matter what. Sort of like Kylie's need to always be in control.

She craned her head to see Sam as he joined them in the living room. "Detective?"

"No, thanks," Sam said.

Her sorrowful gaze lingered on him. "Are you—"

"I'm very sorry for your loss, ma'am," Sam cut in, and ducked his head, clearly uncomfortable.

Chase cleared his throat to save his partner from her continued sad perusal. "Mrs. Hanson, what can you tell us about Mark's behavior before he disappeared?"

She looked at Chase, shell-shocked and confused. "Why would someone kill my boy?"

"That's what we're trying to find out, but we do need to get some questions answered."

Sniffling, she blotted the outer corner of her right eye with one knuckle. "He wasn't a good boy, Detective. I hate to say that, but he wasn't."

"I understand."

"He had troubles," she said. "Drugs. He never told me, of course, but a mother knows these things."

"What kind of drugs?"

"I don't know. All I know is that they made him mean."

Chase remembered Kylie's account of the attack. She'd said that one of the attackers had seemed over the top calling the other one names: *"Giddy one minute and mean the next, like he was high."*

"Before he graduated," she went on, "he was getting into a lot of fights at school. He was so angry all the time." She plucked a Kleenex from a box on the coffee table. "I blame his father. He left us when Mark was ten." She delicately blew her nose before going on. "When Mark went missing, I thought he ran away again. He'd done that several times already, so I didn't report it right away. After about a week . . . he always came back by then, you see, and I was afraid the police would think I cried wolf too many times . . . but this time, after he was gone for six days . . . the most ever . . . I contacted the police." Her chin trembled, and she pressed the Kleenex to her lips. "And now he's dead."

Chase patted her shoulder in sympathy. The awkward gesture was inadequate, but he didn't know what else to do.

As she dabbed at her eyes, Chase gave her a few moments before he resumed his questions. "Do you have any idea who might have had something against Mark?"

"I don't know. Like I said, he got into fights, but I don't know anything about the boys he fought with."

"You don't remember any names?"

"I don't. I . . . I . . ." She teared up again and struggled for words. "I always assumed he started the fight, because of his attitude, so I didn't pay much attention to that. I should have, though. I mean, now that he's . . ." She trailed off and bit her bottom lip.

Chase tugged a fresh tissue from the box and handed it to her. "I have just a few more questions, if that's okay."

She nodded.

"Do you remember Mark ever mentioning anything about Kylie McKay?"

Her grief took on an edge of bafflement. "The tennis player? Like what?"

"Anything at all."

"They went to school together. I believe she was a year ahead of him."

"Did he have classes with her? Maybe talk to her sometimes?"

"I highly doubt it. She ran with the popular crowd. He didn't like those kids at all. Though, I do remember he had a little bit of a crush on her younger sister. What was her name? Judy? Jennifer?"

"Jane."

"Right, Jane. She wasn't like her sister. That's what Mark said anyway."

A new knot of tension began to form in Chase's gut. "Jane wasn't like Kylie how?"

She shrugged. "I don't know. Popular? He really despised that crowd. The 'in' crowd."

"Can you be more specific?"

"Specific how?"

"What, for instance, did he not like about the 'in' crowd?"

"Just, you know, the way a boy of normal means resents classmates that seem to have everything. Money. Designer clothes. Fancy cars. Friends who are cheerleaders and football players."

"Did he talk about resenting Kylie McKay specifically?"

Shocked realization made her mouth drop open. "You think my Mark had something to do with what happened to her?"

"I'm afraid his disappearance has become a part of the investigation into her attack, yes."

"Why?"

Chase hesitated before deciding the poor woman didn't need to be shocked if the news ended up in the paper because of a department leak. "Your son's body was buried at the same site where the baseball bat used in the attack was found."

"But that doesn't mean—"

"Of course it doesn't," Chase interrupted, giving her what he hoped was a reassuring smile. "We're just covering all our bases. I hope you understand."

"I can't imagine Mark had anything to do with what happened to her," she said. "That was . . . it was just vicious and brutal, and Mark might have been an angry young man, but he wasn't . . . he wouldn't . . . he couldn't have hurt anyone like that, especially a defenseless girl. I'm sure of it." Fresh tears spilled down her cheeks. "Do you think the people who attacked her killed my son?"

"We don't know, but we're going to find out." He paused as she blew her nose again. "Do you know if Mark knew or hung out with Quinn McKay?"

Her bloodshot eyes narrowed. "That's her brother, isn't it?"

Chase nodded.

"I saw those stories in the newspaper. He's the one who tried to cripple her, if you ask me."

Chase imagined the entire jury pool of Kendall Falls was similarly tainted. Not that he could do anything about it now. "Did you ever see Quinn and Mark together?"

She thought about it for a long moment. "Maybe."

Chase doubted it. At this point, the woman just wanted to cast the shadow of guilt off her own child. Which meant he'd gotten all the information he could from her. "Mrs. Hanson, do you have a photo of your son from just before he disappeared?"

Rising, she chose a framed photo from the top of the TV and faced him, her gaze imploring. "Will I be able to get it back?"

"Absolutely. I'll make copies and return it to you right away."

Her hands shook as she worked the photo out of the frame and handed it over.

Chase studied it briefly, taking in the dark brown eyes,

brown hair, acne and braces. The guy didn't look the least bit familiar to him, but he would have been a senior when Mark was a freshman, so that wasn't unusual.

"I often wonder how he'd look with straight teeth," she murmured.

# 43

KYLIE WAS FINISHING UP MAKING THE BED—
stalling, really, before venturing out of her room to face
Chase—when she heard a phone begin to ring somewhere
else in the house. It wasn't a regular phone, though. Someone
must have been calling Chase on his cell. But even the ring
tone sounded unfamiliar. When it continued to ring, she went
to the bedroom door and pulled it open. The house beyond
was silent until the phone rang again, coming from the
kitchen.

"Chase?"

She walked down the hall, wondering why everything was
so quiet. Surely Chase hadn't left her here alone. Had he?

In the doorway to the dining area, she paused, surprised to
see a uniformed police officer sitting at the table, his back to
her, his head down on the newspaper spread before him, as if
he'd fallen asleep in the middle of the Sports page. The cell
phone sitting near his hand chirped, but he didn't stir. Chase
must have been called to work, she thought, and called in an
officer to stay with her.

Or perhaps he'd decided he couldn't stand being near her

anymore and bailed. She wouldn't blame him. She'd irritated
the hell out of herself in the past few days. And, really, him
not being here made things easier anyway.

"Hello?" she said, then raised her voice when the cop still
didn't wake up. "Officer?"

She took another step, intending to shake his arm, but that
was when she noticed what looked like thick, red syrup dripping off the edge of the table under his arm.

Her brain stalled, refusing at first to attach meaning to
what that viscous liquid could possibly be. Blood? No way.
*Blood?*

"You're kinda dense, aren't you?"

The voice came from behind her. *Close* behind. She
whipped around, and several things registered at once.
Smooth, black ski mask. Black jeans. Black shirt. Bloody
knife.

*Bloody knife!*

She stumbled back with a gasp, her hip slamming against
the police officer's chair as terror and nausea surged into her
throat. Behind her, the officer's body shifted and slumped.
She whirled toward him, horrified, reaching out to try to
break his fall. She caught his dead weight, but it was too
much and she wobbled to her knees, unable to keep him
from pitching face-first onto the hardwood floor. Terrified—
thinking oh, God, he's dead, oh, God, he's *dead*—she threw
her weight against his side, trying to turn him over to check,
to see, knowing as she did it that it was crazy, that it didn't
matter. What mattered was the guy with the knife.

Then an arm hooked around her throat from behind and
jerked hard, tearing her fingers free of the cop's shoulder and
cutting off her air.

"I've been delivering messages for weeks now," the man
imprisoning her said, grunting between words as he dragged
her toward the living room, "and you haven't been getting it."

Choking, fighting the stars bursting in her head, she
grabbed on to the assailant's arm as her lungs started to burn.
Air. She needed air.

"All you have to do," he growled, "is get the fuck out of town and don't look back. But, no, you're too clueless. I fucking hate clueless."

She reached back with one hand, groping for something, anything to grab on to, perhaps eye holes she could jab her fingers into, to get him to loosen his hold, to let her breathe. When her hand skidded across the front of the cotton mask, she hooked and twisted her fingers into the material, hoping to get a hunk of hair, and yanked. The mask came free in her hand, followed by the attacker's gasp. "Shit!"

He let her go, and she dropped to her knees with jarring impact. The knife fell right in front of her, bouncing and skittering on the floor. She flung out a hand to reach for it, but the intruder swept his foot sideways, sending the blade on a long, smooth slide into the wall board several feet away.

She looked up at him and froze, realizing with a jolt that she could clearly see his face: pasty, unhealthy skin, with dark circles under red-rimmed eyes that were so light blue they were almost clear.

His panicked eyes locked on hers before popping wide with crazed disbelief, and he stumbled back as though she'd spit acid at him. "Fuck!"

Pacing like a wild animal now, he let out a tortured groan between his teeth. "Stupid bitch. Stupid, *stupid* bitch!"

She didn't plan to stick around to see his next move. Pushing to her feet, she lunged toward the living room and the fastest way out. He came after her in a heartbeat, the thud of his feet heavy as he chased her toward the front door and escape. He gained on her quickly and gave her a hard shove from behind, pitching her forward and off balance.

She hit the floor, palms skidding across the carpet, but didn't stay down. She scrabbled up and whirled to face him, panting and assessing. He lunged at her, and she feinted to the left, then surged right and past him, tearing back toward the kitchen and the back door. Any way out. That's all she needed. And a break.

Strong fingers dug into the back of her shirt and jerked backward. She stumbled back as seams gave, and as soon as the shirt ripped free in his hand and cool air washed over her back, she shifted balance and kept going.

She'd taken two more steps when he swept her feet out from under her. She went down hard on her hip, gasping at the agony that shot down her leg and instinctively curling forward around the pain. In the next instant, he was on top of her and, wrestling her desperately wriggling body onto her back, fell across her. He locked her in place, using his entire length to hold her down.

Fighting the panic constricting her lungs, she slapped at him, hitting at anything she could get at, all the while screaming for help in a voice that had already gone hoarse.

He reared back and backhanded her.

Pain burst in her jaw, and she went still, black spots bleeding across her vision.

As she lay there, stunned and tasting blood, he trapped her hands above her head and leaned over her, his breath hot on her face. Eerie eyes, glassy and unfocused, pupils huge, squinted at her from beneath sweaty blond hair.

Oh, God, he's *high*.

"You can identify me," he said, calm now, deadly. "Now I have to kill you."

# 44

"IT'S RED!" SAM SHOUTED.

Chase slammed on the brakes, stopping with a screech of tires several feet into the intersection. Throwing the SUV into reverse and checking the rearview mirror, he backed up a few feet. "Thanks. I didn't see it change."

"No shit. I don't know why you didn't just stay at the safe house with Kylie. I could have handled talking to Mrs. Hanson on my own."

"Kylie will be happier with me gone. She doesn't want me there."

Sam snorted. "Right."

Chase couldn't help but think about the last time he'd seen her—red-eyed from weeping but staring at him with that infuriating expressionless expression. He'd thought he'd had her, thought he'd reached her in a way that no one else had. But just when it seemed he'd broken through her defenses, wham, she'd pulled back and left him dangling in the wind. They almost had it. They *could* have had it all. And, damn it, he hadn't handled the disappointment well at all.

Gripping the steering wheel, he swallowed against the ache in his throat. "I hurt her, Sam. Deliberately. She rejected me, so I hurt her back. And then I walked out on her like a total dick."

Sam studied him for a long, silent moment. "You guys are never going to get it together, so why do you keep trying?"

Chase glanced at him with a rueful, sad smile. "I love her, man. This Quinn thing has fucked up everything. And what was that business from Mrs. Hanson about Jane?"

Sam shrugged. "Sounds like something worth pursuing, in my opinion. Two siblings ganging up on another. It happens."

Chase studied his partner for a moment. The guy didn't even seem engaged in the conversation, as if he didn't give a crap one way or the other whether this case got solved. But, hell, Chase had no one else to bounce his ideas off of. "Do you think Mark Hanson could have gone after Kylie to gain favor with Jane? It was no secret back then that Jane resented Kylie as much as Quinn did." But then he shook his head. "But, damn it, it doesn't make sense. Yeah, the three of them didn't get along all that great, but they were teenagers. Just because there was angst doesn't mean it had to lead to violence. And if Mark *was* one of the attackers, who was the other one and how the hell did Mark end up with his head bashed in?"

"Want to hear my theory?" Sam asked.

Finally. "Yes. My head's spinning."

"Quinn wanted to take his sister down. He got Mark to help, telling him that would impress Jane. Afterward, Quinn feared Mark would rat him out and killed him. Buried the bat and the body separately on the grounds of the Bat Cave and thought that was that. Fast-forward ten years, and his prodigal sister comes home with plans to build on the site where the evidence is buried. He freaks and does everything he can to keep it from being found."

"What about Jane?" Chase asked. "Does she know?"

"Could go either way. Maybe she was in on it, maybe not. We'd have to question her."

Chase nodded. Sam made good points. Chase didn't like them, but they were still valid. But, damn, Kylie was irked enough by his focus on Quinn. Once he turned his attention to Jane—

"I know I've said it before, but I think you should back off on this case," Sam said. "You're not objective. And Kylie'd be happier. Hell, you'd both be happier."

"She'd still probably consider it guilt by association as long as I'm part of the police department investigating her family. No matter what I do, she'll find an excuse to push me away."

Sam sighed. "Then do whatever the fuck you want to do and quit bitching about it."

Chase cast a quick, surprised glance at him. "What's up with you? You've been off lately."

Sam rubbed at his eyes. "Don't worry about it. You've got enough on your plate."

"Sam, come on. I need you focused, and you're—"

"Tina left me. She took the boys."

Chase stared at him, stunned as Sam lowered his head and stared down at his fidgeting hands. "What happened? I mean, Jesus, Sam, I'm sorry. When? Where did she go?"

Sam gave an almost undetectable shrug. "A couple of weeks ago. They're staying with her parents in Orlando."

"A couple of *weeks*?" Jesus, no wonder the guy hadn't been himself. And Chase had been so wrapped up in his own drama that he hadn't noticed his friend was hurting. Way to go, bonehead. "Why didn't you say anything?"

"I thought she'd be back by now."

"What happened?"

"I messed up. I messed up, and she left me."

Ah, hell. That didn't sound good. Chase didn't know what to say to that. Had Sam cheated? He couldn't imagine. His partner seemed so devoted to his wife and kids that Chase had admired, and envied, him at times.

"She'll come back," Sam said suddenly, adding a nod of conviction and shaking his hands apart as though to rid them of nerves. "She has to. She can't keep my kids away from me."

Chase sensed an undertone of despair in the words, and then Sam glanced at him, a sheen of something—tears?—in his eyes.

Chase shifted in the seat and grabbed his cell phone off his belt to call Kylie. He already knew what he'd say: I'm sorry I was such a dick.

KYLIE, BREATHING HARD AND TRYING NOT TO panic—focus, focus, focus—waited, trapped by the weight of her attacker and unable to move.

She was going to die. Like this, right now, right here, and her first regret had silky dark hair and piercing green eyes. She'd wasted so much time, so much . . . everything. Chase loved her, and all she'd ever done was push him away and hurt him. What was wrong with her? She was the biggest, blindest, most stubborn idiot on the planet to run away from love, especially with Chase Manning. She should have run *toward* it, toward *him*. As fast as she possibly could. Now it was too late.

Her attacker changed his grip and shifted to grind a growing erection against her hip. "Before I kill you," he hissed near her ear, "what do you say we have us some fun?"

Her heart stopped—oh, God, oh, God—but she forced herself to stay still, not daring to breathe, biding her time for the perfect moment to fight back. She had to do this right. He'd already proved he was stronger and faster. To survive, she'd have to outwit him.

"You're going to scream when I come," he breathed, his nose in her hair.

Her muscles twitched, and when he released one of her wrists and started to fumble with the button on her jeans, stark, raving fear took control and she began to fight him blindly, biting, scratching, hitting, until he reeled back and partly off her, letting her remaining wrist go and raising his hands to protect himself. She shoved and pushed, grunting with the effort, until she could roll over onto her stomach. Just as she lurched to her feet, the cell phone on the dining room table began to chirp again, making her attacker roll to his knees and twist toward the sound, strange blue eyes wide with surprise.

Kylie dove for the phone on its second ring.

He rammed into her from behind, and they both skidded across the top of the table, crumpling the newspaper and smearing through the police officer's congealing blood, and tumbled to the floor. The attacker landed on top of her, hammering the air out of her lungs.

She fumbled the phone and, paralyzed and gasping for breath, watched it smash against the wall and break apart in the middle of its third peal.

Damn it!

Before she could gulp in air or even begin to struggle, her assailant hauled her to her feet and dragged her, kicking and squirming, into the living room, where he slammed her back against the wall hard enough for black and red spots to splotch her vision. Bracing a bloodied forearm against her throat, he leaned hard into her until everything began to gray.

"You'd better behave or you're dead right now. I'll fuck you dead. I don't give a shit. You'll still be warm and wet."

Terror spiked right into her brain. She couldn't breathe . . . couldn't . . . "I'll behave," she choked out, fighting the spreading dark. "Please, I'll behave."

He eased back, his grin spreading, turning lecherous as he squeezed her right breast through her bra. "That's my girl. Relax, it's going to be the best you've ever—"

Sudden, frantic pounding on the front door jerked his head around.

"Kylie!"

Chase. Thank God!

Kylie brought her knee up with lethal aim and nailed the son of a bitch right in the dick. Howling in pain, he dropped back from her and to his knees, hands cupped around his crotch as his face faded from bright red to dead white. "Bitch!" Spittle flew from his lips.

She edged sideways along the wall, focused entirely on Chase shouting her name, not ten feet away on the other side of the front door. But the intruder blocked her way, and as she tried to slip by him, he lurched to his feet, yelping in pain, and lunged at her.

CHASE JAMMED THE KEY INTO THE LOCK AND drove his shoulder against the front door. Kylie's scream, followed by a loud thud and silence, rang in his ears. "Police! Open up!"

Behind him, Sam frantically called for backup.

The door flew open, and he and Sam roared through it in tandem, guns drawn.

Chase's heart stopped when he saw Kylie on her back on the floor, unmoving, her head turned away from them. Blood was all over her. White noise began to roar in his ears.

A crash from the kitchen snapped Chase's head around and sent Sam tearing in that direction. "I'm going after him," Sam yelled.

"Wait for backup!"

"Check the house!" Sam shouted back.

An instant later, Sam thundered, "Shit!" And slammed out the back door.

Chase raced through the house, gun braced in a badly shaking hand as he quickly searched for intruders, every second feeling like an eternity. His need to get back to Kylie was desperate, mind-numbing, but he had to make sure the house was clear, that no one remained who would sneak up on him. But, God, *Kylie*.

He found Steve Burnett in the dining area, more blood everywhere. The man was dead, and Chase moved on without letting himself feel anything. There wasn't time. Not yet, not when Kylie was in the other room, unconscious and bleeding.

Satisfied the house was empty, he ran back to the living

room, shoving his gun into his holster, and knelt beside her.
Jesus, so much blood, all over her, and her shirt . . . he remembered seeing it in tatters on the floor somewhere. The
motherfucking son of a bitch bastard had ripped it right off
her.

Hands shaking, he pressed two fingers to the side of
her smooth, pale neck. A pulse, please God, I need a pulse.
Please.

Yes, there it was. Strong and steady. His shoulders
sagged, and he let out a choked sound of relief. "Thank you."

She stirred, eyes fluttering. "What . . ."

He smoothed his hand over her hairline, stroked her brow,
her cheek, to reassure her. "It's okay," he said. "You're okay.
I'm here."

He scanned her body, ran his hands over her, looking for
the source of all the blood. Had she been shot? Stabbed?
What? When he found no wounds, he realized the blood
wasn't hers. It was *on* her, as though she had rolled around in
it, but it wasn't hers.

And then her blue gray eyes opened fully, and even dazed
they had never looked so stunning to him. His heart swelled,
huge and hot, right into his throat. Relief had never felt so
overwhelming. "Hey," he said softly, and smiled.

"Hey," she breathed, then turned her head toward the dining area. "There's a police officer . . ."

That was when Chase saw the dark red blood soaking the
beige carpet under her head. His heart knocked hard against
his ribs. Oh, *shit*.

She tried to sit up. "He's . . . I think he's . . ."

He pressed her shoulder down, shaking again. She's
bleeding. Kylie was *bleeding*. "You gotta stay still, baby.
Ambulance is on its way."

"But the officer . . ."

He lowered his forehead to hers, closed his eyes as he
held their clasped hands against his pounding heart. He heard
the sirens in the distance. Hurry, hurry.

"Everything's going to be okay," he murmured, pressing
his lips to her damp skin. "It's going to be okay."

His cell phone rang, and he glanced at the caller ID window without letting Kylie go. Sam. Relieved, he flipped open the phone with one hand. "Please tell me you got him."

Sam was out of breath. "I got him. The fucker's dead."

# 45

CHASE COACHED HIMSELF TO KEEP BREATHING AS he paced the width of the tiny, windowless hospital room then about-faced and strode the four steps back. Small and airless, the room was filled to the brim with a bed, a brown vinyl chair with a nicked-up wooden frame and a corner workstation stocked with simple medical supplies. The sharp odor of disinfectant scented the close space.

His black soles scuffed the white tile floor each time he pivoted, but he kept going, needing an outlet for the rage building inside him. He had to keep telling himself that Kylie was okay. She'd struck her head on the coffee table, and the resulting wound had bled like a bitch, but it was small, no stitches required. The ER doctor had ordered a head CT scan to check for more significant injury but said it was just a precaution.

He glanced at her, his stomach lurching all over again at the absolute whiteness of her still face. She looked small and vulnerable on the bed in the white hospital gown, an IV line snaking out of the back of her right hand. A clamp on her right index finger kept track of her pulse, its steady beat echoed by a monitor next to the bed. He told himself that the darkness of her hair made her look paler than she was, but that didn't stop him from grinding his teeth, especially when he focused on the fist-size smear of purple along her jaw.

The man who did that to her was dead. Sam had had no choice but to kill him in self-defense. And, at the moment, they had no idea who he was.

Chase tore his gaze away from Kylie and hooked his hands behind his neck, leaning his head back and closing his eyes as her account of what happened replayed in his head over and over. That bastard was going to rape her. And then he was going to kill her.

The rage dug his fingers into the nape of his neck until he felt his skin threaten to give under his nails. He needed to get a grip, get control. He was no good to her, to anyone, if he let violence take over. But, God, he wanted to pound the life out of someone, make someone *pay* for hurting her, for terrorizing her. It didn't help that her assailant was dead. *Nothing* helped.

"Hey."

He opened his eyes to see Kylie watching him with a small smile. He fought the urge to let his body fold, to fall to his knees at her bedside. Instead, he returned her smile with his own, lazy, "Hey."

Resting his hip on the edge of the bed, he stroked her cheek with the back of his hand. She was so warm, so alive, and the knowledge stirred up a new surge of gratitude. "How're you doing?" he asked.

"I've been worse." She turned her head against his hand, closing her eyes briefly as though his caress sustained her. Then she opened her eyes and met his gaze. "The police officer . . . he's dead?"

Rage and grief billowed up inside him like rolling clouds of choking black smoke. Steve Burnett had been a good man, a good cop. He nodded slowly. "Yes."

She absorbed the news with a soft, hitching sigh, tears welling into her eyes. "I'm so sorry."

He skimmed his thumb under her right eye, catching the first tear, amazed that she'd let it fall. "Shhh, it's not your fault. He was doing his job."

"That could have been you . . ."

He leaned forward and kissed her, so fucking grateful for the warmth, and responsiveness, of her lips. "It's okay. I'm right here."

She cupped his face with her hands and deepened the kiss, her tongue sweeping between his lips before she tore her mouth away and pressed her cheek to his and held him there, her fingers in his hair, stroking, holding, her body trembling.

He drew back to smooth away the tears spilling over her pale skin, marveling that she was letting herself cry. This was different. *She* was different. She wasn't trying to hide her emotion, wasn't even trying to control it.

"I love you," she whispered, her smile wet but glorious.

The words shook his world, made it light up like the sun had just exploded, and he almost laughed. He wanted to drag her against him, feel the beat of her heart against his body, rejoice in the simple fact that she was alive. But the threat of causing her discomfort held him back, so he cupped her chin, smiled into her eyes and responded with a gentle, reverent kiss.

He felt her sigh against his lips, and a shudder of want rolled through him. The reverence of the kiss turned desperate for a moment, and he had to force himself to back off, to let her breathe.

When they parted, they both shifted so she could snuggle against him, her head resting against his chest. "I'm sorry," she said, stroking her fingers over the triangle of skin exposed at his throat. "I've been a total idiot."

He closed his eyes and ran a hand lightly over her arm, her hair. Everything felt like silk, like life. "I can't argue with that," he murmured. "Can I ask what changed your mind?"

She drew in a shaky breath. "When I realized that I was going to die, all I could think about was how much time I wasted running away from love. Away from you."

His cell phone started to ring, but he tuned it out. Nothing was going to end this moment too soon. Nothing.

She lifted her head to look up at him. "Shouldn't you get that?"

"It can wait."

Smiling, she trailed a finger over his lips, laughing softly as he nipped at it. "We have a lot to work out. Quinn . . ."

He nodded as he drew her closer. "We'll figure it out, Ky. If anyone can, two strategists like us can."

He held her for a long time, listening to her breathe as she drifted in and out of sleep for about half an hour. Eventually, he'd have to show her the picture of Mark Hanson he'd stashed in his pocket. He'd have to ask her if he looked familiar to her at all, as a possible assailant from ten years ago. He'd have to ask her specific questions about the attack today, to try to figure out why the guy came after her in the first place.

"You're so tense."

He glanced down to see Kylie with her head back and gazing up at him, her eyes sleepy.

"No need to worry," he said, stroking the hair off her forehead. "That's just how I always am."

"Do you need to go do something?"

He smiled at the drowsy question. "Like what?"

"I don't know. Cop stuff."

"Are you trying to get rid of me?"

"Not already."

He sighed. "I do have a few questions I have to ask you, if you're up to it."

"Okay." She shifted off him and settled back against the pillows while he got up.

When she focused on him, she looked as tired as he felt, and he considered putting this off for a while longer.

"I'm fine," she told him and smiled. "And I'm not just saying that."

Drawing the photo of Mark Hanson out of the back pocket of his jeans, he handed it to her. "Do you recognize him?"

She peered at the picture for a long moment, her stillness telling him that she somehow knew she was looking at the photo of a suspect in her attack. "He's so young."

She raised her eyes to his, and they were so haunted that

unease settled in his stomach like a greasy burger. "Do you recognize him?" he repeated.

She looked back at the photo, and he heard her breath catch almost imperceptibly. "He's wearing braces."

"And that's significant because . . ."

"I thought at first that the one guy had a razor blade, or something, between his teeth, like he was going to use it to cut me."

A roar began in his ears. Jesus. Every time they talked about it, some new, horrific detail came out.

Her voice cut through the noise in his head. "I realized I was seeing braces, but I never mentioned it for the description. I don't think I even remembered the braces until now."

He tried to think clearly. "Could this be that attacker?"

"I don't know." She shook her head, frustrated. "You could show me a picture of anyone with braces and maybe it would ring a bell."

"What about his eyes?"

She tried to hand the photo back to him without looking at it again.

"Look at his eyes, Kylie."

Her gaze locked with his, and for a moment, her fear was so stark, so shocking, that his breath caught in his throat. This was Kylie McKay without her defenses, and it suddenly terrified him. What if he screwed this up? What if he let her down?

She dropped her gaze back to the photo and examined it until her forehead creased. "We might have gone to school together."

"His name's Mark Hanson. He was in Quinn's graduating class. Do you remember speaking to him or any kind of interaction?"

"It was a long time ago, but no, I don't think so."

"Could he have been a friend of Quinn's? Or Jane's?"

She arched a quizzical brow. "Jane's?"

"I'm just trying to prod your memory."

"I don't know. I mean, he does look familiar, but I don't

know why. I probably just remember seeing him in the halls at school. What makes you think he might have been one of them?"

"He's dead, Ky. He disappeared at the same time as your attack, and earlier today, his body was found at the construction site for the tennis center."

"Oh my God."

As she paled, he took her hand and stroked his thumb over the back of it as he delivered the rest of the bad news. "The side of his skull was crushed, possibly with the same baseball bat used on you."

She stared at him. "Then he was one of them."

"I think so, yes."

"And you think the other one killed him?"

"It's a strong possibility, yes."

She grasped his hand with both of hers and looked him straight in the eye, her gaze so intense his heart tripped. "Quinn is *not* a killer."

He used his free hand to cover their clasped hands. "Trust that I'll do everything in my power to help prove that. Can you—"

Loud voices outside the door, one of them high-pitched and pissed, cut him off.

Kylie cast him a panicked glance. "That sounds like Jane."

"I arranged for a guard outside your door. She can't come in unless you want her to."

"I can't keep my sister out . . ." She trailed off and sat back to rub at her forehead. "God."

"Head hurting?"

"A little."

He gently lifted her chin with his fingers and smiled into her shadowed eyes. She'd really had a crappy day, and it was painted on her face in the dark smudges under her eyes and the ugly bruise on her jaw. "A little?"

"More than a little," she conceded.

"Want me to run interference with Jane?"

"That's not necessary. I can handle her."

"How about I detain her for a few minutes to let you get your thoughts together?"

"That'd help."

He leaned forward and kissed her forehead. "Relax and let me handle things for you for a while, okay? I know you can do it, but you don't have to anymore, not alone."

She caught his face between her warm palms and kissed him on the lips. "Thank you."

As he closed her door behind him, he spotted Jane McKay in the hall, toe tapping in barely restrained impatience.

# 46

"HELLO, JANE."

Kylie's half sister wore perfectly creased khaki slacks and a tucked-in, sunshine yellow linen blouse, her blond hair brushed back behind her ears with bangs falling over her forehead. Her makeup looked freshly applied. She seemed oblivious to the nurses and orderlies buzzing around the nurse's station about six feet away as she eyed Chase as if she were the bull and he waved a fiery red cape.

"Are you the anal-retentive control freak who decided I need permission to see my own sister?"

"Kylie's fine," he said, ignoring her question. "We're waiting on some test results for confirmation."

Jane blinked and let her arms drop to her sides, as though she'd realized she'd let her frustration dictate her priorities. "What happened?"

"A man broke into the safe house and tried to kill her." He carefully watched Jane's reaction to his blunt words.

She took a step back, her hand going to her throat as the heightened color in her cheeks faded away. "And you're sure she's all right?"

"She has some bruises."

"Wait, she was at a safe house? Why?"

"It was a precaution."

"So if she was at a safe house, why wasn't she safe?"

"We're still sorting out what happened."

She squared her shoulders, the determined glint returning to her dark brown eyes. "Then I'd like to see my sister now, detective."

"I have a few questions first."

A blond eyebrow arched in challenge. "I don't have time for questions."

"Make time," Chase replied.

Jane, her chin inching up, shifted her gaze to the police officer standing guard at Kylie's door. "I'd prefer not to do this here, if you don't mind."

Chase glanced at the guard and angled his head. "Take a five-minute break. I'm not going anywhere."

Once the guy was out of earshot, Chase turned back to Jane. "How did you know Kylie was in the ER?"

Jane sighed. "I don't understand why this is necessary," she said, her voice low as she darted a glance around at the ER activity. A baby had started to cry somewhere behind one of the curtained cubicles. "You're acting like I've done something wrong just because I showed up to help my sister."

"Please answer the question, Jane."

"Fine. A friend of mine is an ER nurse. She called me, and I called Quinn. You can tackle him when he gets here, if you want. May I see Kylie now?"

"A few more questions first."

"This is ridiculous—"

"What's your relationship with Wade Bell?"

Jane sighed and folded her arms, looking away as she tapped her foot. "I know you already think you know, but you're wrong."

"Then set me straight."

She stared at the door to Kylie's room for a few moments. "Does she have to know?"

"I don't plan to tell her anything that's going to hurt her unless she asks me point-blank."

Jane's laugh was humorless. "You think my answer is going to hurt *her*? That's unlikely."

"The doctor told me he was with you yesterday morning."

"That's true. But there's no relationship."

Chase's patience slipped. "Perhaps you'd like to clarify."

Jane gripped the elbows of her crossed arms. "Wade and I spent the morning together, yes. But it was nothing." She looked away. "It was a mistake."

"How so?"

Her usual detachment returned, and she met his gaze head on. "I thought he wanted me, but he just wanted a substitute."

"A substitute?"

"Come on, detective. You're not that slow. He couldn't have Kylie, so he settled for what he thought would be the next best thing: me. And I was stupid enough to go for it. But joke's on me. He's still in love with her." Her voice cracked, and she stopped, a muscle in her jaw tensing. She gave him a pained smile. "Can you imagine? Twenty-six and still failing to measure up to big sister."

Chase felt a nudge of sympathy for her, but just a nudge. "You resent Kylie for that?"

Intense bitterness darkened her eyes to almost black. "Hell, yes. Who wouldn't? I've lived in her shadow my entire life. I was never as pretty. Never as athletic. Never as popular."

"Did you resent her enough to have her knee taken out ten years ago?"

"No, detective, I did not."

Her answer was so steady, so practiced, that Chase suspected she'd rehearsed it in front of a mirror. "Where were you when she was attacked?"

Jane pressed her lips together and shook her head before nailing him with a glare. "What's going on here? You can't pin it on Quinn, so you're going after me now?"

"Humor me."

"I was at the beach with some girlfriends."

"You didn't even have to think about it."

"I was wearing a brand-new fuchsia bikini, Banana Boat

sunscreen and cherry-flavored lip gloss. You tend to remember such silly details when you find out your sister's been attacked with a baseball bat."

He couldn't argue with that. He'd used the same psychology when he'd questioned Quinn. But Jane was also a psychiatrist and would know that such details stuck in a person's head after a traumatic event. "Do you remember where Quinn was?" he asked.

"We rode to the ER together."

"How did he seem?"

"Freaked out. Scared. Just like me and our parents. Except, unlike us, he reeked like cheap alcohol."

"So he was drunk."

"Yes," she said. "Very drunk."

"Did he drive or did you?"

"For God's sake—"

"Did. He. Drive?"

"I drove. I had my permit."

"And you drove because he'd been drinking?"

"*Yes*. What the hell is wrong with you?"

He didn't bother to explain that a lawyer would drill her the same way during a trial. "Did you know Mark Hanson?"

She faltered, obviously thrown. "Who?"

"Mark Hanson. He went to Kendall Falls High at the same time you did."

"I don't remember him."

"He was in Quinn's class. Maybe he was a friend of Quinn's?"

"If he was, I don't remember."

"Maybe he was a friend of yours?"

"*That* I would remember."

"Maybe he was a boy who paid attention to you, maybe indicated he liked you?"

"No boys *liked* me in high school, detective. They were too smitten by my sister. And, no, I didn't try to kill or maim her because of it. Are we finished here? I'd like to check on her."

Chase nodded and made a go-on gesture toward Kylie's

room. As she stiffly pushed through the door, he wrapped his hand around the back of his neck. Jane might be impatient and bitchy, but he detected no hint that she'd lied to him just now. None of the guilt radiated off her like it did Quinn. Of course, she could just be a really good actress, but he didn't think so.

Once the guard returned to Kylie's door, Chase walked down the hall a ways and checked his cell phone for the call he'd ignored earlier. Sylvia Jensen's name appeared on the phone's screen, but she hadn't left a message. He thumbed her number to call her back.

"Chase!"

Turning and looking up, he was surprised to see Sylvia hurrying toward him, earrings bouncing, a manila folder clasped in one hand. "I've got something you need to see right away. Is there somewhere we can talk privately?"

At the nurse's station, Chase asked a harried-looking red-head, "Is there an unoccupied room we can use for a few minutes?"

She shook her head. "I wish. We're stuffed to the brim. The staff lounge is down on the right, though. It's usually empty around this time."

As they walked side-by-side to the break room, Chase could feel the excited tension coming off of Sylvia. She had something *really* good.

The small lounge, basically a tiny kitchen with sterile, white appliances, barely had room for a small table with four chairs. As Chase closed the door, Sylvia dropped her folder on the table and flipped it open to several photos of Mark Hanson's skeletal remains with the tarp peeled back. The ratty jeans and T-shirt were remarkably intact. One photo was of a black stocking cap.

Chase reached for it with an intake of breath, and Sylvia nodded. "That was stuffed in his back pocket."

"Kylie said her attackers wore stocking masks like that."

"Look at his shirt," she said.

Chase's heart double-timed. The letters XXL—just as Kylie described—clearly stood out. "Mark Hanson was definitely one of them," he said through stiff lips. Son of a bitch was lucky he was already dead.

"And I've got good news," Sylvia said. She tapped a fingernail that hadn't seen a manicure recently against the image of the shirt, which looked thick with dried blood. "We've got two types of blood. One type belongs to Hanson, and the other isn't in the database. Incidentally, the second type of blood on Quinn McKay's gym shirt? Also Hanson's." She didn't wait for a response before she went on. "There's also blood on Hanson's braces and the tarp."

"On his braces?"

"Yes. He was hit repeatedly. The assailant hit him so violently that he left behind some tissue."

Chase's stomach flipped. "You mean a chunk of his hand?"

Sylvia smiled slightly. "A chunk would be an exaggeration. Let's just call it a large tissue sample." That's what Chase liked about her. She didn't mess with scientific terms and jargon. "Bring me a blood sample from Quinn McKay," she said, "and I can either put him at the scene or help you rule him out."

"What about comparing the tissue sample to Kylie's blood like you did before to see if there's a DNA match?"

"The evidence would be irrefutable with a sample from Quinn. Besides, don't you want to see how cooperative he is when you ask him for some blood?"

# 47

"CAN I GET YOU ANYTHING?" JANE ASKED. "WATER? Another pillow?"

Kylie shook her head, trying to tell herself not to get irritated at her sister's hovering. But Jane had been fussing with everything possible since she'd walked in ten minutes ago. The IV line, the bed coverings, the pillows. Kylie appreciated the efforts to make her more comfortable, but what she wanted most was . . . well, for Jane to go the hell away. Since that probably wasn't going to happen, she would have settled for Jane sitting down and being still.

"Hmm," Jane mused, staring at the heart monitor on the other side of the bed. "That was interesting."

"What?"

"When I asked if I could get you anything, your heart rate spiked."

Oh, hell. Here it comes. Her sister was going to psychoanalyze every twitch. "I must have jarred the thingie," Kylie said, holding up the hand with the sensor clipped to her finger.

"Nope, there it goes again." Jane fixed her with a scrutinizing stare. "You're stressing because I'm here."

"I'm stressing, period."

"Your pulse jumped when I walked in, and it's all over the place now. What gives?"

"I'm sure the third degree isn't helping."

"How am I giving you the third degree? I asked if you want a pillow."

"What followed was the third degree."

With a dramatic sigh, Jane plopped onto the vinyl chair beside the bed. "Fine. I'll just sit here."

Yes!

"Unless you'd prefer I leave."

Kylie most definitely would have preferred she leave, but when she noticed the hurt that Jane failed to hide, she felt like an ungrateful bitch. She needed to appreciate her sister more and get over the hovering. That was just Jane. "I don't want you to leave."

Jane smiled slightly. "Good, because there's something we need to talk about."

Kylie tensed, and she could tell by the way Jane's gaze drifted to the heart monitor that the damn thing had given her away again.

Jane gave her a retiring look. "I'm not going to strap you down and attach electrodes to your skull. I just want to talk."

Kylie tried to force her shoulders to relax. But she had trained herself to go on the defensive with Jane—or perhaps Jane had done the training. Either way, the routine was so ingrained it was like dropping into position to receive a serve from a power hitter. She knew that whatever came hurtling at her would be tough to return.

"I'm sorry," Kylie said. "I'm not myself."

Jane's snort somehow managed to sound delicate. "Please. You've been this uptight for a decade."

Kylie massaged her temple. "You know what I mean."

"Chase suspects me, you know."

Kylie dropped her hand. "Suspects *you*?"

"He just questioned me out in the hall," Jane said.

While Kylie didn't like the fact that he'd questioned her sister, she trusted that he was doing what he thought necessary. "He's doing his job."

"And it's his job to harass everyone in our family? Doesn't he know we've all been harassed enough? Who's next? He'll be all over Mom before you know it." She stopped, gripping the arms of the chair. "I'm sorry. I know I'm not helping."

The admission caught Kylie by surprise, and she sensed a shift in her sister's mood, as if she were doing some internal exercise to let the frustration go. After a long exhale, Jane said, "I had to leave a message for Mom about your . . . accident. She didn't answer her cell."

"You told her I'm all right, I hope."

"Of course. I'm not insensitive." Jane sighed. "I wish she'd already left for Rome so she didn't have to deal with all this, but she insisted on canceling her trip."

Kylie didn't respond. She would have done the same thing, but she didn't plan to argue with her sister.

Pushing up out of the chair, Jane started to pace beside the bed. "Mom's beside herself about Quinn's arrest."

"I know," Kylie said.

"I mean, we're talking about *Quinn*. He adores you. He would never have hurt you like that."

"He didn't adore me back then."

Jane stopped in midpace, her eyes widening with horror. "You don't think—"

"I'm just stating a fact. Neither of you liked me back then. Wouldn't you say it's pointless to pretend otherwise?"

They stared each other down, and Kylie played her sister's possible responses in her head. *Let's explore this further.* Or, her favorite clichéd shrink reply: *How do you feel about that?* Like total crap, thank you.

But Jane didn't say anything for a long moment, her expression unreadable. Then her gaze dropped away and she sat down, shoulders relaxing as though the sigh she released had been what had held them so stiff. When she finally spoke, her voice was quiet, and surprisingly sad. "That's probably the healthiest thing I've ever heard you say."

Kylie let her head fall back to the pillow. "Hallelujah. It's a breakthrough."

Jane's laugh didn't sound at all amused. "And the sarcasm is already back." She began to tap her fingers on the arm of the chair. "You're right, you know. Quinn and I resented you. But we were kids, and we had the emotional range of kids."

"I know that. I've always known that." And, damn it, she thought as she stared up at the ceiling, if she'd kept her mouth shut, Jane would have huffed out already, leaving her alone with the blessed silence.

"You know it wasn't your fault, right?" Jane asked.

Kylie looked at her sister, expecting the Dr. Shrink facade. But Jane's gaze wasn't shrewd or assessing. It was open, curious, concerned.

"Dad's the one who ignored us," Jane said.

"I know that."

"Then why do you feel so guilty about it?"

"I don't—" She broke off at Jane's slightly arched brow. Okay, yeah, she did feel guilty. And the guilt felt like a hard knot in her gut, as though a cancerous tumor grew there. The bigger it got, the more attention it demanded.

"Dad caused the tension in our household, Kylie. He's the one who made you the center of the universe. Not you."

"After I left, did he . . . did you . . ."

"Connect? No. The damage had been done. Neither Quinn nor I thought he gave a fig about either of us, so why bother? I mean, he tried, but it was too little too late at that point."

"I'm sorry."

"Still not your fault."

"I can still be sorry, though. You deserved better."

Jane gave her a tight smile. "Sometimes I think Quinn and I got the better end of the deal. No pressure to perform. No pressure to win. No pressure to please anyone. I don't know how you did it."

"I loved it. Every flipping minute of it. The ride was . . . incredible."

"You still miss it."

Kylie nodded with a sad smile. "Every day."

"Do you think the tennis center will fix that?"

"I don't necessarily think it's something that needs to be fixed. The tennis center will be something new that I'm passionate about, a way to channel my love of tennis. I think I'm going to love it more, actually, because it'll be about kids and other people instead of just me."

"And Chase Manning? Is he a passion?"

Kylie smiled. "Oh, yeah."

"As much as his cop attitude annoys me, I can see he's good for you. Really good."

"Yeah?"

Nodding, Jane put her hand on Kylie's forearm and lightly squeezed. "I have to tell you something about Wade."

"Oh?" Kylie arched a brow, surprised by the shift in topic.

Jane's cheeks pinkened. "He and I . . . well, we . . . uh . . ."

Kylie cocked her head, way ahead of her sister and amused at the way she so uncharacteristically fumbled for words. "Went to the mall?"

Jane rolled her eyes. "You know what I'm trying to say."

"Shared a corn dog? Started a rock band?"

Jane sat back and shook her head, feigning disgust. "I'm trying to be serious."

Kylie laughed. "He's a good man. I'm happy for you, Janie."

"Don't be. It's already over."

"What? You're kidding."

"He . . . well, he's not that into me after all. He's still stuck on you."

"Oh." Damn, damn and double damn. It was their younger years all over again.

Jane shrugged and pushed hair back off her shoulder. "It doesn't matter. I deserve a man who's devoted to me and only me. And I can thank Wade for making me realize that there's more to life than work. I'll always think of him as my wake-up call, even though he hung up on me." Then, her self-deprecation fading, she sat forward and clasped her hands before her. "Have you got a headache? Your eyes are squinty."

Kylie started to say the usual: I'm fine. But the headache had been building for the past half hour. "The pain is starting to drill through my right eye."

"Did they give you something for it?"

"Tylenol."

Jane rose, smoothing the wrinkles out of her slacks. "Tylenol's not going to do much."

"I noticed."

"If you want, I can go see if there's something stronger they can give you."

Kylie smiled. *If you want.* Jane was actually asking permission to help her out instead of barreling ahead. "Could you do something else, too?"

"Of course."

"Maybe find me something to wear out of here? My clothes are . . ." Covered with a dead man's blood. She swallowed and forced herself to focus. "My clothes are ruined."

Jane nodded. "Be right back."

# 48

SAM, A MANILA FOLDER UNDER ONE ARM, MET Chase in the hallway outside Kylie's room. "How's she doing?"

"Shaken up but looks like she's okay." Chase indicated Sam's folder. "What've you got?"

"ID on the attacker. Name's Benny Kirkland. Got a rap sheet as long as a full-grown gator. Drug offenses, assault, breaking and entering, petty theft, loan sharking."

"Please tell me there's a last-known address."

"Sorry. There's a brand-new McDonald's on that corner."

"Fuck." Chase ran a hand through his hair.

"You look like shit, man."

"Thanks," Chase drawled, irritated. "That's helpful."

"When's the last time you ate?"

"Food won't help solve this mother*fucking* case."

"I realize that, but we could grab something in the cafeteria while I fill you in on some stuff."

"I don't want to leave Kylie."

"There's a guard at her door."

Chase cast a glare at the guard, who straightened as if a drill sergeant had just fixed eyes on him, and then at Sam, who looked unmoved by his sour mood. "Fine," Chase muttered.

Sam fell in step beside him. "So what's next? Safetywise, I mean."

"I'm going to hire some security and rent a vacation house in Naples," Chase said as he pressed the "down" button at the bank of elevators. "Something that can't be associated with the police department."

"You think that's necessary? I mean, the guy stalking her is dead."

"Doesn't mean the bastard wasn't working with someone."

"Good point." Sam tapped the manila folder against his palm. "Do you need any help? I could hire security or even set up the rental, if you want. Maybe put it under my wife's maiden name? Get the rental folks to prepare it?"

Chase blew out a sigh. He'd been such an ass earlier, and now Sam was being a good friend. "That'd be fantastic. My hands are . . ."

"Full," Sam said with a sympathetic smile. "Very full."

Chase chuckled and nodded. "Yeah."

They didn't speak on the elevator ride down to the cafeteria level, and then they waited for the other occupants to exit ahead of them before stepping into the hallway and the scent of hospital food. Chase's stomach growled. Okay, maybe this was a good idea after all.

He cast a glance at Sam. "Sorry about the attitude back there."

"No need to apologize. I get it."

"It's just making me crazy, you know. How did that son of a bitch find her at a *safe house*?"

Sam raised the folder. "I've got an answer to that. But, first, we get food."

Ten minutes later, Chase bit into his overdone cheeseburger and chewed. It was probably the worst burger he'd ever had, but it was fuel. He gestured at the folder Sam had set on the table. "So tell me."

Sam flipped open the file. "Like I said earlier, his name was Benny Kirkland. Twenty-five."

"And how'd he find the safe house?"

"He spent some time there himself."

Chase couldn't believe it. "You're kidding. He was a protected witness?"

"Yep. Busted for selling dope a year ago. In exchange for the name of his supplier, he walked. He spent about three months in protective custody."

"Why the hell didn't they lock him up in a cell for that time?"

"Safe house was part of the deal. The department keeps only two safe houses at a time. They recycle them every year or so. I don't know if that was the same house where Benny stayed, but it's got to be."

"Jesus. I made it easier for the bastard to find her than if I'd just taken her home."

"There's more. T.J. Ritchie's description of the man who tried to get him to bust Kylie's windshield? Fits Kirkland."

"Fuck." Chase stared at his decimated cheeseburger. He wondered when Kylie had eaten last. And whether she was sleeping. She had looked so tired. That bastard Benny Kirkland did that to her. He looked up at his partner and told himself not to be grateful Sam killed the guy. At the same time, he wished he'd been the one who'd chased Kirkland. He would have had the satisfaction of putting a bullet in that asshole's brain. And then he wondered . . .

"What?" Sam asked, eyes inquisitive.

Chase realized he must have been staring intently at his partner. "Did he have a gun?"

"Who? Kirkland?"

Chase nodded. "Kylie said he had a knife, but he dropped that in the kitchen. He said he was going to kill her, but he didn't pull a gun on her, and he no longer had the knife."

Sam's face flushed red. "So, what, you're questioning my self-defense call?"

"I don't doubt it was a good kill, Sam. I'm just asking."

"He tried to grab my Glock after I tackled him. We struggled, and I pulled the trigger. Fuck me, Chase. If he'd gotten my weapon away from me, I'd be the one wearing the toe tag."

Chase sat back and drained the rest of his can of Coke. What was his problem anyway? Sam had done the world a favor by taking out the pond scum who'd hurt Kylie as well as who knew how many other people. "Forget I said anything. My brain is fried."

Sam shrugged the tension out of his shoulders, but his face remained set in a scowl.

"So what's Kirkland's connection to Kylie?" Chase asked. Moving on was best.

Sam crumpled up his napkin and tossed it on his cleared plate. "I have a theory. If you're interested."

"Yes. Great."

"I took the liberty of looking into Quinn McKay's finances."

Fuck. That was *not* what Chase wanted to hear.

Sam, shuffling through a pile of papers, went on without noticing that Chase had stiffened. "He makes less than thirty-five grand managing the health club. He has no savings and a ton of credit card debt. The only thing he has that's worth anything is his home. That's doubled in value in the past several years, and, get this, he cashed out equity of thirty grand three months ago."

Chase sat forward. This was something he hadn't expected. "What'd he do with it?"

"Gambling? Drugs? Who knows? But my bet is he chucked away his equity, then went to a loan shark for more. Guess who has a history of loan sharking."

Chase's heart sank. "Benny Kirkland."

Sam nodded. "Bingo. So Quinn bailed on his loan, and Kirkland went after Kylie to force him to make good on his debt."

What Sam said made sense, yet something didn't fit. Or maybe Chase just didn't want it to fit because of Kylie.

"You don't look convinced," Sam said.

"I just . . . I don't know. Something's nagging at me."

"Can you be specific?"

"Nope."

"Then maybe you'll be convinced after you take another crack at him."

"Maybe."

"You want some backup?" Sam asked.

"I think it'd be better if I did it alone, at least at first. He's going to be intimidated by me because of Ky."

Sam pushed back his chair and stood. "If you say so."

Chase rose as Sam started to walk away. "Hey, Sam."

His partner turned back to him, clearly unhappy. "Yeah?"

"I appreciate your help on this. I know things suck for you right now and . . . I've been a major pain in the ass."

One side of Sam's mouth quirked up, and the annoyance that hooded his gaze lightened up. "And you think that's different than usual?"

# 49

As HE AND SAM GOT OFF THE ELEVATOR ON KYLIE'S floor, Chase spotted Quinn and Jane in a huddle, their heads close together and voices urgent but low as they talked.

"Speak of the devil," Sam muttered.

Chase didn't acknowledge the comment, more interested in the content of the two siblings' intense conversation.

Jane saw him first and immediately straightened. Chase didn't have to be a lip-reader to know what she said to Quinn: "Here's Chase."

Quinn turned, and Chase didn't like what he saw one bit. The other man's dark eyes were rimmed in red and bloodshot, his face pale and filmed with sweat. His clothes—denim shorts and a light blue polo shirt—looked as though he'd pulled them out of the bottom of a full-to-the-brim laundry hamper. Chase would have bet money that he'd been drinking away his problems again.

"Quinn, you got a minute?" Chase asked.

Jane's eyes narrowed to killing slits, but she said nothing as her brother nodded.

Chase gestured down the hall. "Let's talk in the lounge."

Before Quinn could take a step in that direction, Jane

grabbed his arm and whispered fiercely, and not too quietly, "Stop acting so guilty."

Quinn cast a miserable glance at her as his face reddened. "Would you just chill?"

"I'll *chill* when you stop acting like you did exactly what they're accusing you of."

"You don't know what you're talking about, Janie, so just shut the fuck up."

"Why don't you just go ahead and confess? You can spend the next five years moping around in prison. That'd probably be a good thing. You can dry out and get—"

"Jane," Quinn snapped.

She clamped her mouth shut and looked from Quinn to Chase and back again before cutting lethal eyes at Chase. "When this is over, we'll see you in court for harassment."

"Frankly," Chase said, "I'd be happy if that's the trial we end up at. Quinn?"

Chase strode to the staff lounge he and Sylvia had used earlier, Quinn a few steps behind him. With the door closed, Chase gestured at the round table surrounded by four chairs. Quinn sat without speaking and clasped his hands on the table's surface. His red eyes looked watery, as though he was trying to suppress tears.

Jesus, Chase thought. The guy was about to dissolve into a blubbering mess. And he reeked of alcohol.

Chase paced for a few moments, trying to get his thoughts in order. He wished he'd taken the time to check on Kylie. She could have grounded him.

Glancing at Quinn, he decided to cut to the chase. Pausing in his pacing, he gripped the back of the chair straight across from Quinn and leaned in. "We found his body."

Quinn barely twitched. "Whose body?"

"Mark Hanson's."

"Who?" Nothing but baffled confusion.

"He was buried on the construction site of the tennis center." Chase paused for dramatic effect. "His skull was bashed in by a baseball bat. Guess which bat."

Quinn jerked as if he'd been zapped by an electrical current. "What? Shit."

"You want to tell me how that happened?"

Quinn sat up straighter. "I have no idea."

Chase resumed pacing and crossed behind Quinn's chair. "Tell me about Benny Kirkland."

Quinn twisted around to watch him. "Who?"

"You heard me. Benny Kirkland. Drug-dealing loan shark extraordinaire."

"I've never heard of him."

Chase grabbed the back of the chair next to Quinn's, lifted it a few inches off the floor then slammed it down, satisfied when Quinn jumped. "Look, why don't we make this easy on everybody? Just lay it all out for me. You resented the hell out of Kylie for everything she was that you weren't and you got Mark Hanson to help you take her out of the game. Then what?"

"No," Quinn barked. "That didn't happen. None of it. No fucking way."

Chase pulled the photo of Mark Hanson out of his back pocket and slapped it onto the table in front of Quinn. "This is the guy. He was a friend of yours. You commiserated about how much you both resented Kylie, and then you ganged up on her and smashed the shit out of her knee."

Quinn stared down at the picture for less than a second then vigorously shook his head. "No. No, I don't know him."

"He was in your graduating class."

"There were almost four hundred people in my class."

"How'd it happen, Quinn? Did Mark try to blackmail you afterward, so you had no choice but to take him out?"

"No."

"Did he threaten to tell Kylie or perhaps your father or even me who tried to cripple her?"

"No!"

"Okay, then tell me about Benny Kirkland. How much do you owe him?"

"Nothing, damn it. I told you I've never heard of him."

"Come on, Quinn. You owed Benny money, and when you couldn't pay up, he went after your sister to force it out of you."

"No! I don't owe anyone any money."

Chase yanked a chair out and sat next to Quinn. Leaning forward, he looked Quinn dead in the eye. "You can't prove it. You can't prove any of it. And we've got the evidence that's going to put you away for a very long time. You're going to prison. Not just for assaulting your sister with a deadly weapon, but for murder. And you're not coming out. *Ever.*"

"Jesus." Quinn's voice broke, and he sat back, dragging both hands through his hair. "Jesus Christ. I didn't do it."

"Prove it."

"I can't!" Quinn surged up out of his chair. "I fucking can't!"

"Somebody bled all over Mark Hanson before he was buried," Chase replied, his calm stark compared with Quinn's slipping control. "We've got experts who'll testify that they're ninety-nine-point-nine percent certain that whoever did all that bleeding was the same person who killed him. We've got his blood and Kylie's blood on your shirt, Quinn, wrapped around the murder weapon."

"It wasn't me!"

"If you tell me how Mark ended up dead, I can help you. Maybe we can work a deal with the DA. You tell me what happened, and the judge goes easier on the sentence."

"I can't tell you what happened, because I *don't know.*"

"Then what's with the guilty act? What were you trying to tell Kylie before she shut you up?"

"I don't know what you're talking about."

"When you said you were a terrible brother. What did you mean by that?"

Quinn sat back down and dropped his head into his hands. For a long moment, he didn't speak, and then he choked out, "I'm sorry. I'm so, so sorry."

"Quinn."

"I should have been there for her," he said, voice muffled

by his hands. "If I'd been there, none of this would have happened."

"Been there when? Ten years ago?"

"Yes." A choked sob seeped into his cradled hands. "I blew her off. I wanted to drink and wallow in my own self-pity, and she lost everything." His breath started to hitch in earnest now, face firmly buried in his hands. "I'm a selfish, pathetic drunk. I was drunk then, and I was drunk this morning when . . . when . . ."

"Benny Kirkland planned to rape her, Quinn. And then he was going to kill her."

Quinn raised his head, eyes squinted and streaming, nose running. "And you think I had something to do with that? My own sister? That's disgusting."

"I've heard about your finances, Quinn. You're up to your eyeballs in credit card debt."

Quinn stared at him, perplexed. "I don't use credit cards anymore."

"You cashed out the equity in your house three months ago. Why?"

"To help Kylie. I invested the money in the tennis center."

That set Chase back a moment. "She'll confirm?"

"Of course, she'll confirm. I wanted to be a part of the project. She didn't want to take it, but I insisted. I wanted . . . I wanted to make it up to her . . . I let her down when we were kids, and I wanted to make it up to her."

Chase thought for a moment. The guy was convincing. But there was only one way to find out for sure if he was telling the truth. "I'm going to need a blood sample."

Quinn gave a quick, eager nod. "Fine, whatever you need."

# 50

KYLIE OPENED HER EYES TO DISCOVER THAT JANE had stepped out while she dozed. Without a watch on, she had no idea what time it was or how long she'd slept. What was taking so damn long on the CT scan? She was tired of waiting for the all clear, especially when she could tell that she was perfectly fine. The earlier headache had backed off, and the nurse had removed the IV some time ago, declaring her sufficiently hydrated. She'd even already changed into the deep purple scrubs Jane had procured for her.

She'd just turned her head to look at the phone, considering calling Chase's cell, when the door opened a crack and her stepmother stuck her head in.

"Is it okay to come in?"

Kylie pushed herself up and grinned. Finally, a guest she could relax with. "Sure, Mom. Come in."

Lara walked in, her usually perfect hair windblown and showing no signs that she'd tried to tidy it. Her face was free of makeup, her blouse and slacks clean but wrinkled, as if Jane's message about Kylie being at the ER caught her by surprise and she'd yanked on the first thing she could find.

"How're you doing?" Lara asked as she brushed a kiss over Kylie's cheek, lingering as though checking for a fever.

"I'm good, Mom. Don't worry, okay?"

"I'll always worry about my children."

"How are *you*? The past few days have been . . ."

Lara settled onto the side of the bed and squeezed Kylie's forearm with a cool, dry hand. "Don't you worry about me. I'm not in the hospital."

"I'll be out of here in an hour or so."

Lara skated feathery fingertips under Kylie's chin in the vicinity of the bruise. "You poor thing. Are you sure you're all right?"

Kylie caught her stepmother's hand and gave it a reassuring squeeze. "I'm fine. I promise."

"I never know with you. You've always downplayed what hurts you."

"Only because you worry too much."

"No, because your father . . ." Trailing off, Lara dropped her gaze to her lap, where she smoothed her right thumb over the thin, wrinkled skin of the back of her left hand. "I should have done more."

Kylie angled her head to see her face better, not used to such vagueness—or lack of eye contact—from this woman. "Done more about what?"

"He pushed you so."

"Dad? He was my coach."

"He wanted you to be a champion."

"Yeah. So did I."

"But it was too much pressure too young. My God, Kylie, he had you on that tennis court four hours a day on top of your schoolwork. And that didn't count weekends."

"I handled it, Mom. It's what I wanted."

"If I'd intervened, insisted he let you do other things, teen-girl things, maybe it wouldn't have devastated you so much when it was all taken away."

Kylie didn't know what to say to that. It never occurred to her that that was an issue, or what those other teen-girl things would have been. She *loved* her childhood. Wouldn't change a thing before that life-altering moment on the path. That's where it all went awry. Where she *let* it go awry.

"I just never knew where the boundaries were," Lara said, "or what being your stepmother meant."

"Where is this coming from? You've always been a wonderful mother. I totally lucked out."

But Lara shook her head, blond hair falling into her eyes. "I let too many things slide because you weren't fully mine. I gave your father too much leeway to do what *he* wanted instead of insisting he do what was best for you. We often argued about that."

"I know. I heard a couple of those battles."

"You did? Oh, I'm so sorry. You shouldn't have had to deal with that. You know, I hope, that none of that was your fault. You were just a child."

"Mom—"

"I wish I could do it all over again. I would have tried to manage things better for you, with your father and between you and Quinn and Jane. I saw their resentment—how could I not?—and I had no idea what to do about it. And then when you . . . I should have tried harder to get you to come home."

Kylie huffed out an exasperated laugh. "Geez, Mom, you want to blame yourself for global warming, too?"

As Lara looked up, eyes miserable and not amused, Kylie scooted to the edge of the bed and bumped her shoulder against her stepmother's. "The best thing Dad ever did for me was marry you. Seriously."

"But Quinn . . . I should have been more . . ."

"He didn't do anything to me, Mom."

"Of course. I know that. But he said such cruel things to you back then."

"That's what brothers do."

"How will we prove his innocence?"

"Chase is a good cop, a really good cop. He'll do the right thing."

Lara smiled. "You love him, don't you?"

Kylie nodded with a broad grin. "Yep."

As if that had summoned him, the door pushed inward,

and Chase strode in. He paused in midstep when he saw Kylie and Lara sitting side-by-side on the bed. "Oh. Am I . . . should I . . ."

"No, no, you're okay," Lara said as she and Kylie both rose. "We were just talking about you."

"Oh?" He quirked a brow at Kylie.

Lara cast him a serious, take-no-prisoners look as she went to the door. "You'll be good to my daughter, detective, or you'll answer to me."

His cheeks flushed, and he straightened his shoulders as though he'd been caught slouching. "Yes, ma'am. Of course."

Kylie laughed as he all but saluted while Lara opened the door and left them alone. "Does she scare you?"

He flashed her a sheepish grin. "A little, yeah. Always did." He walked over and studied her with a critical eye. "You doing okay?"

She nodded and smiled as he drew her into his arms and kissed her. His lips tasted slightly of Coca-Cola, and for a long moment, she lost herself in his flavor, the beat of his heart under her hand, the heat of his mouth on hers, the faint tropical scent of his sunscreen.

When they parted, he didn't release her, just kept holding her close, swaying a little as if a romantic tune played in his head. "Any word from the doctor?"

"Not yet. It's kind of ridiculous, really. I'm fine."

"I'm sure you are," he said, lips twitching.

She rolled her eyes. "I'm not just saying that."

"No more headache?"

"It's mostly gone. Whatever they gave me after the Tylenol worked like a charm."

"Excellent." He kissed the tip of her nose, then sat on the bed and drew her between his legs, where he rested his chin on her shoulder and rubbed her back with one hand.

They stayed like that for a few moments, content in the quiet, until Chase sighed. "I have a question for you. About Quinn."

"Okay." As she moved away from him to sit in the chair,

he held onto her hand for an extra second, as though he hated the thought of letting her go.

Once she sat, he gazed at her, his head cocked. He seemed hesitant.

Sighing, she left the chair and sat beside him on the bed, letting her thigh rest snugly against his. "Just ask me," she said. "I'm not going to get mad."

He shifted to face her. "Quinn says he's invested in the tennis center. Is that true?"

"Yes. I didn't want him to, but he insisted. He used equity from his house."

"Do you know if he's having any financial problems?"

"About five years ago, he had some trouble with credit cards. I helped him out, and as far as I know, he hasn't had a problem since. When the tennis project came up, he said he wanted to pay me back and refinanced his house." Shrugging, she tucked hair behind her ear. "I didn't tell him this, but I stashed the money in a separate account. I didn't want him to lose it if something bad happened."

"Do you know if he'd have any reason to borrow money from a loan shark?"

"A loan shark? Are you serious?"

"Just bear with me."

"If he needed money, I'm sure he would have come to me. I made it clear that if he ever needed what he invested back, I'd write him a check right then and there."

Chase nodded, his forehead creased in thought.

"What's this about?"

"Sam turned up some stuff about Quinn's finances. Must be old information, though. I'll ask him to check further."

"What do Quinn's finances have to do with any of this?"

"Sam suggested Quinn could be behind what's been happening because of money, but it wouldn't make sense for him to sabotage the tennis center when he's invested in it."

"He wouldn't want to chase me out of town, either," she said.

"What do you mean?"

"The attacker today. He said something about trying to get

me to leave town. Quinn was the one who talked me into coming back to Kendall Falls for good."

Chase's forehead smoothed as though something had just become clear. "That's what wasn't fitting. Sam suggested that kid went after you to get Quinn to pay up on a loan, but then why would he have ranted about you not getting the message to leave town?"

"Have you talked to Quinn? I'm sure he could clear all this up."

"Yes. He showed up to see you a bit ago, and I intercepted him to ask him about some stuff our forensics team turned up."

"How did it go?"

"I asked him to provide a blood sample."

"And is he?"

"He seemed eager to, actually."

As much as she believed in her brother, she still felt relieved that he wasn't fighting Chase. "Good. That's good."

Chase nuzzled his nose against her ear. "How about I go rattle your doctor's tree so I can bust you out of here?"

She leaned against him, basking in his solid warmth. "That'd be wonderful. I'm tired of the scenery here."

His hand stroked down her arm before his fingers tangled with hers on his thigh. "Purple's a good color for you. It makes your eyes more blue."

She tilted her head and looked him over. "You've got something else to tell me, don't you?"

"You can tell?"

"You've got a look."

"Hmm, a look, huh?"

"Quit stalling and tell me."

He took a breath. "We're going to hole up at a house in Naples for a while. You should be safe there until this is over."

She stilled. "I thought that since Sam killed the man . . ."

"We don't know what, or who, connected him to you, so it's better to be safe."

"Makes sense."

He caressed her cheek with the back of his hand. "I love you, you know."

She smiled slightly, angling her head into his touch. "I love you, too."

He kissed her, his lips warm against hers. "You don't have to worry about anything. You know that, right? I'll take care of everything."

She closed her eyes and sighed. "You're going to make me very lazy."

"That's my plan."

# 51

THE MORNING SUN GLINTED OFF THE GULF WAVES as Chase stood at the sliding-glass doors of the Naples safe house that overlooked a private beach. Foliage surrounded the peach stucco vacation home on three sides, dissected in front by a half-mile-long narrow, curving driveway. While he couldn't see them, two security guards lurked among the palm, pine and jacaranda trees and shrubs that created as much privacy as anyone could want.

The house and detached garage were nothing to rave about: not even a thousand square feet with one large bedroom, living and dining rooms and a kitchen. The décor was typical Florida: ceramic tile floors and white wicker furniture with cushions sporting large flower prints in peach and pink. Easily cleaned, easily replaced, perfect for vacationers, sloppy or neat.

Chase loved how quiet it was. No traffic noises intruded on the ebb and flow of gentle waves and the back-and-forth singing of birds. The place ought to have been perfect for thinking through a difficult equation. Unfortunately, his problem—this case—had become too massive to get a handle on.

Hearing movement behind him, he glanced over his shoulder to see Kylie in navy sweat shorts and a pink and purple tie-dyed T-shirt. She ambled into the kitchen, her eyes squinted against the bright light. The tan lines on her right leg framed her braceless knee, and he couldn't help but feel a moment of satisfaction that she no longer hid her scars from him. They'd come a long way.

"Hey, sleepyhead."

She gave him a drowsy smile. "Hey."

Walking up to him, she slipped her arms around his waist and rested her head on his chest. He held her, stroking a hand over her back, awed at the ease with which she snuggled against him.

"Sleep okay?" he asked, pressing a kiss to the top of her head.

"Mmm. You?"

"Yep." The truth was, he hadn't slept much since they'd arrived here three days ago, too wired to completely let down his guard. Now that the weekend was all but over without even a false alarm, though, he figured he'd managed to thwart whoever was after her. For now.

"I can tell, you know," she said.

He angled his head so he could meet her gaze. "Tell what?"

"That you haven't slept."

"I've caught a few hours here and there."

She brushed at the hair on his forehead. "You should crash and let me watch over you for a while."

He liked the sound of that but resisted the temptation. "How're you feeling?"

"I'm at a hundred percent. All the sleep has been amazing."

He brushed the knuckles of his right hand over her cheek, watched her eyes darken with awareness of him. He'd deliberately kept his distance since they'd holed up here, wanting her to rest. But now . . .

Lowering his head, he kissed her. Lazy and slow, until she closed her eyes and relaxed fully against him.

"You're so good at that," she murmured. "Everything falls away."

He kissed the tip of her nose. "I'd be happy to do that any time you want."

"Then your lips are going to get chapped."

"I'll invest in some Blistex."

While she was laughing, he took her mouth in another, more intimate kiss, just to take the edge off his hunger. But apparently she was as hungry as he was, because she slid her arms around his waist and deepened the embrace, her tongue tangling with his in a way that had him wanting to back her against the wall and dive in.

He had to force himself to back off, fingers threaded through her hair as he leaned his forehead against hers. "Slow down there, Ace."

"What's the deal?" she breathed as she trailed kisses over his throat. "Don't you want me anymore?"

He chuckled. "Are you kidding me? I want you constantly."

"Then what's the problem?"

"I also want you rested and healthy. It's only been a couple of days since you hit your head."

"My head is fine. The rest of me is very, very restless, though." Her hands roamed down over his butt, and she delivered an affectionate squeeze. "Tell you what. Is there a tennis court nearby? If I can kick your butt, we get to do what I want to do."

"And you think what you want to do and what I want to do are different?"

"We're not doing it, are we? You're being all squeamish about my owie."

"You *did* bleed all over me," he pointed out.

"So now I'll *walk* all over you on the court, and we'll be even."

"I don't know if that tracks, but if you think you can take me, you're on."

"Take you, huh? Interesting choice of words."

He grinned. "Is it?"

KYLIE LAUGHED WITH DELIGHT WHEN THEY FOUND a pair of old tennis rackets and two cans of used balls in the detached garage. Chase bitched about the rickety rackets, but she took a few practice swings and declared them fit for play.

"But what about the balls?" he asked. "I bet they're flat."

She arched a brow at him. "Don't tell me you can't deal with flat balls."

He cocked his head. "Is that supposed to be a joke of some kind at my expense?"

She shrugged. "Take it however you want."

"Are you starting the smack talk already? We haven't even gotten to the court."

"Just warming up."

The walk to a community court that Chase had spotted the first day they'd arrived was lazy and quiet, and Kylie breathed in the fresh air and loved how the birds sang and insects hummed and waves ebbed and flowed on the beach parallel to the sidewalkless road.

"I love Florida," she said. "It's so much more exotic than California."

"But they both have palm trees. And warm winters and tons of sunshine and miles of beautiful beaches. They can't be that different."

"California is definitely missing something."

"Humidity?" he asked. "I could live with less of that."

She linked her arm with his and leaned her head against his bicep. "It didn't have you."

He glanced askance at her, surprised and pleased, then saw the shrewd flash in her eyes and barked out a laugh. "You're totally gaming me."

"What?" She gave him an innocent look. "I wasn't lying."

"From now until we finish this game, I'm not buying anything you say, you sneaky, manipulative—"

"Watch it."

He grinned. "Conniving."

"Be careful."

"Calculating."

"Oh, look, we're here."

Chuckling, Chase followed her through the gate onto the

green, clay court. Forest-green wind screens attached to the surrounding chain-link fence ensured some privacy.

At the net, they divvied up the balls, stuffing them into the pockets of their tennis shorts, before taking their respective sides of the net.

As Kylie bounced a ball, preparing to volley for serve, she called, "So do I need to take it easy on you?"

"Why would you do that?" he asked, springing from one foot to the other to loosen up.

"Well, you're a cop, and cops have a thing about doughnuts."

He stopped bouncing and slapped his palm against his flat abdomen. "Does this look like a Krispy Kreme gut to you?"

She laughed and shook her head. *Hell*, no, she thought, realizing as she pictured his naked washboard stomach that she'd distracted herself with her own trash talk. Get your head in the game, Ace. Eye on the . . . very hot, handsome, sexy guy across the net.

"Any day now," Chase called, bouncing again.

God, he looked good in those tennis shorts, his legs tan and sculpted and . . . just plain yummy. A distracting ache of lust throbbed to life inside her, and she shook her head to shake it out. That's not focusing. But, hell, he'd refused to touch her beyond chaste kisses and brief caresses for three days, insisting that she needed time to heal and rest and blah, blah, blah. She wanted him so much she could scream.

And, she vowed, she'd have him as soon as she put him away.

She volleyed the ball and fell into position, surprised when he whacked the ball back hard and fast. Holy crap. He wasn't a bit stale.

They smacked the ball back and forth several times, forcing each other to run and reach and strain. By the time Kylie lobbed one over his head, she was breathing hard and totally unprepared when he managed to catch it on the bounce and tap it right into the service court where she couldn't possibly get to it in time.

He grinned and celebrated. "My serve!"

They played hard for an hour, sweating and running and grunting, while dark clouds rolled in. As they went into the third set, tied, thunder began to growl in the distance.

"Maybe we should call it a game," Chase called, looking as winded as she was.

"No way." She swallowed and shook her head, trying to catch her breath. "We play to the end."

"You're not supposed to play this hard on that knee," he said.

"My knee is fine." She jogged around in a small circle to show him. "Do you see me limping?"

He rolled his eyes. "You wouldn't let me see you limp if your feet were on fire."

"Do you want to quit?" she taunted. "You want to throw in the towel but blame me for it?"

"Nope. I'm good for another two hours or more."

Another two hours or *more*? She needed to put this guy away before they were both too wrung out to take the physical activity to the bedroom. "Listen, I break your serve, and we're done."

"You think you can break my serve?" he asked incredulously.

"Yeah, I do."

"Right. Bring it." He tossed a ball into the air and fired it at her like a tiny yellow missile.

She returned gently, right to him, as a coach would with a new student. His eyebrows shot up, and when he glanced at her in surprise, she whipped up her shirt with its built-in bra and flashed him with a hoochie-coochie shimmy.

He froze in midstep, eyes flying wide, and let the ball bounce past him unchallenged.

Suppressing a triumphant grin, she repositioned her shirt and tidied her ponytail, cool as you please. "Love-fifteen," she called.

Chase burst out laughing. "That was dirty."

"All is fair in love and tennis," she said, as prim and Jane-like as she could manage.

He stood there and considered her for a long moment, his eyes narrowed.

"What?" she asked, raising her eyebrows. She knew exactly what he was thinking. She was thinking the same thing but wanted him to make the first move. That way, she won.

Finally, he shrugged, hopped over the net and grabbed her hand. "I give. Let's go."


THEY RAN BACK TO THE HOUSE WITH THEIR HANDS linked, laughing as rain began to pelt them.

In the kitchen, they dropped their rackets by the door, and he backed her against the counter, devouring her mouth with his, reveling in the scent of rain and sweat and Kylie. Jesus, she tasted good, like want and heat and everything he'd ever craved from life.

He stood straighter when she smoothed the palm of her hand over the front of his tennis shorts, molding her fingers around his stiffening cock. With a groan, he lifted her against him.

She linked her arms around his neck and her legs around his waist, and he had to coach himself to go slow as he carried her down the hall toward the bedroom. But her sweet scent, her fingers in his hair, her warm, wet mouth on his . . . everything about her was driving him nuts. He had to have her, had to be inside her soon or they were both going to be disappointed.

He braced a knee on the bed and eased her down, never breaking the seal of their lips as he came down on top of her. She cradled him between her legs, moaning in the back of her throat as the ridge of his erection hit her just right. Arching her head back into the pillow, she rasped, "God, you feel good even with your clothes on."

He chuckled, skimming kisses up the length of her throat to the damp underside of her chin while he worked a hand under her shirt. Her gasp puffed into his mouth when his fingers found and rolled an already taut nipple.

"You're going too slow," she murmured against his lips.

He laughed again, and then his eyes crossed as her hands

slipped between them and inside his shorts. She angled her fingers, breathing out a ragged breath when they closed around his hot, aching flesh. "Uh . . ." He trailed off, squeezing his eyes closed and dropping his forehead against hers, every thought erased by the stroke and tug of her fingers. "Uh, I'm not . . . that's too . . ."

She silenced him with a kiss, her tongue sweeping over his lips and inside his mouth. And then she was using her free hand to push his shoulder back while she sat up, still kissing him, still stroking him, shifting their positions so that he was on his back. She sat astride him and removed her hand so she could slide his shorts down and off, her eyes widening as they caressed the part of him that was so hard and ready for action it lay across his lower belly.

"Wow," she breathed. "You are . . . that is . . . amazing."

He would have laughed, but then her hand was on him again, her fingers light and caressing as they skimmed down to his balls. She cupped him there and leaned forward to press tender kisses to his shaft, her tongue running along his length to the tip, and then, oh God, then she slid her lips over him and clamped down with her mouth, her hand suddenly tight on the rest of him.

The wet heat, the swirl of her tongue, whirled his head, and his belly began to burn with the need to thrust and pump and soar. He had to concentrate to keep still, to keep from driving himself into her mouth. But, oh Christ, it was good, it was incredible, and he couldn't stop the guttural groan that ripped from his throat when she began to pump her hand and her mouth on him, working him, taking him into her throat and moaning.

The pressure built, his body preparing to launch, and he put his hands on her shoulders to stop her. "Wait," he gasped. "Wait."

She slowed but didn't let go, as though she had hold of something she really liked and wasn't interested in sharing. God, he loved her.

Okay . . . hold . . . on, hold on. He didn't want to come alone. He wanted to be together.

He tangled his hand in her ponytail and gave a gentle tug. "Come here."

She released him and, with a devilish smile, crawled up his body to kiss him. It was his turn to angle his hand into her shorts, and he found her wet and hot. She moaned as he sank his middle finger into her and rubbed, her breath already beginning to hitch.

"I love loving you, Ky," he whispered against her lips. "I can't get enough of you."

"Show me," she breathed, arching against his hand. "Please show me."

He rolled her under him, skimmed his lips over her cheek, down to her throat, where he slid his tongue over the pulse that pounded under her skin. He loved the taste of her, the way she tensed and sighed when he peeled away her clothes. He loved the way she focused so intently on every stroke of his fingers, every caress of his palms. He loved that when he looked into her face, her eyes were open and watching him, loving him with no hint of wariness.

"I love you," he said.

Her answering smile made his heart soar.

KYLIE BOWED BACK AS HE FINALLY, FINALLY BURIED himself inside her on a long, slow stroke.

He paused above her, his gaze burning into hers, as though taking a moment to savor the emotional and physical sensation of connection. She kept her eyes on his as she dug her fingers into his tight butt and pulled him closer, adjusting the angle of her hips so she could take more, feel more. God, he was so hard, so big. The pressure was heaven.

Everything inside her ached for him. Her heart, her soul, her body. She was amazed at how much she loved him—and how easy it was now that she'd stopped fighting it—floored by how he made her feel alive in a way she hadn't in a decade. Nothing else mattered, and she focused only on the way he loved her, slowly, tenderly, pressing feather kisses to her chin, her nose, her eyelids.

"I love you," she breathed against his skin. "I've never loved anyone but you."

As if in answer, he began to move, to thrust, and she rose to meet him, their rhythm quickly becoming frantic, almost desperate. The pleasure bloomed in small waves that hitched her breath when they rolled and peaked then started again, growing larger, gaining momentum with each thrust. Her muscles tensed, the power of the pleasure gathering, building, and as though he knew she was there, he increased his pace, driving into her, and then, then, he stroked his hand over her breast, caught her nipple between his fingers, and rolled.

The orgasm slammed into her so hard she cried out, her body bucking, blind and deaf to everything but the sensations that exploded inside her. The clamping of her muscles around his hard flesh seemed to prolong the ecstasy, and then he was coming, too, jolting into her, holding her tight against him with an arm around her waist, his face pressed to the side of her neck as he shuddered and shuddered.

Afterward, they lay still for several moments, breathing hard, his body cradled between her slack legs, his softening erection twitching every so often inside her. Easing to the side, he gathered her against him and rolled so that she was on top of him, then pressed a kiss to her forehead.

She shifted to sit up, moaning at the renewed bloom of sensation where they were joined, and moved her hips subtly against him.

He opened his remarkable green eyes and grinned up at her, grasping her hips as she dropped her head back. "More?" he asked.

"Mmm." She sighed, trying to regain her senses. "I don't think I can."

He lifted his hips to bump against her sensitized flesh. She gasped, grabbed at his shoulders to hold on. "Sure you can," he said, a devilish, satisfied glint in his eyes.

She smiled and half closed her eyes. She felt languid, limp. Almost sated. Almost?

His grin spread over his face, and he sat up, his hands

keeping her right where she was on his lap. "Give me a few minutes," he whispered, and spread kisses over her face, her temple, her brow, her cheek. Gently, he pulled the tie from her ponytail and watched, fascinated, as she shook her head so that her hair fell around her shoulders. Then, with his forehead pressed to hers, his breathing, deep and even, caressing her face, he said, "Just stay right here, like this, for a few more minutes."

She could stay like this forever, she thought as she ran her hands over his shoulders, down his arms, reveling in the solidness of his muscles, the heat and glide of his damp, smooth skin. He made her feel safe, protected like never before.

He angled his head to touch his tongue to the hollow of her throat, drew its moist heat up to the underside of her chin, where he nipped with his teeth. She sucked in a breath, her heart lurching. And then his hand shifted off her hip and found her breast, where he slowly, lazily kneaded, stroking and pressing and rolling the nipple under his thumb until it was hard and aching, sending sparks into the part of her body that sheathed him, waiting for him to get hard again, anticipating the moment when he grew and lengthened inside her, evidence that he wanted her all over again, that she turned him on that much.

She stroked her hand up his arm and across his collarbone, down to his chest, where she did her own exploration of his nipples, enjoying the hitch in his breath when she scraped her nails over his puckering flesh. They stayed like that for several minutes, teasing each other, kissing and sucking and stroking. And then, then, she felt the change in him, felt him begin to grow and harden inside her. She arched her head back in giddy anticipation, moaning as he pressed his lips to her throat and his erection filled her to bursting. He seemed bigger than before, his heaviness inside her unbelievably good.

He shifted them together, lowering her to the mattress with utmost care, cradling her head with his big hands as he began thrusting again, slow this time and careful, kissing her tenderly, his tongue against her tongue, stroking and caressing, loving. This time, the orgasm was lazy and slow, building to an almost impossible pressure before blossoming out into clouds of pleasure that spread through her in glorious, worshipful tendrils. He quickened his pace while it shook her, wringing out of her a long, throaty moan, and then he slowed to a stop, kissing the droplets of perspiration from her temples, one hand gently stroking her breast, the nipple so sensitive that each stroke felt like heaven. The continual stroking kept her in the game even as exhaustion pressed down. It took a moment for her to realize he was still hard, his muscles still tensed as he held himself rigid and waited for her to regroup.

"You there?" he whispered, his jaw pressed to her brow, his lips at her temple. The need in him was palpable.

She lifted her hips, languid, complete, took him deeper, shocked to discover that he could still feel so damn good inside her.

He took that to mean she was ready for more and moved, withdrawing almost completely and gliding back in, the stroke long and dizzying. "Jesus," he breathed near her ear. "You're so hot and tight, and you just keep getting tighter around me."

She smiled, breathless and sweaty, wanting this moment, these moments, to never end. This was a good place to be, oh, so good.

He withdrew and pumped forward again, slow still, controlled, his groan long and raw. "I can't wait," he panted, his breathing choppy. "I just came, and I still can't wait." His voice was filled with wonder.

"Then don't wait," she whispered.

He gathered her close against him and pumped his hips, his head thrown back, driving into her almost mindlessly. Another orgasm, sharp and mind-blowing, took her by surprise just as he came, his mouth open and groaning, the tendons in his neck standing out in sharp relief.

Gasping, he collapsed on top of her, his face pressed to the side of her neck, his nose managing to nuzzle even now.

"God," he panted. "God." As though that was all he was capable of at the moment.

She stroked his slick back, closed her eyes. The air smelled of sex and perspiration and the heady scent of satisfaction. They were sweaty and sticky, and she loved it.

"Just give me a few minutes," he murmured against her throat. "I'll make us something to eat."

She lazily stroked his back, smiling when he began to softly snore.

# 52

CHASE SLIPPED OUT FROM UNDER THE COVERS, careful not to jostle Kylie, who slept dead to the world. He took a moment to love how she curled toward where he sat on the edge of the bed, as though even in sleep she sensed him withdrawing and sought to keep the connection.

He lightly caressed her cheek and smiled at the same time that her full lips curved and she settled. He didn't want to leave her—in fact, he wanted her again already. Jesus, he should be sated by now, at least for the day, but no, he couldn't wait to be inside her again, to feel her clench around him during one of those full-body shudders. He loved it when she shuddered. Loved it more when she whimpered and moaned and begged. His name on her lips as she came, wild and out of control . . . he'd *never* get enough of that.

Thinking about it, reveling in it . . . well, hell, he'd focused too much and now he had a growing boner that wanted attention.

"Later," he murmured as he rose and reached for his shorts on the floor by the bed. He really needed to check his messages. And shower. Tennis and sex had left him stinky and damp.

"What're you doing?"

He turned just as he drew his shorts up and found Kylie looking drowsy and spent as she gazed up at him, her head nestled between both their pillows and one arm lazily thrown over her head. The sheet . . . Shit, the sheet didn't quite cover both breasts. One peeked out, the nipple fully awake, the skin surrounding it pink from the attention he'd lavished on it over and over. Christ, that was sexy.

He swallowed and tried to talk himself down. Not a teenager. Work to do.

Except he couldn't remember what that work was . . . Oh, right, messages.

"Go back to sleep," he murmured, bracing one knee on the bed so he could lean over and brush his mouth over her slack lips. "I'll just be a few minutes."

She trailed a hand down his bare thigh. "Don't be long."

He groaned as Chase Jr. twitched to high-alert status. Just because she touched him. He was *such* a horndog for this woman.

"Hmm, what's going on here?" she asked as she propped up on one elbow and smirked at the prominent tenting of his shorts. "Greedy, isn't he?"

"The greediest."

"Then I guess you'd better hurry back."

He quick-kissed her on the nose and headed for the door. "Don't get dressed," he tossed over his shoulder.

Her laugh followed him down the hall.

In the kitchen, he retrieved his cell phone where he'd left it on the counter and scrolled through the menu. Yep, he had a message from Sylvia Jensen.

As he waited for the phone to access his voice mail, he grabbed two glasses from the cupboard and a half-full pitcher of lemonade from the fridge. After all the sweating he and Kylie had done, they'd both need some major rehydration.

Finally, Sylvia's message queued up: "Chase, it's Sylvia. Quinn McKay's not a match for the DNA found on Mark Hanson's body."

Chase just about released a relieved whoop right there in the kitchen. Yes, there was still damning evidence against Quinn, but it wasn't *as* damning. It wouldn't be tough to prove reasonable doubt if it came to a trial.

But now he had to find a way to figure out who *did* belong to that DNA left in Hanson's braces. An idea occurred to him, and he dialed Sylvia.

"Sylvia Jensen."

"Hey, it's Chase. Question: You said the tissue found in Hanson's braces was a 'large sample.' Would the resulting wound have required stitches?"

"No doubt about it. The wound would have been deep and messy."

"Great. Thanks, Sylvia. You're the best."

"You're certainly in a good mood."

"I've got an idea. I'll catch you up later, okay?"

He disconnected the call and pushed his speed-dial number for Sam.

"Sam Hawkins."

His partner sounded as though Chase had awakened him. In the middle of the day? Of course, he and Kylie had just been snoozing, too, so it wasn't as though he had any right to chastise the guy.

"Sam, it's Chase."

"Yeah. Whassup?"

Or, Jesus, was he drunk? He'd definitely slurred his words. Chase quickly shrugged it off. Sam wasn't one to drink in the middle of the day, and he had more important things to talk to him about.

"Sylvia says Quinn's not our guy," Chase said. "I've got an idea, though. We can check ER records from the night of Kylie's attack. Sylvia said that whoever left DNA in Hanson's braces might have needed emergency care."

Silence.

"Sam?"

"Yeah."

"Ten years ago, there was only one ER, at Kendall Falls

General," Chase said. "I'm thinking the son of a bitch might have been there at the same time as Kylie, getting his ripped-up hand stitched."

"Would there still be ER records from a decade ago?"

Sam definitely sounded awake now. Finally. "Probably, in some form or another," Chase said. "Even if they're paper records, we can go through them and see if anything leaps out at us."

"That could take days. Do you know how many people have visited the ER in the past ten years?"

"We're talking about *one day* ten years ago, Sam. Possibly two, if the perp didn't seek help right away."

"You're assuming the records have been well-maintained and organized. And he could have gone to any of the hospitals in the area, too. Fort Myers. Cape Coral. Naples. Even as far away as Tampa."

"Kendall Falls General is a starting point. We can fan out after that."

"What did Sylvia say about it?"

"Nothing yet. I'm running it by you first." Chase stopped and took a breath to try to keep the impatience out of his voice. "Maybe it sounds like a long shot, but it's something. We desperately need something. Quinn's not the guy."

Sam didn't respond.

"Come on, Sam. Are you with me? Did I wake you up or something?" Maybe his partner's marriage problems had gotten him even more down than he'd already been. That'd explain his surliness. But, hell, maybe the man was just ticked at having to work alone the past three days while Chase holed up with Kylie.

"I had a few drinks," Sam said in a contrite voice, confirming Chase's earlier suspicion. "I probably shouldn't be driving."

Chase clamped down on his annoyance. He needed to give his partner a break, considering his separation. "No problem. I can handle this on my own."

Sam hesitated a moment. "I can start making calls from here, if you want."

"That'd be great. Start with Lee Memorial in Fort Myers."
"Will do."
"Thanks, Sam. I'll check in after I've talked to the folks at Kendall Falls General."

After he hung up, Chase took a quick shower, made a phone call, jotted a note for Kylie, let the security guards know he was taking off for a bit and headed for Kendall Falls.

# 53

JANE OPENED THE FRONT DOOR AND GAVE WADE the most bored stare she could muster, pretending to be un-impressed by the bouquet of red roses clasped in his hand. Was it a dozen or, wow, maybe two dozen? Not that it mattered.

Before she could embarrass herself and start babbling about how much she missed him, she fixed Kylie's brand of bland expression on her face and said, "What can I do for you?"

Wade smiled weakly. "I'm here to beg for forgiveness."

Her heart fluttered, but she remained impassive. "Why would you do that?"

"Because when I want something, I go for it."

"You mean, when you can't get what you want, you go for what you consider the next best thing."

He had the sense to wince. "I'm sorry, Jane. I truly am. Please let me come in so we can talk."

She hesitated, suddenly aware that she'd kept him standing on her porch with his flowers long enough to compel neighbors to part their blinds and snoop. She stepped back. "Fine."

He brushed by her, and she shored up her defenses before his spicy scent could invade. When she'd first met him, she'd thought it weird that he wore something as old-fashioned as Old Spice. Now, she found her stomach muscles clenching and her eyes drifting closed just at the thought of that crisp, clean scent.

She closed the door and turned, surprised when she all but walked into his chest. Only the flowers—tea roses, she realized—separated them.

"I have something to say, Jane."

She looked up into his face and had to fight the urge to start crying. She'd really thought she'd found Mr. Right in him.

"Say it and go," she said. "I've got things to do."

He stepped toward her, backing her against the door. "I made a mistake," he said, his voice deep and gruff, as though emotion lurked just beyond his handsome exterior. "I'm sorry, more sorry than you can imagine. Do you want to know why?"

She felt her cheeks flushing but said nothing.

"Because," he said, "I never felt closer to anyone than the way I felt close to you. I hate myself for messing that up."

She met his eyes, felt her own widen at the glimpse of moisture in his.

"I hope that you'll find it in your heart to forgive me some day," he said. "I'll wait as long as it takes."

She couldn't stop herself from smiling at his sincerity. Earnest? Uh, yeah. Earnest as hell. But maybe she could deal with what had happened if it meant she got what she wanted. Him. "I just have one question," she said.

He cocked his head, a smile tempting his lips, as though he sensed he was on the cusp of winning her back. "What is it?"

"Do you have a microphone in your ear so someone can coach you or did you just spend hours rehearsing that speech?"

His smile widened into a grin. "Coach, no. Rehearsal,

yes." He held out the flowers. "And the roses, all three dozen, were completely my idea."

She took the flowers, held them to her nose and breathed in their tealike scent. Then she tossed them over his shoulder onto her new carpet, uncaring about water and dirt and other possible stains, and launched herself into his arms.

# 54

KYLIE WOKE SLOWLY, AWARE THAT SHE WAS ALONE in the bed and that the section of sheet beside her was cool. She took a few moments to bury her face in Chase's pillow. Just breathing in his coconut scent made her feel safe and loved . . . and, wow, tingly and kinda lusty.

Sitting up, she pushed hair out of her face and glanced at the clock: 3:14 P.M. Her stomach growled, complaining that lunch was overdue.

She went into the bathroom for a quick shower, needing the reviving force of cool water streaming over her body. She hoped, with a thrill of anticipation, that Chase would join her. But she soaped up twice and washed and conditioned her hair with no appearance by a ready-for-some-loving man. Sheesh, she must have exhausted him.

Eager to see what he was up to, she dressed in khaki shorts and an orange polo then wandered down the hall toward the kitchen. The house was silent, as if she were the only one there. She got confirmation when she found a folded note sporting "read me" in Chase's scribbly handwriting on the breakfast bar next to a cell phone.

She plucked up the note and unfolded it.

*It's official: Quinn's in the clear! Had to go to work but will call ASAP. In the meantime, hit redial on the cell phone for a surprise. Love you! Chase.*

Smiling, and with tears stinging in her eyes, she sat on one of the breakfast bar stools and let out the biggest sigh of relief she'd ever exhaled. Thank you, God.

Still smiling, and feeling as though a happy dance was in order, she picked up the cell phone and pushed the redial button. After three rings, a familiar voice said, "Hello?"

Kylie straightened up off the stool, her heart leaping. "T.J.?"

"Hey!" he said.

"Oh my God, where are you? What are you doing? How are you?"

His wonderful, boyish chuckle echoed in her ear. "You might want to pace yourself."

She had to laugh. That was advice she'd given him more than once on the court. "Okay, let's start with how are you?"

"I'm pretty good." She could hear the grin in his voice. "I have my own room at the Coopers'. Well, it's really Terry's room. Terry went to college a couple of years ago, and he's spending the summer in Brazil for some school thing. Mrs. Cooper—she keeps asking me to call her Annette, but it seems weird—she really misses him. Oh, and they have a dog, Sandy, who sleeps with me. Isn't that cool?"

She couldn't respond for a moment, stunned at the amount of information he'd shared in one energetic gush. This was not the same sullen, mad-at-the-world T.J. she'd last seen. "Wow."

"Mr. Cooper—Tom—he's a really good tennis player. I wipe the court with him every time we play, which makes him nuts, but he never gets mad. He seems to kind of like it. I don't get that." He paused. "So how are you?"

She started to laugh until tears gathered on her lashes and spilled over.

# 55

CHASE STOOD AT THE FRONT DESK OF THE MEDI-
cal records department at Kendall Falls General while a
young Hispanic woman with glossy black hair, black-framed
eyeglasses, perfect olive skin and unnaturally white teeth
finished up her phone call about a sick Labrador. When
Monica Giraldo, according to the hospital ID hanging around
her neck, hung up, she gave him an apologetic smile that
stretched full, lipstick-free lips. "Sorry about that. I've been
playing phone tag with the vet all day. What can I help you
with?"

Chase showed her his badge. "Detective Chase Manning
with the Kendall Falls PD. I'm looking to get a list of patients treated in the ER on a particular night ten years ago."

She pushed her glasses back on her head. "I'm sorry, but
none of that would be in the database. We weren't electronic
then."

"What about paper records?"

"Paper records from that far back are kept at a storage facility in Tampa."

Tampa. Damn. He'd hoped he'd be able to dive into the
records himself if no one else could do it. He wouldn't be

getting any quick and easy answers now. "But they'd be organized by date?"

"Should be. Sometimes things get mixed up, but yeah." She grabbed a notepad and pencil. "If you give me the date you're looking for, I can have someone up there compile a list of patient names. Once we get the appropriate permissions, of course."

"Could they look at specific injuries?"

She began to chew the eraser end of the pencil as she considered that. "Like what?"

"Hand injuries. Across the knuckles and perhaps this area." He clenched his hand and ran his finger over the fleshy part of his palm. "It'd be a significant injury . . ." He trailed off as he stared down at his fist, his finger rubbing back and forth over that particular spot. Sam's nervous gesture . . .

"Detective?"

Chase looked up, but his brain had started chasing its tail. Sam? No way. No *fucking* way.

Monica tapped the pencil against the cleft in her chin. "What date do you want checked?"

Chase struggled to focus. "Uh, let's go ahead and do three days' worth, if that's not too much trouble."

She winked. "Won't be any trouble for me."

He gave her the dates then asked, "How soon before I can get the list?"

"Could be a week."

Chase withdrew a business card. "Can we put a rush on it? Maybe have it e-mailed to the address on here?"

"I'd have to talk to my supervisor. She's pretty good about doing what she can, though."

"She can call me, if she wants. I'd be happy to explain the situation to her."

A few minutes later, as he pushed out the door into the corridor, his brain resumed its tail-chasing.

Sam couldn't be the guy. He had no motive. He didn't know Mark Hanson. Or, at least, he *said* he didn't know Hanson. He could have lied about that. They were in the same graduating class after all.

But Sam, with all his bulky muscles, certainly didn't match Kylie's description of her assailants . . . except that was ten years ago. Sam might have been a skinny kid back then. Chase had no idea. Quinn, also a rail-thin boy back then, had bulked up just as much, though.

But, no, wait, just wait. Think it through. Don't jump to conclusions. This was *Sam*.

In the elevator, Chase poked the LOBBY button.

The key here was Benny Kirkland. Kirkland tried to get T.J. to smash Kylie's windshield. Kirkland tried to rape and kill Kylie at the safe house. So, okay, maybe Sam hired him. He'd have access to Kirkland's files. Maybe he'd arrested Kirkland in the past or used him as a snitch or just looked him up through the department's system.

But Sam *killed* Kirkland. Why would he kill a man he'd hired?

To keep him quiet, Chase thought, cupping his hand over the back of his neck and squeezing at the insistent knot growing there.

Or maybe Sam had wanted Kirkland to murder Kylie and got pissed when he failed to get the job done. But why kill her? That made no sense. Chase could see trying to run her out of town, considering all the evidence had been found at the site of her tennis project. If she'd left town, she probably would have abandoned the project, leaving the evidence buried. Killing her, though, ran the risk of guaranteeing the project got done, to honor her memory.

A chill at the thought staggered up his spine, and he shuddered as the elevator doors opened into the lobby. He needed to keep thinking, not stall on the horror of losing Kylie.

Okay, what else?

All that stuff about Quinn's finances had turned out not to be true. He'd assumed the information was outdated, but Sam could have lied. Chase hadn't seen any of the supporting paperwork.

And the first safe house . . . Sam could have made up the bit about Kirkland having stayed there himself. Chase had hardly been able to believe that incredible coincidence, but it came from Sam. And he trusted Sam.

Shit. *Shit*.

He *trusted* Sam.

So much that he'd let him arrange the safe house in Naples. Where Kylie was right now. Alone. Sure, there were two security guards outside, but Sam would know exactly how to disarm them. And he knew Chase wasn't there right now. If Sam showed up, Kylie wouldn't think anything of welcoming him in.

Fuck. *Fuck*.

As Chase passed from the frigid air of the hospital's lobby into the humid heat of the afternoon, he thumb-dialed the number of the cell phone he'd left for Kylie, already jogging for his SUV.

She answered, to his relief, just as a mower, damn it, powered up on the hospital lawn. Plugging his free ear with the tip of one finger, he said, "It's me. Give me a second. I have to get in the truck so I can hear you."

He fumbled his keys with a shaking hand but managed to hit the remote unlock button. Once he got in and slammed the door on the noise, he said, "That's better."

Kylie's laugh, seeming so intimate in his ear, sent a chill of a different kind up his back. He loved that sound. The thought of losing that, losing *her*, made his stomach clench into a rock.

"Where are you?" she asked.

"Doing some research at the hospital." He plugged the key into the ignition. "Listen, I . . . well, this is going to come out of left field, but I . . ." He trailed off and shook his head. He could barely get the damn words out. *Sam?* "I have a new suspect. It's . . . Sam."

"Sam . . . your *partner* Sam?" She sounded as shocked as he felt.

"I'm getting a list of patients treated in the ER the same night as your attack. Sylvia thinks the guy who killed Mark Hanson needed stitches in his hand. And Sam has a scar in the right spot." Jesus, it sounded so lame now that he'd said it out loud. Could he be that desperate for a suspect other than Quinn?

His racing pulse started to slow. Okay, he thought, this is wrong. It's not Sam. Sam's a cop. His friend. No way could it be Sam.

He took a calming breath. "Look, I'll know for sure when I get the patient list from the hospital. I just . . . if he shows up there . . ."

"What should I do?"

"Maybe I'm way off. God, Ky, I don't know. But I think it'd be best if you got one of the guards to come inside and stay with you until I get there."

"Okay."

"I'm on my way. Twenty minutes unless there's a ton of traffic."

"Don't worry, Chase. I'll be fine."

He swallowed hard and said a little prayer that she was right. "See you soon. I love you."

"Love you, too," she replied, a warm smile in her voice.

After hitting the button to disconnect the call, he let his shoulders slump and hung his head to rub at his eyes. It's not Sam. Couldn't be. But he'd feel a hell of a lot better once he saw the patient list for confirmation. Either way, he needed to call the lead security guard at the house and put the guys on high alert.

"Chase."

He jerked his head up and met the dark brown eyes reflected in the rearview mirror.

Aw, fuck.

"Give me the phone and put your hands on the steering wheel."

Chase complied. He didn't have to see the Glock to know Sam had it aimed at the back of his seat.

"Don't you know you're supposed to check the back before you get in the car?"

He'd been so distracted by warning Kylie, and that damn noisy lawn mower . . .

"What's going on, Sam? Talk to me. Whatever it is, we can work it out."

Sam's smile went nowhere near his eyes. It looked as dead as Kylie's game face. "You shouldn't have told her."

"I didn't tell her anything she can use. All I told her was I had a suspicion. My suspicions about Quinn were wrong. This one can be, too."

"Nice try."

"Come on, you heard me tell her I wasn't sure."

"This is what we're going to do," Sam said as he stashed Chase's cell in his pants pocket then leaned his weight against the back of the seat and reached around Chase's chest to the gun in the holster under his left arm. "I know you've got one strapped to your ankle, too. Make even a suggestion of a move toward it, and you're dead."

Chase nodded his understanding.

"Take out your cuffs and secure one to your right wrist."

Chase did as he was told, his brain churning out scenarios and discarding them just as quickly. Sam knew his moves. Partners for five years grew to know each other as well as respective spouses.

"Now get into the passenger seat," Sam said, "loop the free cuff through the handle there by the windshield and secure your other wrist."

Chase scooted over, maneuvering his long legs over the center console into the other seat. He threaded the manacle through the curved plastic handle where the windshield met the side pillar of the truck's frame, which was designed to help passengers pull themselves up and into the tall truck, and fumbled to zip-click the free cuff around his left wrist.

"Other drivers are going to see me handcuffed and know something's up," he said.

"That's why we're driving to Naples with the red light on the roof. They'll just assume you're my prisoner. Which you are."

"This isn't going to work, Sam."

"Shut up and don't do anything stupid."

While Sam got out of the back, Chase tested the sturdiness of the passenger-assist handle. It gave as he tugged, but it appeared to be bolted onto the truck's frame rather than glued on, so breaking it off quickly seemed unlikely.

Sam opened the passenger door and removed Chase's ankle piece, then secured Chase's ankles with nylon restraints they normally used on combative suspects. "Don't want you kicking me while I'm driving," Sam said. "That'd be just like you to try to cause an accident and sacrifice yourself to save your one true love."

"Don't do this, Sam, please. Kylie's innocent. She doesn't deserve to . . ." He couldn't say it.

"Die?" Sam supplied with a tight quirk to his mouth. "Maybe I think she deserved to die ten years ago. Ever consider that?"

"But why? What did she ever do to you?"

They both froze as Chase's phone, muffled in Sam's pocket, began to ring. Ignoring it, Sam slammed the door shut. As his partner trotted around to the driver's side, stashing his gun in his under-arm holster, Chase tested the mobility of his legs. He'd be able to snap the restraints with brute strength, but if he did it now, Sam would slap something stronger on him.

Sam stopped in the back for Chase's portable police light, which he secured on the Explorer's roof, before he got into the driver's seat. As he cranked the engine, he said, "Just sit there and be quiet and we won't have a problem."

"You're going to kill both of us whatever I do."

"True, but it'll be easier for Kylie if you behave." Sam shot him a look out of the corner of his eye. "If you know what I mean."

"What? If I don't behave, you're going to torture her before you kill her? Is that really who you are, Sam?"

Sam looked at him fully, his dark eyes black. "You don't know me. You've never known me. So shut the fuck up and be glad this parking lot is too public for me to kill you right here and now. If you behave, I won't make you watch what I do to your girlfriend."

Chase jerked at the cuffs that were binding his wrists. Couldn't help it.

"Give it up," Sam said, voice surprisingly soothing. "You're not going anywhere."

# 56

KYLIE CHECKED HER WATCH FOR THE EIGHT-
millionth time. Thirty minutes had passed since Chase called.
He must have hit traffic.

The security guard pacing the dining-room floor, hand on
the butt of his gun, paused to give her a sympathetic smile.
He looked no older than twenty, with sandy brown hair, sky-
blue eyes and a deep, dark tan. Chase had introduced him
three days ago as Brian. "He'll be here soon," Brian said.

She returned his smile as she folded her nervous hands on
the table. She'd tried Chase's cell phone five minutes ago,
and it had rung until she got voice mail. He must be in a dead
zone, she thought. Relax. Take a breath.

"Thank you for . . . protecting me," she said, and almost
winced. But he was. He'd insisted she sit in the only room in
the house that had no windows, while he paced back and
forth between the entrance to the kitchen and the arched
doorway that led to the living room.

"It's no problem, ma'am."

If she hadn't been so freaked about Sam, she might have
felt old at the "ma'am." Instead, she searched for something
to say, to ease the anxiety that kept trying to grow behind her

eyes. "Are you from this area?" She guessed Boston from his accent.

"No, ma'am. I'm from outside Portland, Maine."

"Ah. It's cold there." Duh. God, she was bad at this when she was distracted.

Brian smiled at her again and nodded. "A lot colder than here. The beach here is a lot more fun." He flashed her a dev-ilish grin. "Especially at spring break."

She laughed. A heartbreaker. He actually reminded her some of Chase when they trained together.

Come on, Chase, where the hell are you? She reached for the cell phone on the table. "I'm going to try him again."

She pressed redial and held the phone to her ear, surprised when she heard the phone ring in the living room. "He's here," she said and jumped to her feet just as the guard, hand tightening on his weapon, turned toward the arched door and blocked her from racing into the other room.

She started to demand he get out of the way, but then his body jerked and he reeled back into her, the violent force of his body slamming her back against the dining room table. She landed on the floor beside him, ribs smarting where she'd hit the table's edge, and stared at the dark stain spread-ing over the front of his white security-guard shirt. He gazed at her with dazed eyes the color of a storm-darkening sky. His lips moved as he tried to say something, and a thick stream of blood trickled out of the side of his mouth.

"No!" Kylie shouted, and scrambled to her knees to grab his limp hand.

His eyes started to roll back, and she jostled his hand and arm. "Don't do that, Brian. Stay with me."

"Kylie."

She shook her head at Sam's voice, wanting to deny what had just happened, refusing to look up and acknowledge him, acknowledge that Chase had been right. Right now, though, all she could process was that Sam had shot Brian, and blood already saturated the security guard's shirt. She needed to stop the bleeding, needed to help him.

But before she could place her hands over the bullet

wound, his body went deathly still, and his fingers slackened between hers. Too late. Oh, God, she'd let shock waste too much time. And now it was too late.

She'd known him for three days, but a fierce grief nearly blinded her. That bastard Sam killed Brian. A sweet security guard with his whole life in front of him. Who lived far away from home and loved the beach and pronounced "car" as "cah" and "drawer" as "draw."

"Kylie."

She coached herself to keep a clear head. Chase would be here any minute. All she had to do was stall. All she had to do was keep her eye on the ball.

Raising her head, she met Sam's eyes and hoped all the hate she felt at that moment didn't shine through. The expression on his face—cold determination—chilled her almost as much as where he aimed his gun. Her right knee.

"I need you to get up," he said evenly. "If you want to keep all that hardware in your knee working, I'd advise you to do as I say. Nice and easy."

She pushed herself to her feet, hoping her wobbly legs would support her. Hurry, Chase, hurry. But then it hit her that she'd heard his cell phone ring earlier—

Her heart jolted as her gaze locked on Sam's. "Where's Chase?"

"You don't need to worry about that right now." He gestured with the gun. "Turn around."

She obeyed, closing her eyes against the sight of Brian on the floor, trying to close her heart to the possibility that Sam had done the same to Chase. But she failed—Chase could already be dead—and black spots splattered across her vision like paintball bullets striking a target. No. Oh, God. No, no, no.

"Hands behind your back."

She didn't ignore the command. She just couldn't follow it as her brain focused on one thing and one thing only. "What did you do to Chase?"

Sam seized her right wrist and jerked it behind her, followed by her left, where he bound them tightly together with

plastic restraints. By the time it occurred to her that he'd had
to holster his weapon to do that, he'd grabbed hold of the
back of a dining-room chair with one hand, and steering her
with the other, dragged it into the kitchen.

After situating the chair in the middle of the kitchen, he
forced her around so that her back was to the seat, as if
preparing to sit, and walked behind her. He grasped her
bound wrists and drew them up and back. Her shoulders
protested the unnatural position, and she bowed forward
with a pained gasp.

"What are you doing?"

"Just relax and work with me."

He pulled her back by the wrists until the backs of her
knees hit the edge of the chair's seat, and she had no choice
but to sit. When she did, her arms were draped over the
chair's back, and she realized his intent. With even minimal
movement restricted, getting up, especially quickly, would be
next to impossible. There would be no way for her to charge
him or otherwise try to disarm him.

He didn't glance her way as he started going through
cabinets, searching for something with desperate determination. Sweat had plastered his green cotton polo to his
sculpted back.

"Finally," he muttered as he withdrew a bottle of Jim
Beam left behind by a previous renter. About four inches of
whiskey sloshed around in the bottle as he spun off the top
and tipped it back for a long swig, his hand visibly shaking.

Kylie, watching his throat work as he gulped the cheap
bourbon, tested the security of the plastic straps around her
wrists. So tight that slipping free wasn't an option, and she
wasn't strong enough to break them.

With less than an inch of booze left in the bottle, Sam
dragged the back of his hand through the sweat dampening
his flushed brow. "Almost there," he murmured, eyes red and
watering. "Just hang on."

Almost where? Oh, God, what had he done to Chase?
"Where is he, Sam? Where is Chase?"

He slammed the bottle onto the counter. "Just shut up."

She tensed when he pulled the gun out of his holster and aimed it at her. "I should have killed you back then. We wouldn't be here now if I'd just gotten it over with. But that pussy Mark ran away, and I had to stop him before he could rat me out."

Full realization clicked, like a whoosh of flame in her face, singeing and airless. "You were one of them," she whispered. "Ten years ago . . . you . . ."

Turning his back to her, he set the gun on the counter, within easy reach, and stared down at the oven as though trying to figure out how it worked.

"Why?" she asked faintly.

"Don't talk to me."

But she had to do *something* . . . stall him, distract him, convince him that whatever he had planned was a very bad idea. She couldn't just sit here and let the growing fear take over, let Sam do . . . whatever he was going to do . . .

"I'm sure you had a good reason, Sam, so I want to understand. Please help me to understand."

He gave his head a curt shake without looking at her. "Stop talking to me like you give a shit. You've never cared about me."

"Of course I care about you. We're friends."

"Friends!" He whirled around and advanced on her, his fingers curled into claws in front of him, like he wanted to grab her by the throat and throttle her. "You were never my fucking *friend*."

If she could have backed away, she would have. This furious, red-faced Sam screaming in her face frightened her more than the gun. "I . . . what . . . I don't know what . . ." She trailed off and said the only thing she thought might help: "I'm sorry."

He pivoted away from her, lowering those clawlike hands to his sides and making fists as he took three strides back toward his weapon on the counter. But when he got there, instead of the gun, he snatched up the whiskey bottle and hurled it at the wall.

Kylie closed her eyes, thinking he'd take his frustration

out on her next. When nothing happened, she opened her eyes to see that he had his head tilted back, the heels of his hands pressed to his temples as though trying to hold in something that was burrowing its way out of his skull. The man was coming apart right in front of her.

And she knew without a doubt that when he finished—or maybe during—he was going to kill her.

"Where's Chase, Sam?" she asked, trying to inject strength into her trembling voice. "What did you do to him?"

He lowered his hands and stared at them as if he'd never seen them before. "I killed him. I killed my partner."

Her head went light, and she fought off the slow, sickening spin, unable to think over the roar in her ears. Chase was dead. Chase was *dead*. But then she shook her head, refused to believe it. "No. You're lying. You didn't kill him."

Sam pierced her with a dark look. "I have no reason to lie. Not anymore."

"I don't believe you." She wouldn't. *Couldn't*. She would sense it if Chase were dead, would somehow *know*.

"I left the Explorer running in the garage and closed the garage door. He was cuffed inside, with no hope of escape. He went to sleep, Kylie. And he won't wake up. Ever."

No, she thought. *No*. Eye on the ball. Focus. *Breathe*. She swallowed the rush of grief. "Why? Just tell me why."

"It's your fault," he said, calm again. "I tried everything to send you running back to LA, everything to stop this moment from coming. I don't want to be this person, this . . . this . . . *bad* person. But it's coming at me like a freight train, and no matter how hard I try, no matter what I do, I can't get off the tracks. And it's *your* fault!"

He lunged forward and backhanded her hard enough to tip the chair onto its back legs. When it slammed back to all fours, Kylie's body snapped forward, held in place by the restraints, and she sat with her head slumped down, quiet and still, fighting the black dizzy spin of pain reverberating inside her skull.

Don't pass out. Do *not* pass out.

The salty, metallic taste of blood in her mouth focused

her, and she started to raise her head, to face the monster who killed the only man she'd ever loved. She'd make him pay. Somehow. Some way.

But she froze at the cold, hard pressure of metal against the top of her head, followed by the unmistakable, heart-stopping slide and click of a cocking gun.

"I should have brought a gun that day," Sam said. "We wouldn't be here now if I'd had the balls. But all I really wanted to do was take something important from you, something you cared about, just like you took something from me."

She didn't move, didn't breathe. Sweat trickled between her breasts, gathered on the tip of her nose. She needed to spit out the blood gathering in her mouth but didn't dare. Instead, she swallowed it and the encroaching terror.

"I'm sorry, Sam, but I don't know what you're talking about. I don't remember you."

"You know how incredibly offensive that is? You changed the course of *my life*, and you don't even remember doing it."

"What did I do? Please tell me what I did."

"Patti Robinson."

Kylie closed her eyes against the sting of tears and perspiration. Oh, God, Chase.

Okay, think, focus. Patti Robinson . . . yes, one of three other girls she and Trisha had hung out with in high school. The five of them had been inseparable. More regret: She'd lost touch with all but Trisha when she fled for LA.

The barrel of Sam's gun dug into her scalp. "Don't tell me you don't remember Patti."

"Of course I remember Patti," she said quickly. "She was one of my closest friends."

"I asked her out. On a date. I bet you don't remember that."

Kylie cycled through memories scattered by two swings of a baseball bat. She vaguely remembered a conversation with Patti about a guy who'd been busted for . . . something. Kylie had advised her not to go out with him alone. Had that been Sam?

"You talked her out of it," Sam said, every word getting a bitter twist. "Said I wasn't good enough for her, that I was beneath you and your popular friends."

Kylie shook her head, heard the scrape of her hair against the gun's tip. "That's not what I said—"

"She ditched me," Sam cut in. "*Ditched* me, made me look like an idiot to my friends. Because you had your nose stuck up so high in the air no one else was considered worthy. You had everything, *everything*, handed to you. You hung out with cheerleaders and football players and could have gone out with any guy you wanted. Kendall Falls worshipped at your feet. The world *revolves* around people like you. And me? I had *nothing*. I was just a dumb skinny kid with zits who got caught smoking pot in the bathroom. The *one* thing I wanted, the *one* thing that could have made my world livable—a girl as sweet and special as Patti—you took away from me without a second thought."

As he adjusted his grip on the gun, Kylie squeezed her eyes closed. "Sam, please—"

"Look at me."

At the higher level of gravity in his voice, her heart stuttered into a new, hyper pace, and she didn't dare move, didn't dare twitch as the ligaments and tendons in her arms began to cramp. Everything hurt. Her shoulders, her jaw. Her heart. Chase . . .

"*Look* at me," Sam said again, and tapped her head with the pistol. "I want to see your face when I blow your brains out."

She lifted her head slowly and met his crazed, red-rimmed eyes. She'd never known hate before. But here it was, and maybe, just maybe, she could understand what Sam must have felt ten years ago when Patti rejected him. This man took Chase away from her, and if she had a baseball bat and free hands, she wouldn't hesitate to swing for the fences.

"Step away from her, Sam."

At the quiet statement, Sam jerked around, toward the door leading into the dining room, where Chase leaned unsteadily against the door jamb.

Kylie gasped, at first relieved beyond belief—he's alive!—then horrified at how bleary-eyed he looked. Perspiration trickled down the sides of his flushed face, and blood bathed both of his wrists and hands. What the hell happened to him?

Sam whipped back around and had the gun aimed at Kylie's chest before anyone could draw another breath. "Don't do anything stupid, Chase," he said. "I mean it."

Chase held onto the frame of the door for support, blinking as though trying to focus. "Same goes."

Sam, having gotten a grip on his composure, cast him a grim look of approval. "So you were able to get free after all. What'd you do? Rip apart the interior?"

"Something like that," Chase said. "Takes longer to die by motor vehicle exhaust these days, remember? Catalytic converters."

"Looks to me like it wouldn't have taken much longer," Sam drawled.

"I got lucky. Now put down the gun."

"No, thank you."

"Then point it at me, not at her."

"No," Kylie said. Her stomach lurched at the thought of Sam, precariously balanced on a very narrow ledge of control, aiming a loaded gun at Chase. "Don't."

Chase didn't acknowledge her plea, or her, actually, his attention laser-focused on his partner. "Sam, please. I'm on your side."

Sam's laugh sounded like a psychotic cackle. "You're on my side? Are you fucking *serious*?"

"Whatever happened in the past, it's the past. We can talk it out. What have you got to lose?"

"Everything!" Sam shouted. "I've got everything to lose! Why the fuck do you think we're here?"

# 57

CHASE STOOD STILL, TENSE AND WATCHFUL AS HIS carbon-monoxide-deadened senses began to sharpen and the roar of blood in his ears retreated. Chancing a glance at Kylie, he tried not to react to the terror sparking in her eyes or the blood on her mouth. Sam, the son of a bitch, had struck her. Chase would make him pay for that first.

"Tell me what's going on, Sam," he said evenly. He'd always had a knack for sounding reasonable while the inside of his head threatened to disintegrate. "I'm sure we can work something out."

Sam's jaw muscles flexed. "I'm going to have to kill you again." His voice broke on the final words. "Christ, Chase, I don't have a fucking choice."

"Tell me why, Sam. Tell me what went wrong."

Sam shifted his aim to Kylie's head. "She. Came. Back," he ground out, punctuating each word with a mimicked recoil of the gun.

Chase's stomach cartwheeled. Jesus! He cast a glance at Kylie, to try to calm her with a reassuring look. The strain of discomfort showed clearly on her face, creasing her forehead and shimmering her brow with perspiration. But instead of staring at Sam in abject terror, she watched Chase with pleading eyes. Her voice seemed to echo in his head when she mouthed: *Be careful. Please be careful.*

Chase's heart wrenched. Sam was pointing the gun at *her*, yet she feared for *him*. He couldn't have loved her more.

"I thought it'd be okay," Sam said, voice wobbling all over the place, "until she decided to build that damn tennis center right *there*. Right where I buried all the evidence."

Kylie cast one last pleading glance at Chase before she shifted her rock-solid focus to Sam. "Tell us about Mark," she said, as steady and calm as she'd been the day she walked out on the court for the Australian Open final. "What did he do wrong?"

Admiration swelled inside Chase's chest. That was his Ky, grace under pressure. He didn't like, however, how she demanded Sam's full attention. Maybe she thought it would help, perhaps give him an opening, but Chase couldn't take the chance that Sam's reflexes would be faster than his at the moment.

Sam edged to the side and, without turning, jerked open the refrigerator with one hand so he could scan the inside door. Spotting what he wanted, he grabbed a bottle of beer and shut the door with his hip. His gaze stayed on Chase and his gun on Kylie while he popped the metal top off the amber beer bottle.

After a long gulp, and apparently fortified by the additional alcohol, Sam said, "Mark couldn't handle it. He freaked out."

"Couldn't handle what?" Chase asked, rewarded when his partner shifted his squinted eyes to him. *That's right, Sam, look at me, only me.*

Sam drank again, so deeply that beer dribbled down his chin, but his gaze never wavered from Chase. "He wanted to do it just as much as I did. Hated that bitch"—he cut his eyes back at Kylie—"as much as I did."

"Sam," Chase said sharply. "I'm over here. Talk to me over here."

Instead, Sam glanced down at his shoes, as though gathering his thoughts.

Chase's muscles twitched, but Sam looked up. "Don't."

Chase raised his hands in a supplicating gesture. "Okay. It's okay. I'm not doing anything. Just tell me about Mark."

"He balked in the middle of it," Sam said, giving his head an incredulous shake. "Can you believe that shit? We've got her on the fucking *ground*, and he *balks*." He paused, his Adam's apple bobbing spasmodically as he pressed the cold bottle to his temple. "Fucking *asshole* starts crying and arguing with me while we've got her on the ground. I mean, Jesus Christ! How am I supposed to get it up with him whimpering in my ear?"

Chase flinched at the implication, and a new roar began in his ears. "You were going to rape her?"

Sam gave the gun an impatient wave. "Hell yeah. We had the prettiest, smartest, most popular girl in school all to ourselves out there in the middle of fucking nowhere. You think we just wanted to hit her in the knee and run away? We had some plans. Some *very* hot plans. She wasn't *ever* going to forget that day."

Chase couldn't stop himself from checking on Kylie. One glimpse of her haunted eyes told him she was back on that path, two threatening figures looming over her and a brand-new terror staring her down.

A chill raced the length of his spine, and his instinct was to step in, to shield her from that, but he couldn't without irking the man with the gun. And that just made him want, all the more, to reach down Sam's throat and rip his lungs out. But the time it would take him to cross the six feet between them, even at a dead run, would be all the time Sam needed to pull the trigger.

So, instead, he vowed to keep Sam talking. Eventually, he would make his partner scream. Sam, the evil son of a bitch, was going to scream and writhe and piss himself from Chase-inflicted pain very soon.

"But Mark screwed it up," Chase said, his tone even, professional. "He freaked out."

Sam drained the rest of the beer, then set aside the bottle with a carefulness that contradicted the gun in his hand. "He kept saying, 'I can't, I can't,' like I'd asked him to put his dick in the mouth of a shark. Fucking pussy. When he took off, I had no choice but to go after him before he ratted us both out." He shifted his attention to Kylie, and his teeth flashed white in his ruddy face. "I got in a few good swings, so the afternoon wasn't a total waste."

"What did you do to Mark, Sam?" Chase asked, his voice sharp. He didn't like the considering way Sam looked at Kylie, as though it had occurred to him that while he hadn't gotten what he wanted that day in the woods, he might be able to get it today.

"Sam," he said again. "Look at me and tell me what you did."

Sam cut his alcohol-glazed eyes back to Chase. "I caught up with him at the Bat Cave. Dipshit was sniveling in the corner, sobbing and crying like a baby. Maybe it was the drugs. We tried something new that day. A joint my dealer gave me, laced with something. I'd never felt better, stronger. Everything was crystal sharp, and it pissed me off that Mark was being such a baby. So I hit him." A smile twitched at the corners of his mouth, as though the violent memory pleased him. "It felt good to hit him, so I kept doing it, just hitting him over and over again. Blood was flying everywhere. And then I saw the bat on the ground where I'd dropped it when I got there, and I picked it up. And swung."

Clasping his gun hand with his left, he brought both back to his shoulder then swept out with a smooth, slow-motion follow-through, knocking an imaginary ball out of the park.

"Oh, God," Kylie whispered.

Chase glanced at her, alarmed at the way her head sagged forward. Was she going to be sick? Had she fainted? He stared at the top of her head, willing her to look up, to look at him. As if feeling his pleading gaze, she raised her head. She was so pale, her blue gray eyes wide with pain and horror and fear. He swallowed back the gush of rage, quickly followed by a groundswell of helplessness. She needed him to do something, and all he could do was stand there and let crazy, insane Sam call the shots.

"Afterward," Sam said, drawing Chase's frustrated attention back to him, "I found a tarp inside the house and rolled him up in it. My hand was bleeding pretty bad by then, so I used my shirt to bind it up real tight before I buried him out back. That left the bat. I went looking for something to use to wipe off my fingerprints and found a gym shirt, Quinn's shirt. When I was done, I wrapped them both in a garbage bag and buried them, away from the body."

He smiled without humor, his eyes looking hollow now, fogged over. "Murder made me strong. Within a year, I was no longer the scrawny loser girls saw when they looked at me. I bulked up, had muscles worthy of a football player. I met Tina, and we fell in love. After school, I became a cop. Believe it or not, I wanted to be one of the good guys. I *became* one of the good guys. I maneuvered my way into place as your partner, figuring that if you ever got a break in the case, or Mark's body was found, then I'd be in a position to steer the investigation. Everything was great for a long time."

He turned his gaze to Kylie, and renewed anger sent a fresh flush into his face. Raising the Glock, he pointed it at her forehead. "Then she fucked up everything *again.*"

She cringed back, gasping when the chair almost tipped backward.

"Sam! No!" Chase took a lurching step toward him, but Sam rounded on him, and Chase froze so fast he was on the tips of his toes, his whole world trembling on a very slippery edge.

Chase raised his hands, his eyes steady on his partner's. "It's good. Everything's good."

The Glock wavered, and Sam firmed his grip. "All she had to do was drop the tennis center and go back to LA. That's all it would have taken."

Chase's mind groped for something, anything. "How are you going to explain the shooting of an unarmed woman bound to a chair? Huh, Sam? How?"

Sam swallowed audibly. "This is your fault, Chase. You know that, don't you? You forced my hand. Gave me no choice but to do this now."

"The ER records."

Sam compressed his lips into a tight line and nodded. "While I was getting my hand stitched up, the doctors were working like mad to save her leg. I practically had a front-row seat."

Chase glanced at Kylie, took in the gray of her complexion. She didn't seem to be in the same room with them anymore, and his heart skipped a beat. Was she going into shock? Oh, Jesus, he needed to do something. He swung his attention back to Sam, determined to end this. "So what's it going to be? You're just going to shoot us? That will open up a whole other, more intense investigation."

The corner of Sam's mouth tipped up. "I'm not going to shoot you." He reached back and twisted the knob on the first burner of the stove. "It's a gas oven. You're both going to die because of an unfortunate, accidental gas leak. And then I'm going to decide the ER records were a dead end and solve the case. Pity that Kylie won't be here to see her brother go to prison."

# 58

As the faint, rotten-egg smell of gas hissed into the kitchen, Kylie raised her head and, struggling to regain her focus, saw Sam blowing out the individual pilot lights. She needed to help Chase, distract Sam so he could do something. But what if Sam shot him? What if Sam killed him? No, she thought. She couldn't risk it.

Eye on the ball, Kylie. Get this right, get it right.

Sam gestured at Chase with the gun. "Grab a chair and sit."

This is it, she thought. She had to distract him now, while Chase had permission to move. Time was running out.

She took a shaky breath. "What about the guy at the safe house, Sam? Did you hire him to do your dirty work?"

Chase gave her an almost imperceptible nod of approval. That's it, he seemed to say. Keep him talking.

Sam rolled one shoulder. "He was a snitch and dopehead. I paid him to sabotage the grounds of the construction site, got him to try to run you off."

"Why'd he approach T.J. to bust the windshield?" she asked. "He's just a kid."

"Who the fuck knows what an addict like that thinks?

Maybe he set him up by getting his prints on the bat. Maybe he saw the security cameras and freaked. All I know is that the kid could ID him, so he tried to take him out with the fire. He was as much of a numbskull as Mark. I should have just done it all myself."

"So, what, you killed Benny because he didn't get the job done?" Chase asked.

"He left behind his fucking weapon," Sam sneered. "Fingerprints *all over* the fucking thing."

"You didn't know that at the time."

"I sure as hell did. I saw him with that knife the day before when I paid him to scare the shit out of her at the safe house. He had his fingers all over it. Once he was ID'd, he would have sung like a canary."

"So he never made a play for your Glock," Chase said.

"You're the *only* one who questioned me on that one. How sad is that? My own partner." He jerked his chin toward the dining room. "Bring another chair in and set it beside hers. The tiniest wrong move puts a bullet in her head."

"How will you explain the security guard, Sam?" Chase asked, still stalling. "It'll be obvious he didn't die from a gas leak."

"I'll take the body with me. Figure something out later. Or maybe I'll just blow the whole damn place. All it'd take is a spark."

"You don't have to do this," Chase said. "There's still time to—"

"I'm done talking!" Sam pressed a clenched fist to his temple, fighting for control. "Get the chair. Get it now."

Kylie held her breath as Chase did as he was told, and Sam turned away from her to crank the burners on the stove full blast.

He'd left her uncovered, was entirely focused on the stove, as if he didn't consider her a threat in the least. Surely there was *something* she could do. And it had to be *now*.

Kylie heaved herself up, taking the chair with her. Sam spun toward her, gun flying in her direction, and she jerked her body sideways, striking him with the chair's legs. He grunted and stumbled back, catching his balance with a hand against the counter. Chase roared into the kitchen, ramming Sam in the belly with his shoulder and sending them both crashing against the refrigerator. Sam somehow managed to hang onto the gun and brought it down with a crack against the back of Chase's head.

Kylie saw blood spurt. "No!"

"Get back!" Chase shouted at her. He slammed his fist under Sam's chin.

Sam's head snapped back, and he stood there for a stunned, suspended instant. Chase went in for another jaw-jarring punch, spinning Sam around with the force of the blow.

Kylie, suddenly facing Sam and realizing she was back in the line of fire, shoved back with her feet, only to have the chair legs hit a seam in the tile at a forceful but awkward angle. The splintering crack of wood echoed throughout the kitchen, and the dizzying sensation of falling spun through her head. She landed on the tile on her side, and pain shot through the elbow that took the brunt of the impact. That was nothing, though, when she realized through the stars bursting in front of her eyes that Sam loomed over her, breathing hard, his face shiny with sweat. Oh, God, oh, no, she was so dead—

But then Chase seized Sam by the shoulder, twisting him back around, and grabbed for his gun hand. They struggled for a long, sweaty moment, smashing through the pantry door and against the shelves inside, sending a rain of cereal boxes and canned goods down on their heads. The house seemed to shake from the force of their bodies hurtling into the opposite wall.

Kylie, secured to the chair and on her side, could do nothing but hold her breath, wincing every time Chase took a blow. She couldn't tell who was winning. They seemed evenly matched, both just as desperate. *She* was the difference. She could put the odds in Chase's favor. If only she could *move*.

She jerked at her wrists, biting into her lip at the resulting pain. This pain was nothing in the scheme of things. She'd endured worse ten years ago. And if Sam killed Chase . . . that was the agony that would kill her.

Come on, come *on*.

And then Chase—her hero—slammed an elbow against Sam's temple, and Sam's eyes rolled back in his head. He slid to the floor, limp.

"You're going away for a long time, fuckwad," Chase growled as he stooped over to snatch Sam's gun out of his hand and holster it. Going down on one knee, he used plastic straps to secure Sam's wrists behind him, his hands steady. She had to admire his efficiency.

"The gas," she gasped. "Chase, the gas."

He lunged at the oven to shut it off, then flashed a grin at her. "Good call, babe."

She smiled, and tears burned her eyes. Other than being a bloody mess, he looked beautifully, wonderfully intact. Her miracle.

He scrambled over to press a quick kiss to her forehead. "Let me get some windows open, then I'll get you out of that chair."

"Okay."

He made fast work of the windows, and as fresh air spilled into the kitchen, Kylie closed her eyes. It was over. Thank God, it was over. All of it. For the first time in ten years, she could breathe easy.

Chase grabbed a steak knife out of a drawer then knelt behind her. As he prepared to saw through the plastic binding her hands, he asked, "Are your hands numb?"

"Some."

"Wiggle your fingers for me."

She wiggled.

"Good." He leaned over her, bracing an arm against her belly to keep her from tumbling forward as he began to work at the straps. "You did good, Ky. Really good. You saved the day."

"So did you."

As her hands popped free, he gently guided her away

from the chair and helped her sit up, where he took her right hand into his and began to stroke her wrist. "Are your fingers tingling?"

"A little." Not that she cared now that she saw up close the shape *his* wrists were in. She grasped his forearm to still him, stomach jolting at the sight of his mangled, blood-coated flesh. "Chase, my God. What did you do to yourself?"

"Messed them up pretty good breaking the thing off in the truck. But it's all superficial. They'll heal." Before she could protest, he grasped the sides of her face with steady palms and kissed her.

Her eyes slid closed, and she fell into the warm, moist glide of his tongue against hers. Nothing in the world existed except this moment.

"I love you," he murmured against her lips. "I'm never letting you go. Never."

"Good, 'cause I love you, too, and I'm sticking around. Always and forever."

# 59

"NERVOUS?"

Kylie glanced askance at Chase's legs as he lowered himself onto the metal riser next to her. His khaki shorts showed off spectacular muscles, and her breath stalled as she remembered how he'd taken her mind off the big day that morning. Oh, yeah, baby. Funny how after six months, he could still make her heart race and her palms sweat just by looking at him.

She raised her gaze to his face, seeing her own reflection in his sunglasses, and smiled. "Nervous about what?"

He chuckled and nudged her arm with his shoulder. "Nice try."

She clasped her hands together and stared hard at center court. "Yeah, I'm nervous as hell. Is this what it was like when you watched me play?"

"Not really. I was too busy checking out your boobs."

Laughing, she shielded her eyes as T.J. walked onto the court with his rackets and bag. "He looks terrified," she said. "Does he look terrified to you?"

"Nope. He looks like a tennis player." Chase slipped an

arm around her shoulders to give her a quick, reassuring hug. "A really fantastic one."

The tension flowed out of her. He was so good at that.

"I ran into the Coopers in the parking lot," Chase said, referring to T.J.'s foster parents. "You'd think the kid was in the finals at Wimbledon."

Kylie nodded. She knew exactly how they felt. "You'd think." She linked her arm through his and edged as close to him as she could get without climbing onto his lap. "Did I ever thank you for getting him placed with them?"

He chuckled, grazing the tips of his fingers over her forearm until goose bumps rose on her skin. "Many times, but I'm willing to let you thank me again any time."

She kissed his cheek. "You're really wonderful, you know that?"

"Well, just for the record, Tom and Annette fell for T.J. on their own. I didn't pull those strings."

"Still wonderful," she said, smiling and resting her chin on his shoulder.

He turned his head and kissed her, slowly and leisurely, until the chill bumps returned and her nipples pressed against his upper arm. "Somebody's cold," he murmured against her lips.

She laughed. "I can't move now until I'm warm again. Oh, wait, I'm already warm." She nipped at his earlobe. "Really warm."

He cleared his throat, then awkwardly crossed his legs and made a big show of taking in their surroundings. "This is quite a crowd," he observed, his voice strained.

Kylie had already taken in the hundreds of spectators filling row upon row of metal bleachers, a phenomenal crowd for a junior tennis tournament. It helped that the newspaper had run a story that morning about T.J. Ritchie, the tennis sensation being coached by Kylie McKay. The story included a nice little plug, too, for McKays' Tennis Center, opening next year. The bank had stuck with Kylie despite the delays. Cash infusions from both Jane and Lara helped.

After a few minutes, Kylie rubbed her palm up Chase's

arm, keeping the gesture soothing rather than sexual. "Better yet?"

"Not as long as you keep touching me."

She moved away from him with a soft laugh. "Fine, I'll keep my distance."

He caught her chin and kissed her quickly. "Just for now, though, right?"

Heat seared through her at the low, promising tone of his voice. "Just try and keep me away."

He grinned, then glimpsing someone a few rows down, he jumped to his feet. "Oh, hey, there's Rhonda and Maddy."

Kylie rose, too, and greeted Chase's former wife and daughter, grateful for all the activity to distract her from her nerves and Chase.

Maddy ran up and gave her a tight hug. "Hi, Kylie!"

"Hey, kid. How's it going?" Kylie returned the girl's embrace, sharing a smile over the top of her head with Rhonda, who had to be the most amazing ex-wife on the planet. She seriously didn't seem to harbor any ill will toward Kylie at all.

Maddy peered at the tennis court. "Is T.J. playing yet?"

Chase tapped Maddy on the head. "Hey, don't I get a hug?"

Giggling, she wrapped her arms around his waist. "Hi, Dad."

"Thanks for dropping her off," Chase said to Rhonda.

Rhonda, a petite blond woman with hazel eyes, plopped down on the bleachers. "I'm here to watch. Rumor has it this kid's going to be the next Kendall Falls tennis star."

"When are they going to start playing?" Maddy asked.

Kylie drew the girl, who was all elbows and long legs and smelled faintly of her dad's sunscreen, onto the seat next to her. "It won't be long, Squirt."

"T.J.'s going to win," Maddy said. "Just watch."

"It doesn't matter if he wins or not," Kylie said, inwardly looking forward to watching T.J. kick his opponent's butt all over the court until the other kid fled, sobbing for his mommy. "It's how he plays," she said to Maddy.

"Dad says that's bullshit. He's supposed to win."

"Maddy!" Rhonda exclaimed in parental horror, even as she covered her mouth to hide a laugh.

Chase shrugged at Kylie's reproachful glance. "Well, it's true. Isn't that the point?"

Kylie sat up straight. "The point is that he develops into a mature, professional player."

"And *wins*," Chase said, then grinned before he chucked Maddy under the chin. "Your nose is turning red from the sun already, kiddo."

"Hi, everyone!"

Jane, in a sundress and floppy yellow hat that sharply contrasted Kylie's own khaki shorts and white tank top, waved from a few rows down. As Kylie waved back, she couldn't help but be amused that Jane dressed up even for a junior tennis tournament.

Their relationship had improved considerably in the past six months. Of course, Jane had focused her psychoanalyzing attention on Quinn these days. Luckily, she'd appeared to have learned that a lighter touch was often more productive.

Jane gestured over her shoulder as she made her way toward the empty seats in front of Kylie and Chase. "Sorry we're kind of late."

"You're fine," Kylie said. "Match hasn't started yet." She shifted to see behind Jane, curious about the "we." Spotting Wade Bell, she smiled and returned his wave, thinking how perfect they were for each other. She hadn't seen Jane this happy . . . ever.

Seeing who followed behind Wade, she grinned. "Trisha, excellent!" And then she saw who accompanied Trisha and squealed. "Quinn! I thought you had to work."

Her brother hugged her and pecked her on the cheek. "Playing hooky. Don't tell anyone, okay?" He waggled his eyebrows toward Trisha, as if to say, "Look who I brought!"

Kylie couldn't stop grinning. Holy cow. Quinn and Trisha hanging out together. She could hardly believe it.

Chase signaled Maddy. "Come here a sec, Madster. We need to sunscreen that nose."

"I want to sit next to Kylie during the game," Maddy said, giving her chin a stubborn set.

Chase chuckled. "Don't worry. We can share."

"So," Quinn said as he and Trisha settled down behind Kylie. "Big day, huh?"

She gave a nonchalant shrug. "Another day, another match."

"Yeah, right," Quinn said with a snort. He glanced at Trisha, pitching his thumb toward Kylie. "She's about to take off like a rocket."

"I can tell," Trisha said.

Kylie laughed. "Don't light my fuse."

"Hey, have you guys seen Mom yet?" Jane scanned the crowd. "She said she'd meet us."

Emotion thickened Kylie's throat. The whole family was going to be here. She didn't think everyone had ever turned out for any of *her* matches, even the championship ones. They were all here for her now, though, and that's what mattered.

She checked center court to see that T.J. and his opponent had begun their warm-up volleys. "Here we go."

Chase slid his hand over hers and linked their fingers. "Marry me?"

She looked at him with a gasp. "What?"

He hugged her arm to his side and leaned in close to nuzzle her cheek. "Don't worry. I'll ask again later when you're not so distracted."

The players on the court were introduced, and the stands shook with cheers at T.J.'s name. Kylie saw his eyes widen before he looked toward her and grinned.

He won the coin toss for first serve, and a hush fell over the spectators while he threw the ball high into the air and slammed it at his opponent in perfect grace.

Ace.

While the crowd erupted in cheers, Kylie scooted closer to Chase and put her lips near his ear. "Yes."